**They were a family steeped
in honor and conflict.
War brought out
the best in them and
exacted a bitter price . . .**

———❦———

RODNEY HIGGINS: As a young ___ l officer he
broke the rules in order to joi_____ _t for the
killer battleship *Bismarck*. B_ ___ ____ in the
bloody waters of the Pacif___

NATHAN HIGGINS: ___ _____ __an, the
quick-tempered yo__ ___ __ __s family's
wealth and histor_ ___ _____ _o stay out of
the fight as long __ ___ ___ __ _e went to battle
and discovered the ___ ___ __ _y was . . .

RANDOLPH HIGGIN__ __ _ daring young pilot
he had flown against the Germans in the War to
End All Wars. Now he was strapped into a Spitfire
in defense of London, the oldest pilot in his wing,
a man haunted by the demons of a love he had
desperately avoided . . .

•

LLOYD HIGGINS: A brigadier general commanding a brigade of tanks in North Africa, he outfoxed
the Desert Fox himself, Gen. Erwin Rommel . . .

•

BRENDA HARGREAVES: Widowed twice by World
War I, the matriarch of the Hargreaves-Higgins clan
still retained her voluptuous beauty. And in her
sparkling blue eyes were the unfulfilled promises
of love, the knowledge of war, the terror of two
sons out to destroy each other . . .

ALSO BY PETER ALBANO

• • •

WAVES OF GLORY

Published by
POPULAR LIBRARY

TIDES OF VALOR

PETER ALBANO

POPULAR LIBRARY

An Imprint of Warner Books, Inc.

A Time Warner Inc. Company

POPULAR LIBRARY EDITION

Popular Library® and the fanciful P design are registered trademarks
of Warner Books, Inc.

Cover illustration by Ron Lessor
Cover design by Jackie Merri Meyer

Popular Library books are published by
Warner Books, Inc.
666 Fifth Avenue
New York, N.Y. 10103

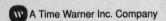 A Time Warner Inc. Company

Printed in the United States of America

First Printing: October, 1990

10 9 8 7 6 5 4 3 2 1

This book is dedicated to Thomas C. Dante, a generous man who is devoted to his family and in return is loved by those fortunate enough to be related to him. A man of integrity, he is respected by all who know him.

ACKNOWLEDGMENTS

The author makes the following grateful acknowledgments to:

Master Mariner Donald Brandmeyer for his generous help with ship handling both in port and at sea;

Patricia Johnston, RN and British citizen, who assisted with medical problems and descriptions of the English countryside;

William D. Wilkerson and Dennis D. Silver for advising on flight characteristics of aircraft in all aspects of flight including the stress of combat;

Kevin Eldridge and John Maloney of the "Planes of Fame Museum" in Chino, California, who gave freely of their time to answer questions about the Rolls Royce Merlin engine;

John McCoy of "The Museum of Flying" in Santa Monica, California, for contributing his expertise on the Spitfire fighter;

Craig Michelson of the "Heritage Park/Military Museum" in El Monte, California, for allowing me to inspect the museum's unsurpassed collection of World War II armored vehicles and answering my endless questions;

Mary Annis, my wife, for her careful reading of the manuscript and thoughtful suggestions;

Robert K. Rosencrance for lending his technical and editorial skills in the preparation of the manuscript.

I

The North Atlantic
May 27, 1941

THE North Atlantic was gray and brooding, swirling mists and banks of fog obscuring the early morning sun and lending a leaden hue to the surging swell. Chains of atmospheric depressions swept across the frigid waters with gale-force winds, building sea upon sea, unchecked rollers sweeping implacably across the length of the ocean like an endless procession of gray hills.

High on the square, citadel-like bridge of battleship *King George V*, Lieutenant j.g. Rodney Higgins, USN, focused his glasses and leaned against the steel windscreen. Tall with sandy hair that spoke equally of Kansas wheat fields or California beaches, his broad shoulders tapered to the narrow waist and powerful legs of the trained fullback. Set in deep sockets, the American's intense blue eyes had the look of a man who could discuss poetry with Byron or savage a countryside with Attila the Hun. The jaw was square and strong as if fashioned by Rodin's chisel, nose straight and aristocratic, hinting at English antecedents. The entire visage was that of striking good looks—an aspect of matinee-idol perfection that inevitably turned female heads.

Sweeping his sector, he grunted in frustration as time and again his lenses were fogged by swirls of mist. Nearby, the sea was as hard and cold as slate, while on the eastern horizon, where occasional shafts of feeble sunlight broke through, it appeared like molten chrome. To the far north towering clouds massed and rolled across the horizon, flashing lightning as if doing battle, giant mushrooms colliding, blending, and darkening the horizon with solid sheets of rain. Turning his glasses astern, he caught glimpses of the rest of the force; battleship *Rodney*, battle cruiser *Repulse*, carrier *Victorious*, and escorting cruisers and destroyers charging through the mists like gray ghosts.

The cold was bitter, borne on the brunt of Arctic winds that mourned through the rigging and ripped the tops from the chop in gray-white sheets. The shock of the frozen air whipped Rodney's breath away in solid banners of vapor, causing him to gasp like a drowning man. Tears streamed from his eyes and across his cheeks, icy spray scoring his face like frozen sand and coating his lips with salt. He tried to contract his big bulk into his navy great coat and cinched his muffler until it almost strangled him. But the cold found its way in, between his gloves and sleeves, seeping around the muffler as if it were liquid. He tried to put it out of his mind. Pressing the glasses tighter against his eyes, he cursed the terrible visibility. The pride of the *Kriegsmarine*, battleship *Bismarck*, was out there somewhere. He had to find it before it found them.

Bismarck. Formidable with an awesome reputation most professionals knew was not completely earned, the great ship was a rework of the old World War I Baden design. Typical of World War I naval architecture, the German battleship had a low armored deck and lacked the dual-purpose secondary guns being adopted by the British and Americans. Eight hundred twenty-three feet long with the unusually wide beam of 118 feet, she was armed with a main battery of eight fifteen-inch guns and was capable of thirty knots. She was intricately compartmented and would be hard to sink. But the old design left her rudders and steering gear poorly protected, her communications and data-transmitting systems exposed. Worse, because her fifteen-inch ammunition was poorly fused, many of her shells would not explode. However, she was a convoy killer with massive secondary batteries: twelve 150-millimeter guns; sixteen 105-millimeter guns; sixteen 37-millimeter guns; twelve 20-millimeter guns. And she had already killed the pride of the Royal Navy, battle cruiser *Hood*.

Horror had filled the Allied camp when on May 21 *Bismarck* and her consort, the eight-inched gunned cruiser *Prinz Eugen*, sailed from the Kors Fjord near Bergen, Norway. There were eleven convoys at sea; one, bound for the Middle East, was loaded with troops. Battle cruiser *Hood* and the new battleship *Prince of Wales*, completed only two weeks earlier and still suffering teething problems with her fourteen-inch turrets, put to sea in a line ahead from Scapa Flow and made for the Denmark Straits—the eighty-mile-wide passage between Greenland and Iceland. Here cruisers *Suffolk* and *Norfolk* had sighted the German ships and broadcast an alarm. *Bismarck* turned, opened her firing arcs, hurling several salvoes at her tormentors. Unharmed and continuing to broadcast sighting signals, the cruisers turned away and began shadowing just out of range or concealed by the mists. *Hood* and *Prince of Wales*, steaming just south of the exit to the Denmark Straits and skirting the Greenland ice, charged in.

May 24 was a day that rocked the British Navy, shattering confidence and depressing an entire nation. At 0552 hours at a range of twenty-five thousand yards the action began. Exchanging salvo after salvo, *Hood* and *Prince of Wales* concentrated on *Bismarck*, *Bismarck* and *Prinz Eugen* firing on *Hood*. Eight minutes after the action began, one of *Bismarck*'s shells penetrated *Hood*'s deck and plunged into her magazines. A flash like the birth of a new sun leapt from the sea, the whole bow of the ship hurled up out of the sea before the fore part of the ship began to sink. A giant black cloud of smoke covered the area like a pall and when it cleared, *Hood* had vanished. There were three survivors.

Prince of Wales, with two turrets out of action, turned away but not before hitting *Bismarck* with two fourteen-inch shells, one of which crashed through her bow and started a leak in a fuel bunker. Losing oil, *Bismarck* turned south, shaping a course for St. Nazaire. *Prinz Eugen* steamed off to the north to carry out commerce raiding.

May 25 was another bad day for the British fleet. *Norfolk*, *Suffolk*, and *Prince of Wales* lost *Bismarck*. Worse, believing *Bismarck* was returning to her base by making for the Iceland-Faeroes gap, *King George V*, *Rodney*, *Repulse*, and *Victorious* turned to the northeast, away from the German battleship. But that afternoon *Bismarck*'s commanding officer foolishly sent a long, thirty-minute message boasting of the victory over *Hood*. Picked up by radio direction finders, the English ships reversed course and closed in. But *Bismarck* was 110 miles ahead of her pursuers. Nothing short of a miracle would bring her to action. And the British were running low on fuel, too; *Prince of Wales* breaking off and heading for Iceland to replenish; *Repulse* making for Newfoundland with her tanks nearly dry.

On May 26 antique Swordfish biplanes flying from *Ark Royal*, which was steaming north from Gibraltar with battle cruiser *Renown* and cruiser *Sheffield* of Force H, found *Bismarck*. Throughout the day the old planes dogged her, reporting her position. They never let go. That evening fifteen Swordfish attacked *Bismarck* with torpedoes. Two hits were scored; one exploded amidships on the port side doing no appreciable damage while the second struck her starboard quarter, damaging her starboard propeller, wrecking the steering gear, and jamming her rudders. The great battleship began to turn in circles and her speed dropped to eight knots. The British had their miracle.

Lieutenant Rodney Higgins dropped his glasses and grabbed the teakwood rail below the windscreen as *King George V* slammed into a huge swell with the violence of a maddened bull, sending banners of gray-white water flying to both bows, sounds like great bass drums booming through her hull. Built with a low bow for zero elevation firing of her forward turrets, *King George V* challenged and fought the seas, crushing the swells and shouldering them aside arrogantly when other ships rode over. A two-fisted, barroom brawler of a ship, she gave her crew a rough ride, defying the Atlantic's worst efforts with her 38,000 tons and 110,000 horsepower.

Clutching the rail, Higgins reflected on how he, an American naval officer and a neutral, could find himself in the middle of a naval battle fought by the British and Germans. In essence, he was a stowaway—a neutral observer attached to the American embassy who had been aboard *King George V* (the British affectionately referred to her as *KG V*) when the first warning had been broadcast by cruiser *Suffolk*.

Rodney's first impulse was to return ashore as ordered by the ship's public-address system. But an inexplicable compulsion, a fascination for battle—the killer of many, yet the domain of only a few—drew him, pulled him like metal shavings to a magnet. *KG V* was about to embark on a great adventure, lend her name to a footnote of history, live it and, perhaps, die with it. He knew he risked a hideous death and possibly a court-martial, if he survived, but he rigged a flimsy excuse of illness and sleep and remained in his tiny cabin until he felt the battleship rise to the North Atlantic swell as it sortied from Scapa Flow. Then feigning surprise and embarrassment, he emerged from his cabin.

The British were surprisingly sporting about the whole flimsy deception, handing him a greatcoat, "battle bowler" (steel helmet), binoculars, and actually assigning him as a lookout on the starboard wing of the navigation bridge. "By Jove, we never have enough good eyes on the bridge," the navigator, Commander John Reed-Davis, said the morning Rodney reported to the bridge. A Sandhurst graduate and a true professional, the tall, slender, middle-aged commander had brown, thinning hair streaked with gray, hollow cheeks, and blue-green eyes that glinted with good humor on the surface, but steely resolve, characteristic of his race, burned in the depths. And then, clapping the young American firmly on the back with his tongue firmly in his cheek, said, "Remember, Mr. Higgins, you're a neutral. If it comes to hand-to-hand combat, cast off the Krauts grappling hooks but keep your cutlass in its scabbard." He laughed while the other members of the bridge force chuckled.

Every member of the crew Rodney met from the nineteen-year-old Midshipman Ian Longacre to the commander of the battle fleet, commander-in-chief of the Home Fleet Admiral Sir John Tovey, had made him feel welcome. In fact, he even sensed the powerful bond of camaraderie that binds all men together on the eve of battle—the mutual sharing of mortal risks that made brothers of strangers. He was served hot chocolate laced with rum in a white mug with the ship's logo in gold, referred to as "Sir" by the enlisted men and "Mr. Higgins" by the officers. He became aware of the feeling of isolation and desperation endured by these brave people in the darkest of hours, Britain standing alone against the conquering, invincible madman, Adolph Hitler.

The year 1941 had seen a parade of disasters. German forces had smashed through the Balkans, conquering Greece and Yugoslavia in a mere three weeks. A British relief force was driven into the sea and took refuge on Crete. Incredibly, the British army on Crete was overwhelmed by an airborne assault. A new general named Erwin Rommel took command in North Africa and swept up the British forces and drove them back into Egypt, trapping over twenty thousand British troops in a Libyan port called Tobruk. Convoys attempting to relieve Malta were smashed. London was hit by the deadliest raid of the war, hundreds were killed, Westminster Abbey, the House of Commons, and the British Museum were all hit. At sea, U-boats were sinking ships at will. The only bright light came from the Italians. The British routed them whenever they met. But everyone knew the Italians couldn't fight, anyway.

Surrender, conciliation, even a negotiated "peace with honor," were out of the question. The mad "paper-hanging corporal" would be fought and beaten. The tradition of Nelson was there, the spirit of Drake. Nevertheless, the English needed more than tradition and spirit to survive. They needed America. Their warmth and congeniality were easy to understand. Of course, he was welcome.

The bugle calling the crew to "close to action stations" had been blown before dawn. Now Rodney had been at his station on the starboard wing of the navigation bridge for over an hour, searching the dark mists and finding absolutely nothing. Everyone knew that *Bismarck* had been damaged and everyone knew U-boats were about, prowling just below the surface, ready to sink the most powerful ship with salvoes of torpedoes. Between 0200 and 0300 lookouts had reported flashes over the far southeastern horizon and there had been reports of destroyer actions on the fleet circuits. But nothing was sighted. Probably just more lightning. It was all around.

Leaning forward Rodney could see the ship's long graceful bow, forecastle, and turrets A and B; A with four Mark VIII fourteen-inch guns, B with two. Aft, X turret mounted four more great cannon. In all, the ten guns could deliver an awesome 21,200-pound broadside at a range of 36,000 yards. However, the quadruple turret was an unusual arrangement; not one American ship used four-gun turrets because of the crowded conditions, slow rate of fire, and dangers inherent in loading the big guns. But *KG V* had been built in the late thirties under the restrictions of the London Naval Agreement of 1936 and her design had suffered. Still, she was a solid gun platform and powerful, the first ship to carry the 5.25 inch dual-purpose gun capable of an elevation of ninety degrees. Rodney Higgins had counted sixteen of the rapid-fire weapons mounted in twin turrets lining her sides from the bridge to the boat deck.

KG V's armor was designed on the "all or nothing" principle with a newly devised vertical external belt and increased thickness over the magazines. It was also deepened below the waterline where capital ships were vulnerable to plunging fire and the main horizontal armor was raised one deck to protect against the threat of aerial bombs. Discarding torpedo bulges, her builders, Vickers-Armstrong, Newcastle, relied on the double bottom and a longitudinal bulkhead with two watertight compartments sandwiching an oil-filled compartment between the bulkhead and the hull for torpedo protection.

Glancing over his shoulder, Rodney Higgins could see the foretop with its main gun director, lookout stations, banks of recognition lights, radar and radio antennas, searchlights, and signal halyards. One deck below was the flag and signal bridge while aft was the chart house, WT (wireless transmitter), and captain's and admiral's night cabins. Just abaft the superstructure were her two stacks; the first mounted too close to the bridge, occasional clouds of acrid smoke and fumes enveloping the crew whenever the ship was struck by a powerful following wind. The second was set well aft, just behind the two aircraft hangars and crane. "Two blocked" during the night, the battle ensign whipped proudly from the gaff, just forward of X turret. Visible along her sides and cluttering the superstructure were nests of pom-poms; dozens of the unreliable 1.1-inch AA machine guns (the Americans called them "Chicago Pianos"). All were manned, the helmeted heads of their crews appearing like clusters of chamber pots.

" 'E's out there, sir," Nives Quinn, a young cockney lookout from Wapping, said. Standing next to a gyro repeater with his glasses to his eyes, the young able seaman moved his glasses through his sector with the short jerky movements of the trained lookout. The son of a "costermonger," as fruit vendors were known in London's East Side, the short, burly Quinn had a particularly venomous hatred for the Germans who had killed his brother at Dunkirk. Typical of the battleship's crewmen, Quinn had started his training at sixteen and was a thoroughly trained and experienced professional. Only twenty-two years of age, the set of lines around Quinn's eyes and mouth were those of a much older man. "The buggers' knickers are in the twist," Quinn said, dropping his glasses to his waist and waving furiously at the hazy horizon. "You'll see, guvn'r—ah, I mean Mr. 'iggins."

Chuckling, the American refocused his glasses. Nothing. Nothing at all. He shifted his search to the east where the sun was fighting a losing battle with the clouds, smudging the seascape with bloody carmine and dull brass. The sun was not rising, it was hemorrhaging. Was nature's bloody display a harbinger? Would he die this day? If so, he would die in good company. With Englishmen. His father had been an Englishman, Commander Geoffry Higgins, the hero of battle cruiser *Lion* in the battle of Jutland who had saved his ship from a cataclysmic magazine fire at the cost of his own life—a frightful death in the incandescent heat of burning gunpowder. There had been a Victoria Cross, posthumous, of course, but Rodney had seen it only once. His mother had put it away where it could never be found or even seen again. He had heard her sobbing to his grandmother once, "It was a lousy trade—a monkey's paw."

His mother, Brenda Higgins. He saw her face gazing down at him, silken auburn hair in long folds to her shoulders, blue eyes glowing with love. In her middle age, Brenda Higgins was still one of the world's great beauties and wealthiest women. In fact, she was such a striking woman that even the unusual beauty of his "steady," Kay Stockard, seemed inconsequential when the women were together. His mother would be bitter and filled with horror if she knew of his foolish deception and risk. She had sacrificed two husbands and a brother to the gods of war—had bitterly opposed Rodney's entrance into Annapolis while coddling his war-hating brother, Nathan.

Restlessly, Rodney turned and glanced into the pilothouse. With the lids of its steel scuttles dogged closed, its interior was still very dark in the feeble morning light. Rodney could see a dozen men manning their stations, swaying gently with the motions of the ship like silent drunks. The soft green light of the compass repeater and binnacle tinted by the dim red glow of battle lamps rheostated down to their lowest settings gave an eerie aspect to every countenance. With the lower half of his face illuminated by the binnacle, the wheelman's features glowed faintly with the green hue of a week-old corpse. There was another green glow at the back of the compartment—the newfangled radio detection and ranging machine (the British called it by the acronym *Radar*). Higgins watched the remorseless sweep of the beam, but it showed nothing, too, except ships in their own formation.

Admiral Tovey and the ship's captain were in the armored conning tower with Commander Reed-Davis and the plotting team. The OOD (officer of the deck) was an experienced commander named Willard Blackstone. Standing just behind the helmsman and next to a manifold of voice tubes suspended from the overhead, Blackstone was in contact with the admiral and captain by both speaker and voice tube.

The speaker squawked and then Rodney heard Blackstone's basso profundo strident enough to fill Yankee Stadium, "Starboard ten."

"Starboard ten, sir. Ten of starboard wheel on, sir."

"Steer one-one-five."

"Steer one-one-five. Passing one-one-zero, sir."

"Midships."

"Rudder is amidships, sir. Steady on one-one-five."

"Very well." Blackstone turned to the rating manning the engine-room telegraphs. "Full ahead together. Give me revs for twenty-nine knots."

There was a clang of bells and almost immediately the changed beat came up through the soles of Rodney Higgins's shoes as the four great Parsons turbines six decks below delivered every one of the ship's 110,000 horsepower to the four propellers.

"One-hundred-thirty-two revolutions, twenty-nine knots, sir."

"Very well."

Rodney stared into his glasses to the south and east where

Bismarck was supposed to be but saw nothing but the same frustrating curtains of mist. At flank speed, *KG V* was straining her engines and pouring oil into her eight three-drum Admiralty boilers at a lavish rate that would run them out of fuel in a few hours. There must have been a report from a shadowing destroyer or cruiser. What other explanation was there for the change in course, the fuel-consuming speed? A U-boat? He felt a tremor. Was that it? But there were no torpedo tracks. No wildly charging destroyers ripping the depths with depth charges. Every ship was holding station as before. It must be the *Bismarck*. But, damn, where was she?

Blackstone's voice: "Radar?"

"No new targets, Commander."

Blackstone's retort was filled with the frustration felt by every man, "Dash it all! Where are the buggers?"

Rodney felt a new presence on the bridge. It was the navigator, Commander Reed-Davis. Raising his glasses and pointing, the navigator said, "We've reports our Swordfish got two hits, Mr. Higgins."

Rodney dropped his glasses and let them dangle at his chest. "I know, sir. Should slow her a few knots, sir."

"Not if she took one up the arse, Lieutenant."

"You mean her steering gear is damaged, too?"

"You bloody well know it. The Fourth Destroyer Flotilla reports she's steaming at a reduced speed on an erratic course to the south of us. We'll bring her to book straightaway. And don't let this waiting about get on your wick. Keep a close watch." The commander returned to the conning tower.

Every man leaned into his binoculars like statues frozen by the Arctic winds. A tingling like electricity raced through Rodney's body. The air was frigid and his breaths puffs of steam, yet the tremor was not from the cold. It came from within. Fear. The coldness of formless dread. The moment of truth was near and he was feeling the atavistic stirring of mortal peril. His reaction was the same reaction of all frightened men in the presence of other frightened men on the eve of battle. He squared his massive shoulders, stood as tall as his six-foot-one-inch frame would permit. Then, for the first time in his young life, he found a sudden insight into men and battle, realizing pride in manhood would not allow him to be less than any of the men who surrounded him. He smiled slyly to himself.

The speaker gave a preliminary squawk and then crackled with the gunnery officer's voice: "All hoists filled, armor-piercing, full-charge powder, temperature of cordite sixty-three degrees, wind force five from two-eight-five."

"Very well."

The hoists were filled with silk-bagged powder and projectiles like unlighted fuses to the magazines. A hit, a tiny piece of burning silk, could ignite a chain of bags that could destroy the ship. It was rumored *Hood* had died this way. It was common knowledge that battle cruisers *Invincible*, *Indefatigable*, and *Queen Mary* had all blown up after magazine fires at Jutland. Suddenly Higgins felt an amalgam of fear and helplessness—the helplessness all men feel when their lives are committed to battle by other men. Tovey in his steel tower, committees of faceless admirals at Whitehall, even Winston Churchill at 10 Downing Street, had taken control of his fate, deciding if he were to live or die. And he did not belong here; yet, at that moment, would not have been anywhere else. Bewildered by his mercurial emotions that changed direction and clashed as aimlessly as the seas in the eye of a hurricane, he brought his glasses up and clenched his jaw.

Staring through his binoculars a swelling excitement pushed his fears and doubts aside, his five senses fine-tuned—becoming the primeval sixth sense of the predator. He was both the hunter and the hunted, playing the most horrifying yet exhilarating game on earth—searching for like creatures of like intelligence. The air itself seemed to change, charged with static that brought up the hair on the back of his neck and made it tingle. A ship moving through the darkness filled with men determined to kill you gives off an energy you can feel. He wiped his glasses, narrowed his lids, hunched against the windscreen looking for a shudder in the patterns of sea, a shadow in the mists, the hint of something moving where nothing should move. Then, abruptly, the sun broke through the low-scudding clouds to the east, hurling shafts of brilliant sunlight like silver javelins to play upon the sea.

He gave a start as a dark shape on the far southeastern horizon stopped his glasses in midsweep. His heart barged against his chest furiously and he was suddenly incapable of swallowing. With trembling fingers he made fine adjustments to his focusing knob, pressed his glasses against his eyes until they watered with pain. Black smoke. A ship hull down. At that instant, it seemed that time slowed and his vision was suddenly concentrated to brilliant clarity. Clearly, he saw a director with its tube and lenses protruding like the ears of a startled rabbit. A great mast, the tip of a single raked stack. A British destroyer? Impossible. Not with a director that large, a single stack, massive upper works. It was a capital ship. Clearing his throat, he masked his excitement with a strained, flat voice, "Ship bearing zero-four-zero . . ." Hesitating in momentary confusion, he realized he was using American terminology instead of British. Correcting himself, he began again, "I mean, ship bearing green forty, hull down."

Seaman Quinn shouted, "It's 'im. Tally bloody ho! Kraut at green forty."

Leaping from the pilothouse, Commander Blackstone charged out to the wing of the bridge, hunched over the gyro repeater, and peered through the gun sight of the bearing ring. He read the azimuth, but before he could utter a word the foretop lookouts were heard, "Ship bearing green forty, range twenty thousand." Then the radar operator's excited shout as the target came onto his scope. Blackstone raced back into the pilothouse.

The sighting report spread throughout the ship like wildfire. Tinnily, the admiral's voice came through the speaker, "Ship's main and secondary armament load. Make the hoist,

'Engage vessel bearing green forty, range twenty thousand. Fire when ready.' "

Battle. They were going to fight. Lieutenant Higgins felt the excitement charge his veins with sexual intensity, heard the hum of blood in his ears, felt the warmth of it on his cheeks. Incongruously, Kay Stockard's nude body flashed in his mind—slender, long-limbed, hot, and trembling. Kay. He missed her. Maybe, he loved her. But why was he thinking of her now? He shook his head. Wondered at the mad kaleidoscope racing through his brain.

Rodney heard a hum overhead and Kay vanished. Looking up he saw the director turning slowly toward the enemy. A trained gunnery officer, in his mind's eye he could see the entire intricate fire-control system at work and the men who made it function: the main director's trainer and layer hunched over the eyepieces of the range finder, turning their cranks and bringing the split image of the target into a tangible whole; the control officer, spotting officer, rate officer, and cross-leveling officer poring over their instruments and plotting sheets. And far below in the transmitting station in the bowels of the ship—the brain of the fire-control system—were the deflection officer, clock operator, range operator, spotting plot operator, all working furiously over their fire-control table, computing speed of target, range, deflection, temperature of powder, curvature of the earth, even factoring in the number of times the guns had been fired. Then a continuous stream of elevations, ranges, and deflections were transmitted to the four turret captains who in turn relayed the data to their trainers and layers. An intricate system, but it worked with murderous efficiency.

Rodney heard the whine of electric motors and the whir of turret-training rack and pinion gears as below him turrets A and B swung to starboard, the six fourteen-inch guns pointing toward the stranger like tree trunks. He heard Quinn muttering, "I've 'ad a bloody jugful o' you Krauts. Killed me brother, you did—sank 'ood, bonked London. Now thank the Lord for what you're 'bout to get, you bloody sods.'' He giggled and salivated.

''Starboard ten,'' Blackstone said. ''Steer one-two-five. Ahead standard together.''

The mists pulled back like the curtains at the Metropolitan, the sun finally winning its battle with the haze and fog. Higgins could see the upper works of the intruder quite clearly. It was the *Bismarck*. Obviously not in full control, she was idling north and east on a meandering course. But she appeared intact, eight fifteen-inch guns trained to port, directly at Lieutenant j.g. Rodney Higgins. The American felt his guts turn to ice water and his Adam's apple became a stone that clung to the back of his throat. His mouth had never been so dry.

Battleship *Rodney* was bearing off on the enemy in a reckless head-on approach, unmasking all nine of her forward-mounted sixteen-inch guns. *KG V* was closing the range and slowing. *Bismarck* must be damaged. Turning toward *Bismarck* reduced the range but cut down on X turret's firing arcs. A silence so heavy it was a palpable force had settled over the ship. With blowers secured and vents closed, *KG V* seemed to be holding her breath. Higgins could only hear the gentle ticking of the gyro repeater and the sluicing of water as the ship's stem slashed through the water. Then the voices of the gun-control personnel putting the guns on target broke through the gunnery circuits. ''Guns loaded,'' came from the turret captains. ''On target, on target,'' came from the trainers and layers.

Immediately the American heard the calm voice of the director-layer piped down from the main director, ''Director-layer sees the target.'' Rodney caught his breath. Those few simple words meant the man was ready, guns loaded, finger itching to pull the trigger. He heard Admiral Tovey's shout through the speaker, ''Shoot!'' There was a high, festive tinkling of a chime much like the gay sound of bells on the harness of a horse pulling a sleigh through Christmas snow.

Despite clinging to the windscreen, Rodney was staggered by the concussion as six fourteen-inch guns fired as one, brilliant orange flame leaping thirty feet from the muzzles. The Vesuvian eruption lighted the sea and reflected from a cluster of low-streaming clouds, the ship jerking with the shock like a harpooned blue whale. Dust and chips of paint rained in the pilothouse. Flung high into the air, the bearing ring clattered on the steel deck. Quinn scooped it up. Rodney heard the radar man curse: his set had been knocked out of commission.

Although the American had clapped his hands over his ears, the great booming sounds of thousands of pounds of nitrocellulose exploding assaulted his ears as if he were sitting in the percussion section of a great symphony orchestra, played by mad musicians. Immediately a great cloud of brown smoke stinking of cordite enveloped the bridge with a smell like burned solvent and vaporized Vaseline. Thankfully, it was swept away abruptly by the stiff breeze. All eyes watched for the fall of shot. Taught a bloody lesson by the High Seas Fleet at Jutland, the British had given up on single ranging shots and adopted the Germans' "ladder" method of ranging. Firing full salvoes, the spotters looked for ladder short, ladder long, then down ladder and rapid fire. "Short!" rang through the speaker.

Battleship *Rodney*'s six sixteen-inch guns flowered to life in a single gigantic hibiscus-orange flash followed by a billowing cloud of brown smoke. At that instant, Lieutenant Higgins saw a sight that froze his blood, sent tremors of horror racing up and down his spine like the clawed frozen feet of a hundred loathsome insects. *Bismarck*, looming large in his binoculars, had opened fire, the flash of her main armament lighting up scattered patches of fog and low clouds with scarlets and yellow like the open door of a giant blast furnace. With his glasses pointed directly at the muzzles, the blast leapt at Higgins with a glare that sent afterimages winking off his retinas. Hell. He was staring into the bowels of hell.

He dropped his glasses, blinked his watering eyes, and then he saw them—the most frightening sight he would ever see in his life. Eight fifteen-inch shells were actually visible, stubby purple-black pipes arching slowly in the clearing blue of the morning sky and dropping down toward him—directly at him, Lieutenant j.g. Rodney Higgins, USN. He stared with disbelief and a thought all men have when first exposed to enemy fire roared through his mind: *They're trying to kill me—Rodney Higgins. Why me? What have I done to them?*

Bismarck's salvo was at least two hundred yards short, a great curtain hundreds of feet high rising majestically into the sky, the flash of exploding lyddite drowned immediately by the sea. One round was short, a defective barrel or broken driving band on the shell. Its impact was flat and it skipped across the surface like a flat rock thrown by a boy across a pond. Lazily, it sailed toward *KG V*. Mesmerized like a man menaced by a coiled cobra, Higgins watched the one-ton projectile leap from a crest not more than seventy yards away, turn end over end, flail the surface with first its base and then its AP tip like a ponderous pinwheel, and then finally crash in a burst of spray, disappearing into a cresting swell not more than fifty feet from the bridge. Rodney released his pent-up breath with a hiss.

The gunnery circuits crackled with flat, dehumanized voices, "Elevation two-four-zero-zero minutes, direction forty-seven degrees, deflection thirty-seven left, range one hundred minus eighteen thousand, four-zero-zero . . ."

Blackstone's commands could be heard over the crackle of the speaker: "Starboard ten."

"Starboard ten. Ten of starboard wheel on, sir."

"Course one-three-zero."

"Course one-three-zero. Passing one-two-zero, sir."

"Midships."

"Rudder amidships, ship steady on one-three-zero."

"Very well. All ahead together two-thirds. Give me revs for twenty-four knots."

They were closing on the enemy, coming to point-blank

range. Cruisers *Norfolk*, *Dorsetshire*, and the escorting destroyers scurried out of the line of fire, like small boys leaving the arena to the heavyweights. The great ships were built to duel at ranges that exceeded twenty miles. Yet, the men who commanded were rushing in close—near enough to fire over open sights. It would be a barroom brawl at murderous ranges where the great ships would pound each other to pieces like giants wielding sledgehammers against egg crates.

The ship rocked and staggered, the main armament firing again with barrels nearly horizontal. More waiting and watching. Huge fountains leapt a hundred yards beyond *Bismarck*. "Long! Long!" the cockney shouted. "We've bracketed the buggers."

Battleship *Rodney* fired and *Bismarck* let go another salvo. But the German was forced to divide his fire against his two attackers. His shells roared over both targets. Higgins not only saw them, but he heard them this time, ripping overhead with a thundering sound like the Twentieth Century Limited. Four geysers shot into the sky two hundred yards beyond the battleship.

"Ranging! Ranging," came from the director. "Secondary battery on target."

The gunnery officer's voice: "Main armament, down one hundred! Deflection eight right! Barrage! Commence! Commence! Secondary battery shoot!"

Lieutenant Higgins groaned as eight 5.25-inch guns in four turrets on the starboard side of *KG V* came to life with harsh cracking sounds like the tip of a whip snapping in a man's ear. Firing eighteen rounds per minute, per gun, the battery set up a continuous drumfire, a torrent of shells deluging the enemy. Six fourteen-inch guns crashed out another salvo.

Higgins had his binoculars on *Bismarck* when at least five one-ton projectiles struck her amidships. Strakes of plates, chunks of a splintered whale boat, and an entire crane that appeared intact shot into the sky on the tips of flame-red explosions. He could see the bodies of a dozen men cartwheeling in the air like rag dolls. Cheers. "We've taped the buggers!" Quinn screamed. "Kill 'em!"

Blackstone's calm voice: "Port ten."

The equally calm reply from the quartermaster: "Ten of port wheel on, sir."

"Steady up on zero-nine-zero. Watch your head, Quartermaster. All ahead together one-half."

There were new sounds overhead. Ripping canvas, warbling and sighing. *Bismarck*'s secondaries; 150-and 105-millimeter shells fired from at least fourteen guns that should bear on *King George V*. But the fire was wild, the German had taken too many hits. If her directors had not been destroyed already, they had been damaged, perhaps knocked from their circular ball-bearing mounts.

They were so close to *Bismarck* Rodney Higgins could see small details: her forward director turned toward him; the emerging sun reflecting from the glass on the bridge; life rafts hanging from the superstructure; searchlights mounted on her upper works and single raked stack; her rigging, antennas, and even her battle ensign whipping from her mainmast. Her guns were pointed at him, the fire of her secondary armament continuous rippling red flashes, her main battery firing about every thirty seconds. Big shells hurled waterspouts as high as her masts all around the great ship, spray reaching out in vast circles to mark the power of each one. Flashes winked and smoke puffed where she was struck by 5.25-inch projectiles. They could do terrible execution, but it would take big shells to sink her.

Battleship *Rodney* veered to the south across *Bismarck*'s bow to keep her firing arcs open and to stand clear of *KG V*'s fire. Again and again *KG V* fired, her big guns at zero elevation now. The hits came. Fourteen- and sixteen-inch shells poured in, their soft steel AP caps weakening the German's face-hardened armor before the shell proper plunged through. For three quarters of an hour annihilation rained on the battleship.

Bismarck's A turret was flung into the sky, number-one gun flying off like a twig in a gale. The main director was blown into the sea like a piece of trash thrown into a garbage pail. The mainmast tilted slowly and then plunged into the water like a tree felled by an ax, trapping every man in the aft director and drowning most of her lookouts. Struck by at least a half-dozen hits, the bridge disintegrated in a cyclonic whirl of shattered plate, glinting fragments of glass from her scuttles and recognition lights. Bodies and pieces of bodies rained into the water. Her stack exploded and flames leapt up amidships, black smoke roiling, clinging to the sea in greasy rolls. Plates, men, and secondary turrets shot into the air, fires burst from her hull, and ready ammunition began to explode and burn on her main deck. Slowing, she began to wallow deep in the swells. But Y turret fired defiantly until a full salvo blew it off its barbette and it skidded across the fantail and toppled overboard.

Rodney Higgins shuddered. The exhilaration of battle, the blood lust was fading. Men were dying horribly, blown to pieces, trapped in flooding compartments or flung about in engine compartments by the compression and concussion of big shells, blasted into the machinery and chewed to death by gears and flailing pistons. He tried to depersonalize as all men do in battle. *She was a ship. That's all she was*, he told himself. But at three thousand yards his binoculars almost took him aboard the wreck. He could actually see men being killed, blown high into the air, dismembered. His stomach was suddenly sick and empty. Was this the triumph of battle—the garden of glory? These witty, warm, jolly Englishmen were killing hundreds and enjoying it.

Quinn's eyes were wild and saliva streaked his chin. "Stuff that lot, guttersnipes! Fill your Kraut bellies with British steel." He laughed, waving his fist, eyes glinting with the savage joy of a predator making his kill. Rodney turned his glasses back to the stricken enemy.

Bismarck was dead in the water, guns silent, burning from a dozen fires. Although she was down by the head, she appeared in no danger of sinking. Her superb compartmentation and excellent damage-control parties were keeping her afloat.

Her executioners were so close, their shells fired on flat trajectories could blow away her upper works, but her hull was relatively immune to the heavy shells. An old naval adage wisely suggests, "Let water into them. Air won't sink a ship." Admiral Tovey had come to that realization. Plunging fire was needed. They had to open the range.

"Port ten," came from the pilothouse. Then Higgins heard Blackstone give a series of commands that turned the ship away from *Bismarck* and opened the range at a high speed. Dutifully, three destroyers assumed escort stations; *Cossack* ahead, *Maori* off the starboard beam, *Zulu* to port. Battleship *Rodney*, escorted by two other destroyers, continued firing at the helpless German at close range while *KG V*'s X turret fired over her fantail. At a range of fourteen thousand yards, the battleship turned and unmasked her entire main battery. Now, with a longer range, the barrels were elevated and the big shells would arc high and then plunge into *Bismarck*'s bowels and hopefully sink her. The secondary battery fell silent.

The bombardment continued for almost an hour, yet *Bismarck* refused to sink. Quinn was delighted. He jumped up and down and actually danced a jig while humming a music-hall ditty. " 'ave a jugful, you bloody tiffies."

Suddenly Reed-Davis was on the bridge, standing next to Rodney Higgins and staring into his glasses. He licked his lips and muttered, "That'll settle their lot." He turned to the American, "What do you think of your first battle, old boy?"

"The battle was over long ago, Commander."

"What do you mean?"

Higgins waved. "She's helpless. In a battle, your opponent can fight back."

The Englishman bristled. "They're Huns. They've bloody well earned what they're getting."

"They're men and this has become an execution. Why don't you take prisoners?"

Reed-Davis waved irritably. "Her battle ensign is still flying—look for yourself."

Swinging his glasses, Higgins saw a flag whipping from a stub of the mainmast. His voice was filled with incredulity, "You'll kill hundreds because of that rag?"

The voice was acid. "That's what this lot's all about, Lieutenant." Whirling on his heel, he vanished back into the conning tower. Higgins returned to the windscreen, seething with anger. Quinn stared through his glasses sullenly as if he had heard nothing.

"Cease fire! Cease fire," echoed through the ship. Immediately the cease fire gong rang at each gun station.

Quinn turned to the conning tower and spoke as if the admiral could hear him. "Bonk 'em, your nibs! Some of them buggers ain't bought it yet." He eyed the American angrily.

Rodney Higgins sighed with relief, the silence washing through his ears like a soothing salve. Everyone knew they were low on fuel. He suspected the admiral would let escorts finish off *Bismarck* with torpedoes. Tovey's tinny voice coming through the speaker confirmed his suspicion, "We're very low on fuel. We will disengage and return to port for fuel."

Quinn shouted, "No!" and shook a fist at the conning tower.

Tovey continued, "I am ordering *Dorsetshire* to finish off our enemy." There was a cheer. "Well done. I'm proud of every man jack of you. Each of you has made his mark on history—a mark that will stick in Hitler's craw like unboiled cabbage. Well done. Well done."

There was a rumble that came through the closed vents, dogged doors and scuttles; from the engine rooms, handling rooms, turrets. Thousands of boots thudding against the steel decks and floor plates, and the cheers swelled and echoed through the ship. It was the joy of victory, the tribal scream of the victorious warrior who was holding his enemy's head on high for all to see. Quinn added his voice. To Rodney, he seemed to be hearing the cry of a wild beast dipping his fangs into his quarry's entrails. He stared at the dying German as *Dorsetshire* moved in with her torpedo tubes ready and felt no joy, no feelings of triumph.

"Fall out action stations. Port watch to defense stations," came through the speaker.

Men stirred in the pilothouse and there were the sounds of scuttles being opened, doors and hatches undogged and locked in open positions, and the welcome sound of blowers coming to life. The great guns came back to battery and the turrets were trained fore and aft. There were excited shouts as men began to be relieved on the bridge and foretop. Crawling out of the small hatches under the foot-thick armor at the rear of the turrets, gunners still encased in their flash-resistant clothing began to pour out of A and B turrets. They gathered in groups at the rail, gesticulating at the dying battleship and talking excitedly.

Then, as *King George V* turned for home, *Dorsetshire* fired three torpedoes into the wreck. Looking back at the horizon, Rodney saw the great ship finally roll over, her red-leaded bottom rocking and kicking up spray, her three bronze screws still turning. Higgins felt a start of horror; there must still be live men in her engine rooms. Within minutes, she vanished, only a black cloud lingering. Quickly, the smoke yielded to the wind and faded away, leaving nothing to mark the grave of over two thousand men.

Lieutenant Higgins lingered by the windscreen. He wondered about the strange gamut of emotion that had wracked him and wrung him dry of feelings. He had felt the blood lust of battle, triumph, and then near despair when he realized men were really being killed. But had he not trained for this? Pointed his entire life at this moment? But never in his training had he ever conceived of actually killing anyone. And then a revelation on a day of revelations—*nothing prepares a man for battle except battle itself*.

He should not have felt despair—regret. *Bismarck* had been the enemy of *KG V* and he had been part of *KG V*. With a little luck the Germans would have killed him just as they had killed the crew of *Hood*. And they would have celebrated his death with cheers and backslapping. He was convinced of one thing: the battleship was the supreme power at sea. Nothing could stand up to her power.

The kaleidoscope was racing again and he felt exhausted. He pounded his temple with a clenched fist. He needed a drink. And he needed to see home again. Yes. That was it. He was due for a leave. He would return to his home on Fifth Avenue. To his mother. To Kay Stockard.

II

Return to New York
June 18, 1941

CARRYING a heavy canvas barracks bag in one hand and a briefcase in the other, Lieutenant j.g. Rodney Higgins flagged down the 1936 De Soto cab. He was home at last. Standing on Twenty-third Street where it butted into the East River docks and looking east, the skyline was studded with Manhattan's forest of skyscrapers. Raucous sirens wove through the city's peculiar dull roar of rumbling subways, noisy cabs, and street traffic. He could even smell it. Feel the press and energy of two million crowded souls. It was all back. The town of towns. He loved it. "Sixty-first and Fifth Avenue," he said, slamming the door behind him and settling back into the lumpy upholstery. The cabbie pushed the flag down, grunted, and roared away from the curb.

Rodney's ship, the old tramp steamer *Bristol Spirit*, had arrived at the Hudson River's Pier 36 just forty minutes before. It had made the crossing in complete secrecy. The lieutenant still felt the grime of the antique freighter and yearned for a long luxurious bath in his old tub. *Just twenty minutes*, he told himself as the taxi turned up Sixth Avenue.

It had been a long, grueling trip with incessant U-boat alarms sending him to his boat station at all hours. And the ship had steamed alone with only her American flag for protection. But everyone knew the U-boat captains respected nothing. Just the week before, the American steamer *Robin Moore* had been sunk. But *Bristol Spirit* was steaming back to America with empty holds. To the Germans, she was a low-priority target. Everyone knew that, too.

His first sightings of the New York coast had been exhilarating. Standing on the forecastle, he and a dozen other passengers—officers and noncoms who had been attached to the RAF, BEF, and Royal Navy as observers since 1939—had strained their eyes for the first glimpse of home. There was a ripple of excitement as New Jersey's Sandy Hook was sighted in the dim early morning light. Then Rockaway Point and Coney Island where he had spent many exciting days as a youth loomed to the north and east. At a maddeningly slow speed, the old steamer creaked into the Lower Bay, passed Norton Point, and entered the Narrows. Looking around happily, Rodney saw the green shore of Staten Island crowding the restricted passage from the west, Brooklyn's Owl's Head Park to the east.

There had been shouts when the Statue of Liberty came into view. Growing up, Rodney had seen her a hundred times. The lonesome figure had been nothing but a three-hundred-foot pile of weathered copper to him then. Today, she was different. Holding her torch higher than ever, the grand old lady welcomed them and seemed to bless them at the same time. To Rodney, the streaked greenish face appeared warm, alive, and beatific. Two young officers broke into a chorus of "Chattanooga Choo Choo." Two sergeants began to jitterbug.

Someone pointed to the Empire State Building. Its 102 stories reaching for the low clouds dominated the Manhattan skyline of metal-clad, steel-ribbed, glass-shrouded towers and rising clouds of steam. Everything that represented America was there—strong, reassuring, rich, and stable after the bloodletting in the North Atlantic. It was colossal. It was romantic. It was their country. More murmurs of excitement like young schoolboys on their first field trip.

The passage through the Upper Bay had been made at a snail's pace. All around the bay was thick with freighters, tugs, tall-funneled ferryboats, sludge (honey) barges, launches, lighters, motor yachts, train flats. The most powerful fireboat in the world, *The Firefighter*, passed, making for the Upper Bay.

Looking around at the heavy traffic, a lieutenant said to Rodney, "Thicker'n whores on Broadway."

Rodney chuckled. "Safer. None of these ships can give you a dose of clap."

"I'll drink to that," an old, gnarled top sergeant named Christopher Lester said, leisurely scratching his crotch. A native of Chicago and at least sixty years old, Lester's sleeve was crowded with "hash marks" that reached to his elbow. Then eyeing the other passengers slyly, the sergeant mimicked a medic's voice. "Skin it back and milk it down," he crowed, arching a bushy gray eyebrow. There was a roar of laughter.

Crossing the East River estuary they glimpsed the Brooklyn Navy Yard where gray-clad warships and transports were nested, gantries and cranes drooping over them like old birds with broken backs. They passed Liberty Island, Ellis Island, Governors Island, Fort Jay, and entered the Hudson River where most of the city's 103 piers jutted into the stream like an interminable row of black teeth. Everyone stared at the interned French liner *Normandie*. Moored at the foot of Fourteenth Street, the one-thousand-foot-long leviathan looked pathetic and forlorn in her rust-streaked gray paint. Two German freighters were moored astern of her. Armed guards could be seen on the pier and walking the decks of the ships.

With the help of a tug as dilapidated and old as herself, the old steamer finally made her turn and was warped into her berth at Pier 41 on Manhattan's West Side. Rodney and the rest of the passengers were ready to disembark as soon as the first line was secured. It took at least twenty minutes to lower and rig the gangway. Each clumsy gaffe by the crewmen was analyzed by the waiting passengers with colorful expletives. "Get on the ball! Get your finger out your ass!" a middle-aged infantry captain from Boise bellowed. A former sergeant major, he continued the harangue with his sergeant's vocabulary, "You assholes can't even rig a simple plank. We should make you walk it, you six-fingered fuck-ups!"

Now Rodney was eyeing his hometown from the cab eagerly, like a first-time tourist. The sleazy irregular structures of lower Sixth Avenue; the vast, impersonal slab of mundanity called the RCA Building; the asymmetric facade of Rockefeller Center with its flower gardens and roof gardens; midtown with its smart shops, grand hotels, plush offices, theaters. Unlike the austere traffic of London, New York's was multitudinous—brightly painted, endless, vigorous, and confident. The flash and panache of it was like a tonic. He had missed it. Lord, he had missed it.

The cabbie was a slice of New York, too. He was a short, dark man who chewed on the end of an unlighted cigar incessantly. Either the back of his hairy neck had not seen soap and water for days or he was a very dark Italian or Spaniard. It was also obvious his origins were in Brooklyn. "Youse from New Yawk, Lieutenant?"

"Yes. Just got back from England," Rodney said, contemplating the neck.

"Then you ain't up with them bums?"

"The Dodgers?"

"Yeah."

"The English papers aren't interested."

"No wonder we had a rev'lution. They ain't civ'lized."

They both laughed. The cabbie continued, "The bums ain't doin' shit. I seen 'em yesterday. Pee Wee Reese an' Mickey Owen ain't hittin'. The pitchin' stinks."

"What about Dixie Walker, Cookie Lavagetto, Dolph Camilli?"

Rodney had made a mistake. The cabbie had a live one and he knew it. Waving his arm for emphasis, he launched into a long soliloquy about the incompetence of the manager, Leo Durocher, the hitting, pitching, analyzing each player in minute detail. The villains were the aristocratic Yankees who he obviously loathed. The Dodgers were a team of the people, a team for the common man. Rodney grunted, nodded, and stared out of the window. Fortunately, a rush of traffic as they approached Fifth Avenue finally brought silence to the front seat, the cabbie wrestling with the wheel as he weaved and dodged in the usual reckless fashion of a New York cabdriver. Rodney held his breath, but the cabbie had talked himself into silence.

With a screech of tortured tires, the big De Soto made the turn up Fifth Avenue—"The Avenue" to old New Yorkers—wide, the street of millionaires, the habitat of the best families and ambitious, expensive whores. Broad, handsome, it was ornamented with elaborate twin-light lamp standards, ending in a formal archway at Washington Square. The sidewalks were teeming with fashionably dressed men and women. On the side streets, shabby men hawking everything from apples to diamonds, even a few prostitutes looking for an early afternoon "John." Nothing had changed. Nothing would ever change.

Finally, with the green swath of Central Park visible to the left, the battered De Soto roared past Sixtieth Street and screeched to a halt in front of the Higgins mansion. Rodney felt a boyish warmth of remembrance, the ineffable joy of homecoming known to those who have risked their lives in battle and had wondered repeatedly about their chances of ever seeing home and loved ones again.

He would take them by surprise. Was his mother home? He should have phoned Brenda from the dock, but had decided against it when he thought of delighting in the surprised joy on her face. His grandmother, Ellen Ashcroft, should be home. Perhaps his divorced aunt Betty and her daughter Marsha would be there. But Marsha was in college and Betty liked to spend her time at Tiffany's, Cartier's, and the surrounding smart shops—so they said. He suspected lovers. His worthless brother, Nathan, had moved out, but made frequent appearances with his slatternly girlfriend, Margaret, especially when he was hungry. One way or other, like it or not, he would see them all and soon.

He felt a twitch of deep remorse. Kay Stockard was out of town. She had written him about a trip to Hollywood to discuss fashion ads for *Harper's Bazaar* where she held the post of assistant advertising director. He needed her in the hot, carnal, physical way all men need a woman. But he could not have her. She would not return for at least two weeks. And it had been such a long time. Just the thought of her brought a discomforting heat to his groin. He squirmed in frustration.

The sight of his home tore his mind from the hot memories. He feasted his eyes on the immense three-story brownstone that dominated the corner of Sixty-first Street with all the cold aloofness of a king's crypt. Yet, now, at first glimpse, it seemed strangely warm and cozy to his hungry eyes.

Neither palazzo nor chateau as were most of the other palatial residences of "Millionaires' Row," his home was an eclectic blending of flat, medieval lines and Tuscan arches. Crowding the street with its facade of high windows and ornate cornices, the immense building was separated from gawking passersby by a high iron-grillwork fence capped inhospitably by a grim phalanx of pikelike points.

Bounding from the cab, clutching his canvas bag and briefcase, Rodney chuckled in high spirits. He tipped the cabbie lavishly and turned to the door.

"Thanks, Lieutenant," the cabbie said, examining the bill in his hand. "See youse at Ebbets Field." He roared away with a clash of gears and cloud of blue-black smoke. Rodney waved.

Travers the butler answered the pounding. At first the balding, portly old gentleman, still splendid in his formal livery, could only stare openmouthed. Then a warm handshake and a call to "Mrs. Hargreaves!"

She met him in the entry, a huge, circular room bigger than *KG V*'s wardroom. It was hung with Rembrandts, Titians, and Holbeins, had a Garnier chandelier overhead, and was floored with gray and white marble set in a checkerboard pattern. Flinging her arms around him, Brenda's emotions took Rodney by surprise. Although he had not written her of his experiences on board *King George V*, she had learned from friends in high places in the Navy Department of the risks he had taken.

She broke into sobs that quickly became cries of recrimination and anger. "Why? Why did you do it? You're like your father—your stepfather. They couldn't wait to get killed—to die gloriously—earn their goddamned medals." She pounded his chest with her tiny fists, crying and kissing his neck, his cheeks.

He held her close, muttering, "Mother. Mother, please." Again and again he told the lie of illness and sleep while the servants, Travers the butler, Antoine the cook, and his mother's personal maid of over twenty years, Nicole, watched misty-eyed.

Finally, taking Rodney's hand, Brenda led him into the parlor. With a ceiling of rich Chinese fabrics, a collection of Japanese and Chinese bronzes, and walls of red silks and velvets, his grandparents had dubbed it the "Chink's Room." Brenda pulled her son down onto a plump velvet sofa and gestured to the butler who had limped into the room behind them. Torn by shrapnel at the Argonne, Travers's left leg had withered to half the size of his right. With a fused knee, he used it more like a cane than a leg.

"The usual, sir?" the old gentleman asked, beaming down on the lieutenant.

Rodney nodded. Travers stumped to a sideboard and returned with a Johnnie Walker and seltzer for Rodney and a glass of Chateau Lafite-Rothschild for his mistress. After placing a silver service with ice and liquor on a low giltwood pier table in front of them, he exited quietly. Taking a deep drink, Rodney sank back, feeling the warmth of the liquor spread. The tensions began to drain.

"You won't do something as stupid as that again, will you, Rodney?" his mother began.

"As what?"

"Risk your neck for nothing. That's what."

The lieutenant smiled. "Of course not, Mother." He took another drink. "And, Mother, no one was hurt—*KG V* wasn't even hit."

She covered her mouth. "Rodney. Please. Please. You know how I lost your father, stepfather, my brother Hugh. They'd tell me the same stories. No one ever took any chances. But they're all still dead."

The young man drained his glass and recharged it. He changed the subject. "Grandmother? Nathan? Aunt Betty? Marsha? Where are they?"

"Your aunt Betty and grandmother Ellen are shopping. Marsha's taking classes at Columbia and your brother Nathan doesn't live here anymore." She turned away and he could see she was upset.

"Moved? Where does he live?"

"Greenwich Village and sometimes he sleeps in Central Park."

"Central Park?" He took another deep drink.

She looked up. "The park's safe—you know that, Rodney. He says he likes to commune with nature."

"He's been communing with that communist, Earl Browder, and a bunch of radicals, Mother."

"I know. But he says he's found something."

"He should find a job and he'd better hunt for himself, too. He doesn't know what he is." He could feel the Scotch spreading, and the cold motif of the room began to take on a warm glow.

It was Brenda's turn to change the subject. "How long is your leave?"

"Three weeks."

There was anguish in her voice. "Is that all?"

"I'm sorry."

"Your next duty?"

He toyed with his glass. "I've applied for battleship duty."

"Why?"

"That's where the power is. I want to be at the heart of it. I think I'll get *Arizona*. She's been moved from Long Beach to Pearl Harbor. The whole battle fleet moved last year."

"You were impressed by your—ah—last experience."

"They're safe, Mother. Floating steel fortresses."

"Tell that to your father, the boys on *Hood*, *Bismarck*." She covered her mouth.

"We aren't at war, Mother."

She looked at him, the blue of her eyes heightened by moisture. "No, but Roosevelt is sure trying to correct that situation. We gave the British fifty destroyers, there's Lend-Lease, we're escorting ships, the Germans are sinking our ships . . ." A sob cut her off.

He held her close, pressed his lips to her temple, felt the effects of liquor and fatigue sapping his energy. "Mother. I need to soak myself—rest. The old ship never had enough water and . . ."

"Why, of course. You must be tired." She smiled up at him. "Your old room is exactly as you left it. Take your bath and get some rest. I'll phone Nathan's apartment. We'll have a family dinner together." She ran a finger through the stubble on his chin. He detected a tension in her voice, "Your girlfriend, Kay, is out of town."

"I know. She wrote me." He came to his feet.

The liquor, the hot-water tub, and then a thick turkey sandwich served to drop Rodney into a deep sleep. And he was back in the comfort and security of his own room with its heavy four-poster bed, massive oak furniture, rich drapes, and thick Aubusson rugs. Deep in his sleep he sensed a presence before he heard the light footsteps. Opening his eyes, he saw the delicately molded features of Nicole the French maid looming over him.

She was more beautiful than he ever remembered. Although he knew she was at least forty, she looked ten years younger. Her skin was clear like fine porcelain without a hint of wrinkles even at the corners of the eyes and mouth. True to her genesis near Toulon in the Cote d' Azur, her hair was black, cheekbones high and tinted by her Latin blood the color of ivory, nostrils straight and small, mouth perpetually curved in an uncertain pout that gave it a sensual twist. Her breasts were large and pointed, a tight white apron nipping her black taffeta dress in at her tiny waist. He remembered stealing looks at her when she walked past when he was very young, perhaps not thirteen. And he noticed her even more as he grew into adolescence. It was like watching music, full-formed womanly hips and buttocks that flowed sinuously with each step. He had always wanted to touch her, but never dared. Once, when he was a junior in high school, she had played a prominent role in one of his erotic dreams. Everyone knew her lover had vanished with his entire regiment at Verdun. She had never married. Her whole life revolved around Brenda and the Higgins family.

Her huge dark eyes were peering into his. "I am sorry, Monsieur Higgins. I did not mean to awaken you. I brought you your favorite pillow." She placed a goose-down pillow on the bed next to his head.

Rodney had no memory of his "favorite pillow," but tucked it under his head anyway, with a smiling, "Thank you, Nicole."

The maid's eyes moved over the sheet-covered form. "I missed *le galant homme*. I worry." She leaned closer. "I lost my love, Henri, at Verdun and *mon père* at the Marne in *La Grand Guerre*. And now my Rodney, fighting the Boches, too. And maybe I lose him." Her hand was cool and soft on his forehead. Boldly, she traced a finger down his cheek.

He could never remember Nicole touching him before. When he had been very young his governess, Bridie O'Conner, had cared for him, his brother, and sister while Nicole spent her time with his mother. She had always been distant, aloof. Now, she was leaning very close and her eyes held not just concern; there was warmth there. Was it the heat of desire? He had read it in the eyes of many women before. And the long dry months had taken their toll of Rodney. Despite his will, the barrier of decades, the impossibility of a dalliance with a maid in your own home, he felt the fire begin to rise like an aphrodisiac from deep down. He reached up and took her hand.

There was the sound of uneven footsteps in the hall. It was Travers. Rodney was shocked back to cold reality and the maid stepped back. "Is there anything else, monsieur?"

"No, thank you, Nicole. You are dismissed."

The footsteps faded. "He is gone, monsieur." She stepped closer.

The timbre was curt, "I said you are dismissed, Nicole."

"*Oui*, monsieur." She whirled and left the room.

The dining room was large and eclectically furnished, filled with the sounds of people talking and eating at the same time. The long mahogany table was George III, cabinets and sideboards Hepplewhite and Duncan Phyfe, the enormous chandelier Waterford crystal. The walls were hung with a Van Dyck, a Renoir, and two Picassos of the blue period. In a corner stood his mother's pride: an ancient satinwood-cased grandfather clock by Eli Terry, *click-clack*ing with the peculiar sound of its wooden movement.

Now his mother, Brenda Hargreaves, looked up at him from the opposite end of the table. In the soft glow of candlelight, she was lovelier than ever, the anguish of the early afternoon gone. Her auburn hair flowed to her shoulders like silk, her flawless skin glowed with good health. The widely spaced blue eyes were as deep and dark as the Atlantic at sunset, the fire of candlelight reflecting from her pupils like dancing gold leaf. The warmth was for her son—back, safe, seated at her table again.

Most of the family was seated. On Rodney's right hand sat his adoring grandmother, Ellen Ashcroft, who had been widowed since 1931 when her husband, John, had either fallen or leapt from the twentieth floor of the New York Stock Exchange. Born in 1870, she was still a nineteenth-century woman with Victorian values and prejudices. She was the quintessential "grandmother," short, gray, and matronly with a round pudgy face and bright eyes that danced with joy whenever she looked at Rodney and her other grandchildren. Retaining some of New York's finest couturieres, she still managed to appear dowdy and matronly even when dressed in the most stylish gowns.

Beside Ellen sat Rodney's aunt, Betty. In her early forties, she had arresting blue eyes like Brenda's. However, her red hair was frizzled as if she carried an electrical transformer at the base of her skull, charging every strand with a hundred volts. The tangled bristles reminded Rodney of Albert Einstein's wild hairdo. Her once-beautiful face had been marred by incursions of fat. Spread wide and appearing soft like a sack filled with gelatin, her once-petite figure had suffered, too. She had outraged her parents and been disowned when at the age of seventeen she married an Italian barber, Dominic Borelli, and moved to Los Angeles. Betty divorced Dominic in 1927 when she discovered his affair with his manicurist. She had never remarried. Instead, she had taken a succession of lovers, showing an insatiable appetite for young men. Rodney had often caught her staring at him with hungry eyes. He always looked away uneasily. Currently, it was rumored she was seeing a boy not twenty years of age. She had two children; twenty-one-year-old Tony who was attending the University of Southern California and a nineteen-year-old daughter, Marsha, who was sitting next to her mother. Mother and daughter had taken up "temporary" quarters in a suite on the third floor two years earlier. Betty was comfortable financially, enjoying a million-dollar trust established by her parents after she divorced the Italian.

Because Marsha had been raised in Los Angeles, Rodney had seen very little of his cousin. She had a deceptive appearance. Delicate like a Dresden doll, the exquisite lines of her face gave a misleading cherubic appearance. However, her hot eyes and sensuous walk revealed her true nature; an erotic view of the world and a developing voracious appetite for men similar to her mother's. Disdaining Bryn Mawr, she was attending Columbia University and majoring in art. Rodney always felt she was majoring in boys. In fact, there was already a blossoming scandal about her and a middle-aged professor.

An empty chair was opposite Aunt Betty. Rodney felt a hollow, languishing emptiness as he stared at his half-sister's place at the table. Rodney adored Regina. His beautiful, intelligent half-sister, Regina Hargreaves, had married a Polish Jew, a premed exchange student she had met at the Metropolitan Museum of Art while a freshman at Bryn Mawr. They had moved to Warsaw just in time to be caught by the German invasion of 1939.

The family had warned Regina, objected to the Jew, Josef Lipiski. "Stay away from foreigners," Grandmother Ellen had cautioned her. "Look at your aunt Betty. She married a 'Wop' and see what happened to her. 'Kikes' aren't any better. Marry a nice white man of good breeding." Everyone agreed except Regina. Rodney felt the statement was repugnant and said as much. His half-sister had smiled warmly at him while his grandmother looked pained.

They had had four letters from Regina in 1940, sent through the Swiss Red Cross. Thus far, in 1941, not a word had sifted out of tortured Poland. The family only knew Regina, her husband Josef, and their one-year-old child Rose were living in the Warsaw ghetto. Once a month Brenda and Betty sent packages loaded with food and clothing. Those sent in 1940 had been acknowledged, but not a word in 1941. Rodney was convinced the Germans were stealing everything.

Rodney's eyes moved to his brother, Nathan, who sat to his left. Wearing a heavy black beard like a nineteenth-century philosopher, Nathan was a college dropout who hated war and loved Karl Marx. He was an admirer of the isolationists: Henry Cabot Lodge, William E. Borah, Gerald P. Bye, Charles A. Lindbergh, and the vociferous Burton K. Wheeler. A draft dodger, his efforts to avoid service had been aided by Brenda's claim he was essential to the operation of Ashcroft Mills.

To Rodney's knowledge, his brother had never worked. Built big like Rodney, Nathan's once athletic, powerful physique was turning flaccid. As unpredictable as North Atlantic weather, he showed quick, tempestuous mood changes and a hair-trigger temper. In fact, as youths, they had fought often with fists. Once, at an American Legion baseball game when they were on opposite teams, with bats.

Nathan's most impressive feature was his heavy black eyebrows. Meeting at the bridge of his nose like valances, they sheltered his piercing brown eyes that glowed ominously with inner heat like coals of an open fire fanned by a vagrant breeze. Nathan disliked bathing. He smelled. *Rasputin the Monk*, Rodney thought to himself.

Wolfing her *salade de tomates* in a chair next to his brother sat Nathan's girlfriend, Margaret Hollister. A tall, raw-boned girl who obviously hated brassieres, she had big disassociated breasts that stabbed obliquely from each other like the eyes of a cockeyed man. Her harsh features reminded Rodney of a youthful Marjorie Main. Margaret dressed carelessly. Her hair was unkempt, dresses commonplace and sometimes soiled, and she exuded the aroma of a neglected body. "Natural musk," Rodney had heard her say once to a smirking Nathan. She, too, was a follower of Karl Marx. She, too, was from a wealthy family. Rodney wondered how she and Nathan could ever stand each other's odors in bed. *Maybe they wear clamps on their noses*, he thought ruefully.

His mother's new "friend," Hamilton Babcock, sat at Brenda's right hand. A middle-aged man, balding and with a developing paunch, Babcock was one in a series of "friends" and earlier "uncles" who his mother had entertained, often privately, in her own quarters since Rodney was a little boy. Divorced with two grown sons, Hamilton owned a majority interest in Spectrum Electronics, one of the nation's largest manufacturers of radio equipment. He was also president of the company and chairman of the board. Everyone knew Hamilton wanted to marry Brenda, but, as usual, Brenda showed no interest in matrimony. He had a sharp toothy smile, and the most dulcet voice this side of the Royal Shakespeare Company. But there was something unsettling about the man, a latent malevolence that glowed in the mottled gray-green eyes every time he looked at Rodney. Rodney felt uneasy whenever in the man's presence.

As Nicole and Travers scooped up the salad plates and replaced them with bowls of a soup called *bourride*—Antoine's artful blend of mixed fish, herbs, and spices—Hamilton turned to Rodney, "Heard you were in on the kill of *Bismarck*."

"I had some help." Everyone chuckled. Rodney described the action, not mentioning the fact he was the first to sight the German.

Nathan looked down the table at his brother. "Every shell turned a profit for Vickers-Armstrong," Nathan said suddenly. All eyes moved to Rodney.

The lieutenant laughed. "A debit in Hitler's ledger," he countered.

"Boys, please," Brenda said. Nathan slumped back and drained his glass.

"It must've been a glorious thing to see," Babcock persisted, gray-green eyes hard as if they had been lacquered.

"Glorious? The sinking?" Rodney moved his eyes from guest to guest before answering. "It was a slaughter. It was hideous." He saw the pained look on his mother's face and regretted his words. He gulped his wine and held up his glass. Nicole filled it with Chablis Premier Grand Cru and moved around the table, filling the other glasses. Gesturing with his glass, he said, "To the British—a brave people who don't know when to quit." Everyone drank except Nathan and Margaret.

Brenda held up her glass. She looked at Nathan and then Rodney, "To your uncles Lloyd and Randolph Higgins. As long as they're alive, Hitler can't win."

Glasses were drained and again Nathan and Margaret refused to drink.

"What's wrong, Nathan?" Rodney said with a voice that singed. "Can't toast capitalist swine?" Silence flooded the room like water through a broken dike.

Nathan turned to his brother, his bushy eyebrows meeting at the apex of his scowl. "Yes. Our uncles have been exploiting their workers at Carlisle Mills . . ."

"Enough!" Brenda cried. "We're not here to hear you two argue." Her sons fell silent. But Nathan glared at his brother, the brown pinpoints highly polished marble.

Hamilton Babcock interrupted in an attempt to salvage the situation, "Uncles Lloyd and Randolph? They're English?"

"Yes," Brenda answered. "They're my brothers-in-law by my first marriage to Geoffry Higgins. They were both wounded in the first war. Randolph is a fighter squadron commander with the RAF."

"Isn't he too old to fly?"

A snicker circled the table. "Everyone knows that except Randolph."

"Not combat."

Brenda nodded. "I hope not. In his letters he claims he spends his time flying a desk."

"But you don't believe him?"

She shook her head and stabbed a finger upward. "He's a creature of the air. Loves to fly more than anything else on earth. He was one of England's first flyers. In fact, he learned to fly with A. V. Roe, Tommy Sopwith, Geoffrey de Havilland. They would fly together, design their own aircraft, build them—they did it all." She turned to Rodney, "You saw Randolph?"

Rodney welcomed his mother's change in mood. "Yes, Mother. I saw him at Fenwyck. Got to spend a weekend there. Saw Aunt Bernice and cousins Trevor and Bonnie, too. And Randolph's desk must be equipped with machine guns. Trevor told me there's a rumor he's had a dozen kills in the last year, but tries to keep it quiet—gives credit to his men. He's afraid of being grounded." Murmurs of excitement and disbelief circled the table. Rodney continued, "Uncle Lloyd's still in Africa."

Hamilton asked Brenda, "With the Eighth Army?"

"Lloyd's a brigadier general with General Richard O'-Connor's staff in North Africa," she answered.

"O'Connor was captured by Rommel. The Germans have been gloating about it for a month."

"Not Lloyd. He'd die first. I got a letter from him last week," Brenda said.

Hamilton downed the rest of his wine. His glass was quickly refilled by Nicole who turned and recharged Rodney's glass. Leaning too close, her breast brushed against his shoulder. He took a quick drink and began eating his soup. He felt heat on his face.

Hamilton continued, "They're businessmen?"

"Yes, of course," Brenda said. "They own two thirds of Carlisle Mills, Limited, in Manchester. We're partners. I inherited one third of the business when Geoffry was killed." A cold look like a sheet of ice hardened the lovely features. "When he was burned to death at Jutland." She glared at Rodney. Nathan snickered.

Brenda's enormous wealth came home to everyone at the table. Sole owner of Ashcroft Mills that had been deeded to her by her mother after her father's suicide, she also held a share of one of England's largest textile mills. Two years earlier, Rodney had heard the British holdings estimated at a value of over three million pounds. No doubt, with lucrative war contracts, it was worth much more. The value of Ashcroft Mills was in the tens of millions. Rodney saw Hamilton dampen his lips with the tip of his tongue.

Nicole continued to circle the table with the wine decanter while Travers quickly placed the entree in front of the diners. It was one of Antoine's specialties, veal in cream sauce that he called *blanquette de veau*. It was served with marvelous glazed carrots and delicate potato puffs. Rodney felt more thirst than hunger. Draining his fourth glass, he held it up. There was a flash of taffeta and the glass was full again with the straw-colored liquor. Brenda glared disapprovingly. Nathan smiled and held up his glass, too.

There was a momentary silence as the diners attacked the gourmet meal. Ellen broke the silence by timidly turning to Margaret. "Do you think the British can hold out?"

"With our help," Margaret Hollister said, spraying her words through a mouth full of food. "Roosevelt's declared his own private war. He's arming the British and everyone knows it." She waved a fork for emphasis. "We're escorting their ships."

"Herbert Hoover said the only way we can aid the British was to stay out," Marsha asserted, entering the conversation. Obviously eager to see Rodney's reaction, she stared into his eyes with a bold, confident look for one so young.

"Stay out?" Margaret said.

"Yes," Marsha said, turning to Margaret, fine hair swaying with the movement like a silk sheet. Marsha's hair was remarkable and she obviously took pride in it. Worn in the style popularized by the actress Veronica Lake, it was the color of roasted chestnuts and as lustrous as watered satin. Flowing down to her shoulders, it flickered with glowing red stars and highlights each time she moved. Brushing a strand from her eye, she continued, "He says we're not even prepared to defend ourselves."

"Tell that to Roosevelt," Margaret replied curtly, thumping the table. "And we're stuck with him for another four years."

Marsha turned back to Rodney but before she could speak, Nathan interrupted her. Eyeing Hamilton ominously, he spoke and his slurred words made it clear he was feeling his wine, "Your company stands to make a pile if we get into this one—radios, electronics equipment . . . You must stick pins into your Lindbergh and Wheeler dolls every night."

Margaret laughed so raucously that she choked on a piece of veal. A full glass of wine drunk in two gulps washed the meat away. She wiped her mouth with the back of her hand.

Hamilton's eyes widened. Beginning at his neck, a red flush crept slowly upward to his cheeks. "See here . . ." he began.

Brenda interrupted. "Nathan," she cried. "That was rude."

Nathan tried to sit upright, but slumped to one side, turning his big bearded head from side to side. The apology was so grudging it was not an apology at all. "Sorry," he offered. "Didn't mean to offend." Margaret snickered.

Rodney felt his own anger rising through the half-eaten entree and at least eight glasses of Chablis. "Hitler's getting ready to clobber your ol' buddy Stalin, dear brother," he said sarcastically. "And Stalin has it coming. He started the war."

Brenda sank back, hopeless resignation on her face. Everyone else stared at the brothers. "Started the war?" Nathan repeated incredulously.

Rodney thumped the table with a clenched fist for emphasis. "In 'thirty-nine Stalin was negotiating with both the Allies and Germany. He made a nonaggression pact with Hitler because he knew if Hitler's rear was safe, he would attack Poland. In fact, they even agreed on how to carve up Poland before the war began." He sank back and took a drink. "Of course Stalin started it. He wanted Germany, England, and France to slaughter each other and then he could walk in and take over Europe."

"Nice speech, brother, but just the usual capitalist propaganda," Nathan shot back, suddenly appearing to sober. "It's the Rothschilds, Rockefellers, and DuPonts and their gang of greedy international bankers counting their profits in blood. Look to them if you're looking for warmongers."

Marsha spoke, dark eyes fixed on Rodney and flashing provocatively as if backlighted. She was enjoying the passion of the exchange and rising to it. "There've been rumors for weeks about German troops massing on the Russian border."

Nathan dismissed the girl with an imperious wave. "More propaganda. Wishful thinking on the part of the capitalists."

Marsha would not be put off. She recited a litany of destroyed nations: "Poland, Czechoslovakia, Denmark, Norway, France, Yugoslavia, Greece . . ."

Nathan interrupted her, "Imperialistic, capitalistic swine who had outlived their time."

Eyeing the pair, Rodney felt restraint fading, an amalgam of frustration and anger growing. "Our own sister's trapped in Warsaw," he said grimly. "Don't you give a damn?"

"She made the choice when she married the Jew," his brother retorted hotly.

Rodney's voice cracked like breaking ice, "And Adolph Hitler is a humanitarian—a fighter for Marxism?"

"He's brought changes."

"He's also a Fascist. How can you, a warrior for the downtrodden workers, support him?" Silence, a thing of weight and substance, filled the room, coating everyone. All eyes were on the brothers. Brenda remained silent. It seemed she knew her sons had to have this thing out. Her eyes were very sad.

Rodney answered his question with a question, "Is it because he has a treaty with the champion of the world's workers, Joseph Stalin?"

Nathan leaned forward, fists balled on the table. He spit out his words, "This isn't the nineteenth century, brother. The people will no longer be exploited, will . . ."

"Will what?" Rodney interrupted. "You hated Hitler until August of 'thirty-nine—until he and Stalin signed their nonaggression treaty. Then you fell in love with him. Now the Germans are massing on the Russian border. They'll attack Russia before the summer's out." His face twisted into a sarcastic grin. "That'll end your love affair. Mark me. You'll jump out of that bed."

Nathan chewed his lips and then skinned them back abruptly, revealing yellow, food-clogged teeth. "Nonsense! Wall Street's wishful thinking—propaganda to mislead the masses."

Rodney narrowed his eyes, the timbre of his voice acid with derision, "You live well for a hater of capitalism." He circled a finger over his head. "Plain but simple fare for the champion of the oppressed workers. House on Fifth Avenue, French cuisine." He held up his glass in a mocking salute, "The best liquor money can buy . . ."

Nathan's face darkened like the shadow of a squall at sea. His voice rumbled from deep down, "We live in a tenement—in Greenwich Village. We . . ."

"But you manage to find mother's kitchen every day."

Eyes flaming, fists balled, Nathan bolted to his feet. "That's a lie and I won't take that from anyone!" he shouted, voice reeking with anger and outrage.

Coming erect, Brenda cried, "Nathan!" Everyone else remained silent. Ellen slumped, a look of horror contorting her features. Betty had a frightened look on her face as if she had walked head-on into the Frankenstein monster in a dark hallway. Marsha's eyes glowed with the passionate fascination of one viewing the slaughter of gladiators in Rome's coliseum. Margaret grinned through a mouth full of food and belched. Hamilton Babcock had an amused smile on his face. He sipped his Grand Cru. Travers stood by the door, supporting himself on the doorjamb, face impassive. A crestfallen Nicole was a statue behind her mistress.

For the first time in his life, Rodney ignored his mother. The effects of the liquor and his anger took charge. The fires flared deep, the internecine rage that only one brother can feel for another gripped his mind like the jaws of a steel trap. He was right and he knew it. Nathan was a traitor, a bum who mooched off of his mother. Even the servants complained about Nathan and his friends raiding the refrigerator and pantry, sometimes twice daily. The remnants of his control melted away like ice in the summer's sun and he leapt to his feet, eyes glinting cold blue light like bayonet tips. "Hypocrite! Draft dodger! Anytime you care to . . ."

Brenda was on her feet, her face a book of anger and grief. Her voice cracked like a whip, "Enough! Both of you. You are not only rude to me, you are rude to my guests. That's unforgivable—unconscionable."

Nathan sagged, turned to his mother. "Sorry, Mother." He gestured to Margaret. "We were just leaving."

"Excellent idea," Brenda answered.

Glowering at his brother with unabashed hatred, Nathan left. Margaret followed him, glancing spitefully at Rodney.

An hour later, Rodney was still seated at the table, glaring at the linen tablecloth and drinking. "You are sure you want more *vin*, monsieur?" Nicole asked. Rodney nodded. She half filled the glass and stood quietly at his side. Everyone had left. His heartbroken mother claiming she needed fresh air had gone for a ride with Hamilton in his new Packard Custom Super Eight convertible sedan. Even Travers retired after the table had been cleared.

Rodney looked up at the maid's sad face. "Go to bed, Nicole."

She shook her head. "Nicole stays with Rodney, *s'il vous plaît*?"

A trace of a smile began to turn the corners of his lips. "Okay. But I'm one helluva bore tonight." She smiled at his improving spirits.

He finished the wine in a room filled with silence except for the *click, clack* of the big grandfather clock. Finally, fatigued and with heavy eyelids, he struggled to his feet. He was very unsteady. Nicole took his arm and he did not object when she helped him up the stairs. He collapsed backward on his bed fully clothed, arms flung out like a dead man.

Soft hands with delicate fingers removed his shoes and

loosened his collar. Quickly his shirt was pulled off. Then the fingers found his belt, undid the buckle, and unbuttoned his trousers. Several hard tugs failed to pull his pants down. He was too tired, saturated with alcohol, to raise himself. The hands gave up, but remained for a moment, casually running over his hard abdomen, the flanks of his slender hips. It was pleasant. He drifted off.

Sighing, Nicole pulled the heavy drapes, threw the wall switch, blotting out the last trace of light as she closed the door behind her. In complete blackness, Rodney fell into a deep sleep.

His sleep was fitful. Feverish. His brother's baleful face. The heartbreak in his mother's eyes. The faces of the others—Hamilton Babcock, his grandmother, aunt, cousin, all staring wide-eyed. The wine soured and gurgled in his stomach. Suddenly his skin was hot. Bolting upright, he tore off his clothes. The sheets felt cool on his bare flesh. He rolled in them like a little boy and fell back into a sleep so deep he felt drugged.

Then the dreams came like a theater's curtain opening on a terrible tragedy. He was alone at sea on the deck of a great warship. There was a ferocious storm. A towering wave washed him over the side and he was falling. But there was no water. Instead, he twisted down into an infinite vortex like the black eye of a hurricane. Lightning flashed in jagged streaks, burning in unearthly fires and turning the twisting column into the color of blood. Fierce wind currents buffeted. He tumbled. Spiraled down with his arms and legs extended. Twirled. Then fell head over heels. He wanted to scream. He tried to scream, but his voice was paralyzed. Slowly a great cavern formed and rose to meet him—a maw lined with serrated teeth like rows of daggers. It was a mouth—the jaws of a loathsome reptilian creature about to envelop him. Pitiless black eyes bored into his. Foul breath gagged him. It roared, thrashed, whipped its scaled green tail. He tried to scream, but his vocal chords refused. Then, just as suddenly, the beast vanished and he saw her. Kay Stockard. It was a miracle. The stormed stopped. Time stopped. All was peace. Calm.

She was a nude wraith—a spirit drifting toward him from the far end of the tunnel with her arms extended. The long, slender perfect legs, round, pointed breasts, the heat of desire burning in the green eyes. He felt his arousal. Reached for her. Then a voice told him this was a dream. Like so many dreams he had had when he was a young boy. The kind other boys would make nasty jokes about. But her hands felt real —had substance. And her arms were around him, lips on his, mouth open, wet and hot, tongue searching deep, challenging his. Then the pointed breasts were against him, stomach, pelvis, thighs, pliable and molding to his body in a frantic effort to destroy the last vestige of space between them.

Never had he had a dream like this. He pushed her onto her back and pressed her down into the mattress with his weight. *Dear God. Please don't let me wake up*, he cried to himself. But this was no dream. She was real. The flesh was hot and silky and yielding under his hands. Hair long and flowing like satin. Frantically, he kissed the pulse in her throat, the round, swollen breasts. Ran his hands over the hard stomach, the smooth curve of the muscles of her sides and thighs, not believing what he had found. Her breath was short in his ear and she breathed as if she were gulping air. He reached between her legs. She gasped and began to tremble. Spread her knees. Pulled him into a position as old as mankind. Stiffened and moaned as he gripped her buttocks and thrust deep into her. Then she locked him into the crucifix of her limbs, meeting and riding his frenzied assault with twisting, thrusting hips.

He lost himself in the pure essence of unleashed desire that he had never known before.

When it was over, she slid from the bed, slipped on a silk negligee, and walked to the door. Before closing the door behind her, she turned, long hair swaying and glowing like a halo in the dim hall light behind her. Her voice was soft, "You were very good, cousin."

He whipped the brush in the shaving mug with furious circular motions, foaming lather running down the sides and flicking onto the mirror. He looked into the mirror with loathing. The eyes were bloodshot and watery, the blond stubble on his cheeks and chin glistening in the light over the mirror like dead wheat. He didn't see Lieutenant j. g. Rodney Higgins in the mirror. No, indeed. He saw a beast. An animal who had copulated with his cousin. The fearful beast in his nightmare had been himself. It was a warning. He should have known.

Animals mated with their mothers, sisters, cousins. He was an animal. It made no difference that he had been drunk. Asleep. It made no difference that Marsha had ignited the whole thing. Had invaded his dream and stolen it. The only thing that counted was that it happened. Marsha was a slut. Worse than that, she had morals that would shame an alley cat. He should have been forewarned at the table. Although he had only seen her a half-dozen times in his entire life, he had seen that look burning deep in her eyes before.

He brushed a thick layer of shaving cream on his face as if he were trying to hide from himself. He stropped the long straight razor with short, snapping motions and then skimmed uneven swaths of cream and stubble from the smooth skin. But the mind raced on. He had to face his mother, grandmother, aunt, and maybe Marsha in a few minutes at the breakfast table. His mother was brilliant and probably knew. Would know by just watching him. By judging his attitudes, emotions, looks. And his grandmother was no fool. The servants. Everyone could sense a sexual thing between two people. It was impossible to hide. And they all knew Marsha better than he did—except for one thing, of course.

His stomach rumbled and he tasted a revolting gorge of sour wine and bitter acid. He'd leave. Had to leave. It would never happen again, but he couldn't live under the same roof with that carnal bitch in heat.

The razor pulled and he winced. Quickly he stropped the razor again and then scraped the last hair from his chin. After wiping a few thin runnels of cream from his cheeks, he slapped his face with bay rum. Then he turned to the door.

When Rodney entered the breakfast room, a large alcove off of the kitchen with a bay window to let in the morning sun, no one was there except Travers. Ellen took her breakfast in her room, but the other members of the family usually ate together. Rodney's favorite breakfast was already on the table; cornflakes topped with strawberries, rye toast, and milk. As Rodney seated himself, Nicole entered and poured a cup of steaming black coffee with the obligatory, "*Bonjour*, monsieur." The tone seemed cold, eyes narrow and blank.

Rodney answered with a "*Bonjour*, Nicole." The maid left.

Travers volunteered some information. "Your mother kept a late hour last night, sir. She sent word to the kitchen that she would be a little late this morning." He placed a copy of *The New York Times* on the table next to Rodney. "The paper, sir."

"Thank you, Travers." The butler left.

Sipping his coffee, Rodney felt the veil of anxiety lift slightly. Maybe his mother had not even been home when Marsha entered his room. Maybe she had been satisfying her own desires. He hated to think of his mother that way. Somehow it seemed dirty and beneath her. But years ago he realized Brenda had her needs—and she met them. At least, she didn't do it with young boys. She had probably spent most of the night with Hamilton. But everyone else had been home.

He poured some milk over his cereal and added a single spoonful of sugar. He opened the paper. The front page was sickening. More reports of Allied disasters in North Africa. The island of Malta was being pulverized by German and Italian bombers. It was the most bombed place on earth. More sinkings by U-boats. And German air raids on England continued despite heavy losses. There were more rumors reported from Sweden and Switzerland of large German troop movements along the Russian border. He drank more coffee. "They're going to do it," he said to himself.

Travers entered, carrying the silver coffee service. He volunteered more information, "Your aunt and cousin left early, sir. They had an appointment at the university."

"Oh?"

"Something about a sorority." He refilled Rodney's cup.

"Thank you, Travers."

As the butler left, Brenda entered. Wearing a green silk robe, she appeared beautiful despite fatigue that had awakened incipient lines at the corners of her mouth and eyes. As usual, her hair was perfectly coiffed, her face touched with just the right amount of cosmetics. Immediately Travers and Nicole materialized, fawning over their mistress, pouring coffee, placing her toast and mixed fruit in front of her. "Thank you, thank you," Brenda said. The servants fled the room as if they knew something unsavory was about to happen.

After sipping her coffee, Brenda opened the conversation casually, "Your aunt and cousin had an appointment at Columbia."

"Travers told me."

"Marsha's joining a sorority."

Rodney nodded at the good news, not trusting his voice.

"She's moving out today."

Rodney felt small consolation in knowing he could remain at home. His mother had been blunt. She knew or suspected something. He felt she could pierce his innermost thoughts like a torch in darkness. Despite a lack of appetite, he brought a spoonful of cereal to his lips, tried to focus his eyes on the *Times*.

If Brenda's mind was occupied with Marsha, she dismissed the girl quickly. It was Nathan. As always, Nathan was paramount. She studied Rodney over her cup. "You were awfully hard on your brother last night, Rodney."

"I'm sorry, Mother. But he wasn't exactly polite to me."

"You were too harsh."

"I won't take insults from anyone, Mother. If it will please you, I'll leave."

A pained look tightened her face. "You know that wasn't necessary. You only have three weeks. I want you here—at home. You belong here."

Sighing, Rodney pushed the paper aside. "I'll avoid him, Mother—avoid arguments when I see him." He took her hand. Stared into the blue eyes rimmed with fatigue. "You're working too hard, Mother."

"I was out late."

He knew the statement was true, yet a screen. Brenda kept her hands firmly on the operations of Ashcroft Mills. Perhaps this was her man, the substitute for her first husband lost on battle cruiser *Lion* and the second snatched away from her during a bloody raid on the German works at Ostend. Each morning her chauffeur, Desmond Hallcraft, drove her to the Chrysler building at the corner of Forty-second and Lexington. The offices of Ashcroft Mills occupied the entire sixty-second floor. Despite young, energetic managers, Brenda oversaw the operation with unusual business acumen; especially the negotiating of new contracts. Huge orders for uniforms, tents, and sheets were pouring in from the government. In addition, direct lines connected her to the offices of Carlisle Mills, Limited, in London. Liaison had always been difficult and clumsy.

In Rodney's happiest memories were frequent trips to England, usually in the summer, when he, Nathan, and Regina were out of school. The trips were made necessary because of a provision in his father's trust prohibiting sale of the interest and requiring conveyance of the holdings to Geoffry's sons upon Brenda's death.

Rodney loved those days. England was beautiful in the summer, especially in Kent where the Higginses' great ancestral manor house, Fenwyck, sat majestically, surrounded by its manicured sylvan grounds. Many joyous afternoons were spent there racing through the maze of hedges, flower gardens, trees, and orchards with his brother, sister, and cousins, Trevor and Bonnie, who were the children of Lloyd and Bernice. When they tired of hide-and-seek and kick-the-can, they invented new games; sheep and herder, policeman and bad men. And he loved his grandparents, Walter and Rebecca Higgins, and his uncles, Randolph Higgins and Lloyd Higgins, and Lloyd's wife, Aunt Bernice. Walter Higgins died in 1927 and Rebecca followed in 1930. However, the vacations continued and Rodney grew very close to his uncles and cousins, Trevor and Bonnie.

Rodney's favorite had been the perennial bachelor and flamboyant pilot, his uncle, Randolph Higgins. "You've heard from Uncle Randolph?" Rodney asked. "You still write him? It's been over three months since I saw him."

"Of course. I just got a letter from him last Tuesday. He's well and his squadron is operating in the southeast of England. That's all I know. Apparently, the rest is classified. He just writes about family, food shortages, and his men." She drummed the table. "You saw Bonnie and Trevor?"

"Yes, Mother. Bonnie is a nurse and is engaged to a midshipman named Boggs. Trevor is a lieutenant in the navy."

"You met this Boggs?"

"Yes. Nice chap." Rodney did not mention the instant dislike he had seen between Boggs and his Uncle Randolph. Rodney finished his coffee and gestured to Travers who refilled the cup. "Randolph's too old to be flying fighters, Mother."

The timbre of Brenda's voice was edged with bitterness. "He's like your father. He's got to be in the thick of it and his squadron's in the southeast where the fighting's heaviest." She turned away, face a rictus of anguish.

"But most of the Blitz is over, Mother," he reassured her. "The Luftwaffe came off with a bloody nose." He knew there had been strong feelings between his mother and Randolph who had never married. It had been more than the bond of affection expected between brother-in-law and sister-in-law. Even as a little boy, Rodney had seen the looks—hot, deep looks reserved for lovers or those who wished to become lovers. But he had never seen physical contact; not a touch, not even a handshake. It was as if neither dared cross this barrier, not even casually.

Brenda stared down at the intricate designs in dark blue and rich golden hues of the Maksoud rug under her feet, spoke to the past in a halting voice, "Randolph's too conscientious—dies with every dead boy. He was shot, crashed, burned, and broke down in 1917." She looked up, her misty eyes searching for reassurance. "You think the worst of it's over—you think he's safe, now, Rodney?"

"Why of course, Mother. We all know the heavy fighting's over and I'm sure he spends most of his time in his office like a good CO should. He's probably relaxing in an easy chair, reading the London *Times* right now."

III

MAJOR Randolph Higgins eased the throttle of the Spitfire Mark VB a notch by pulling back on the lever attached to the quadrant on the left side of the cockpit. A finger on a control handle on the instrument panel thinned the mixture and then a quick adjustment of the black knob of the propeller lever on the throttle quadrant brought the propeller to coarse pitch. He watched his rev-counter drop to two thousand rpms, manifold pressure thirty inches, and airspeed to 180 miles an hour. With its twelve cylinders starving for petrol, the Rolls Royce Merlin skipped a beat, trembled its objections, and then settled down into its usual steady roar. It would take no more. A red light low on his instrument panel caught his eye. The fuel low-level indicator light was glowing its warning. Grunting, he reached forward and turned the selector switch to the fuselage reserve tank. He had another fifty minutes in the air. No more. He banked toward the Channel, leaving the East Sussex coastline behind.

It was an unusually clear day with almost unlimited visibility. The sky was heron-egg blue marred only to the west where fast-moving caravans of clouds stretched low over the horizon. Reflecting the rays of the sun, the fluffy tops were gilded with silver and platinum while dark grays shadowed their undersides. Off the East Sussex coastline, he could see thermals of gulls circling on wide-stretched pinions over a cluster of fishing boats, wings glinting like polished metal in the sunlight.

The entire summer had brought warm, soft sunny weather. True, from time to time scuds of rain had swept in from the North Atlantic and early or late mists and fog had blotted out the coastline. Only a week before sudden blasts of cold winds drove across the Channel, herding thick thunderclouds before them. Everyone had been taken by surprise and both Germans and English canceled operation. Because changes of weather usually came in from the Atlantic and moved eastward, the RAF knew what the elements were going to be before the Luftwaffe. All British fighters stood down before the full fury of the storm struck. Intelligence reported that the Germans had lost a fighter and a Focke-Wulf long-range patrol bomber.

Staring through his bulletproof windscreen, Major Higgins could see the coast of Belgium to the east, Calais almost directly ahead, and France to the southeast. The coast of Normandy was visible all the way to Le Havre and he could see inland hundreds of miles, the tableau of the vast landscape obscured only in the far distance by a bluish ground haze. Clusters of houses, roads like brown streaks, and the ribbons of canals were visible. Here and there railroad tracks caught the sun and reflected the light like burning threads. He could see inland as far as Saint Omer, Fauquembergues, Etaples. Freshly plowed fields appeared as brown patchwork interspersed with the lush green of maturing oats and barley. Stands of trees stood guard like battalions of silent green sentries. And it was occupied—all occupied by the Germans.

The major liked his Spitfire Mark VB. Very advanced aerodynamically, the Spitfire was the first all-metal fighter built in Britain. It was a sturdier and faster aircraft than the Hawker Hurricane that had been the most numerous RAF fighter during the height of the Battle of Britain. Powered with the new Merlin 45 engine, his fighter had 1440 horsepower and a top speed of 370 miles an hour. It was equipped with the three-bladed De Havilland constant-speed, variable-pitch propeller that was a vast improvement over the two-bladed wooden club attached to the shaft of the first Spitfire he had flown—the Mark I. His firepower had been improved, too. The Spitfire Mark I had packed a good punch with eight 0.303 Browning machine guns. However, now with the newly strengthened B-type wing, his machine could deliver a much heavier weight of fire from its battery of two drum-fed Hispano-Suiza twenty-millimeter cannons and four 0.303 machine guns.

Although the major had flown for thirty years, designed aircraft with Tommy Sopwith and Geoffrey de Havilland, single-handedly modified the S.E.5 into what was to become the famous S.E.5A of the Great War, held flying license number twenty-three, flight still seemed an impossible adventure. Often, especially alone at high altitudes sucking on his oxygen like a baby at his mother's teat, he felt like a gnat suspended in an infinite void. There was nothing between him and disaster except a flimsy wing bending with the invisible blows of the air, a straining engine, and a fragile structure of aluminum and wire. At these moments, he knew he was experiencing something far beyond a triumph of human skill; it was a miracle.

Flying was a singular existence. In the air a man found his own spirit, passed through an invisible barrier and emerged into a different universe. Here he found a new awareness of his body, yet fathomed only a bare perception of it. This was the realm of the gods and he became a ruler of a sort who controlled his destiny with a bare touch of rudder, a breath on the stick. The essence of reality was here and the prospect of horrible death was a constant companion. Lurking danger tortured some men. It was a tonic to the major. These were the moments when he was most alive. What predator, no matter how savage or courageous, stalked a quarry that could shoot back with machine guns?

He scanned the horizon with the short jerky movements of the experienced fighter pilot, never focusing on one spot, but, instead, moving quickly around the vault of the sky, depending on his peripheral vision to detect fly specks that could sprout wings and turn into Messerschmitt (ME) 109s in a blink. But there was no sign of the enemy. Things had been quiet for weeks. Something was brewing in eastern Europe and apparently everyone knew it except the Russians. Rumor had it Hitler was preparing a very unpleasant surprise for his new bedmate, Joseph Stalin.

Still, the Luftwaffe's *Luftflotte Zwei* (Air Fleet Two) continued with occasional harassing raids on the south coast and London had been hit once just a week before by a dozen Heinkel 111s in a sneak night raid. And Major Erich Kochling's *Jagdstaffel Vierter* (Fourth Fighter Squadron) still operated out of its field west of Hardelot Plag on the Pas de Calais. The inventor of the "finger four" subunits or Schwarm tactics, Kochling was a ruthless butcher who boasted fifty-two victories. Twenty-four had been easy kills in Spain where he had flown with the Condor Legion, his 109s sweeping the skies clean. Twenty more were hapless Polish antique aircraft destroyed in 1939. However, eight British roundels decorated the Nazi killer's tailfin. Two had belonged to Randolph's men.

Randolph's mind wandered back to 1917 and his old enemies of the Western Front; Oswald Boelcke, Manfred von Richthofen, Hermann Göring, Ernst Udet, Werner Voss, Max Mueller, Erwin Boehme, and the sadistic Bruno Hollweg. In four years he had flown against all of them, fought most of them, and in a strange, twisted way even respected them. All except Bruno Hollweg. Hollweg the butcher. He still thrilled with the memory of killing the swine. Now it was Kochling. Another war. Another killer. Another personal vendetta. Would it ever end? At age forty-six he was the oldest fighter pilot in the RAF. Oldest in the world, as far as he knew. But he would kill Kochling before he died. Had to. He punched the instrument panel so hard the needle on his altimeter quivered.

Everyone said he was too old when he applied for flight duty. But the prime minister, his old friend Winston Churchill, had intervened for him. His only other support came from the elder statesman, the doddering Lloyd George, who everyone ignored. Despite the sometimes bitter objections of Fighter Command's Hugh "Stuffy" Dowding who pointed at Randolph's burn-scarred leg and old wounds, the prime minister persisted and saw to it Randolph was given command of Number 54 Squadron based at Detling. Randolph had solemnly promised both Churchill and Dowding he would never fly in combat. However, the promise had been forgotten the first time the major squeezed into the cockpit of a Spitfire.

The old touch was still there. His ravaged leg strong again from years of exercise had no trouble kicking the fighter into the sharpest of turns. He had had twelve kills in the past year—a pair of the slow, heavy Messerschmitt Bf 110 *Zerstorer* (Destroyer) fighters better known as "Göring's Folly," three dive-bombing JU 87 Stukas for target practice, a Dornier 17 "Flying Pencil," which he broke in half from below where it had little protection, four tough but lightly gunned Heinkel 111 bombers, and two Messerschmitt 109s. Both of the 109s had been from Kochling's Jagdstaffel Vierter. He and the German were even on that score. Thankfully, Stuffy Dowding's office had remained silent.

The ME 109 was formidable. Almost as fast as the Spitfire, it was not as maneuverable and had a short range, which made it a poor escort for bombers. Nevertheless, it was a sturdy aircraft and could strike with terrible destructiveness with two twenty-millimeter Oerlikon cannons and two Rheinmetall Borsig thirteen-millimeter machine guns. Its inverted Daimler-Benz V-12 engine was fuel injected, never faltering in the most violent maneuvers while the Rolls Royce's carburetor was known to choke in steep power dives. The wise

RAF pilot never tried to dive with the ME. And German fighter pilots were the best the Luftwaffe could find. They were superbly trained, experienced, and daring. Many had cut their teeth in Spain and all had enjoyed the Polish massacre.

The white cliffs and beaches of England were behind him and the coast of France loomed close. Time to turn. You don't make a fighter sweep over the continent with three aircraft. Moving the control column to the left and gently balancing with rudder, he banked to the north. Glancing from side to side he caught glimpses of his wingmen, Flight Lieutenant Cedric Hart off his starboard side and Pilot Officer Ian McBride to port. As usual, both were holding station perfectly as if attached to his elevators by invisible umbilicals. Randolph smiled. They were the best.

Twenty-three-year-old Hart was from Hinkley Point in Somerset. The son of a barrister, he was a taciturn lad with a temper like gunpowder and the killer instincts of a scorpion. He had four kills. McBride was a twenty-one-year-old Scotsman from Achanalt, a small town in the beautiful Strathconon Forest of the Highlands. His father was a blacksmith and young Ian had developed powerful muscles from years at his father's forge. His brain was as big as his muscles and he had qualified for RAF training despite a minimum of schooling. He was also a killer with seven confirmed victories.

Staring down over his left wingtip, Randolph had a clear view of the Channel, which was only about twenty-five miles wide at this point. It was deceptively peaceful. Reflecting the sky, it was a deep azure, the frothing small chop sparkling with sunlight like chips of diamonds. Such a beautiful day —such a beautiful day to be killing men.

At the low altitude of six thousand feet, he could see two trawlers and a minesweeper escorting two freighters north toward the Thames estuary. The ships were so slow they appeared like five insects pinned to a collector's blue mat. Group had reported E-boat activity out of Calais and Bologne.

But he saw no white scars on the sea—the sure sign of the motor torpedo boat. Indeed, all was calm; almost too calm. He disliked flying this low. He was giving the Germans most of the sky. This was a job for Coastal Command, for big, lumbering Short Sunderland flying boats. Not his Spitfires. He glanced anxiously into the glaring orb of the sun. Saw nothing.

Randolph stiffened as his earphones came alive with the hiss of a carrier wave. Then the familiar calm, carefully modulated voice of the control officer at Sector Control crackled in his earphones. "Wolf Red Leader, this is Cricket Control. Do you read me? Over."

Randolph keyed his microphone. "Cricket Control, this is Wolf Red Leader. I read you loud and clear. Over."

The voice returned with the timbre of a schoolmaster assigning a reading of Thackeray, "Wolf Red Leader, this is Cricket Control. I've got some work for you in sector one-five-two. Five plus bandits at angel three on a westerly heading. Your vector zero-three-zero, climb to angel ten and intercept."

Randolph's mind churned and digested the information. Radar had picked up some German aircraft flying low and headed for the Thames estuary. Probably mine-laying bombers—the fast Dornier 217 that could sneak in at over three hundred miles an hour, drop its mines or bombs, and be gone before intercepted. The information had been relayed from Fighter Command to Group, to Sector Control, and then to his flight. A marvel of efficiency, the system had tipped the Battle of Britain in their favor a year ago. However, it had its flaws. It had never measured altitude accurately and often it missed high-flying fighters.

After snapping his oxygen mask securely to his helmet and turning the flow valve to "On," his throat tingled and felt raw as he breathed pure oxygen. Randolph spoke into his microphone, "Wolf Red, this is Wolf Red Leader. We have some unexpected guests in sector one-five-two. Follow my lead and we'll prepare a warm welcome for them."

"Roger. Sure an' I'm chillin' the champagne now," came from McBride.

A curt "Roger" came from Hart.

Randolph's hands moved instinctively in a flurry of movements honed by years of experience. In quick succession he punched the throttle hard open against its stop, changed the pitch of the propeller to fine, and pushed the mixture control knob to rich. Then he pulled back hard on the yoke at the top of the control column. As the horizon dropped beneath the cowling he spoke into his microphone, "Cricket Control, this is Wolf Red Leader. Request top hat."

"Wolf Red Leader. This is Cricket Control. Wolf Yellow will provide top cover at angel twenty. Taking station now. Over."

"Roger." Randolph felt new confidence. A three-plane section from his own squadron would give him top cover. The yellow section led by his best friend, the tall, skinny Freddie "Coop" Hansen, had been patrolling the sector just to the north. A friendly Canadian and former bush pilot, Hansen had accumulated over two thousand hours in the air before joining the RAF. With a slow, wry smile, tall, sparse build, Hansen so resembled the film star Gary Cooper he had been immediately given the sobriquet "Coop" when he first joined Fifty-Four Squadron the year before. At age thirty-five, he was considered elderly but not grandfatherly like Randolph. With a remarkable twenty-one kills in only eleven months, he had been mentioned in dispatches and awarded the DSO. His wingmen were Flight Officer Preston Donovan, a young Welshman from Carmarthen, and Flight Sergeant Michael Sturgis from East London. Donovan was a replacement with only sixty-three hours in Spits. Sturgis was experienced with two kills and three probables.

Pushed back into his seat by the acceleration, Randolph watched the white needle of his altimeter wind clockwise around the dial. Quickly he scanned his instruments. At full war emergency power, the Merlin was straining at its mounts, vibrating the airframe, and sending the oil and coolant temperature readings to crowd their red lines at 105 and 121 Celsius. Passing twenty-eight hundred, the rev-counter, too, was approaching the danger area while the manifold pressure gauge neared its maximum reading of sixty-seven inches. The airspeed indicator showed 340 miles an hour.

He was gaining altitude, the flyer's treasure; it could be so easily traded for speed. He pushed the safety cover from the firing button and caressed it gently with his thumb. Reaching up, he threw a switch and his electric reflector gun sight came to life, the tiny dot in the center of the reticle glowing red. Staring through the gun sight, he felt a familiar warmth deep down in his groin—an atavistic heat he always felt before bedding a woman or killing a man.

Searching the sea, the flight leader cursed. The big elliptical wings of the fighter blocked most of his view to the north. "Wolf Red Leader to Cricket Control. I can't see the bloody buggers." Randolph knew women were stationed at the plotting tables at Fighter Control. But, by now, they were accustomed to RAF profanity.

"Wolf Red Leader, they are beneath you and five miles to the northwest. Good hunting."

"Thanks awfully, old boy. I'm awfully keen to meet those chaps straightaway," Randolph murmured, mimicking the velvet soft tranquillity of the controller's voice.

Leveling, Randolph centered his controls and dropped his port wing. Then he saw them exactly in line with the tip. Five bombers flying very low in a loose V and headed for the Thames estuary just as he had anticipated. Minelayers or bombers, it made no difference. They were out to kill Englishmen. Callous swine sitting high in the air who dropped their death casually while they joked and gloated. But not these five.

A hasty glance told him all he needed to know about the intruders: two big BMW 801 radial engines, long tapering fuselage, twin fins, the long tail cone housing the ridiculous petal-type dive-bombing brake, a thirteen-millimeter machine gun in a dorsal turret and another in a ventral mount. The fast deadly Dornier 217. But it was no match for the Spitfire.

A last look around and then a glance up-sun. This could be a trap. Throw easy meat to a patrol of fighters and then hit them with a high-flying ambush. He had seen it work in 1915 and it still worked in 1941. *Watch out for the Hun in the sun*, rang through his mind. A whole Staffel could be up there at thirty thousand feet and he would not know it. He saw nothing and prayed Coop Hansen's Wolf Yellow was up there. He keyed his microphone, "Wolf Red, this is Wolf Red Leader. Tally-ho! Five Dorniers at ten o'clock low. Like whores at the palace. Give them a jig-a-jig they won't forget. Number One take starboard; Number Two take port. Break!"

With acknowledgments from both Hart and McBride echoing in his earphones, he pulled back hard on the column, kicked left rudder, and split-essed into a screaming dive. He pointed his nose at the second bomber on the left, avoiding the lead plane. In this way, fewer guns could be brought to bear on him. McBride would take the last plane to port, Hart already was bearing off to the right after the last Dornier to starboard. The airspeed indicator had passed 360 and was still climbing. Turning like a watch with a broken main spring, the white needle of the altimeter chased around the dial counterclockwise, passing the big needle again and again.

Randolph felt a familiar vibration as the big wing began to flutter. Although it was a two-spar wing, the front spar took most of the load. Combined with the leading-edge skin, the front spar made a torsion box of great strength. The most advanced design in the world, it could take tremendous stresses, but it still vibrated in full-power dives. Cursing, he brought the bouncing reticle to the fuselage of the Dornier.

They had been seen. The Dorniers bunched closer like frightened geese. Hunching forward, Randolph skinned his lips back and gritted his teeth, thumb poised over the red button. He brought the bomber to the center of his range finder. It filled two rings. Two thousand yards. One thousand yards. Flashes from the bombers. Glowing fireflies left smoking threads as they arced toward him and fell off. "Too far," Randolph snorted. "Amateurs!"

A bare breath of pressure on the left rudder pedal turned the fighter slightly, setting him up for a one-quarter deflection shot from the rear, the glowing dot moving to the forward part of the fuselage where the four members of the Dornier's crew were bunched together. "Four Huns with one burst." He chuckled to himself.

More tracers rose to meet him slowly and accelerated as they passed. There was a thump as his wing took a hit. The Dornier filled all three rings of his range finder and the luminous bead was fixed on the fuselage. He had his killing angle. He thumbed the tit. After the first gun camera pressure, he felt the recoil, the 6,650-pound aircraft bucking and shuddering as two cannons and four machine guns exploded to life. Flames leapt from the leading edge of his wings and streams of empty brass cartridge cases tumbled and showered into the slipstream from their chutes in the wing, glinting in the sun like gay New Year's Eve confetti. Randolph saw his tracers hammer home. But his hits were far back on the fuselage, not forward in the crew's compartment. "Fuckin' bloody buggers!" he screamed, forgetting his microphone was open, but not caring who in the world heard him, anyway.

Pulling the stick back gently, he marched the hammer blows up the Dornier's fuselage, shells and bullets chewing into the aluminum like a saw through dry kindling. Chunks of metal were ripped from the fuselage, exposing frames, stringers, and longerons. Torn aluminum tumbled into the slipstream like trash. The power turret exploded, most of the gunner's head and chest streaming behind the bomber like a red-gray haze. Then the cockpit was blasted by at least four twenty-millimeter shells, Plexiglas and chunks of aluminum whipped into the slipstream, bouncing from the tail assembly and slashing the starboard fin off at its root as if it had been chopped off by a giant cleaver.

With a dead crew, the big bomber dropped off on its starboard wing and at full power careered across the sky, cartwheeling wildly toward the Channel. Screaming with joy, Randolph plunged past. The Channel was rushing up at him and his attack had carried him much closer to the Kentish coast than he had anticipated. He was low. Too low. The Channel filled his windshield. Hauling back on the stick, he caught a glimpse of the inshore water. Smudged with cloudy blue, it was calm and smooth as oil. He could even see the line where it met the upwelling of the deep water quite clearly, sharp as a blade, the surface beyond it dark and ruffled by the chop.

As his dive flattened, his weight was multiplied by at least a factor of six. Heavy as a boulder, his head crushed down and his chin dropped. He felt the strain on his neck and spine. His vision starred and darkened and he seemed to be staring into a tunnel as his peripheral vision faded. He felt his guts drop and push against his harness. The flesh of his cheeks sagged, his nose ran, eyes watered, and there was a terrible roaring in his ears as blood drained from his brain. The Spitfire vibrated and then, as the dive flattened, bounced up and down, wings bending and trembling with the terrible strain like a stricken bird. With its top unlatched, his flare box cover banged up and down like a door in a gale. He slammed it shut, felt a wetness in his crotch. Urine was staining his underwear and creeping through his flight suit. Next, his bowels would go. Randolph shook his head, screamed into his mask, trying to relieve the strain. The dribbling urine stopped.

The sea was just below and the coast of Kent ahead. He was so low his propeller kicked up an ostrich plume of water. At at least 430 miles an hour, the fighter rocketed over the white strip of sandy beach and then inland, gaining altitude grudgingly. Struck by thermals rising from the hot surface below, trembling and buffeting, the fighter's controls became heavy and sluggish. It yawed from side to side over the countryside like a Lambeth drunk. Trying to clear his head by shaking it furiously, he caught a glimpse of land so close it looked irregular instead of featureless as it appeared from great heights. The usual mosaic of green and brown was now plowed fields with clearly defined furrows, pastures with animals grazing indifferently. Clusters of trees had become orchards, stands of beech and oak. There were farmhouses, rock walls, fences, a brown dirt road, a stream meandering and frothing through an emerald slash of undergrowth. He whipped over a haystack, the tornado of his backwash leaving a cloud of straw whirling behind it. Chickens screeched in terror and anger, running pell-mell in every direction. Farmers stopped plowing, women and children ran from houses and stared up with white faces.

The plane seemed to have a mind of its own, refusing the stick. The yaw had become a "Dutch roll," the aircraft twisting from side to side, nose weaving in a deadly figure eight. If the nose dropped, he would be fertilizer scattered over acres of England's best farmland before he could blink. Frantically, Randolph worked his controls to regain balance, used full aileron and elevator to keep the fighter from flipping on its side. Like the thoroughbred it was, the fighter corrected and began to fly straight and level as an arrow.

Randolph felt his guts freeze as a cluster of towering oaks loomed directly ahead. Shaking his head to clear the last cobwebs, he horsed the stick back again. The plane fairly leapt skyward over the treetops and banked away. A last glance down at the oaks and he saw a redheaded girl waving something pink and dainty. *Her drawers, by Jove*, ran through his mind. "I'll drop in again for a longer visit," he shouted. Balancing with left rudder and centering his controls, he convulsed with laughter as the fighter pulled out of its turn and pointed its nose toward the sky. The horizon disappeared below his cowling and the girl vanished. Blue sky filled his windscreen. There were more men to be killed. There was no more laughter.

Climbing high over the Channel, he saw two black plumes and four white parachutes. Hart and McBride had scored. He could see two surviving Dorniers fleeing to the east. Then he saw his wingmen, low on the water, pulling from their dives and curving after the Germans. Then his earphones crackled with words that froze his blood. "Wolf Red and Wolf Yellow, this is Cricket Control. Six bandits closing on sector one-five-two, high and to the east." He cursed the controller. How could the man be so bloody calm?

Freddie "Coop" Hansen's voice responded, "This is Wolf Yellow Leader. Got the bastards. Am engaging."

Randolph keyed his microphone, "Wolf Red, this is Wolf Red Leader. Disengage bombers. Follow my lead. We have some work upstairs."

"Roger. Let's go oop an' stuff their arses with twenties, Major," McBride said.

"Roger," came from Hart.

With his wingmen formed tight again, the section screamed skyward. Randolph's confidence and exhilaration of the kill had melted, replaced with an amalgam of anxiety and dread. Yellow Section was outnumbered two to one. And Preston Donovan was a new man. He could see a tangle of contrails at twenty thousand feet. Anxiously, he threw a switch on his radio. The fighter frequency was alive with the shrill voices of near-hysterical men fighting for their lives in aerial combat.

The first voice he heard was Coop Hansen's: "One-oh-nines overhead. Donovan, do you see them?"

"I can't see 'em. And your RT (radio transmitter) sounds bloody awful."

Sturgis came back with his usual obscene bluntness, desperately trying to jar the new pilot, "Bugger all, man. They're at two o'clock high. Open your bloody eyes."

"Donovan! Do you read me?" Hansen asked.

"Affirmative. Tell me when to break."

"Aircraft above and behind. Muck in everyone—tight."

"Six o'clock. The buggers are on our arses!"

"I can't see 'em in my mirror," Donovan pleaded.

"Bonk your bloody mirror. Are you blind?"

"Break right! Here they come!"

"Turn hard! Hard right, Donovan. Those bastards can't turn with us."

Staring upward Randolph could see the trails weave and entwine like a deadly, burgeoning spider's web.

Sturgis's shriek of victory: "I stuffed the bugger! Fry, you bloody bastard."

High above his cowling Randolph saw a bright orange flame trailing a black ribbon of smoke. A funeral pyre. Sturgis's kill? Maybe it was a Spitfire. He punched the instrument panel. Urged the fighter on with, "Come on you bloody bugger." But he knew the fight would come to him. Dogfights inevitably deteriorated into a series of altitude-killing turns, banks, and rolls, with every pilot dropping his nose to maintain and regain speed. The melee was bound to plunge downward as he climbed.

Pointed straight down and twisting slowly into a spin, the burning plane plunged past far to the east like a meteor. Thick nose, deep-set cockpit. Peaked tail and low-slung wing line. A ME 109. Then he saw the Luftwaffe insignia on the fuselage that had almost been blacked-out by soot and the crosses on the wings were clear. A glimpse of the tail and a black and white chevron on the vertical tail plane identified it as a member of *Jagdstaffel* Four. Kochling's squadron.

The frantic voices returned. Coop Hansen was screaming: "Donovan! Behind you. Two of 'em. Break left!"

Sturgis broke in, "No! No, Donovan. You can't dive with the buggers! Pull up! Pull up!"

"Sturgis! Look out! Two behind and below."

"I see 'em, Coop. Turn with me you gutter tiffies."

Hansen's funereal voice: "Donovan's bought it. Save your own arse."

Now the combatants were very close, distinct. They would be in range within seconds. Randolph switched off his receiver and spoke into his microphone, "Wolf Red, this is Wolf Leader. Individual combat. Break! Break!"

A Spitfire with two Messerschmitts on its tail snapped into

a half roll and dove directly at Randolph. The Germans were split and converged on the Englishman like the arms of a Y. The ME to Randolph's right led his companion and was ruddering into a near-perfect killing angle. He had a bright yellow propeller boss. Blood-red flames winked and leapt from his wings and cowling, tracers smoked into the Spitfire. The canopy dissolved and two cannon shells nearly blew the pilot in half. The fighter began its final spin. There was a big *NK* painted on the side of the fuselage. It was Coop Hansen's new wingman, Preston Donovan. Dead at nineteen.

Randolph felt hatred seethe deep down like bitter acid. He wanted the yellow spinner. A touch of rudder brought the glowing red dot to the Messerschmitt. He knew Hart and McBride would see his move and take port and the other ME. Anyway, at a combined closing speed of over seven hundred miles an hour, there was no time to give orders.

The German was no coward. He banked to meet the major head-on. The corner of Randolph's eye told him the other German was busy, veering off desperately as Hart and McBride raced upward to meet him.

Randolph and the German began firing simultaneously. Tracers whipped past. Thumped into his wing like a pneumatic hammer. Ripped a long tear in his fuselage. He saw his shot strike home, chunks of metal fly free like paper in a gale from the leading edge of the ME's wing. The German's engine filled his windshield. The yellow spinner was going to spear him between the eyes. He would ram the Hun. Why not? Could there be a better way to die? He was old. Tired. And Preston Donovan would be avenged.

The Jerry lost his nerve. At the last instant, he pulled back on his stick and passed over so close that Randolph's canopy was sprayed with glycol and the turbulence caused the Spitfire to bounce as if it had hit a runway with its wheels up. He had shattered the enemy's air cooler. Without glycol, the Daimler-Benz would overheat. The German had to turn for home or burn. Trailing a misty white banner, the ME half rolled into a dive and headed for the coast of France. Pursuit was useless. A Spitfire could not dive with a Messerschmitt. Donovan had found that out. Anyway, Major Erich Kochling was up there somewhere. He had a score to settle.

A bright flare caught Randolph's eye. The ME to port had exploded into flame, Hart and McBride hosing it with bullets and shells. The burning fighter rolled over on its back and a brown-clad form dropped out of the cockpit, tugging on the D-ring of his parachute. Too soon the white umbrella opened, caught a mere tip of flame from the plunging fighter, and then flared into orange flame of its own like a struck match. Trailing his shrouds and a thin trail of black smoke, the German tumbled head over heels, arms extended as if he were trying to slow his descent. Randolph shook his fist. "Wave your arms. Fly! Fly! Think about it all the way down, you bloody killer." His laughter was uncontrolled.

The laughter stopped abruptly. McBride was in trouble. His engine was backfiring orange flames from its exhaust ports, leaving oily black gouts of smoke like pockmarks in the sky. The Scotsman banked slowly toward the English coast. "Wolf Leader, this is Wolf Red Two," came through Randolph's earphones. "I've a bit o' trouble with the ol' mare. Caught soom Kraut lead in the balls, I did. Sorry to quit this lot."

"Take her home, ol' laddie," Randolph said, ruddering alongside and waving. "But hit the silk if she quits on you. Don't be a hero."

"No hero here, Wolf Red. I've a lassie waitin' for this lad's joystick. Wouldn't wanna disappoint her now, would I? Roger an' out." Trailing smoke, McBride's fighter swooped toward home.

Craning his head back, Randolph searched the sky to the east. Then he saw him. Erich Kochling trailed by his wingman. High and far to the east his garishly painted orange-and-green-striped Messerschmitt was locked in a duel with Coop Hansen. Sturgis was far to the south fighting a single

109. Randolph keyed his microphone, "Wolf Red One, this is Wolf Red Leader. Join the scrap at three o'clock, I'll take the one at ten o'clock. Break!"

Kicking left rudder and pulling the stick back and to his left, Randolph peeled away from Hart who banked to the south. Using the superior acrobatic ability and speed of the Spitfire, Coop Hansen was holding his own. Closing on the dogfight, Randolph could see Kochling's wingman darting in after Hansen while Kochling, in his usual manner, lurked above looking for a chance for an easy kill; preferably, a shot at a cripple.

Suddenly the wingman broke away and headed for Randolph. Kochling dove on Hansen who turned to meet him in a sharp climbing turn. Desperately, Randolph pulled back on his stick. Altitude. He needed priceless altitude. Now the approaching ME was slightly below him. An almost imperceptible movement of the stick to starboard, balance with rudder, and the German came into his range finder. One quarter above and at six hundred yards. He would chance it. He squeezed the tit. The fighter shook with concussions and his tracers ripped into the 109's fuselage and tail. He cursed. Too far. He wanted the engine. The man.

He kicked left rudder but the German half rolled brutally into a dive. Randolph knew he could not dive with the Messerschmitt, but he already had the advantage of speed. He had a good chance. He stood on his wingtip and flipped the fighter over into a near-vertical dive and turned like a corkscrew until he could see the Jerry only seven hundred yards ahead. But he was pulling away already. Streaking downward, engines screaming like berserk banshees, the two fighters turned on their axes slowly, the Englishman trying for a shot, the German turning away. England, France, Belgium, and England again revolved about Randolph's cockpit. The Channel rushed up.

The German gradually flattened his dive as he began to run out of altitude. Bringing the glowing bead to the wing of the ME, Randolph broke into the leering grin of a death's head. Six hundred yards. Pulling back hard on the control column, he ran the chord of the German's arc, cutting the range quickly. He had his killing angle and he was close. He punched the button at a hundred yards. With centrifugal force draining blood from his brain, his vision was cloudy and blurred. But his shot struck home, winking red and orange as strikes ripped the enemy's port wing and marched toward the fuselage. The hood flew off and the canopy dissolved into a glittering cloud. But the Jerry was still under control and actually pulling away. "Die, damn you. Die. I'm burning out my guns!"

The wing root. The ME's weakest point. A seesaw touch of rudder pedals with delicate balancing of ailerons and elevator moved the nose of the fighter back and forth in flat turning movements. The German was sprayed as if he had been caught by a garden hose. Three, four explosions and the entire wing bent up at the wing-root fillet and broke away, exposing ripped ganglia of broken control wires and color-coded hydraulic lines. Red fluid sprayed into the slipstream. Immediately the fighter wrenched violently to the right, cartwheeling wildly. No longer a graceful creature of the firmament, it tumbled and corkscrewed across the sky, a stricken bird stripped of its power to fly, dying in agonized gyrations and coming apart as if it had been assembled with bailing wire and paste. It hit the Channel, bouncing and disintegrating in a huge column of water, spray, and flying debris. The severed wing splashed into the sea a mile away.

No cheers. No joy. Before the German was dead, Randolph already had the control column horsed back into the pit of his stomach, clawing for altitude. Kochling and Hansen had drifted far to the north and their fight had carried them below five thousand feet. Coop was in trouble. Climbing, he trailed a thin ribbon of black smoke. "Coop! Break left! Break left!" Randolph screamed into his microphone.

Hansen half rolled and turned toward Randolph. At that moment, he was caught by a half-dozen twenty-millimeter shells that blew the heads off an entire bank of cylinders and sprayed his hot exhaust manifold with raw petrol. Blowtorch orange flame roared back and enveloped the cockpit. Gracefully, the fighter rolled to its back and a lone figure dropped out of the cockpit. Instantly, the bright white canopy of a parachute blossomed overhead. Swinging like a pendulum, Hansen descended slowly toward the Channel. Kochling turned toward the parachutist.

"No!" Randolph screamed.

The ME bored in like a shark for the kill. Hansen raised his pistol and fired. There were bright red flashes on the cowling as the ME's pair of synchronized machine guns fired. Hansen's body jerked and quivered like a man jolted by high voltage, great thirteen-millimeter bullets ripping his chest and stomach open like invisible meat cleavers. Broken ribs, torn lungs, and heart exploded from the carcass in a red storm of blood, to fall like a gory rain. His intestines dropped and hung between his legs like a tangle of swaying gray snakes. Chin down to his chest, arms hanging straight down, Coop splashed into the water.

Sobbing, filled with horror, hate, and grief, Randolph Higgins pounded his instrument panel and raced after the orange-and-green-striped ME 109. In the strange way of aerial combat, the sky appeared to be suddenly empty of aircraft. The Spitfire and Messerschmitt seemed to have all of the heavens to themselves. Randolph wondered—as all fighter pilots wondered—how a sky that had been churning with dogfights in one moment could be completely empty a moment later.

Kochling had turned for home and was picking up speed in a shallow dive. He was very close to the surface, perhaps under a thousand feet. Randolph was higher, had superior speed, and was closing the gap. Randolph flashed over Hansen's body, trailing his chute that had stretched the shrouds full length in the water like a sea anchor. The butchered section leader was floating on his back, held on the surface by his Mae West. His arms were outflung like a cross. A huge red cloud stained the water around him like a dye marker.

Higgins hunched forward, set his jaw, choked back the sobs, and wiped the tears off of his cheeks with the back of his glove. This was David A. Reed again. His best friend in 1917 murdered by Bruno Hollweg as he sideslipped his burning Nieuport. He seemed to be repeating his life. The same enemies, the same dead young men, the same hunger for vengeance. Was this some kind of hell? Maybe he had died back there during the first one. Maybe he was destined to repeat the agony of seeing his best friend killed over and over. Certainly, God in his infinite mercy could not devise a more hideous punishment. God! Infinite mercy! He had turned his back on the Western Front and abandoned the Channel, too.

Kochling was in trouble. He could dive faster than his pursuer but was running out of altitude. His 109 was slower than the Spitfire and could not turn with it. He was desperate and made the move of a desperate man. He pulled back on the stick savagely and half rolled at the top of his loop, executing a perfect Immelmann turn. It was the move of a veteran and a brave man who would not allow himself to be caught from behind by an enemy and butchered with impunity.

But Randolph already had set up a one-quarter deflection shot from the left and above. At two hundred yards the Englishman opened fire. The bead was on the Jerry's cockpit, but the strikes hit along the fuselage and tail, blowing off the aerial mast and blasting a chunk of plywood out of the wooden tail fin. Fabric streamed from the rudder.

Banking hard, the German fired. But he only had a two-second burst as the Spitfire rocketed past. He missed. Both pilots pulled back hard on their control columns and Immelmanned back toward each other. At nearly four hundred miles an hour, each aircraft devoured miles, even in the tightest of loops. Finally, spinner to spinner they charged each other like two knights trapped rigidly in the lists, lances lowered, intent on disemboweling their enemies.

Both were low on ammunition, both held fire, thumbing

their buttons at only two hundred yards. Randolph felt joy leap as a cannon shell blew off the ME's starboard ejector exhausts and cowling fasteners. The right side of the cowling bent up like wet paper and tore off. Flame and black smoke exploded from the Daimler-Benz.

There was a thump, then a jar as strikes ripped a huge chunk from the top of the Spitfire's port wing, exposing the two spars, ribs, braces, the breeches and ammunition trays of the two Browning machine guns. Then a single hit on the wingtip from an Oerlikon shot out the aileron control pulley. The aileron flapped in the wind on its hinges like a loose shutter in a gale and immediately the left wing dropped. For the first time, fear flowed in Higgins's veins and a cold claw clutched at his heart. He throttled back and the jarring vibrations lessened.

Horror and fear turned to joy as the ME slowed and dropped below the Spitfire, to bank sharply to Randolph's left side—to the side pulled down by his damaged wing. Holding the control column dead center and countering the drag with slight right rudder, he allowed the damaged wing to pull the aircraft to the left and down toward the ME. Kochling turned his fighter directly into the Englishman's sights. Not believing his good fortune, Randolph screamed, "Götterdämmerung, you butcher!" He jammed the button down hard. There was a hiss of compressed air. "No! I can't be out of ammunition." The guns remained silent.

The German passed only fifty yards ahead. Carefully, Randolph eased the Spitfire alongside. He had to see this man—this insensate killer, the focus of his existence. Curiously, Kochling turned and stared directly into the Englishman's eyes. He was blond, young with a yellow fuzz on his cheeks as if he were a first-year-man at Eaton trying to grow his first beard, but too young to make it good. He waved a hand overhead making a zero with his thumb and forefinger to indicate he, too, was out of ammunition. Randolph waved a fist, "I'll kill you next time, bloody killer." The German threw up a mocking salute and laughed. Then trailing smoke he banked for France.

Randolph was in too much trouble to bother with Kochling further. Carefully working his rudder pedals and control column, he turned the nose of the fighter toward England and the coast of Kent. There was an irregular beat in the Rolls and oil streaked the fuselage and splattered the windshield. He turned on the windshield washer but the blade served only to smear the oil. Cursing, he turned it off.

Trying to restore trim and gain altitude, he was forced to use right rudder and the stick to counteract the terrible drag of the damaged wing that was trapping the airflow and pulling the port wing down. Another chunk of aluminum skin ripped off and he could see the breech of the cannon, ammunition drum, more formers, stringers, ribs, control wires. His airspeed dropped. Knowing he was in danger of stalling, he increased power, dropped his flaps ten degrees, and pushed the pitch control to full increase. Nevertheless, the trapped air sucking at the gaping hole in the port wing still dragged like a loose anchor, forcing him to rudder hard to the right and ride the control column in the same direction.

With the port wing drooping five degrees, the Merlin squirting oil from its stub exhaust ports, the oil pressure gauge showing under fifteen pounds and dropping, the tough, doughty fighter still climbed. Nodding with disbelief, Randolph eyed his altimeter that was slowly passing twenty-five hundred feet. If he was forced to bail out, he had the altitude. He turned his frequency selector to Sector Control and spoke into his microphone, "Cricket Control, this is Wolf Red Leader. Mayday! Mayday! I've caught one and I'm in a bit of a jam. Inbound five miles off the coast of Kent on course two-seven-five, angel two. Sector one-five-two."

The familiar silken voice filled his earphones, "Wolf Red Leader, this is Cricket Control. Have alerted air-sea rescue. Keep the cork in and good luck, old boy. Hope you make it."

"I say, thanks awfully. That's white of you, old man." Randolph's laugh was wild and funneled into an open microphone. He quieted himself and then shouted a response that shocked half of England, "I've had a jug full of you. Stuff the cork twice up your arse, you bloody, icy-calm chambermaid. Come up and scramble with these bastards and then see how calm you are." He switched off the radio and continued to chuckle to himself. Hansen's dead body stretched in the water was burned on his retinas and kept flashing pictures to his numb brain. He shook his head, blinked his eyes to no avail.

The coast of Kent passed below and the downs were ahead. Fenwyck Manor. His childhood home at Fenwyck was only a few miles ahead. Mercifully, Hansen faded. But his mind, still boiling with the frenzy and horror of combat, raced with crazy thoughts. Maybe he could drop in. Bail out, work his shrouds, and land on the vast lawn. Surprise his sister-in-law, Bernice, the servants. His brother Lloyd was in North Africa. He was due for a leave but maybe he was dead. Perhaps, his nephew Trevor was home. His niece Bonnie might even be there with her new army officer beau, Lieutenant Blake Boggs—a pimply-faced, weak idiot if he had ever seen one. He had seen his nephew Rodney Higgins there two months earlier when the young lieutenant stayed a weekend. Fine lad. He had the good looks of his mother Brenda. God, Brenda. Dear, beautiful sister-in-law Brenda Higgins Hargreaves. The most magnificent woman he had ever known. He loved her still and always would.

A backfire and flash of flame from his ports jarred him back. His oil pressure was almost zero and the coolant temperature was in the red. The Merlin was burning up. He stared down, looking for the emergency field at Kelvedon. Saw nothing but woods and here and there a plowed field. He banked carefully to the south and his home airdrome. Then it happened.

The engine began to vibrate as if it were trying to shake itself from its mounts. There was a muffled explosion and the right side of the hood flew up and bright orange flames spewed over the right side. He could smell burning petrol and oil and the cockpit filled with smoke. Heat came up through the floorboards and he could feel it through his boots. In seconds, the fire would break through the fire wall. He felt horror course through his veins like ice water. He had burned once in a S.E.5A. Crashed in no-man's-land. Was he to repeat that, too? But he had no parachute then. He had a parachute now and he was at three thousand feet. The thought calmed him. "Might be time to quit you, old girl," he said out loud.

He was answered by a ripping, wrenching sound of metal strained beyond its limits and the left wing bent up at the fillet and then flopped back down again. He felt the port main wheel drop and bang loosely on its pivot. More skin ripped loose. Then the entire wing broke off just inboard of the cannon and carried off most of the tail as it tumbled into the slipstream. Immediately the fighter plunged to the right into an incredibly tight spin like a maddened dervish.

Randolph felt himself flung against the side of the cockpit and there was a sharp pain in his shoulder. With speed born of panic, he groped for his harness pin and pulled it free. Then in quick motions he tore off his mask and helmet and yanked the rubber ball hanging over his head. The canopy ripped away and wind like demons unleashed by the devil swirled and shrieked around him. Then, hooking his elbows on the cockpit rim, he pushed with his feet and elbowed himself up. But the centrifugal force of the impossibly tight spin battered him against the side of the cockpit, tangling his jacket in the aluminum quadrant of the throttle and mixture control. He was trapped. It was his pocket, hooked like an anchor.

Screaming in a frenzy of fear, the major pushed with all the power of his muscular arms and his good left leg. His head was above the windscreen and a hurricane of wind tried to suck him out. He worked himself up but the jacket was caught in a vise, pulling down over his shoulder but refusing to break free. Around and around he whirled, the doomed fighter beating him against the sides of the cockpit. A solid maelstrom, the wind clawed at his flesh, rippled the skin of his cheeks, tore spittle from his mouth and blinded him. Down, down he plunged into the nightmare, timeless, witless, and helpless. But a sliver of brain still functioned, still fought for survival in the eye of the hurricane.

Screaming, cursing, he pushed and kicked. There was a ripping of leather and a quick release and he fairly shot out of the cockpit, barely clearing the remnants of the tail. He grabbed the D-ring, pulled hard. There was a sharp report like a pistol and the parachute opened. Then, impossibly, all was quiet. He was floating in a paradise of silence.

Above, the peaceful sky was a calm blue. Below, his fighter was twisting and disintegrating. It corkscrewed into a pasture with violence rarely seen on this earth, the explosion scattering pieces of debris in a quarter-mile radius. A black, ugly plume surged into the sky and orange flames roiled fiercely. Randolph shuddered.

He was low, perhaps five hundred feet. He worked his shrouds, drifting away from the smoke. Below he could see green fields, orchards, quaint thatched houses, horses, cows, and people. Standing alone or in groups on roads or in front of houses, they stared upward with the usual white faces and pointed. He drifted toward a tiny hamlet with a church spire topped by a cross with a finial like a dagger. "That cross can kill," he said to himself. Fumbling with the shrouds, he spilled air and drifted away from the threatening cross and the half-dozen houses of the village. Now he was very close to the ground and the earth that had seemed so remote and faceless was rising fiercely to meet him.

A young woman carrying a pail was staring up. She was standing next to a rock wall on the edge of a meadow and was very close. Randolph felt himself drifting toward the wall. More frantic pulling of the shrouds and suddenly he dropped straight down. When he hit, he buckled his knees and rolled forward, arms covering his face. He tumbled, tangled in the shrouds, and then felt himself dragged across the ground toward the rock wall. Cursing, he dug in his heels and strained hard. The parachute tangled in the rocks and some small elm. He was down and alive. He unhooked the harness.

He ran his hands over his body, legs, arms, head. His left shoulder was sore and there was blood on his cheek, but nothing was broken. Like all men who survive combat, the thought, *It's over and I'm still alive*, ran through his mind over and over.

He pulled up his knees, wrapped his arms around them, and stared straight ahead, trying to comprehend what had just happened to him. His mind was numb as if his brain had been severed at the base. Shock. Nature's way of protecting man from the horrors he could visit upon himself had deadened not only his brain but also his senses. It took him a full thirty seconds to realize he was sitting in a small potato patch and someone was standing beside him.

A slender, beautiful blond young woman of about twenty was by his side. She was holding a pail of milk. Although she was slender, her plain cotton dress could not conceal the lovely curve of her hips, the small peaked breasts. Her blue eyes held the compassion of a mother who had just discovered her baby had stumbled over a rock and required her attention to soothe his hurt. There was a quiescent glow in their depths—a tranquillity that wiped away the horror of killing and brought back a feeling for peace and life. To Randolph, he was staring at an angel.

After placing her pail of milk carefully on the ground, she leaned over the pilot and touched him gently on the forehead. Her palm was cool. "Are you all right?" she asked in a soft, high voice filled with concern.

Randolph smiled. "Quite fit, thank you." He tried to rise but found his legs were like rubber.

Carefully, she placed an arm under his elbow and helped him to his feet. The world turned but immediately began to slow. She clung to his arm tightly. He could hear shouts and the pounding of boots as a group of farmers rushed across the meadow. She gestured to an opening in the wall and Randolph could see the thatched roof of a house nestled in a group of trees. "Would you like a spot of tea?" she asked casually.

Randolph chuckled. "Why do you think I dropped in?"

IV

Return to Fenwyck

NUMBER 54 Squadron was based on a farm just to the east of Detling. A huge wheat field had been cleared and two crisscrossing asphalt runways laid. At the end of each runway was a dispersal hut for ready pilots and a concrete tarmac large enough to park four fighters. Each hut was connected to the small control tower with telephone lines. The RAF had learned the bloody lesson of dispersal early in 1940 when several squadrons had been caught on the ground with their aircraft bunched and wiped out.

There were four wooden-framed, canvas-covered hangars that were near duplicates of the flimsy Besson-neau hangars of the Great War. A machine shop had been assembled in the barn, two long barracks buildings built for the enlisted men, and a row of small huts for the pilots' quarters. A kitchen had been built between two mess halls; a small room for the officers and a larger hall for the men. A compact but complete surgery was tucked behind the mess halls.

Randolph's headquarters was in the farmhouse. A former

stagecoach station, the large two-story building was nearly four hundred years old. Built of enormous beams—some were a foot wide and two feet thick—the walls were plastered with a mixture of sand, gravel, mortar, and horse hair, which was used as a bonding material. In the early years it was known as the Santa Marta Inn because the huge ceiling beams had been salvaged from the wreck of the Spanish galleon, *Santa Marta*, which grounded on the rocks off Dymchurch after losing her masts in a battle with Sir Francis Drake. In the early nineteenth century the railroads put the stagecoach company out of business and a prosperous farmer named Donald Barrington bought the station. Here four generations of Barringtons cooked, ate, slept, fornicated, were born and died. In 1939 the RAF took possession and the airdrome was built.

Tourists would have called the old house "charming." To Randolph, it was "a filthy old rattrap." His bedroom was at the head of the stairs and he worked in the large main room that had been the public room of the old inn. At this moment, for the first time, he was receiving medical attention in his own headquarters.

Stripped to the waist and seated at his desk, a battered, old oak piece contributed by Detling's constable, Randolph was at the far end of the room next to a huge fireplace. Randolph grunted as the old squadron surgeon, Captain Wayne Chatfield, examined his bare left shoulder with a delicate but firm touch. The flyer's right leg ached from calf to thigh where his old, layered burn scars had been stretched when he had parachuted to the ground. The impact had been severe, like jumping off a barn, and both knees reminded him of the impact with dull, persistent aches. These things he kept from Chatfield, but the ripped cheek and bruised shoulder could not be concealed.

There were seven other men in the room watching the proceedings with keen interest. Randolph's batman, Sergeant-Major Forrest Woodhouse, was watching intently over the doctor's shoulder. A twenty-five-year veteran and a survivor of the battles on the Somme, he had been blown sky-high by a forty-two-centimeter Wipers Express in 1917. With a broken shoulder, six broken ribs, and a fractured hip, he had been offered a medical discharge. He refused, accepting limited service, instead. Faithful and diligent, he had a knack for anticipating his officer's needs. He had already handed Randolph his second Haig and Haig and water. He had been crestfallen when the pain in the major's shoulder had forced him to cut the blue tunic off of Randolph with scissors. But coagulated blood on the right collar and sleeve would have probably ruined it anyway.

Seated at his desk, which was nothing more than a battered old sideboard with a typewriter, was the squadron clerk, Lance Corporal Timothy Evans. A towheaded youngster from Acle in Norfolk, he was eager, energetic, and was a fast learner. His large gray-green eyes were misty with concern as he watched the proceedings.

Randolph's adjutant, Captain Edwin Smith, hovered nearby nervously. In his early fifties, he was a veteran of the old Royal Flying Corps and had seven kills over the Middle East where he had flown Sopwith Camels against General von Falkenhayn's best flyers. In 1917 he was the first Englishman into Jerusalem and never let anyone forget it. Brazenly, he had landed his Camel inside the city just after the Turks evacuated and before General Sir Edmund "Bull" Allenby made his storied triumphal entry. Allenby never forgave him. Now with crippling rheumatism, which he vehemently denied, he was relegated to administrative duties that he despised. However, he executed his responsibilities with panache and a high level of efficiency.

Still in their flying kit, Pilot Officer Ian McBride, Flight Lieutenant Cedric Hart, and Flight Sergeant Michael Sturgis sat against a side wall, smoking and drinking. All stared at Randolph with deep, penetrating looks as if they could not believe the major was actually there. All had been convinced the major had been killed.

Chatfield, an old RAF doctor who had come out of retire-

ment "for the new bash," was at least sixty-five years old.
With a bare stubble of white bristles, his pate gleamed as if
it had been stropped with Kiwi. His sagging face was deeply
creviced like a relief map and his rheumy blue eyes were
strangely striated with uneven green lines. But there was
confidence there—the confidence that came to eyes that had
seen everything. Steely resolve gleamed there, too. Regardless of rank, his decisions, his authority, prevailed.

Chatfield had a brilliant, incisive mind and loved chess.
Often, in the evenings, he and Randolph spent hours at the
board. Usually these matches were futile, because more often
than not, their efforts ended in drawn games instead of check-
mate. Randolph had immense respect for the physician and
considered him one of his best friends.

Everyone leaned forward as Chatfield raised the flyer's left
hand shoulder high. Randolph winced and was unable to
suppress a groan.

"Severe contusions, abrasions, and some subcutaneous
bleeding," the doctor said to himself. Then the old surgeon
reared back and used the lower magnifying lenses of his
bifocals. "The X rays show no broken bones, but, upon my
word, Major, such a lot of lovely colors—purple, yellow,
black, a dash of green." He lowered the flyer's arm gently
and stepped back.

"How bad, Doctor? How bad?" Randolph asked impatiently. He emptied his glass and held it up. Immediately
Sergeant-Major Woodhouse recharged the glass from a make-
shift bar on a battered sideboard next to the clerk's desk.

"Why did you refuse attention from the army doctors at
Bethersden?"

"They're butchers."

Chatfield smiled at the oblique compliment. "Then who
cleaned the head wound? The temple?" He gestured at the
long red laceration that began just forward of Randolph's
right ear and extended down to his cheek.

"A civilian—a girl. I landed on her potato patch."

Chatfield narrowed his eyes and mused, "And you injured it when you bailed out?"

"Quite right. I already told you that. Why do you ask again?"

The old doctor tugged on his chin with a thumb and forefinger. "Because it looks like it has been professionally cleaned and dressed." He leaned forward. "And it looks as if it's been healing for a week."

Randolph sat quietly for a moment, mind filled with thoughts of the fascinating girl—Elisa Blue, she had told him as he left—and her beautiful cottage. His voice softened. "No, Doctor, just two hours—two hours ago."

Chatfield said, "I'll dust it with sulfa and bandage it. But it doesn't look as if it needs either."

Evans spoke up, bringing the war back and blotting out the warm memories, "You scrubbed two Jerries, Major?"

"Quite, I know," Randolph acknowledged, feeling sudden, inexplicable irritation.

"Confirmed?" the adjutant, Edwin Smith, asked.

"I don't give two bloody stuffs for the whole lot," Randolph growled and then fell silent. Everyone looked at one another uneasily.

"Yes. Confirmed," Hart offered. Misreading Randolph's silence, the flight lieutenant pressed on enthusiastically, "I saw them both and so did most of the eastern seaboard. I boffed a Dornier and a ME, McBride got one of each, Coop Hansen got a ME. Two Dorniers and two one-oh-nines got away."

Randolph slammed his fist on the desk so hard a bottle of alcohol leapt off and shattered on the floor. Hart recoiled like a man encountering a cobra in a dark forest. The major's face was flushed like sunset and the veins in his neck swelled like a tenor reaching for a high note. "Blast it! Kochling got away and Preston Donovan bought it and Coop was butchered by Kochling." Silence like a heavy, viscous liquid dropped on the room, coating everyone and everything. Eyes were averted, seeking the floor, the ceiling, anything but another man's eyes.

The major drained his glass and Woodhouse made another trip to the sideboard, returning with a full glass. Shifting his gaze from man to man, the squadron leader showed a mercurial change in mood, suddenly speaking softly and sarcastically, "Think of the glory—the honor Coop and Donovan bought. Their heroism will be reported in *The Times, The Guardian, Gazette*. They'll be mentioned in dispatches, be awarded the DSO, and their families can display them on their mantels. Marvelous trade." He grabbed a maintenance report with his good hand and held it before his eyes as if he were reading a citation. He mimicked the clipped, singsong voice of a bored staff officer, "His Majesty the King has been graciously pleased to approve the award of the Distinguished . . ." He threw the document into the air and it drifted like a pendulum to the floor.

Randolph let his hands drop on his chest and interlaced his fingers. Staring at the ceiling he said, "Perhaps we should take a verse from Brooke or Henley. If some bloody drivel is too nonsensical to mouth, make a poem of it." Suddenly he was a poet, waving a hand effeminately, " 'Some corner of a foreign field forever England,' or perhaps, 'England, my England, Take us and break us: we are yours, We shall die to the song on your bugles blown.' " The gaze circled the room, found nothing but shocked, astonished eyes. "Coop and Donovan heard the bugle." He drank through a chuckle, rivulets running from the corners of his mouth, off his chin, and onto the hair of his bare chest.

Randolph was not finished, "Or why not just forget the poets and simply congratulate them for dying in the clean Channel sky away from doctors' scalpels, pans, and tubes—free of chanting priests and stinking incense? Salute their freedom from the aches and infirmities of old age. Perhaps we should celebrate their good fortune by singing, dancing"—he held up his glass—"drinking, find women, bonk 'em until they can't walk." He laughed until his eyes watered. "Yes. That's it. Celebrate the transformation from flesh to fantasy. Jolly good fun for all." He held up his glass. "To the freedom of death in the summer of its power." He drained it, but alone. The other men in the room could only stare at one another in shocked wonder and concern. They had never seen Squadron Leader Major Randolph Higgins in this state.

Chatfield spoke softly yet with the assurance of one holding all the cards, "Sir, you can't fly for at least a fortnight."

Randolph slammed a fist on the desk. "I've got to!"

"Sorry, sir. I can't clear you." He gestured. "With that shoulder you would only kill yourself and maybe some others."

Randolph downed another drink and sank back with a long sigh. His sixth drink, the liquor was finally taking affect. Slowly, he turned to his adjutant. The words were slurred and filled with resignation, "You'll be in charge, Captain Smith."

"Yes, sir. We can handle the lot, sir," Smith assured him. The three pilots nodded agreement.

Nursing a fresh drink, Randolph spoke to his desk, voice rising again, "I've got to bring Major Erich Kochling to book."

"Not for at least a fortnight, Major," the doctor said calmly. "And, sir, keep the lid on. The war can roll merrily along without you." The bold statement caused an exchange of anxious looks. However, Chatfield had the look of a man who knew his ground and was ready to stand it.

Randolph smiled. "You think I'm going off my wick, Doctor?"

"That can happen to any of us—especially you flyers." Chatfield turned his lips under and spit out his words as if they were rotten fruit, "That could lead to permanent grounding, Major. You know that. If I may suggest, Major Higgins, you're due for a leave." He gestured at the shoulder. "And you are in need of rest and rehabilitation. Go home. Nothing is as bracing as that. Your brother is waiting . . ."

"My brother Lloyd? Brigadier Lloyd Higgins?" He glared at his clerk, Lance Corporal Timothy Evans.

Evans's smooth, young face collapsed in a ruin of anguish. "I'm sorry, sir. Group rang us up just before you returned. With your injuries and the rest of that lot it slipped my mind and . . ."

"Dash it all, man. It didn't have far to slip." Higgins turned to the doctor. "A two-week leave—at your orders."

Chatfield smiled. "Group is cutting your orders now."

Randolph smiled for the first time, "Confident old bugger, aren't you. You'd send Dowding to blighty, wouldn't you?"

Everyone chuckled more with relief at Randolph's change in mood than at the jest. Chatfield nodded. "Quite so, if he had a shoulder like that." He began to put his instruments back in his bag. "Get the rest you need, sir. And if I may suggest, you have a beautiful estate. Return to Fenwyck, sir."

"Quite," Randolph said, rising. "I'll return to Fenwyck."

Driving from Detling to Fenwyck, Randolph gunned his Jaguar SS (Swallow Sports) two-seater, using every one of the 125 horsepower of the big 3.5-liter engine and his gear box to whip around army lorries, horse-pulled wagons and carts, and occasional civilian vehicles. With the top down, he was lashed by wind that sent his brown hair flying and brought water to his eyes. He smiled, mind wandering back to the open cockpits of Nieuport 17s and S.E.5As. Those were the days when a man challenged the skies with wood, canvas, and glue, and no parachute. Took the flimsy crates to twenty-two thousand feet, sucking on an oxygen tube and not really believing it could all be real.

Thoughts of the old fighting scouts revived memories of his own youth and the advancing years that were stealing it away. A glance in the mirror showed only minor incursions of gray hair at his temples, his skin, weathered by years in the cockpit, tanned and rough but still unlined. A vital, alert gleam had reinvigorated the brown of his eyes. "Old Wayne

Chatfield knew what he was talking about," he said to himself.

A stab of pain caused him to wince. His left shoulder was very sore. When he worked the accelerator, brake, and clutch, both knees ached and his right leg throbbed from calf to thigh where his old, layered burn scars had been stretched.

Despite the horror and rage of the last dogfight and his aches and pains, Randolph's spirits were elevated by the marvelous performance of the Jaguar and the anticipation of seeing his brother Lloyd. Brigadier General Lloyd Higgins —smart and as clever as a fox. In December his Fourth Armored Brigade had led the rout of the Italian Tenth Army at Sidi Barrani in Egypt, brilliantly flanking the "Eyties" by swinging south into the deep desert and driving them back into Libya. Then Churchill's intervention in Greece that emasculated the Desert Army, the rout by Rommel, and Lloyd's near capture when a German motorized column captured General Richard O'Connor's headquarters. But now Lloyd was home after two years in Africa. And unhurt. Unbelievable.

Roaring past a stalled Bren gun carrier, he forced a half-dozen soldiers to leap aside. "Blimey! Slow it!" an old sergeant bellowed after the tiny sports car.

"Why?" Randolph shouted over his shoulder into the swirling dust and staccato blasts of the exhaust.

Entering Kent the little machine climbed a gentle grade to enter the weald where magnificent stands of oak, beech, hornbeam, and elm crowded the road, making the way ahead appear like a green corridor walling off a brown-black ribbon. "Robin Hood, where are you?" the major shouted. "There are blackguards afoot. In fact, they're all over the bloody continent." Wildly, he threw peals of laughter into the roar of the engine, the wind, and the hiss of tires on pavement.

The beauty around him drove away dark thoughts and brought back the girl. Elisa Blue. Just the thought of her calmed him. She had helped him up after his jarring parachute landing. Took him to her cottage—a tiny, thatched, rock-walled building about as large as his adjutant's storeroom. But Elisa's home was immaculately clean, filled with bluebells, primroses, violets, fuchsias, and live ferns growing to the window light. In his dazed state, he had learned little of her except she was apparently alone. She had served him tea, cleansed his wound. There had been pounding at the door, of course, as anxious farmers trooped to see the heroic pilot. But Randolph shouted them off, claiming, "I'm fit."

Actually, he had been captivated by the delicate, ethereal beauty who sat next to him on an old but beautifully covered sofa. She moved close, spoke softly to him of the flowers, the animals and crops as she cleaned his face and wiped blood from his neck. The war was not there; not in the cottage, not in her mind. Oddly, he felt like a little boy again, sick, with his mother leaning over his bed ministering to him. And the girl seemed to exude the force of life, contrapuntal to everything he did in the sky. He had wanted her for himself. Needed her like a dying man needs a transfusion. It could only be for a short time, but he wanted that time. Too soon, they heard the lorry. "You'll come back, Major?"

"Of course. But I may not be able to give you any notice."

Her smile had been warm, filled with the promise of life. "I'll be here, Major. Whenever you choose to come. I have made cherry wine. It's almost ready." She took his hand. "Please have summer wine with me."

He would never forget that magical moment—the moment he had lost himself in the depths of her blue eyes that were deeper than the Channel he had just flown over and sown with death. "You have my word."

A bump in the road and the little motor car was very nearly airborne. Frantically, Randolph fought the wheel and then geared down. "Like a Nieuport in a crosswind, old girl," he said to the Jaguar. The little car settled down, purring and racing through the woods like the cat whose name it bore.

The woods gave way to fields of oats, barley, hops, and wheat as the Jaguar charged into the great plain that extended through the counties of Sussex, Surrey, and Kent. Orchestrated by the breeze, hay, oats, and barley undulated gently in waves like swells running from a storm, while hop bines twisted up tall, rigid poles in fields as densely planted as forests.

Wheat caught his eye, waving its golden heads in the summer sun. Submarines had put it there. Terrible losses to the undersea prowlers had forced the planting of vast new fields. He gritted his teeth. Gripped the wheel tighter and glanced at the golden fields again. Like Elisa's hair. A much more pleasant thought. Strange, how the girl's memory endured—could push the war aside; even submarines, Kochling, the lot.

He passed more lorries and Bren carriers at such a speed, the vehicles seemed to be at a standstill. Then he entered the part of Kent that was free from spring frosts and had sparse summer rainfall. Fruit country. Orchards of orange pippins, cherries, and plums began to appear, branches sagging heavily with the bounty of the fruit. Here and there in pastures nestled in the orchards, sheep and cattle grazed, sometimes tended by young boys and girls. Invariably, they waved at the flashy little two-seater. Randolph waved back. This was England. This was home. How could a man not love it?

A few more miles and the North Downs were near. Wye and the Romney Marsh would be just over a low rise to the southeast. He smiled. He was almost home. The narrow dirt road to Fenwyck would appear to his left just before Wye. There it was. Almost hidden by beechwood and elms.

With a squeal of tires, he whipped the small car hard to the left and entered the lane. He smiled. "Home. Home . . ." he said, over and over.

Turning off the narrow road, the Jaguar entered a circular drive that led to Fenwyck's Victorian porch and two great oak doors that opened on the huge manor house. Originally a medieval castle that had dominated the entire countryside, Fenwyck had been destroyed by Oliver Cromwell's ruthless Ironsides during the civil wars of the seventeenth century. Rebuilt in the haphazard Tudor style of the time, Fenwyck was built of brick with stone trim and timbered gables. In the bright sunlight of early afternoon, the blue slate of the saw-toothed roofline reflected the sun like a choppy sea. The impression was that of size; an enormous three-story building with at least two dozen chimneys—each of the eighteen bedrooms had its own fireplace—massive timbers, and intricate stonework. The house had been designed, built, enlarged, rebuilt, and lived in by men who wanted the world to know they had enormous wealth and did not care one whit how they spent it. Randolph's great-great-grandfather Henry who bought the house in 1760, great-grandfather Oliver, grandfather Neville, and father, Walter, had been cut from this cloth.

The grounds were Elysian. The great lawn, which was over a hundred years old and a full acre in size, was cut into rigid geometric patterns by a low maze of hedge. It was the best time of the year for flowers. Rioting with vivid blues, reds, yellows, and muted combinations of all colors of the rainbow, beds of roses, violets, chrysanthemums, and bluebells bordered the walks and nestled in beds close to the house. In the distance, the sun was caught by treetops that reflected the sunbeams in flashes of silver and gold as the gentle breeze swayed the foliage.

Randolph drank it all in hungrily like a swimmer too long underwater who surfaces to fill his lungs with sweet air. Then joy unbounded as he saw his brother Lloyd and sister-in-law Bernice waiting for him on the porch. Screeching to a stop in a cloud of dust, Randolph leapt from the car and raced up the steps despite the pain in his knees. Lloyd met him halfway. Then Bernice. In a moment the trio was locked in an embrace, the brothers throwing British restraint to the winds. Then Lloyd stepped back, staring at his brother while Bernice clung to Randolph, kissing and hugging him.

"God, Randolph, we thought you bought it this time," Bernice said, voice quavering.

Randolph did not question her knowledge. With friends in high places in the Air Ministry, his every move was well known to every member of the family. Five feet three inches tall, she only came to his chest. She was still attractive, but her flaxen hair had turned gray and years of worry had left lines trailing off in hard slashes from the corners of her eyes and mouth. She was very thin and felt fragile enough to break. He released her and clasped his brother's hand.

At six feet three inches, Brigadier General Lloyd Higgins was two inches taller than Randolph. He was one of the few men Randolph ever had to look up to. The desert sun had done terrible things to his brother. Sparsely built since his youth, Lloyd now appeared to have had most of his flesh burned off his bones, leaving him gaunt and slightly bent. Hanging in creases and folds, his uniform looked as if it had been tailored for a man a stone heavier. His wind-scoured and sun-leathered face was a craggy ruin, large sagging pouches like quarter-moons underscoring his eyes. His Roman nose looked larger than ever, bushy gray brows beetling, and his mouth a colorless slash. But the gray-blue eyes were clear, alert, and gleamed with intelligence.

Lloyd looked Randolph up and down. "Daresay, you look well, brother. At least fourteen stone, I'd wager." His eyes ran over the bandage extending from the right temple to Randolph's cheekbone. "Been in a bit of a scrape, I hear."

"A little rough going over the Channel—shot up and bailed out." Randolph touched the bandage gently with a single finger. "Just a nick I picked up when I quit the old girl." He smiled with a warm new thought. "But it's healing very quickly."

"Oh, God, Randolph," Bernice said, kissing his cheek gently.

"It's nothing, nothing at all, Bernice. Not even stitched." Randolph gestured at the door. "I need a tot."

"I'll second that," Lloyd said, mounting the stairs.

They were met at the door by a trio of senior servants, headed by the old butler, Dorset. Randolph could not remember when Fenwyck had been without Dorset. He had to be at least seventy-five years old, but admitted to only "six decades and seven.'' Of medium height, the old butler had a full head of hair as white as an alpine ski slope, clear, almost unlined skin, and the dignified, rigid bearing of a ramrod. Gripping Randolph's hand, he said in a clear, resonant voice, ''Welcome home, Mr. Higgins.'' His dark eyes were brightened uncharacteristically by a film of moisture.

''Good to see you, Dorset,'' Randolph said. Then he shook the hand of Andre Demozay, the chef.

A fiftyish Frenchman from Marseilles, Demozay had joined the family in 1938. The man had a wife and two children still in France and he claimed the Vichy government would not permit their emigration. A former *poilu*, Andre was a survivor of the horror of Verdun where a million men died in the carnage. The spirit of France died there with the flower of her youth. ''They shall not pass,'' old Marshal Pétain had cried. And the Germans did not, but the cost was the soul of France.

Randolph always suspected that André had left France to avoid military service but his credentials were never challenged. Randolph dropped the Frenchman's limp hand and moved to the third servant, Bernice's personal maid, Emily Burns, who curtsied stiffly.

Emily was a slender, plain, middle-aged woman from Ledbury in Worchester. Flat-chested and narrow-hipped, the woman appeared to be as barren as a Dover chalk cliff. She had never married and Randolph had often wondered if she had ever had a man. Men, lust, and sex seemed out of her ken and she appeared content to serve as Bernice's maid and, often, her confidante. Similar to Dorset, her whole life was the Higgins family.

Lloyd led his brother through the huge entry, past the grand staircase, a Chinese Chippendale monstrosity imported from Indochina by their grandfather Neville, down a long, thickly carpeted hall past a dining room, morning room, breakfast room, gun room, business room, finally entering their father's old study just before a turn in the corridor that led to the servants' quarters.

Randolph's mind ran with warm memories. Around the turn in the hallway, the second door on the right had belonged to Brenda's maid, Nicole, when the girl was still an "underhouse parlor maid." He had known that door well, the small room, the bed, the French girl's smooth, hard body and frenzied passion. The first time she had been only eighteen and he twenty-two. She had been insatiable, like an animal, screeching, writhing, and sometimes clawing. It had gone on for over a year and Randolph always suspected his father had placed Nicole so that her room was conveniently located at the foot of the rear stairs that led directly to Randolph's room on the second floor at their head. Nevertheless, he broke it off after a year, feeling revulsion at the sordid, pedestrian affair. It was 1917 and he commanded Number 5 Squadron on the Somme. The killing on the Western Front was in full swing and he lost himself in wild flings with women he met in London. In those days, they were everywhere, flaunting their availability in Piccadilly, the Palace, Ritz, Berkeley, and on almost any street, if you wanted that kind. Nicole had been brokenhearted, but soon consoled herself in the arms of a young lieutenant. Soon after, she became Brenda's personal maid and she was moved upstairs into a room across the hall from Brenda; her *maitresse*.

Following Lloyd and Bernice, Randolph entered his father's old study. It was unchanged. Everything was just as Walter had left it on the day he died. A male sanctuary, no expense had been spared to make it one of the most richly furnished rooms in the house. It boasted paneled walls lined with glass-doored bookcases, hardwood floors covered with layered rugs, and rows of sporting prints hanging on the walls or, in the Victorian tradition, resting on the shelves of the bookcases. Dominating the room was a ponderous serpentine writing desk still laden with Walter's racks of carved pipes, empty tobacco tins, and ash receivers. Close by on a Regency carved walnut sideboard were cut crystal decanters filled with liquors. Despite the lavish furniture, the showpiece of the room was a magnificent eighteenth-century Carlin long-cased clock, veneered with tulipwood and ebony, and box and banded with purple-wood. Clicking softly but regally in a corner, the timepiece showed sidereal time with a green hand and the date could be found in a panel below the center. Even the signs of the zodiac were shown, painted in gold leaf around the dial. Topping the elaborate mechanism like a king's crown was a spectacular gold gilt group of Apollo driving his chariot.

Moving to the sideboard, Lloyd poured stiff drinks of scotch for Randolph and himself and a glass of Bordeaux for Bernice. He handed the drinks to Randolph and Bernice who seated themselves on a plump sofa facing the desk. Lloyd took the chair behind the desk. He sank back, sighing, and held up his drink. "To us, brother, together again," he said, staring warmly at Randolph. The trio drank.

Randolph held up his glass. "May we settle the hash of the 'Frog of the Pontine Marshes' and 'the Austrian paperhanger' soon—chop, chop."

Lloyd and Bernice chuckled and shouted "Hear! Hear!" at the acrimonious sobriquets assigned to Benito Mussolini and Adolph Hitler by the British press. They all drank.

Bernice turned to Randolph. "I got a letter from Brenda." She held up two sheets of paper neatly lettered in ink.

Feeling a slight warmth on his cheeks, Randolph sipped his drink. He was sure both Lloyd and Bernice were aware of the strong feelings—the powerful attraction—that existed between Brenda and himself. The years had taught him such things were impossible to hide even when platonic. He managed a casual, "Really. Any news?"

Sipping her wine, Bernice glanced at the letter, telling Randolph of Rodney's return to New York, of Betty and her daughter, Marsha, who lived with Brenda.

"Betty married that worthless 'Eytie' barber—Dominic, ah . . ."

"That's right—Borelli."

"By Jove," Lloyd interrupted. "It amazes me that that

lad Rodney was in on the kill of the *Bismarck*. Stout fellow. Could've sat on his backside on the beach instead of risking his neck. Always knew he had backbone. Blast it, wished I'd been here when he stayed the weekend.''

Bernice looked at her husband. ''He's a big, strapping, brilliant fellow, Lloyd. He was a big star in that insane game Americans call football. He told us all about *Bismarck*—the sinking, the whole lot.''

Randolph nodded agreement. ''You're quite right about American football. It's played by homicidal maniacs who leave their brains in their lockers. But Rodney was a tough little nipper. Remember the brawls he had with Trevor and Nathan? Sometimes both at the same time. Made a mess of the garden, smashed their toys. Horrified Mother and amused Father.'' The brothers drank and chuckled at their memories of long ago.

The pair fell silent as Bernice read on, telling Randolph of their niece Regina and about her entrapment in the Warsaw ghetto with her husband Josef Lipiski and baby Rose.

''Beastly rumors out of Poland.'' Randolph drummed his armrest.

''Relocations,'' Bernice offered.

''Worse,'' Randolph said. ''Murder. Mass murder.''

''I can't believe that. After all, the Germans are human beings.''

''Are they, sister-in-law? My Polish pilots have told me otherwise. Some of them get letters smuggled out through the Balkans and into Turkey. They claim there have been wholesale executions.''

''No!'' Bernice cried in disbelief, covering her mouth with her hand.

''I say, brother,'' Lloyd interrupted. ''I have no love for the Jerries, but the Afrika Korps has always observed the Geneva Conventions—treated our chaps humanely when they've captured them—fed them, tended their wounds.''

Randolph said to his brother, ''Hitler's virulently anti-

Semitic and Rommel is cut from a different cloth. Rommel's an aristocrat, Hitler's a common guttersnipe—capable of anything, and you know it.''

Bernice shuddered. "I hope you're wrong, Randolph.''

The flyer eyed his sister-in-law over his glass. "I hope I am, too.'' He emptied his glass with a quick toss of his head. Stepping to the sideboard, he recharged his glass and did the same for his brother's. Returning to his seat, he discreetly changed the subject, asking about Lloyd and Bernice's children, Trevor and Bonnie.

"Trevor's stationed at Portsmouth. He thinks he'll pull destroyer duty. He's gotten himself involved with a Wren,'' Bernice said.

"Serious?'' Randolph glanced at Lloyd.

Lloyd shrugged and turned his palms up. "I've never seen her.'' He turned to his wife. "You've met her, love.''

Bernice nodded. "Several times. She's sweet and seems to love Trevor.''

"Bonnie?'' Randolph asked. "Still a nurse at Chatham and still going with that useless Blake Boggs?''

"You're too harsh on the lad,'' Bernice said, smiling at Randolph's obvious overprotectiveness of his beloved niece. "And, yes, she's still at the naval hospital at Chatham.''

"She can do better than Boggs,'' Randolph said. "Much better.''

There was a low cough. Dorset was standing at the door. "Sorry to disturb you, Mrs. Higgins. But Andre has a minor crisis in the kitchen. May I impose on you.''

"Of course,'' Bernice said, smiling. Turning to Randolph, she said, "He's making a special dish in honor of your return and I promised to confer with him.''

Randolph laughed. "A major campaign?''

"Right.'' She placed her glass on the sideboard and left.

The brothers refilled their glasses and sagged back in silence. They were alone, finding an intimacy that only brothers can know—a commonality of mood and thought reserved for men of the same womb who had been close for a lifetime and loved and respected each other very deeply.

Thoughtfully, Lloyd lit a cigarette. Randolph remembered the rancid odor of the Goldflakes and Abdullahs his brother used to smoke and was thankful to notice the green Lucky Strike label on the package. Lloyd exhaled a huge cloud of blue smoke and toyed with his drink.

Randolph broke the silence, "It's been a tough go in Africa, Lloyd?"

"Dash it all, we bloody well put the wind up them and botched it," the brigadier fumed bitterly. He took a long drink and stared at his brother over his glass. "Do you know that Graziani had a quarter-million troops in Libya and Egypt?" Randolph raised an eyebrow. "And O'Connor boffed his arse with thirty thousand. That was the entire Western Desert Force—the whole lot." He refilled his glass and poured another for Randolph. He slammed his fist into an open palm. "We had them, brother. Captured a hundred eighty thousand of them. They were finished. All of North Africa was ours for the taking and then Wavell gutted our army and sent our best lads to bloody disaster in Greece and Crete." He pulled on the cigarette like a thirsty man gulping water.

"It was the War Cabinet—Anthony Eden, Alan Brooke . . ."

Lloyd waved a hand in irritation. "No, Randolph. Wavell made the decision. He was the commander-in-chief, Middle East. O'Connor and I fought him, but he was CIC. He must have been daft." He gulped half of his drink in two swallows. "Then Rommel came in with his corps—the Fifth Light and the Fifteenth Panzer, both equipped with the Panzer Three tank. The Panzer Three is faster than our Matildas, outguns them with its fifty-millimeter gun against the Matilda's two-pounder. And they're bloody tough. At Halfaya Pass I personally hit one with three two-pounders before it blew up." He pulled on the Lucky Strike hungrily, spoke through the exhaling smoke, "And their eighty-eights!" He slapped his forehead hopelessly, stubbed out his cigarette, and lighted another.

"I know about them, Lloyd. I've come under fire from them over the continent. It's a vicious ack-ack gun."

Lloyd narrowed his lids. "Well, let me tell you this, brother, it's the best antitank gun in the world. I've seen it open our Matildas like tins of bully beef at a mile. It fires a twenty-pound shell at three thousand feet per second with unbelievable accuracy and fifteen to twenty rounds a minute." He tossed off the remainder of his drink and refilled his glass. He continued, voice heavy with bitterness, "In just one month, Rommel swept away everything we had accomplished in our entire campaign, drove us all the way back into Egypt. Captured General O'Connor and most of his staff. The only thing that stopped him was the lack of supplies." He tapped the desk with his knuckles. "I got back to Egypt with four tanks and mine was damaged."

Randolph rotated his glass slowly, watching the amber liquid swirl gently to the lip of the glass. He spoke thoughtfully, clipping each word as if his lips were scissors, "You insist on leading your brigade."

"Quite right. I'm in the lead tank with my command pennant flapping from the WT antenna."

"For the whole world to see?"

"Quite."

"You've turned down major-general. You could have your own division, Lloyd."

The brigadier smiled wryly. "And command from the rear from a safe dugout. Is that what you mean?" He shook his head. "If I'm to send men to their deaths, the least I can do is lead them there." He tapped ashes from the end of his cigarette and stared hard at his brother. "Randolph, you bloody well don't have room to get on my wick. Don't you think I know you begged and bullied your way into your command. You could be a colonel with a safe billet at Group." He chuckled. "You must be the oldest fighter pilot in the history of aviation, yet, you fly at the head of your squadron. Well, I'll bloody well lead my lads, too.''

Randolph laughed with his brother. They were too much alike. Neither could mislead the other and Lloyd had him backed into a corner. He escaped to a new topic. "Rommel's got a nest of Aussies to contend with at Tobruk.''

Lloyd nodded. "Tough buggers. The Ninth Aussie Division and other Dominion troops. Over thirty thousand. Trapped.''

"That many?"

"Afraid so."

"Any chance to relieve them?"

Lloyd shrugged his shoulders. "We need a lot of reinforcements. Armor with bigger guns straightaway. That's why Auk sent me.''

" 'Auk'—you mean John Auchinleck the new CIC?"

Lloyd nodded. "Quite. Wavell got the boot all the way to India, you know.''

"Auk's a good man?"

"Quite so. We want the new American M-Three tank—the Yanks call it the General Grant. It has a seventy-five-millimeter gun, good armor, and can do twenty-six miles an hour.''

"Can you get them?"

Lloyd drank deeply, pulled on his cigarette, and exhaled slowly. "We signed contracts for them in 1940, but I haven't the foggiest. That's really why I'm here." He gestured at the door. "You know I don't tell the Missus everything. I have appointments with Viscount Alan Brooke, Anthony Eden, and in a week the PM.''

"Churchill. Good! He'll listen. He gave me my squadron.''

Lloyd tapped the desk restively. "It's not Winnie, it's his advisers—the War Cabinet. They're bloody stupid. If they want to win this bloody bash, they've got to stop the endless twaddle and give us the men and equipment.''

"What about our new Crusaders and Valentines?"

Lloyd shook his head hopelessly. "Still too slow, too light, and armed with two-pounders. We need the Grant and I hear the Yanks have a superb new tank in their M-4 Sherman." He tapped the desk and licked his lips. "Love to get my hands on a brigade—just a brigade." He sighed. "I'd settle Rommel's hash—send him to bed with the bedouins."

"What about the Arab? Whose side is he on?"

"His own."

"I don't understand."

Cigarette dangling from the corner of his mouth, Lloyd refilled both glasses and sank back in the chair. He took another deep drink before answering, words flowing swiftly but slightly slurred. "You've got to understand this, brother, the Arab has absolutely no honor, no integrity. He's the most corrupt human being on earth. It's a point of honor to lie and cheat—do anything to best someone—anyone. They bully the weak and run like jackals from the strong. The only thing that they honor is baksheesh—bribery. For two bob an Arab'll sell you his soul and then double deal with your enemy. They steal from us—from our dead and Axis dead. I shot two of them stripping the rotting corpse of a Tommy at Sidi Suleiman." He smiled like a man recalling the delights of a love affair. "I put half a belt of three-oh-three ball into them. One of the most satisfying experiences of my life." He eyed his brother. "Enough of the Western Desert and those creatures, how goes it with you, brother?"

With the liquor spreading through him like warm fingers, Randolph began to feel a pleasant glow. He spoke slowly, "I have a fine squadron."

"Bad show yesterday?"

The glow vanished. "Lost two fine lads."

"To Kochling's *Jagdstaffel*. Major Erich Kochling."

Randolph was stunned. "How did you know?"

"I've heard of him for over a year and Bernice found out yesterday when she heard from the Air Ministry after you were shot down. Besides, Kochling flies a garish orange-and-green-striped machine and your bash with him was seen by thousands. Don't you realize that, brother?"

"Why of course—quite right," Randolph said, sipping his scotch.

"He's another Bruno Hollweg, brother. Another personal feud. Right?"

Randolph palmed his forehead as if he were wiping confusion from his mind. "I honestly don't know, Lloyd. I just know I've got to kill him. He butchered my best friend in his parachute."

"Lord, no."

There was a long silence in the room, both brothers drinking and avoiding eye contact. Finally, Lloyd spoke, finding a topic they had quibbled over for years, "Serious about any woman, brother?"

"Not that again, brother," Randolph said with resignation. "Yes, I know some women."

Lloyd chuckled. "I know that. You've known scores. I mean love—marriage. You aren't getting younger, old boy."

Randolph pinched the bridge of his nose and stared at his glass, trying to organize his thoughts. Drinking on an empty stomach, the liquor was making itself felt. "You mean a man alone keeps poor company, brother?" he managed.

The brigadier chuckled. "Well put."

Randolph smiled and then grew serious. He waved. "I don't know if there's any love out there. Not now, not in wartime. I meet women, I'm attracted—but love them?" He shook his head, drained his glass, and walked unsteadily to the sideboard while Lloyd eyed him curiously. After renewing his drink, Randolph sank back in his chair and thought for a long moment before he found the right words. "You really want to know how I feel about women—about love?"

"I just asked you, Randolph."

Randolph sighed and then spoke slowly and deliberately, "Men and women don't meet, court, and love in wartime, Lloyd. 'Love,' whatever that might be, is a pretty name, brother. That's all. There is no time. People collide and rebound from each other like billiard balls. The conventions, rituals, the obligations, and, yes, the morals, as you know them, are gone—you should know that.'' He tilted the glass up and drained it. His brother remained mute. ''Don't you see, brother, men and women do not 'love' in wartime, they desire, demand, and take. I may sound cynical and coldly pragmatic, but, remember, there is nothing as pragmatic as a five-hundred-pound bomb. Love has been banished for the duration.''

Lloyd held his cigarette before his eyes and watched the thin ribbon of smoke stream to the ceiling where it flattened into a blue cloud against the paneling. ''Pragmatic? Perhaps. But to say you're cynical, Randolph, would be the understatement of the decade.''

''Sorry, brother.''

''They're all the same to you?''

''I didn't say that, Lloyd.''

The brigadier stared at his brother in confusion. ''But you just said . . .''

Randolph interrupted with a wave. ''In fact, I met someone quite different just yesterday.''

''The girl who cleaned your wound?''

Randolph nodded. ''A strange girl—a very strange girl.''

''You're shedding your cynicism fast, brother,'' Lloyd snorted.

Randolph went on as if he had not heard, ''She wants me to return—for summer wine.''

''It's summer.''

''I know. I'm going tomorrow.''

''But there's no love.''

Randolph laughed softly. ''Of course not. There can't be. Good Lord, man, I just met her yesterday and I was in a daze. She's probably younger than Bonnie.''

''Then, why see her?''

''Why not?''

There was a presence at the door. It was Dorset. ''Dinner is served, gentlemen,'' the old man announced.

The brothers rose unsteadily and left the room.

* * *

Elisa Blue actually lived only an hour's drive from Fenwyck. East of the estate, her cottage was in East Kent south of Shepherdswell. Turning off the main road at Elham, the Jaguar entered a lane like a dirt track, lined with trees and thickets of shrubs and wildflowers. Slowing, Randolph geared down as the rev-counter dropped below two thousand rpms and the high-compression engine began to lug. There were potholes and rocks, the springs of the little machine compressing and rebounding as the tires bounced over the uneven surface. Randolph cursed, fighting the wheel and working his accelerator and four-speed gear box. His knees began to ache and the long scar on his right leg sent pangs of pain up his side. Then a narrow beam of sunlight caught his eye, turned his head, and he was suddenly aware of the rare beauty around him. He forgot his aches and pains. The road suddenly became smooth and the Jaguar seemed to glide.

He had never seen such lush countryside. As he slowed the car and looked around, silver shafts of sunlight broke through the branches and fronds, painting the leaves and flowers theatrically, bringing out rare hues of lilac, heliotrope, amethyst, scarlet, and salmon pink in clusters of honeysuckle, bluebells, daisies, poppies, buddleia, red campion, and many other flowers Randolph did not recognize. He saw wild blackberries, mistletoe, holly, chestnuts, and fruit crowding through thick growths of rhododendrons, hollyhocks, foxgloves, nettles, ferns, golden saxifrage, and hazel. When he could see the ground, it was carpeted with mat-grass and honey fungus like round toy stools for tired elves. Oak, poplar, willow, and elm crowded the road in elegant ranks like dancers on the stage of the Royal Ballet, soughing and swaying in the coying breeze and splashing the ground and passing motor car with ever-changing patterns of light. Sparrows, nightingales, and pigeons whirred through the branches in flocks while jackdaws scolded the intruder angrily. Giant butterflies delicately clothed in vivid blues, yellows, and reds staggered through the air in swarms like party confetti. It was breathtaking. Awesome. And Elisa was here. Elisa was everywhere. He knew he was very close to the cottage without really understanding why.

The girl had not left his mind from the moment he met her. But it was hard for him to believe she was what he had actually seen—a delicate, unearthly creature as gossamer as a wisp of cloud slipping past his cockpit. He had been dazed by the hard landing, in shock from the sight of Coop's frightful death. But she existed. He knew that. She had cleansed his wound and invited him back. And now, he would see her again.

He heard the brook before he saw it, splashing and gurgling ahead of the slow-moving vehicle. Cresting a small rise, he found it below, a gravelly stream hurrying through the wood on its way to the sea, running across the road so that he had to ford it where the rocks had been cleared. In first gear, he splashed through the stream and then climbed the rise on the opposite side. Then he saw her cottage. It was unmistakable.

In a small clearing, it was as he remembered—stone and thatched with a patchwork of swarthy Kentish brick and tile running through the masonry where it had crumbled over the years. Flowers grew up to the building in casual patches and there were animals everywhere. Chickens in a coop, a cow in a small barn, a half-dozen unpenned rabbits, and a goat tethered to a willow behind the coop. Behind the house, the wood had been cleared and he could see small patches of potatoes, cucumbers, turnips, carrots, and many other vegetables. Berries vined up onto trellises, cabbages squatted in long leafy rows. To the south was the wheat field and the small meadow where he had landed. There was order and peace everywhere. An island. A vacuum. His memory was accurate. There was no war here. No fighter sweeps. No maddeningly calm voice in his earphones coldly ordering his lads to their deaths. No eviscerated Coop Hansen and grinning Erich Kochling. And then he saw her.

Dressed in a bright white spotless cotton dress nipped in at her tiny waist by a shiny patent-leather belt, she walked from behind the house. Braking the Jaguar to a stop, Randolph leapt to the ground, knees suddenly free of pain. Facing the girl who was very near, he caught his breath. She was lovelier than he remembered. The long fine hair was truly golden and in the playful breeze it moved and flowed cloudlike around her shoulders. The huge dark eyes spoke of Celtic heritage, sparkling blue like a tropical summer day. Her features were delicate with a fine straight nose and high molded cheekbones, lips chiseled like the petals of a rose. Balancing her head like an orchid on a stem, her neck was long and regal. Her smile showed perfect white teeth as she extended her hand. "I've been expecting you, Major," she said with a voice that rang as clear as fine leaded crystal.

Holding the soft white hand in his, he was trapped in the blue depths of her eyes, realizing just how attractive she was. Not just physically or sensually. There was mystery and delicacy there and the fresh innocence of a child-woman as if she had stepped from the canvas of a Renoir painting. "You're real," he blurted. Feeling foolish, he released her hand and blushed like a schoolboy.

Her laughter was the sound of the brook he had just crossed. "I'm afraid I am, Major."

He composed himself quickly. "Elisa Blue."

"Yes. And you're Major Randolph Higgins."

"I've come for my summer wine."

"Yes, Major. Your summer wine. I've been waiting for you."

She took his hand and led him to the door.

He had not been mistaken about the cottage. The main room was filled with flowers: he saw them on two end tables flanking the sofa where he had sat when she washed his cheek, on the hearth of the rock fireplace, on a small sewing table in the corner, and on the heavy dining table next to the small kitchen. There were four windows in the room, artfully draped and curtained with lacy materials one rarely saw in an English farmhouse. Potted ferns on the sills grew in each one. Everything was in harmony like the foliage crowding the lane he had just driven; the colors of the flowers, the curtains, the patterns of the ferns, the lovely sofa. And it appeared as if each object had even been chosen for size and shape, then carefully placed to complement and harmonize with everything around it. It all exalted life.

She led him to the sofa. As he followed her she seemed to glide as if she were moving to music. The lovely, intricately woven themes of Mozart and Haydn came to his mind. He seated himself but she remained standing. "I'll get the wine," she said.

She walked to the kitchen, which was only a small alcove sealed off from the room by a low wooden wall and pastel-colored curtains hanging from the ceiling. He could see a few shelves and a hand pump over a spotless porcelain sink. The floor was of oak, hand-hewn and roughly fitted. A curtained doorway in the far wall sealed off what Randolph was sure were rooms added in recent years. He guessed they were bedrooms and storage rooms.

She returned, handed him a glass filled with red liquid, and sank down on the sofa next to him. She placed a bottle on the table before them. "Cherry wine, Major, as I promised," she said. She touched his glass with hers. They drank.

"Marvelous," he breathed, holding the glass up to the light. It was clear, unclouded, and sparkled like a tropical sunset. "Never tasted anything as exquisite—delicate."

"Thank you, Major."

He took another sip. "How did you know I'd return?"

"I knew."

"I took quite a thumping—was half off my wick. Might never have found your digs again without a parachute."

She laughed. "You had no trouble."

He nodded. "Came directly."

She ran a finger over his cheek. "How is your injury?"

"You did a fine job. It's healing very quickly and didn't require a single stitch."

"And your shoulder and your knees?"

"How did you know?"

"It was obvious."

He rubbed his shoulder gently and flexed his knees and chuckled. "Seem to be fit."

"You carry old wounds?"

"Yes. From the first one."

"Why do you fly?"

"You think I'm too old!"

"No. Too tired. You need a rest."

Surprisingly, Randolph was not offended by the boldness of the statement. Instead, his curiosity was aroused. "You know a lot about me."

"I've seen you before. When I was a little girl you were driving like the wind on the Hythe road in your little motor car, nearly hit our wagon. Made my father very angry. And I saw you twice at the marketplace in Hawkinge. You live at Fenwyck. Your family has lived there for generations."

He emptied his glass and she refilled it. "And you, Elisa, you live alone?"

"I'm not alone." She waved her hand in an encompassing gesture. "I have my animals—my flowers."

"But where is your family?"

She refilled her glass. "My mother left the world when I came into it." She sipped her wine, stared hard at the floor. "My brother went to sea in the *Rawalpindi*."

Randolph felt an electric prickle on the back of his neck. The merchant cruiser *Rawalpindi* had been sunk in 1939 by *Scharnhorst* and *Gneisenau* with terrible loss of life. "I'm sorry. And your father?"

"He's with the East Whittlesey Fusiliers in Singapore."

Randolph smiled reassuringly. "Well, that's a quiet theater."

She nodded. "Yes. His letters complain of the boredom." She looked up, a bright fresh smile on her face. She waved, "You like my home?"

"It's enchanting. You have an eye for beauty."

"I love life, Major. I love living things."

"You have a lot of animals—a big farm." She nodded

agreement. "You can manage the lot all by yourself?" he asked.

"I can take care of the gardens and the animals."

"You have wheat."

"Yes. The army helps out, you know."

"At harvest and planting?"

"Yes. They send young men. There's quite a demand for wheat, Major." She drank her wine and stared at him over the glass and then took him by surprise, "What's it like up there? Do you feel closer to God?"

He mulled the question over and took a small drink. "You make marvelous wine, Elisa."

"Thank you, but you didn't answer my question."

He sighed, sank back, and spoke slowly, "You mean when other men aren't trying to kill you?"

"Yes. Please leave out the killing."

Randolph chose his words carefully, but spoke the truth of his feelings, "You're by yourself. Totally, and in control of your own destiny, Elisa."

"I didn't ask that. I asked about God."

"You're closer to the ultimate reality."

"I don't understand."

"Of what you are, can be."

"You don't believe in God?"

"I can only believe in myself and my men. God has never stopped a machine-gun bullet."

"You're a cynic."

Randolph laughed. "My brother said the same thing yesterday."

She took his hand. "You should laugh more often, Major. Your smile is brilliant—warm. I'm happy the skies sent you."

"Sent me?"

"Yes." She brushed his cheek with her lips. It felt like cool satin against his flesh. "Come back tomorrow. I'll make you a dinner you won't forget."

She moved closer and he could feel her arm, her hip and

leg against him. Her eyes had not only caught his, they trapped him. Strangely, he felt nothing sensual or erotic in her closeness. But instead, there was a deep feeling of happiness—an ineffable joy a man might feel in finding a part of himself he had lost long ago. He felt young again but the feeling reversed and for the first time the gulf of years between them came home. "You need a young man. I have a niece and nephew older than you, Elisa."

The blue of the eyes was heightened by moisture and she stared at him with the naiveté and honesty of a child. "I need you, Major. Come back tomorrow, please." She grinned shyly, but held his eyes and wrapped her two tiny palms round his big hand. "I'll prepare you a feast fit for Olympus."

"I loved your summer wine. I'll return."

They drank and talked of the farm, animals, crops, the sky, and flying. The words flowed around Randolph like leaves stirred by a vagrant breeze, his mind, his whole consciousness captured by the strange girl so close beside him. Words were only a device to keep her at his side. The hours passed and finally he rose. "Got to leave—sorry," he said sincerely.

Her voice was heavy with disappointment, "So soon?" She came to her feet.

He pulled her close, brushed her cheek with his lips. He felt her tiny hands gripping his shoulders, her body against his. "Tomorrow," she whispered. "Promise?"

He wanted to kiss her, taste her lips, her mouth, hold her so tight she blended with him. For the first time in his life, he held himself back. Somehow, it would have been obscene. He said simply, "I promise."

They walked to the door hand in hand.

The next day, Randolph arrived in the middle of the afternoon, carrying a large bouquet of orchids his grounds man had grown in Fenwyck's hothouse. It was the best choice he could have made. She held them, caressed them, running a finger carefully over the delicate blooms as if she had to reassure herself they were real. She threw an arm around his neck and kissed his cheek, murmuring, "Thank you, Major. I've seen them at shows but never in my life have I ever had orchids of my very own."

He could only answer, "I knew you'd like them." He held her very close.

He almost groaned as she broke away and rushed to the kitchen. In a moment, she returned, carrying a vase filled with the gorgeous blooms. Chortling and laughing like a child on Christmas morning, she placed them on the table in front of the sofa. Suddenly she whirled, voice filled with anguish. "I'm sorry. I'm a terrible hostess. Would you like some wine?" She took both of his hands in hers.

He already felt heady just from her presence. "Not yet. Show me your place. Let's walk, Elisa."

"Of course."

She led him to the door and into the yard where the Jaguar was parked. Randolph felt a pang of discomfort. Suddenly the red machine did not belong here. She gestured at the animals and tiny outbuildings and spoke with pride, "I have a cow for milk, eggs from my chickens, and"—she pointed to her garden—"over there, potatoes, cucumbers, beets, carrots, leeks, onions." She gestured at a small glass-covered shelter. "And in there, I have some luck with tomatoes and lettuce."

Everything was as neat and spotless as her cottage. Not a weed grew in her garden. Randolph shook his head in disbelief. "You do all of this by yourself?"

She smiled proudly and nodded. He stared at her for a moment as the sun freed itself from a cloud and sent brilliant beams to bathe her. Moonlight was made for most women, the sun was created for Elisa. She wore it like a garment especially woven for her. Sunbeams played in her hair, turning it into a canopy of gold sparkling with gems. It painted her face with lustrous shades of ivory and falling snowflakes, and for the first time, he noticed tiny freckles like golden dots on her nose and cheeks. "You're beautiful," he said, holding her close. "So very beautiful." Sighing, she snuggled and held him.

Then, laughing, she broke away, took his hand, and led him down a path into the woods. She knew each plant, each bird, and described them as if talking of members of her family. She walked close to him, always touching; sometimes reaching for his hand, sometimes grasping his shoulder, his arm, or pressing a hip against him when the path narrowed. She was life itself, the warmth of her touch and the music of her laughter rejuvenated him and he was young again. Just walking beside her erased the wounds, the pain, the heartache of dead comrades, made him feel vital and strong.

They crossed the brook by removing their shoes and leaping precariously from stone to stone, giggling when they slipped and splashed water up to their knees. Finally across, wet and giddy with the magic of the moment, they pulled on their shoes and reentered the forest.

"This is the most beautiful place on earth," he said honestly.

She said nothing, but stopped him with a hand on his arm. Then she moved close and circled his neck with her arms. He ached for her with a deep yearning, wanting ache. Her mouth came to him eagerly and this time he could not deny himself.

Her lips were soft warm silk and she groaned as she clung to him. He kissed her nose, her cheeks, her forehead, her temple, her hair while her breath came hard and warm and she cried out with delight.

Suddenly her hands were on his chest and she pushed gently and reluctantly. "Dinner," she whispered. "I've prepared a feast for my major."

She led him back to the cottage.

They sat close together on the sofa, sipping their after-dinner wine. Despite the absence of meat, the meal had been superb. First came a salad of lettuce, tomatoes, celery, and beets followed by a thick bean soup flavored with thyme, garlic, and onions. The entree was a baked dish of potatoes, eggs, cheese, spinach, and leeks delicately flavored with herbs. A superb carrot cake topped with whipped cream was the surprise dessert.

"You're a magician," he said, drinking his wine and holding her hand.

She stared straight ahead and then surprised him with her question. "Why do you do it, Major?"

"What?"

She stabbed a finger upward. "What you do up there?"

"I'm not sure." He drank and then circled a finger around the room. "Maybe I do it so you can keep all this."

"And you can keep Fenwyck?" She stared at him and he felt as if he were being penetrated by blue light. "You defend the realm?" He averted his eyes. "That's not really true, is it?" she said.

"I'm not sure."

"You do it for the other men, don't you? Only for them. Your 'lads.' "

He stared at her, amazed at the perceptive mind that had hit squarely on a truth he had found hard to admit to himself. "I think you're right. That might be all of it—the lot. King and country, the empire, could be rot."

Her voice was suddenly deep, not coming from her throat but from her soul. "You can't be less of a man than they are or they less than you. So you kill and die and I will walk without you, drink my summer wine alone."

Wordlessly, he stared at her, unable to believe the depth of feeling in her voice, that she could truly love him so soon, with such force, such strength. The great blue eyes hardened like marble. Her words cut deep, "You came from the sky and the sky will claim you."

He felt helpless, could only say, "Don't say that."

"I'll lose you forever."

"You can't love me—you hardly know me and I am older . . ."

She interrupted him, "I've always loved you." She pulled

his head down and kissed him fiercely. He felt the urgency in her lips, held her close, and pressed her down into the sofa. She moaned and trembled like a leaf in a freshening wind. She kissed his cheeks, his eyes, ran the tip of her tongue over the small ridges at the corners of his eyes and mouth leaving warm trails of saliva. "My major—my major," she whispered. "Stay with me, hold me for the whole night—if that's all we can have."

He sat upright, turned away. "No, Elisa. I—I can't do that. I can't let that happen between us."

She kissed his neck and then turned his head by placing a palm on each cheek and found his lips. They held each other in a long embrace and he could feel her tiny hands pressing on his back, small hard breasts against his chest. He wanted her more than anything he had ever wanted in his life. He had found whores and easy women at the Imperial, the Palace, and a dozen other places. He had even picked them up off the streets in Piccadilly. It was sex on demand, no love required. Perhaps, a quid would be exchanged, but, usually, not even that. Just the demand, the relief, and the parting. "No. No, I can't stay."

She would not release him. "Nothing can happen between us that should not happen between us."

She stood, pulled him to his feet. Her kiss was hot now, and she molded her pliable body to his as if she had been made to fit him. He groaned, drank of the wet heat of her mouth, and ran his hands down her back, clutching. He felt resolve, control melting, replaced by a primal fire deep in his groin that spread quickly like flames through a vale of dry mat-grass.

She gasped through his kisses. "I want my arms around you for the whole night, feel the life within you and take it for myself."

Never in his entire life had he heard words like these. He managed, "It wouldn't be right."

"Nothing could ever be so right." She took his hand and led him to the curtained doorway.

* * *

When the Jaguar roared up to Fenwyck's great porch at midmorning, Randolph was still dazed by Elisa and the night they had spent together. He had never known anything like it. The guileless, innocent blue eyes had not misled him. Yet, there was no tension, no restraint, no self-consciousness. She came to him as naturally as a bee seeks honey in a fresh bloom, a brook finds its way to the sea. Together they disrobed and she displayed herself eagerly, pulling him onto the bed and guiding his hands over her when at first he still held back. When he did touch her, she stretched and twisted, making small sounds of delight deep in her throat. He stiffened when she traced a finger over the ugly layered scars that began below his chest and covered his leg. She kissed them, ran her tongue over them like the tip of a small warm brush. She told him she loved him and everything he was and he believed her. Finally, he lowered himself onto her and she twined herself around him like a vine around an elm.

Instead of the wild urgency he had found in his unions with other women, with Elisa it had been slow, stately, and deliberate. With his body deep in hers, mouth glued to hers, their breath became one, heartbeats pulsed together, and they even seemed to blend their blood, their thoughts. They were truly one as he had never known before, and he savored the moment, prolonged it. Then driven by a hunger as old as humanity, their movements hastened until she finally cried out incoherently, dug her fingers into his back, twisting and kissing him frantically. And then as the night wore on, and they found each other again and again, she cried out in passion and joy, "I love you! I love you!" And at those special moments, he heard himself use the same words.

But now, as he left the motor car and mounted the stairs, those words brought guilt. Did he mean them? Could he ever mean them? And he had used them again at the door when he left and she had held him and purred in his ear, "You're mine, now, Major. My love." And then she pulled back and held him with her eyes. "You'll return for more summer wine?"

"Nothing can keep me away," he had answered sincerely.

"Tomorrow and the day after and every day of your leave?"

"Yes. Tomorrow and every day of my leave." And when he left, it was like tearing himself away from part of his own body. Her last words were, "God go with you, my love."

He found Lloyd in the library. His brother was smoking and reading. The brigadier looked up as his brother sank into a chair. "Haven't seen much of you for a couple days, old boy. The farm girl?" He raised an eyebrow.

Randolph nodded. "Yes. Elisa Blue."

"You look a bit under it. A new toy?"

Randolph bolted erect. "Mind your tongue!"

"Easy, old man. Didn't mean to offend." Lloyd reached to a small table beside the desk and poured two stiff drinks of Haig and Haig. Randolph accepted his and sank back into the soft leather. "Got some encouraging news, Randolph." The flyer raised an eyebrow. "Top secret and all that rot, but we'll get more new tanks—Matildas and the American 'Honey.' "

"The Honey is a light tank. What about the Grants and Shermans?"

"Not until next year. But our artillery is being beefed up—more twenty-five-pounders, seventeen-pounders, and the new six-pounder antitank gun. It'll gut the Panzer Three. There'll be a major buildup and the Western Desert Force no longer exists, now it's the Eighth Army." He punched the desk. "In a few months we'll take the offensive, punch Rommel with an iron fist he won't forget." The voice was jubilant.

"You're sure?"

"Got it from Winnie himself."

Randolph raised his glass, "To Winston Churchill, the best PM the realm has ever known."

"Hear! Hear!" The brothers drank.

Lloyd eyed his brother with a sly smile. "Got some other news for you, brother." He took a drink. "A RAF mission is to be sent to the States—look over some new aircraft. The PM told me he personally submitted your name to the Ministry to head it."

Stunned, Randolph felt a hot spring uncoil deep in his guts. "It's that blasted Dowding," Randolph snarled. "They all think I'm 'round the bend."

Lloyd shook his head. "No, brother. You just happen to be the best qualified pilot in the RAF."

"And the oldest," Randolph said bitterly.

Lloyd lit a Lucky Strike and exhaled a cloud of smoke. "You'll still keep Number Fifty-four squadron. You'll be temporarily detached."

"Who'll command it?"

Lloyd pulled on his cigarette. "I don't know."

Randolph emptied his glass. Lloyd recharged it. "A lot of my lads could die without me," the pilot said.

Lloyd nodded knowingly. "I command, too, brother. I know how you feel."

The conversation was cut short as a breathless Bernice hurried into the room. "It's happened! It's happened!" she shouted excitedly. The men stared curiously. "It's just come over the wireless."

The brothers looked at each other. "What came over the wireless, love?" Lloyd asked.

"Germany has attacked Russia. Millions of German troops are pouring into Russia." She poured herself a glass of Bordeaux and found a chair.

"Well bugger all. They really did it," Lloyd said to himself. "Stalin started this bloody war and now that swine is being led to the slaughter. Poetic justice."

"The 'paper hanger' made a mistake," Randolph said, forgetting his anger.

Lloyd shook his head. "They'll strike for Kiev, Leningrad, and Moscow—probably with three separate army groups. That's the German way. Take them in a month or two and

Russia will be finished and Hitler will have his lebensraum (living space), oil, and the greatest wheat-growing region on earth. He'll be stronger than ever.''

Randolph raised a hand to indicate disagreement. "Napoleon took Moscow and you know what happened to him.'' He drank and then spoke thoughtfully, "Geography and weather will do in the Jerries. Mark me.''

Lloyd shook his head. "Poppycock. By the time winter arrives it'll all be over, brother.''

"We'll see.''

"Quite. We'll see.''

V

THE two weeks following the invasion—Operation Barbarossa to the Germans—the news from Europe was shocking and the repercussions struck the shores of every nation on earth like waves driven by a hurricane. The Germans destroyed whole Russian armies, taking hundreds of thousands of prisoners. Within a week, the Russian air force—the largest in the world—ceased to exist. German panzers took Lwow, Brest-Litovsk, and Minsk, the capital of Byelorussia over two hundred miles deep in Russia only six days after the invasion. Pogroms were rumored in Latvia and Lithuania and it was said thousands of Jews were being rounded up and sent to camps. Finnish, Rumanian, Hungarian, and Italian forces joined in on the attack on the staggering Russian giant. The advance was so fast, the punishment so cataclysmic, it looked like nothing could stop the juggernaut.

Churchill reacted quickly, declaring, "Any man or State

who fights against Naziism will have our aid. Any man or State who marches with Hitler is our foe." Immediately, a British mission under Sir Stafford Cripps was dispatched to Moscow to discuss military and economic aid.

President Roosevelt threw his support to the Russians, too. In order to keep Russian ports open for arms shipments, Roosevelt exempted Russia from the neutrality statute. He sent his personal aide, Harry Hopkins, to Russia to confer with Stalin and promised to aid the Soviet Union, releasing all Russian credits in the United States. U.S. Marines occupied Iceland, Trinidad, and British Guiana to relieve British troops who were recalled to England. The State Department explained the occupations: "To prevent the occupation by Germany of strategic outposts in the Atlantic to be used as air or naval bases for eventual attack against the Western Hemisphere."

In the last week of his leave, Rodney Higgins was stunned by the events just as all other Americans. Each morning at breakfast he scanned the *Times* and found nothing but reports of more German victories and Russian disasters. Usually, he saw his mother, grandmother, and aunt at the breakfast table. Nathan had not been seen for over two weeks and Marsha had returned twice since moving into a dormitory at Columbia. Rodney had managed to avoid her on both occasions. On this Monday morning Rodney faced his aunt across the table while Travers and Nicole served them. Brenda had not yet finished dressing and Ellen was taking her breakfast in her room—a practice that was becoming more and more frequent.

"More bad news from Russia," Betty said, gesturing at the headlines.

"Depends upon your viewpoint," Rodney offered.

"What do you mean?"

Rodney sipped his coffee and thought with chagrin of his aunt's mind that seemed so feeble when compared to his mother's. How could two sisters be so unalike? He managed a smile and concealed his impatience, "If you're an America Firster or a member of the German-American Bund you're celebrating."

"You mean Fritz Kuhn and the rest of those vermin?" she said with rare insight.

"There are thousands of them, Auntie, and they're Americans. They have a constitutional right to their podium—their voice."

Betty looked up from her poached eggs. "I'll bet Nathan and his friends are upset."

"Upset?" Rodney laughed, almost choking on his cereal. "They're hung in black crepe. The Communist Party has reversed itself one hundred eighty degrees. Now Lodge, Borah, Nye, Wheeler, Lindbergh, and Randolph Hearst are the villains. Roosevelt, Hopkins, Cordell Hull, Frank Knox, Henry Morganthau, and Henry Stimson are their heroes. Roosevelt can't do enough. They're screaming for intervention."

"It was such a surprise."

Rodney paused while Nicole refilled his cup. She had returned to her habit of leaning just a trifle too close to him, sometimes even brushing his back with a large pointed breast. The contact stirred a mixture of emotion, not all unpleasant. "Not really, Aunt Betty. Hitler set it all down years ago." Betty raised an eyebrow. Travers and Nicole paused and stared at the young lieutenant. "He said it all in his book, *Mein Kampf*, which means 'My Struggle.' It was required reading at the Academy."

"If I may say so, sir," Travers said in a rare moment of articulation, "*Mein Kampf* is the bible of the Nazi Party, required reading in German schools."

Rodney smiled at the butler. "Right." He returned to his aunt, "In it he told of his plans to invade Russia to get the living space—lebensraum, he called it—that Germany needs."

"Just like that. Take it by force."

"Why of course, Aunt Betty. And don't forget, to the

Nazis, the Russians are of an inferior race, Slavs degenerated by centuries of mixing with Mongoloid stock. Why Hitler's even referred to Russians as men with Slav-Tartar bodies set with Jewish heads. In *Mein Kampf* Hitler describes them as a mass of born slaves.''

"Slaves for the Third Reich, Rodney?"

"Why, of course."

All heads turned as Brenda entered, dressed in a perfectly tailored green business suit. Her blue eyes were rimmed with red and it appeared as if she had not slept. Before she reached her chair, Travers had filled her cup and Nicole had exited to the kitchen to fetch her grapefruit and single soft-boiled egg already prepared by Antoine. Sensing her grim mood, everyone remained silent while Brenda sipped her coffee. Brenda spoke to her cup, "Nothing can stop that madman." She sipped her coffee. "Not a word from Regina—not a word." Nicole placed a sliced grapefruit before her. Brenda ignored it.

Rodney stared at his mother. "Rumors, Mother. And how in the world could a letter get through from Warsaw now? Communications are cut off. Even radio transmissions are being jammed. We'll hear from her soon—when things return to normal."

"Normal! Normal!" Brenda cried. "What's that? The lunatics have taken over the asylum! War! War! My life's been cursed with it."

Silence dropped on the room like a heavy wet blanket. There was only the clatter of bone china as coffee was drunk. Brenda turned to Rodney and placed a soft hand on his. "I'm sorry, son," she said contritely. "Got up on the wrong side of the bed."

The lieutenant stared into his mother's eyes, "It's all right, Mother. We're all worried." A tiny smile turned up the corners of his lips, "Truly, these are the times that try men's souls."

She returned his smile with a sad little turn of her lips. "Thomas Paine knew what he was talking about, Rodney."

Betty looked at Nicole who returned a blank stare. Travers smiled.

Brenda brightened with a new thought, "Have you heard from Kay Stockard?"

Rodney felt his cheeks warm. "I got a letter yesterday. She's staying in Hollywood for at least another month. In fact, she's been offered a position at Paramount in their design department."

"Kay's a clever girl," Brenda said. "Very talented."

"Yes, Mother. She's very talented."

"Do you think she'll take the new position, Rodney?"

"There's a good chance. She was offered the position by the woman who heads the department, Gertrude Foot. And you know her family is from Pasadena and it's only a few miles from Hollywood."

"Too bad. I'll miss her."

"Not as much as I," Rodney said before considering the impact of the words.

His mother busied herself with her grapefruit and Nicole turned her back and hurried into the kitchen with a tray filled with dirty cups.

Nathan returned that afternoon. Rodney was in the library reading when he heard loud, boisterous voices in the kitchen. Disturbed by the noise, the lieutenant lay aside the paper—he had been reading two of his favorite correspondents, Dorothy Thompson and H. V. Kaltenborn—and pushed his way through the swinging doors. The kitchen was a large room with a six-burner, hooded range at one end and two ovens stacked one on top of the other next to the range. A long salad table was placed in the middle of the room, laden with chopped lettuce, tomatoes, celery, herbs, bowls of half-prepared potato and macaroni salads, and jars of Antoine's own special dressings. Two refrigerators were pushed against a far wall. Tabletops, counters, appliances, and hood all gleamed of stainless steel.

Immediately Rodney saw Nathan and Margaret Hollister

seated at a small table in the corner with chicken breasts and drumsticks in their hands, bowls of potato salad, macaroni salad, and a half-empty bottle of Haig and Haig Pinch in front of them. Nicole was busy at a small counter, polishing silver. Antoine pushed a huge ham roast into the top oven and then leaned over the stove top seasoning a large pan of onion soup. Travers sat in front of the call board, smoking and reading *The New York Times*. For a moment no one noticed Rodney. Nathan looked up.

"Hi, loving brother," Nathan sneered, waving a drumstick. Obviously feeling his liquor, he slurred the words. Margaret snickered and dug her teeth into the meat. The servants glanced at the newcomer.

Rodney felt a familiar heat uncoil in his guts like a hot spring. "Well, well," he said evenly. "The champion of the proletariat is back—back with his appetite and thirst. I thought you provided for yourself?"

"Aw, shit, man. You motherfuckers were going to throw this shit into the garbage, anyway. We just intercepted it." Margaret laughed raucously, spraying bits of partially chewed white meat. The servants stared at Nathan in disgust.

Rodney walked across the room and stopped close to his brother. An atavistic rage crept over him and he felt control slipping. At that moment he hated his brother. He lashed out, "I hear Hitler's a son of a bitch—has been for a whole two weeks. No hero anymore. No trouble with that, brother?"

Nathan dropped his drumstick and gulped down a huge swallow of scotch. "That Fascist pig and his lackeys must be stamped out or the whole world will be enslaved."

"You're humming a new tune, Nathan."

"The world changes, brother. Keep up with the times instead of marching to that reactionary drum of yours."

Rodney boiled over. "You loved Borah, Wheeler, Lindbergh, and the rest of those isolationists until June twenty-second. Then, suddenly, they were traitors and Roosevelt and Churchill were your heroes. That stinkin' rag the *Daily Worker* reversed itself in twenty-four hours." He leaned for-

ward, fists balled. "The whole Communist Party is schizo-
phrenic and you, personally, are a contemptible hypocrite."

Slowly Nathan came to his feet, eyes flashing a warning.
"Watch that big mouth, brother," he warned. The servants,
Margaret, all stared wide-eyed. An oppressive silence gripped
everyone.

Feeling anger possess him like a rapacious beast that had
lain in ambush all these years, Rodney challenged, "Do you
think you can close it, brother?"

"You're chicken shit, Rodney," Margaret said. She hurled
a drumstick that bounced off his tan shirt, leaving a greasy
smear. Rodney shifted his eyes to the girl. It was a mistake.
He never saw the fist. For a moment he thought someone had
clubbed him from behind. His head snapped backward and
he reeled as a big bony fist caught him on the side of the
head. Gongs rang in his ears and lights like comets flashed
across his retinas. His cheek felt numb and at the same time
there was a coppery salt taste in his mouth.

He had been in many fights in his youth. In fact, he had
even been thrown out of two football games when he knocked
down linemen who punched and gouged at his eyes in pileups.
He leapt back and avoided the second punch of the combination. The sneak punch had been cowardly and rage came
on him with startling ferocity as if a ravening beast had
jumped on his back and dug into him with claws and fangs.
He heard the beast growl in his ears, it was his own voice.
His veins were charged and his senses had not been so alert
since *Bismarck*. He crouched, weaved with his massive fists
raised, and shook his head clear. Nathan stepped toward him.

Nathan was flabby and out of shape but still dangerous.
Rodney stared at his brother's face; it was impassive and cold
like an executioner. There was no boxing. The space was too
confining and both fighters were so intent on destroying his
enemy, there were no calculated moves, no thinking—just
actions and reactions.

"No! No! *Gentilhommes!*" Nicole cried while Antoine
stared silently, soup spoon in hand.

"Gentlemen, please," Travers pleaded. The pleas were ignored. Travers reached for the phone.

The punch came from the level of Nathan's knees. This time Rodney was ready, ducking and riding away from it. The huge fist as big as the ham roast in the oven whistled past his temple, scraping the flesh away from the outside corner of his eye and brushing his hair straight up. The counterpunch was instinctive. Exploding from his crouch like a loaded spring and with all of his 190 pounds behind it, Rodney's fist slammed into his brother's armpit. He was sure he felt ribs crack. The impact was so hard, he felt his own teeth jar in his head and a sharp pain shot up his forearm.

Nathan stopped in midstride, grunted, spittle flying, and his breath hissed like an open pressure valve on a steam boiler, but he swung a right hand that caught Rodney on the cheek. The impact twisted Rodney's head, hair lifted from his scalp and for an instant stood erect like clipped wheat. Saliva and blood flew from the corner of his mouth. Both men jumped back. Margaret laughed with glee and took a huge bite of chicken breast.

Thinking his brother was badly injured, Nathan charged like a corrida bull, swinging short arcing punches. He had misread his brother. Lefts and rights rained on Rodney's arms and shoulders as he retreated. He ducked, weaved, then stepped inside the attack, bringing a fist up hard into Nathan's soft midriff. His brother doubled forward, bearded chin crashing down on Rodney's shoulder. Nathan grabbed him in a bear hug. Clinching, punching, screaming into each other's faces, the brothers staggered against the long salad table, upsetting it and sending it crashing to the floor with bowls of lettuce, celery, tomatoes, potato and macaroni salads, long-handled spoons and forks and a half-dozen jars of dressing that broke and spilled their oily contents onto the linoleum. Losing their footing and spinning like a pair of drunken dancers, they bounced against a wall with such force two pans fell from their hooks. They broke apart, stunned.

Nicole screamed, Travers shouted into the phone, and Antoine ran from the room, carrying the huge pot of boiling soup.

Numbly, the two combatants stared at each other. "Had enough, brother?" Rodney said.

The answer was a guttural shout like an enraged bull and a wild charge. Counterpunching, Rodney gave ground. Blows rained off his shoulders, arms, glanced off the side of his head punishingly. He slipped in some oily salad dressing and balanced precariously on one foot. Yelling with triumph, Nathan brought a fist up that caught Rodney on the side of the head. His head jerked to the side, teeth clashing together and lacerating his tongue. Droplets of sweat flew from his hair and scalp like a halo. The gongs rang again and a door slammed in his head, vision starring, penetrated by small winking lights. His knees bent like reeds in a heavy rain. Desperately, he swung, felt his fist impact his brother's nose. There was a crunch like teeth biting into a crisp apple as flesh flattened, gristle broke, blood and mucus flew. Rodney felt a fierce joy surge.

Now both brothers were treading salad dressing like first-time ice skaters on a frozen pond, slipping, sliding, clutching each other, crashing into the cutting block, and tumbling to the floor with it and a dozen knives and cleavers. They rolled across the floor, shrieking into each other's faces, punching, coating themselves with salad dressing, potato salad, macaroni, lettuce, and squashed tomatoes. Rodney swung again and again, some blows dying in the air, others skinning his knuckles on the linoleum, and yet others cracking against bone and muscles. His brother began to weaken.

Desperately, Nathan grabbed a cleaver. Nicole screamed. Travers shouted a warning. Antoine reentered the room and tried to grab Nathan's arm but was knocked down when the brothers rolled into him. Margaret bellowed, "Slice him into hamburger, baby!" and then laughed with glee.

Grabbing Nathan's wrist, Rodney forced the hand and the murderous blade straight up. Then he elbowed his brother's body away slightly and brought a knee up hard into Nathan's crotch. He felt his brother's genitals flatten from the blow and the strength went out of Nathan like air out of a punctured balloon. The cleaver clattered to the floor.

Margaret screamed, "You fight dirty, you son of a bitch!"

With a shout of triumph, Rodney rolled on top of his brother and straddled him, knees pinning Nathan's arms to the floor. Looking down into the battered face, he saw one eye purple and closed, lips swollen and bleeding, nose twisted with blood, and mucus streaming from both nostrils. He hated his brother for his hypocrisy, his treachery, the humiliations and frustrations of a lifetime.

But most of all, he hated him for mocking every value Rodney held dear, deriding the very things that gave his life meaning. He was not satisfied. At that moment, he wanted to kill him. He raised his fist.

Then the whirlwind struck him. It was Margaret Hollister, crashing into him from behind with all of her 160 pounds. The impact was like a battering ram and the black curtains dropped again. The force of the charge knocked him flat on his face and he skidded face first into a heap of potato salad and a broken jar of mayonnaise. The girl was on his back, clawing, cursing, howling like a banshee. Then Nathan was on his feet, staggering and then falling on top of the combatants. Rodney felt the breath crushed out of him and he was convinced he would strangle on the salad and mayonnaise. Mercilessly, Margaret's blows rained on the back of his head, ears, and neck while she shouted "Motherfuckin' pig!" over and over. There was a high-pitched scream like steam from a kettle and Nicole leapt onto the pile. Her weight toppled the mass of bodies. Clawing, screaming, flailing, the four rolled in a single contorting mass across the floor.

The sound of the one voice in the world that could stop them crashed through the room. "Rodney! Nathan!" their mother screamed. But the brothers were deaf. The punching, cursing continued. Then strong hands gripped and pulled. Travers, Antoine, the groundsman, Crag Watson, and two policemen pulled the combatants apart and held them. Nicole, sobbing out of control, staggered out of the room, brushing salad from her black taffeta. Cursing, Margaret returned to her chair. She downed a full glass of Scotch. The two brothers, held by the five men, were pinned against the wall.

Following the rule of bloody, vicious fights, the combatants were "fought out," not only drained of energy, but of emotion. They were both pliable as rubber and almost docile as they were held against the wall. But hatred still burned deep in Nathan's eyes.

"Would you like them booked?" one of the officers asked.

Brenda looked at the officer sadly, "I am embarrassed to admit it, but they are my sons."

"Both of them?" the officer asked incredulously, obviously concluding Nathan and Margaret were intruders, or, at worst, thieves.

"Yes, both of them." Brenda turned to the boys. "My sons. My God," she said, voice heavy with heartbreak. She stepped close and the brothers stared at their mother. "What have I done that was so terribly wrong?" she said. "Where did I fail?" She seemed to be speaking to herself. "Both from my womb, same father, same blood. How can this happen? Caine and Abel over again?"

The boys remained mute.

Brenda shook her head. Her voice returned, octaves lower, "It's kill, kill, kill. The whole world's insane and the insanity infects my family, is in my sons."

Nathan looked at Margaret and signaled her with a toss of his head. "We'll leave," he said softly. Brenda nodded and he was released. He and Margaret left hand in hand while the officers watched them warily.

Only after the door closed behind Nathan was Rodney released. "I'll leave, too, Mother."

She looked deep in his eyes with a sadness that tore at his soul. "Stay, Rodney—stay until your leave is up. Four more days. I asked you before and I still want you here with me."

"Yes, Mother."

"Nathan will be gone soon, too."

"What do you mean, Mother?"
"He joined the Marine Corps yesterday."

That evening Rodney was unable to eat the roast ham because of his sore jaw and tongue. Salad had no appeal— the taste of potato salad and salad dressing was still in his nose—and he confined himself to onion soup loaded with croutons and cheese. A Jell-O dessert went down easily. After dinner, he, Brenda, Ellen, and Aunt Betty moved to the sitting room where his mother's pride, a huge Majestic Superheterodyne radio, squatted gaudily in a corner. With a large four-foot mahogany cabinet festooned with strips of gleaming chrome, it had a huge cyclopean dial near the top. Its controls resembled the diving station of a submarine and it flashed with more lights than the Marquee on the Radio City Music Hall.

Rodney was glad it was Monday evening. This was the night for the Lux Radio Theater and Brenda never missed a single production. In fact, she was addicted to the radio, listening religiously to "Fibber McGee and Molly," "Myrt and Marge," "The Incomparable Hildegarde," "The March of Time," "Burns and Allen," Fred Allen's "Town Hall Tonight," "The Jack Benny Show," and many more. When the war broke out in 1939, she began searching the dial for correspondents. The voices of William L. Shirer, Edward R. Murrow, Dorothy Thompson, Winston Burdett, and Howard K. Smith began to boom through the big speaker each afternoon and evening. Rodney was hoping the radio, anything, would take her mind from the terrible scene in the kitchen. Sullen and depressed, she had not spoken a dozen words to anyone for the entire evening. He was glad when Hamilton Babcock entered and sat next to Brenda on a long sofa in front of the radio. Hamilton always listened to the program with Brenda. Brenda switched on the radio and Rodney sank back in his chair.

Cecil B. DeMille's limpid, dulcet voice filled the room like cold oil, speaking in awed tones of this evening's gripping dramatization of "Dark Victory," starring Clark Gable and Josephine Hutchinson.

Just as the orchestra was reaching for the thundering crescendo that would introduce the first act, the knock came and Travers entered the room. He coughed. Brenda turned off the radio with a quick, irritated twist of a knob in the corner of the giant eye. Travers's voice was apologetic, "Sorry to interrupt, madam. There's a gentleman to see you."

"Who is it?"

"He didn't say, madam."

Sighing, Brenda stood. "Show him in."

"He is already in, madam."

Rodney and Hamilton came to their feet and faced the door with Brenda.

RAF Major Randolph Higgins entered the room. In his serge woolen, blue-gray, perfectly tailored uniform, he looked taller and broader than ever. His thick brown hair was highlighted with silver-gray strands and lines clearly slashed downward from the corners of his eyes and mouth showing the years of strain and the toll of time. But in a way, his growing maturity, erect, assured bearing, broad shoulders, and trim waist made him appear more attractive than ever. His face was still very handsome with a straight aristocratic nose, square jaw, and fine unwrinkled skin. His brown eyes were flashing as if backlighted and held only Brenda in their gaze. He raised his arms.

Brenda choked, covered her mouth with a closed fist, and then made strange squeaking sounds deep in her throat as if she were incapable of forming words. She rushed into his arms and for the first time in his life, Rodney saw his mother and Uncle Randolph touch each other. It was far more than a touch. They held each other tightly while Brenda kissed his cheeks, his neck, and finally his mouth. Hamilton came erect in a rigid stance and his lips slashed back from his teeth in an inverted crescent. Finally, Randolph pulled back slightly and Brenda found words, "Oh, God, you're alive. You're alive," she sobbed. "My dear, dear Randolph. I've been so worried."

Ellen and Betty crowded around, prying their way in to kiss and hold the pilot for a few moments. Nicole entered and walked up to Randolph timidly. She was crying and tears streamed down her cheeks. It was a bold move for a maid, but the Frenchwoman seemed not to care—and neither did Randolph. He held her very close and she whispered in French in his ear and then kissed his cheek. He smiled and whispered something back in French. Then she curtsied and left. Instantly Rodney sensed an intimacy—a feeling that something deeply personal had happened between the pair long ago.

Finally, Rodney made his way through the crowding women and grasped his uncle's hand. "I say, you look well, nephew," Randolph said, smiling broadly. The women fell silent. "And it was marvelous having you at Fenwyck for a weekend."

"It was great being there and you, too, look fit, Uncle."

"Sinking the *Bismarck* did wonders for you."

"A tonic, sir. Like to do it again." Everyone except Brenda laughed.

After a quick introduction to Hamilton, Randolph sat between Brenda and the businessman. Brenda held onto Randolph's hand possessively. Hamilton's eyes were as cold and hard as highly polished marble.

Travers entered and at a signal from Brenda moved to a corner bar where he poured bourbon for Hamilton, scotch for Randolph and Rodney, and wine for the women. Brenda raised her glass, "To Randolph Higgins, the mysterious major who can materialize anywhere, anyplace, anytime."

Everyone laughed and drank. Randolph asked about Nathan. Brenda, showing astonishing aplomb, explained that he no longer lived at home and that he had joined the Marines and was waiting to be called. Randolph nodded approvingly and sipped his scotch. "And what do you hear from Regina?" he asked cautiously.

Brenda bit her lip. "Nothing. It's been months."

"Daresay, deucedly mucked situation there," Randolph said. He explained how Lloyd was home for a short leave and assured everyone the family was well. He did not mention Bonnie's fiancé, Blake Boggs.

"Will Lloyd be home long?" Betty asked.

"Betty, that could be a secret," Brenda cautioned.

Randolph smiled enigmatically. "Not really. He's been in North Africa for almost two years and is home on a short leave. Since both 'Lord Haw Haw' and 'Axis Sally' not only named his brigade in broadcasts that covered half the world, but, also, Axis Sally actually named Lloyd, personally, as the commanding officer, I can't see any harm in telling you."

"He'll return to North Africa?"

"Probably. He's got to settle some logistical problems first—those *are* secret."

"And you? Why are you here? How long will you stay? Can you stay with us?" Brenda asked.

Randolph threw up his hands defensively. "I've got to catch a train at oh-two-hundred." There was a groan.

"Can you tell us your mission?"

Randolph sipped his drink. "Some of it." He ran his eyes over the room. "You know I'm a fighter pilot." He looked at Brenda. "And, Brenda, you know in the early days I designed aircraft with Tommy Sopwith and the lot." Brenda nodded, never taking her eyes from Randolph as if she were not yet convinced he was sitting next to her. "Everyone knows we—the RAF, Coastal Command, the Royal Navy— have been shopping for aircraft here, in the States, since 'thirty-nine."

"You're here to buy aircraft?" Ellen said quickly.

"In a way. You see, there's a new fighter being built on the West Coast by the North American Company called the P-Fifty-one, Mustang Mark One. It's powered with an Allison engine. I test-flew one in England."

"Isn't this secret?" Betty asked.

Randolph laughed. "You can buy any one of a half-dozen aircraft magazines on any news kiosk in the United States for a dime and find schematics of not only the P-Fifty-one, but also your Lockheed P-Thirty-eight Lightning, the Curtis P-Forty, the Bell . . ." He slapped his forehead. "The German and Japanese general staffs subscribe to all of them. Your magazines provide them with some of their best intelligence."

"I can't believe that," Ellen said.

The pilot shrugged. "It's true. Buy one."

Rodney said to Randolph, "How does the P-Fifty-one compare to your Spitfire?"

Randolph shook his head. "Not too well. However, I had the lads put a new Rolls Royce Merlin Forty-five engine in one and that made a fighter of it. With the Rolls, it could be the best fighter in the world."

"So you're going out to California to persuade?" Brenda said.

Randolph smiled. "The engines are already there. I'm to advise and perhaps test-fly."

"Then you'll leave here in a few hours and we won't see you again?" Brenda said thickly, eyes moist. She took his hand in both of hers.

The Englishman smiled down at Brenda, "I'll be back, sister-in-law. There's a new fighter in development here on the East Coast called the Republic XP-Forty-seven."

"Why the Republic plant is on Long Island," Brenda said. "At Farmingdale." And then joyously, "You'll be nearby."

"Quite right. And I'm to test-fly a prototype at Mitchell Field that is very close to the plant. The XP-Forty-seven is a big, rugged machine with a huge Pratt and Whitney engine. I hear it's very much like the new, powerful German fighter called the Focke-Wulf One-ninety. If you wish to learn more of the project, just drop by the nearest news kiosk and pick up a magazine."

"Then we'll see you again?" Brenda said.

"Perhaps in only a fortnight or so—if you're unlucky."
Everyone chuckled except Hamilton.

Rodney nodded to a row of ribbons Randolph was wearing
on his tunic just below his white-drab silk wings. "You've
added a DFM to your DSO."

Before Randolph could answer, Betty asked in confusion,
"What? I don't understand."

Rodney nodded at the ribbons that were centered directly
under the RAF monogram and silk crown of the wings. "The
Distinguished Flying Medal and the Distinguished Service
Order."

Awed, Betty eyed the decorations. She blurted, "How
many Germans have you killed?"

"Betty!" Brenda said reproachfully.

Silence crept through the room and Rodney's aunt flushed.
"Sorry," she said humbly.

"Nonsense," Randolph said, smiling broadly at the embarrassed little woman and saving the situation gracefully.
"I had thirty-six confirmed in the first one and fourteen in
this war."

"Fifty kills," Hamilton Babcock said with disbelief.
"You've probably killed a hundred men?"

A silence as cold as an Arctic gale chilled everyone. There
was a long silence.

Randolph broke the silence. "I've spent more time in this
business than any other man on earth. I have a fine
squadron—fly with the finest lads in the world. We fly machines and destroy machines." He stared hard at Hamilton
who stared back. "The Crown pays me for my work and I
do it. I don't collect scalps."

"See here," Hamilton said, eyes wide, face flushed. "That
wasn't necessary."

Everyone stared at the two men who glared at each other.
Rodney sensed the argument was not over flying at all, but
over Brenda.

Randolph continued, "It was necessary. When the Jerries

try to destroy your country, you do your bit to stop them.'' The timbre of his voice became sarcastic, ''This is not a cricket match. Sometimes, people are injured, even killed.''

Brenda raced in to salvage the situation, ''Of course we understand.'' She glared at Hamilton. He turned away sullenly and then stood.

''Got to be going,'' he said, moving toward the door.

''So early?'' Brenda said.

''Yes. I start inventory tomorrow.'' Randolph did not stand and no handshakes were exchanged. Hamilton left.

With Hamilton gone, a relaxed ambiance settled on the room. Brenda moved her eyes back to Randolph and narrowed her lids as she stared at the faint red line tracing down from his temple to his cheek. She ran a finger over it. ''You've been wounded?'' She let her finger linger on his cheek and moved closer.

''Just a scratch. Got into a devilishly awkward situation when my Spit shed a wing and most of its tail. Can't fly half an aircraft, you know. Almost bought the farm. Made a clumsy botch of it when I bailed out of the old bird and tore up some poor girl's potato patch when I landed.'' The smile vanished and a strange, distant look crossed his face fleetingly and he stared over everyone at the far wall. The smile returned just as suddenly. He looked at Brenda. ''Nicked my face on the way out. Nothing at all, Brenda.''

Brenda shuddered. Rodney felt a sudden chill. Despite the laughs, the boisterous company, the spirit of love and family, death was in the room, permeating everyone and everything. He took a big gulp of Scotch.

They talked for hours of family, the war, the future, hopes and ambitions. Rodney told Randolph of his hopes to get battleship duty. ''And your second choice?'' the pilot asked.

''Submarines. I did six months on an old S-boat when I was first commissioned. Only got out of Long Island Sound twice, but I enjoyed the duty. It's a different world.''

''Quite so. The Germans have been teaching us,'' Randolph said bitterly. He glanced at his watch. ''Got to get on my horse. Sorry and all that. Two of my lads are waiting for me at Grand Central. At least, I hope they are. They've spent the last few hours in a nearby pub.'' He turned to Brenda. ''Please have the butler call a cab, sister-in-law.''

''Nonsense,'' Rodney said, rising. ''I'll take you.''

''No need, old chap.''

''Of course we'll take you. And I'll go, too,'' Brenda said, coming to her feet.

''We'll all go,'' Ellen said as she and Betty rose.

Nicole followed the laughing, talking group to the door. She stood behind some heavy drapes when the group exited. Randolph never saw her.

The next morning at breakfast, Rodney got the phone call. Travers answered the ring and casually announced, ''The President would like to speak with you, Mr. Higgins.''

Rodney looked up from his coffee. Betty, Ellen, and Brenda exchanged a confused look. Rodney asked, ''The president of what?''

''The President of the United States, sir,'' Travers insisted.

Rodney laughed, convinced some of his old friends had learned he was in town and were pulling a prank. He looked at his mother and aunt and pronounced gravely, ''Must have some staggering international problems he can't solve. Just take a few seconds and I'll set the world right.'' He rose and walked to the phone. Taking the instrument and covering the mouthpiece, he asked the butler, ''You said he claimed he was the president?''

''Yes, sir.''

''And it wasn't his secretary?''

''No, sir. The gentleman announced himself as President Roosevelt.''

Rodney wondered how the butler could keep such a straight face when the call was such an obvious farce. Smiling, he brought the phone to his lips and spoke with mock reverence, ''Lieutenant Rodney Higgins here, Mr. President. I'm ready to solve any and all international problems too difficult for you and your staff.'' The women laughed gleefully.

The familiar, cultured voice that filled Rodney's ear was a marvelous imitation of the voice he had heard on the radio numerous times during the famous fireside chats. ''Is your Grandmother Ellen Ashcroft there?''

''Why, yes?''

''Ask her if she can remember the summer of 'twenty-eight when Eleanor and I met her and your Grandfather John Ashcroft at Martha's Vineyard.''

Smiling, Rodney asked Ellen the question and his grandmother nodded her remembrance. ''She says 'yes,' '' Rodney said into the mouthpiece. The women all hunched forward. There was no more laughter.

''We had dinner at the Bayside Inn. Joe and Rose Kennedy were there and so was Al Smith. Your grandparents were the only Republicans in the bunch.'' He chuckled.

With new seriousness, Rodney relayed the information. Ellen nodded and came to her feet. ''I remember—I remember quite clearly. The Kennedys, Al Smith. He was in his wheelchair and Eleanor . . .''

The voice continued, ''Now do you believe me?''

Still not completely convinced, Rodney asked, ''Why do you call me personally? Why not a secretary? Why the president?''

''Because I'm here in my office, unable to move from my chair, and the phones are at my right hand. Why not?''

Rodney sighed and looked at the women who stared back in amazement. Somehow, he believed the voice. ''What can I do for you, Mr. President?''

''I want to see you tomorrow afternoon at sixteen hundred hours in the Oval Office. Can you make it? I can send a car from the Brooklyn Navy Yard and have you driven.''

''I'm awaiting my orders.''

''I'll send to the Navy Department and Knox will have them on my desk when you arrive. Will you need the car?''

"I'll take the express this morning, if that's all right with you." *Knox*. *Frank Knox*, ran through Rodney's mind. The secretary of the navy personally delivering his orders to the President of the United States? Ludicrous! Unbelievable, but apparently true.

"Fine."

"May I ask what this is all about?"

"You were present at the sinking of the *Bismarck*."

"Yes, sir. I submitted a written report."

"I know. It's on my desk. I want to discuss it with you face-to-face—much more can be learned that way. I'll have time tomorrow afternoon after a meeting with my cabinet. I'd appreciate it if you'd come." And then cautiously, "Another American had an experience similar to yours. I want you to meet him."

"I'll be there, sir, at sixteen hundred hours."

He hung up and faced the women. They stared back silently. "It was no prank," he said and walked to his room.

Lieutenant Rodney Higgins, splendid in his dress blues, was led to the second floor of the White House by a marine guard. Sucking in his stomach and holding his breath, Rodney was ushered into the Oval Office. The president was seated behind a ponderous, handsomely carved desk.

Even seated, Franklin Delano Roosevelt appeared to be a big man. Just as his pictures had shown over the years, he was extremely handsome. His hair was sandy with gray and white strands shining in the overhead light, his forehead broad and deep and showing permanent lines of worry. Framed by his pince-nez, the eyes were large, intelligent, and seemed to measure Rodney the moment he entered the room. The long, straight nose complemented the strength and determination of a chin and jaw that were square-cut and obstinate. Rodney imagined the face when young had probably appeared chopped from oak by an artisan using a hatchet. But now, fifty-nine years and strain had softened the lines and newly formed sags and wrinkles were beginning to erode the near-classic features. It seemed incongruous that the noble head, broad shoulders, and deep chest were supported by withered, useless legs that were kept hidden.

There were two other people in the room. A middle-aged woman with a pad and pencil sat behind a small revolving desk next to the president while across the room, a short, young ensign sat in a large easy chair. He wore flyer's wings on his blue coat. The ensign appeared ill at ease. In fact, Rodney could see tiny beads of perspiration on the young man's face.

Beaming, the president spoke, "Lieutenant Rodney Higgins?"

"Aye, aye, sir. Reporting as per your orders, Mr. President."

"Pardon me if I don't rise," Roosevelt said. "I have a small problem, you know." He gestured to the ensign who had risen. "This is Ensign Leonard B. Smith—the other American I mentioned on the phone." He glanced at the woman and Rodney sensed there was information here that was not to be shared—not even by a personal secretary.

Rodney took Smith's hand and found the grasp strong and assured despite the young man's obvious nervousness.

"Ensign Smith must leave in a moment but I wanted you two to meet. You share an experience no other Americans can claim." He turned to the woman. "This is my secretary, Marguerite LeHand."

The secretary stood and extended her hand. About fifty, she still showed traces of a beauty long faded. She smiled sweetly and said, "How do you do."

Rodney responded appropriately and following the president's gesture sat in a large chair next to the ensign.

Roosevelt turned to his secretary, "That will be all for

now, Missy. Please type up the memoranda for Knox and King and have them on my desk in the morning.''

"In your office in the west wing or here?" she asked, rising.

"West wing, please."

"Yes, Mr. President." The woman left.

As the woman closed the door behind her, Rodney's eyes scanned the room. It was not as impressive as he had imagined the office would be where the most powerful man on earth worked. In addition to the two desks and the occupied chairs, there were four more leather chairs and four side tables with ashtrays. Glass-doored bookcases lined one wall. There was a large fireplace with models of cruisers and destroyers on the mantel. The nautical motif was carried further by marine paintings and prints covering the walls. Rodney recognized one painting, the famous "The Return of the Mayflower," depicting the arrival of the first American warships in European waters in 1917. Rodney remembered Roosevelt had been assistant secretary of the navy at that time.

The president's desk was incredibly cluttered. There were stacks of reports, two pen and pencil sets, a clock, a half-dozen writing pads, a small bust of John Paul Jones, packs of cigarettes, family pictures, two ashtrays both half-filled with cigarette butts, a lamp, and two miniature pigs. Pencils were scattered throughout the litter.

Roosevelt waved. "You like my decor, Lieutenant? Nautical enough for you?" He chuckled.

"Yes, sir. I would say a friend of the navy lives here."

Roosevelt laughed and the ensign smiled. The president reached to a side table next to his desk. On it Rodney saw rows of bottles: bourbons with Old Taylor, Mammoth Cave, Old Crow, Old Fitzgerald, Seagram's Seven Crown, and Seagram's VO labels; Scotches with the fine Haig and Haig, Johnnie Walker, Chivas Regal, Teacher's, White Horse logos and many more. There were gins, cognac, vermouth, olives, onions, even a small bottle of grenadine next to a bowl of sliced lemons. "Have a drink with me, gentlemen?" the president asked, pulling a pitcher of martinis from the table and placing it in front of himself. Then, Rodney spotted the empty cocktail glass. The president had already had a drink. Roosevelt filled his glass, speared an olive with a toothpick, and dropped it into the cocktail.

Smith rose and brought an empty glass to the president. Pouring bourbon into the ensign's glass and topping it with a bubbly squirt of seltzer, Roosevelt looked up at Rodney, "You have a little catching up to do, Lieutenant."

Rodney smiled. "A little of that Johnnie Walker Black Label, straight, and I'll go right by you, sir, like Jesse Owens past Hitler's supermen."

The allusion to the black American's embarrassing victories over German athletes in the Berlin Olympics in 1936 caused Roosevelt's big laugh to fill the room. It took him a moment to compose himself. Then, after handing the ensign his drink, he half filled a glass with Scotch and gave it to Rodney who had walked to the desk. Both officers seated themselves.

The president became serious, "To England and the brave stand of the British people," he said, holding his glass high.

"Hear! Hear!" the officers chorused. They all drank.

Eyeing both young men, the president took a pack of Camels from his desk and offered them to the officers. Both refused. Carefully, he took a cigarette from the pack, gently twisted it into an elaborate holder, placed it in his mouth, and lighted it with a gold-plated lighter. Sagging back and tilting the holder at a jaunty angle, he took a deep drag and exhaled an enormous cloud of blue smoke. Staring upward at the smoke, he said, "Two packs a day—forty nails in my coffin." Both officers chuckled politely. "I wanted both of you here because of your contributions to the sinking of *Bismarck*." Rodney stared at Smith with a puzzled look. He had not only never seen the young officer before, he had never even heard of him. But, obviously, he had done something important. Roosevelt continued, "I have already told Ensign Smith of your sighting of *Bismarck* from the bridge of *King George Fifth*." Smith nodded and smiled.

"Thank you, Mr. President. But there were a few other men involved. I didn't sink her single-handedly," Rodney said, sipping his drink.

Roosevelt roared with laughter. "Yes, but I have been informed you picked her out of the mist even when radar was having problems. It's not in the ship's log because you were present as a neutral observer and technically not a member of the crew. However, I know you were posted on the bridge as a lookout—got it directly from Whitehall."

"Thank you, sir," Rodney said modestly.

The timbre of the president's voice became grave and slightly hushed. He nodded at Smith. "Ensign Smith's part in the sinking is secret and must remain so—you understand me, Lieutenant Higgins?"

"Yes, sir."

The president emptied his glass and refilled it from the pitcher. Speaking through a cloud of smoke, he continued, "You know that *Bismarck* vanished after sinking *Hood*. The Royal Navy lost her completely."

"Yes, sir. We were headed away from her toward the Iceland-Faeroes Gap when she made a radio transmission and a PBY (Consolidated Catalina flying boat) picked her up."

Roosevelt smiled broadly and nodded at Ensign Smith. "Meet the pilot."

Rodney was stunned. An American naval officer flying for the British. It was illegal, violated the Neutrality Acts and a half-dozen other laws and regulations. He stared at Smith who had his eyes fixed on the president.

"Now, you understand why Ensign Smith's part in the battle must be kept secret. Congress would roast me and Hitler would have a field day." Chuckling, he took another sip. "Actually, Lieutenant Higgins, we have seventeen of our navy pilots flying as 'advisers.' " He gestured at Smith with his glass. "Ensign Smith provided the British with some of the best *advice* of the war." He laughed boisterously at the jest. Again, the officers laughed politely. Both officers leaned toward each other and grasped hands. "Good work—good work, Ensign," Rodney said.

"You did all right yourself, Lieutenant," Smith said.

The president beamed. "Now you know why I wanted you two to meet. But keep in mind, Lieutenant Higgins. Top secret."

"What I hear here, remains here," Rodney said.

"Excellent." Roosevelt drank and refilled his glass. He gestured and Rodney brought his glass to the desk. Roosevelt refilled it. However, Smith emptied his and tabled it.

"With your permission, Mr. President," he said, rising. "I'll leave." He glanced at his watch. "I'm due at the Pentagon in an hour."

"Of course."

Ensign Leonard Smith shook hands with both men and walked to the door. "Nice seeing you, Lieutenant," Roosevelt said.

Smith froze with the door half open. "*Lieutenant?*" he said with surprise.

Roosevelt laughed. "Remember, I'm your commander-in-chief. I just promoted you."

"Thank you, sir." The young flyer closed the door behind him.

Obviously feeling his drinks, the president was in an expansive mood. He recharged both their glasses and lit another cigarette. "I have a fine staff," he said, staring at Rodney. "Secretary of the Navy Frank Knox and Secretary of War Henry Stimson are two of the best." He smiled broadly as if what he had said was loaded with subtle humor. But Rodney missed the humor completely and stared quizzically. "They're both Republicans," Roosevelt explained. "Broadens my base—helps pull some of Congress's teeth." Rodney chuckled appropriately. Roosevelt continued, "My chief of staff, General George C. Marshall, is a fine soldier. And I have others, all hand-picked. Harry Hopkins, my special envoy—he's in Moscow at this moment conferring with Stalin.''

"Yes, sir. Fine men, Mr. President.''

"You wonder why I bring them up?''

Rodney stared back silently, wondering if this could really be happening. A casual and apparently intimate conversation with the President of the United States? A president who was obviously feeling his drinks? A president who was obviously lonely. The whole incredible dream gave Rodney a queer twinge, almost of conscience, to see the obvious pleasure his commander-in-chief was finding in his presence. It was odd to know that he, a junior officer, was respected and his opinions sought after by the most powerful man on earth.

Roosevelt answered his own question, "Because there is one thing they all lack.'' He drank and stared over his glass at Rodney. "They haven't been there—they don't hear shots fired in anger, and even if we were in this, and God forbid that, they would not.'' He stabbed his cigarette at Rodney. "Leonard Smith's been there. You've been there. You've heard the shells fly over. You've heard them explode.'' He hunched forward. "You saw a naval battle—a great ship destroyed and you did it voluntarily.''

"I was curious, Mr. President.''

Roosevelt laughed. "You know what curiosity did to the cat.'' Rodney chuckled and emptied his glass. The president recharged it and the lieutenant sagged back into his chair. "What did you think of *Bismarck*?''

Rodney described the battle and the difficulty the British had in sinking the German battleship.

"Do you think they scuttled her?''

"No, sir. She took dozens of fourteen-inch and sixteen-inch hits. She was not returning fire and she was well down by the stern before *Dorsetshire* put two torpedoes into her. The Royal Navy didn't need any help from the Nazis.''

The president patted some papers on his desk. "You want battleship duty?''

"Yes, sir."

"You have it. Your orders are already cut. You will report aboard USS *Arizona* as assistant gunnery officer by twenty September. Report to the naval base in Long Beach, California in one week and you will be provided with transportation to Pearl Harbor on the first available transport." He nodded at the half stripe beneath the full gold stripe on Rodney's sleeve. "And make that half stripe a full one as of right now."

"Thank you, Mr. President."

The president thumped the desk thoughtfully. "You have had an experience few men can boast and you are very intelligent, Lieutenant. I want your opinion on several matters." He rummaged through some papers. Rodney wondered how anyone could run the country in such a mess. After muttering a few oaths, Roosevelt gestured at a half-open door beyond the fireplace. "I must have left my notes in my bedroom on my nightstand. Would you get them, please? Your name is at the top of the list."

"Of course, sir." Rodney rose and a slight movement of the floor told him he had had perhaps one drink too many. He shrugged and managed to walk a straight line into the president's bedroom. Although the bed had been neatly made, the room was as littered and cluttered as the president's desk. There was a heavy wardrobe—there were no closets in the White House—two rocking chairs and a pair of nightstands flanking the bed. Jumbled together on one was a Bible, a novel by Pearl S. Buck, pencils, aspirin, nose drops, cough syrup, an ashtray, and an unopened pack of Camels. The other nightstand held a pitcher of water with a glass, pads, pencils, stacks of documents, and a prayer book. On a marble mantel above the fireplace were a small collection of ceramic pigs, horses, and dogs with family snapshots propped behind them. A tail of a horse was prominently displayed over the fireplace.

Rodney walked to the nightstand holding the pads and found one with a list of questions. At the top he found his name. He returned to the Oval Office and handed the pad to the president. The president handed Rodney another full drink. Holding the glass, the lieutenant returned to his chair. He stared at his president. He had heard men of power—men in high places—were lonely men. President Franklin Delano Roosevelt was starved for conversation. He was convinced he was looking at the loneliest man in the world.

The president sipped his martini and grinned slyly. "You're wondering about the horse's tail?"

"A little odd, sir," Rodney conceded. And then with a tongue loosened by liquor, "I half expected to see Hitler's face under it."

Roosevelt laughed until he gasped. He finally managed, "You have a wonderful sense of humor, Lieutenant. I've got to remember that one. Maybe I'll put Adolph's picture there. It would certainly be appropriate." He smiled slyly. "But again, I might insult the horse's anatomy." Both men laughed uproariously. Finally, Roosevelt raised a hand and explained through the chuckles, "My father raced trotting horses. That's the tail of Gloucester, his most famous horse. We all loved the animal."

Finally regaining his composure, Rodney gestured to a painting of Eleanor Roosevelt hanging over the door. It had been obviously painted when she had been very young. Curling naturally, her long fair hair shimmered in the light, eyes shone a dark blue, skin fine and creamy. Her waist was small, flaring gracefully to full, womanly hips. To Rodney's surprise, she actually looked sexy and only remotely resembled the dowdy, plain, middle-aged woman the nation now knew. "Lovely picture of your wife, sir."

Looking up from the pad, Roosevelt said, "Oh, yes, Eleanor. She was an attractive girl. I miss her. She's in Sacramento meeting with some Democratic women's club." He thumped the pad thoughtfully and returned to his favorite subject, "What do you think of the Royal Navy's fighting ability, Lieutenant?"

"They're tenacious, courageous, and consummate professionals," Rodney answered. And then he added, "They showed little interest in taking prisoners after *Bismarck* sank."

"There were reports of U-boats around, you know."

"I know, Mr. President."

He glanced at the pad, "Do you think the battleship can fight off attacking aircraft, Lieutenant?"

"Yes, sir. Too much firepower. They'd never get through a battleship's barrage."

"You've heard of Taranto?"

"Of course, sir. It's an Italian naval base. The British attacked it last year."

Roosevelt nodded. "According to G-Two and Naval Intelligence, the Italians lost three battleships to just twelve Fairey Swordfish torpedo planes."

Rodney sipped his Scotch. "But they were taken by surprise and they were Italians. Everyone knows they can't fight."

Roosevelt laughed. "True." There were more questions about *Bismarck*'s ability to absorb punishment, effectiveness of armor, damage control, and turret fires that damned the British and destroyed four battle cruisers in two wars. Roosevelt spoke casually of the new Iowa class of battleships. Revealed how he personally had participated in the design of the turrets that separated each turret into three separate compartments surrounding each breech with the powder hoist in each sealed off in its own narrow room. "Like a tiny, sealed closet that opens a panel just long enough to discharge powder bags into the loading tray and then springs snap it shut," the president said proudly. He waved at a bronze of a tiny vessel on the corner of his desk. "That was my idea, too."

"The subchaser?"

"Right, Lieutenant. I was assistant secretary of the navy during the war and I insisted on the small, wooden, cheap escort vessel."

"And the North Sea mine barrage?"

The president nodded. "I pushed for that, too." He shuffled some papers on his desk. Took Rodney by surprise, "What do you think of the Japanese?"

Sipping his drink, Rodney pondered for a moment. "Tough, treacherous fighters. Knocked the Russians around in 1905. Sank most of their fleet in the Korean Straits."

The president sucked on his cigarette. "And they started the war by taking the Russians by surprise at Port Arthur."

"They're samurai—that's their way, sir. According to the code of Bushido, the samurai should try to destroy his enemy with a single, quick fatal stroke. That explains the sneak attack on Port Arthur."

"You're very knowledgeable, Lieutenant."

"Thank you, Mr. President. We have a fine Naval Academy." He took a tiny sip of Scotch. "Sir, may I ask if you think they might deliver a quick stroke in our direction?"

"Only if they're mad, Lieutenant."

Rodney hunched forward. "But the Japanese mind can seem irrational to us. He'll do the unexpected—that's what we can expect. And their rear—Manchuria—is secure. After all, they did sign a neutrality agreement with Stalin."

The president nodded grimly. "Yes. Stalin turned Hitler loose with his nonaggression pact in 'thirty-nine and now, you think, he might be doing the same thing with the Japanese?"

Rodney nodded. "Looks that way, sir."

The president's face was set in a hard line. "Several of my staff have expressed the same concern. In fact, my chief-of-staff has written a paper on that very problem." He drummed the desk restlessly before continuing. "We know the Japanese are dangerous empire builders, Lieutenant." Rodney remained silent while Roosevelt showed his knowledge of the Japanese by reviewing Japanese expansionism that began in the nineteenth century with the acquisition of the Kurile, Bonin, Ryukyu, and Volcano islands. Quickly he sketched her war with Russia where she won control of Korea and the southern half of Sakhalin. A cheap commitment to the Allied effort in the Great War won her the Marianas, Caroline, and

Marshall islands with the exception of Guam. Then Roosevelt described the thirties when Japan invaded Manchuria and annexed it as the puppet state of Manchukuo. ''Now they have their Tripartite Pact with Germany and Italy, their nonaggression pact with Stalin.'' He slapped the desk angrily. ''And that gutless Vichy government is actually inviting them to move into French Indochina, threatening the Burma Road. The Japanese have a consistent, inexorable policy of conquest that has never changed with emperors or governments. There, your samurais have been consistent and predictable.''

Rodney was not shocked by the information that was well known to him. However, the president's grasp of the consistent, unified drive for territory and power over the decades was startling, showing his incisive, penetrating intelligence. He gave old history a new look. The eyes of the handsome face with its almost fixed expression of good humor gleamed incongruously with emotion and just as incongruously seemed to be searching Rodney's eyes for approval.

''But, sir, the Konoye government has tried to be conciliatory.''

Roosevelt shook his head grimly. ''Prince Konoye—Emperor Hirohito—don't really rule.'' He looked up. ''You've heard of General Hideki Tojo?''

''Yes. A real hothead.''

Roosevelt nodded. ''Konoye is finished. Tojo will be taking over within a month. He leads a band of army fanatics who believe Japan is destined to rule in Asia with what they call 'The Greater East Asia Co-Prosperity Sphere.' They will be satisfied with nothing less than complete conquest of China. And keep in mind, we've embargoed oil and scrap iron and the Kwangtung Army still persists in its war in China regardless of what the politicians in Tokyo try to do about it.''

''The generals answer to no one.''

''Correct, Lieutenant. They're a bunch of Caesars. They crossed their Rubicon in China and I intend to freeze their assets here, over one hundred fifty million dollars of it, and see how Tojo likes that. The British and Dutch will cooperate in any sanctions we impose." He looked up suddenly. "Do you think we could goad them into a war?"

Rodney was shocked. The President of the United States was asking him if America should go to war. Maybe he was drunk. He gulped his drink. "They're samurai." He shrugged and turned up both palms in a gesture of futility. "Who knows? Is that what you want, sir?"

Roosevelt shook his head. "It's the last thing. It would be the wrong war with the wrong country—if there could be a right war. But we can't let Chiang Kai-shek down. China is the only power in the Far East that can stand up to the Japanese." He tapped his desk, his quick mind moving to another problem. "You're a navy man. You know the Nazis pose the greatest threat to this nation, not the Japanese."

Rodney walked to the desk and the president refilled his glass. He returned to his chair and, strangely, despite the drinks, the loose, giddy feeling of drunkenness had abated. Instead, he felt pleasantly relaxed and alert. "You are worried about the Royal Navy?"

"Of course. If the Fascists take over the Royal Navy and the French Fleet at Toulon, we would be hopelessly outnumbered, and of course, the Japanese would not remain neutral. They'd all jump on us."

"A year ago, sir, that was a grim possibility. But, now, the British are growing in strength and Hitler must defeat the Russians."

The president pulled a document from a disorderly stack. Drank and smoked in silence for a few moments. His voice was grim. "Today, Lieutenant, the Wehrmacht overran the Minsk pocket and Vitebsk. According to British Intelligence and the OSS (Office of Strategic Services), almost three hundred thousand Russians were captured, twenty-five hundred tanks, and fifteen hundred artillery pieces lost." He took another drink. "How long do you think the Russians can hold out? They're losing whole armies."

"It'll be a long war, sir."

"A long war?"

Rodney nodded. "Geography, weather, and numbers, sir. All against Hitler."

Roosevelt shook his head. "I hope you're right, Lieutenant. But I'm afraid the Russians will be finished within two months or less." He punched his desk angrily. "And I warned him!"

"Warned who, sir?"

"Stalin! I sent my Under Secretary of State Sumner Welles to see the Russian ambassador, Constantine Oumansky, last March and Welles warned him that we had information that a German attack was imminent. Of course, those idiots in the Kremlin wouldn't listen." And then sarcastically, "After all, Hitler had signed a nonaggression pact with them." He pulled on his cigarette.

Rodney was stunned. "But how, sir. How did you know?"

Roosevelt smiled but there was no humor on his face or in his voice. Instead, a warning, "I'm afraid, Lieutenant Higgins, that information might be dangerous for you to know."

"I understand, sir."

Roosevelt moved on. "When Russia falls, England will be in grave trouble and we're the next domino."

"We're the 'Arsenal of Democracy,' sir."

Roosevelt laughed at the quote of his own words. "True. And with Lend-Lease we have no problem with British credits. But we must see that our cargoes reach the British—that they continue to fight the good fight, our fight."

"Escorts?"

"Yes. I'm ordering our navy to escort American cargoes as far as Iceland."

"I've heard. There has been scuttlebutt."

Roosevelt chuckled. "Naturally. That's the navy." He put the holder to his lips, inhaled, and leaned back luxuriously as the smoke filled his lungs. He exhaled slowly as if he were enjoying every breath of carbon monoxide and speck of hot ash. "What you hear here, stays here."

Rodney smiled. "Of course, sir. We've already made that agreement—not that it was necessary, Mr. President."

"Of course." The eyes caught Rodney and held him. "I enjoy talking to you, Lieutenant. You're from the line, the trenches in a way, with a refreshing viewpoint. I rarely have an opportunity to talk with someone like you. My advisers are lost in grand strategy, world-shaking economic decisions, for the most part. It's interesting to meet a man who has your perspectives."

"Thank you, sir."

The president sighed. "It's time for a bite. Would you care to join me for dinner?"

"Thank you, sir. But I've got to return to New York—to be with my family." He glanced at his watch. "With a little luck I can catch the twenty-one hundred train."

Roosevelt nodded and placed his cigarette in a brimming ashtray. Rodney stood and walked to the desk. The hand clasp was firm and forceful. "I want to see you again, Lieutenant."

"I'd be honored, sir."

Roosevelt scribbled a number on a sheet of paper and tore it from a pad. "This is a confidential number. I want you to have it. You can always get through to Missy and if I'm here I'll talk with you." He handed the sheet to Rodney.

"I'm honored, sir." Rodney felt sudden confusion. "Is there anything in particular . . ."

The president interrupted him with a wave. "No. You're not a spy—a confidential agent. You're smart and perceptive. If you see something in your service that you feel the President of the United States should be informed about, use that number. Consider yourself my man in the field, and that's all."

"Thank you, sir," Rodney said, pocketing the sheet of paper.

"I enjoyed our conversation, Lieutenant. I may send for you again."

"I'm at your disposal, Mr. President."

"Here are your orders," Roosevelt said, extending a long brown envelope. "Cut by the secretary of the navy and handed to you by the President of the United States."

"No one, absolutely no one, will ever believe this," Rodney said, pocketing the envelope.

The president grinned broadly. "I know. But, someday, when you have grandchildren, tell them anyway. They'll believe you."

"Until age ten, sir."

Roosevelt nodded. There was a warm glow in his eyes. "I know. I have two granddaughters. They still believe me." He narrowed his eyes. "Before you leave, I'd like to know if there is anything you'd like to ask me?"

Rodney thought for a moment and a dark memory clouded his mind. He spoke earnestly, "Yes. I have a sister in Warsaw. She married a Jew." Rodney heard the president catch his breath. "Have you heard anything—anything at all I haven't found in the papers?"

Roosevelt shook his head. "Only that all Jews in the Baltic states have been ordered to wear the Star of David and mass relocations are going on."

"Pogroms?"

The president bit his lower lip. "British Intelligence has picked up rumors of some massacres in Poland and Russia."

"No!" Rodney cried in an agonized voice.

"Rumors, Lieutenant, rumors," Roosevelt pleaded. "All kinds of wild stories are coming out of Russia. This information came from Swedish sources. They reported a massacre of Polish officers and intellectuals in the Katyn Forest near Smolensk. One report puts the date of the killings in the spring of 'forty. But that seems impossible. They don't even know who to blame, the Russians or the Germans. In any event, we have no confirmation of any of this. I really can't believe any of it is true."

"I understand, sir," Rodney said, feeling some relief. He grasped the firm hand again and left the room.

VI

The Warsaw Ghetto
July, 1941

B Y the end of 1940, the Germans had crammed all of
the Jews of Warsaw into a deadly pen two and a half
miles long and a mile wide. Surrounded by a ten-foot-
high brick wall topped with barbed wire and imbedded glass
splinters, the ghetto was shaped like a flat-headed mushroom.
In all, the ghetto covered almost nine hundred acres of slums
in the northern section of the city. There were twelve exits
guarded by "Polish Blues" (police) and by vicious Lithu-
anians. Most of the solid blocks of tenements were two to
six stories high and dated to the nineteenth century. Plumbing
was primitive or nonexistent, sanitary conditions appalling.
Into this foul, festering pressure cooker designed to hold
150,000 residents, nearly a half-million Jews were jammed.

They squeezed into every corner of every room, averaging
a dozen to each room. They overflowed into the halls and
stairwells. Some slept in courtyards, others on sidewalks.
Maggoty potato soup made with straw, twenty grams of
bread, an ounce or two of groats, a tiny portion of condensed

milk, were the principal daily fare. Seldom did a resident consume more than three hundred calories in a single day—far below what a human being needed. Starvation and disease were endemic. Each morning corpses littered the sidewalks and gutters. "Death squads" picked them up and carted them to fields in the northeast section where they were buried in mass graves.

Oppressed people learn the art of survival. House committees were established in each building to help the poorest. Gardens were cultivated in every patch of ground, even on balconies and roofs. Risking instant execution, children crawled through sewer pipes and tiny breaches in the wall to the "Aryan side" to trade family possessions and jewels for food. Professional smuggling proliferated, Jews and Poles alike engaging in highly organized operations that involved bribed guards and corrupt German officials. They ruthlessly exploited their customers while living lavishly among the starving. However, most people began to eat more than their meager daily allotment, thwarting the Nazi effort to destroy ghetto morale, the will to survive. Still, starving skeletons and bloated children staggered through the streets and the death squads collected their harvest each morning.

Josef Lipiski lived here, worked here, and was convinced that he would die here. With his wife, Regina, and year-old daughter, Rose, he lived on the first floor of an old three-story brick building in the heart of the ghetto. Located at the corner of Leszno and Karmelicka streets, the building was a block west of the Thomaka Synagogue. Because Josef had completed his premedical training in the United States, he was proclaimed a "physician" and placed in charge of the "Leszno Hospital" after the old doctor, Abraham Chernowitz, dropped dead during a cesarean section he was forced to perform without anesthesia. The patient and baby soon followed the doctor. They were all thrown into a mass grave the next day.

Josef Lipiski was an impressive man. The son of Warsaw's most respected tailor, he was tall and slenderized by poor nutrition, giving the impression of towering height far beyond his six feet. The breadth of his shoulders under his threadbare shirts was wide and powerful. His hair was very dark and uneven in color—appearing as if lampblack had been combed through strands the color of ocher. Very thick and unevenly cut, he wore it brushed back from a wide, unlined forehead. The head was broad at the temples, features large, the bones of his jaw and cheeks and forehead weighty and massive-looking as if they had been fashioned by a stonemason. His most impressive aspect was his eyes. Big and brown, they were set in deep sockets where they glowed with a penetrating perception that proclaimed to all that this was a man of great intelligence and character—a man to be reckoned with.

The hospital was located on street level in a storefront of what had been a bakery. The surgery, where Chernowitz and his patient had died, was in the shop itself. The ward of sixteen lice-ridden straw mattresses occupied the workroom and storage area. Often, three people crowded each mattress. To call the facility a hospital was a macabre joke. Usually, there were no linens. Most of the patients suffered from malnutrition or typhus or both. They came with their own blankets and usually died under them. There were three other "hospitals" in the ghetto. All three were staffed by older, experienced physicians. However, the conditions were the same and the death rates astronomical. Each morning, bodies were carried from all four facilities and stacked on the side-walks for the death squads.

The hospital brought Josef several advantages—he had his own flat behind the bakery and enough rations to keep his family alive. Also, because of the increased rations, he had a large staff of volunteers who tended the patients around the clock.

In their three-room flat, the Lipiskis actually found privacy—a rare commodity, indeed. The living area had a battered couch, two chairs, a lamp, and a large bookcase filled with Chernowitz's old medical books and journals. Two packing cases served as tables. The kitchen was a small alcove with a two-burner stove, cutting block, and wooden sink. The baby slept on a straw mattress in the corner while Josef and Regina's bed was in a small curtained area. At first, with his father, Janus, mother, Leja, and teenage sister, Sara, living in the apartment, too, conditions were crowded. However, in May, his parents and Sara had been sent with a work party of nearly two thousand other Jews to help build a new camp at a small town on the Bug River called Treblinka. The Germans claimed Treblinka was to be a model work camp with abundant recreational and cultural facilities. Janus and Leja had volunteered while Josef remained as an assistant to Doctor Chernowitz.

Usually, in the evenings, Josef found time to play with Rose, who could already walk and was learning her first words. These few moments were the only moments of joy he could find in his existence. There had been no letters from Treblinka. In fact, no one had received a single letter from members of the work party. However, in the evenings, playing with his daughter, Josef could put the terrible worries aside for a few moments. At these times, he could hold his daughter and watch his wife as she cleared the table and washed the dishes. He still marveled at Regina's beauty.

Strongly resembling her mother, Brenda Hargreaves, Regina Lipiski possessed the elegant grace of an orchid in full bloom. Josef loved everything about her. Like her mother, her hair was auburn and long and she wore it like a cloud flickering with sunbeams. Her skin was jade, eyes large and dark, hinting at Celtic origins in the deep past. Josef guessed this came from her British father, Captain Reginald Hargreaves, after whom she was named. He loved Regina's long, slender neck, vaulted cheekbones, soft, sensuous lips cut in perfect sweeps like the wings of a butterfly. He loved her large silky white breasts, narrow waist, and hips that flared like the curve of an Egyptian vase. He was glad there was no resemblance to her grandmother, Ellen Ashcroft, a bigot who hated "Wops," "Spics," "Kikes," and every other ethnic group not descended from English stock.

Ellen was typical of all the other bigots he had met and learned to loathe in America. He found them all hypocrites who stridently espoused their patriotism and the Bill of Rights, and then excluded Jews and other "undesirable foreigners" from their neighborhoods, clubs, schools, and even their part of the bus. At least, in Poland, a Jew knew he was hated, his oppressors wearing their hatred on their sleeves as boldly as the yellow Star of David the children of Israel were forced to wear. Nothing was hidden, there was no hypocrisy, it was hate and be hated.

Eyeing his wife, he could not wait for the baby's playtime to end—for the moment he and Regina could move to the curtained alcove in the corner where he could find her hot, naked body and lose himself in her and for a few moments forget the anguish of their existence. But she did not belong here. There was a good chance she could escape this hell. He pushed aside the warm thoughts and opened an old argument.

"You've got to leave, Regina," he said. "You're a Gentile—we should try to get you out—find refuge with an Aryan family. There are some good *goyim* on the other side. Maybe, even send you to Switzerland and back to the States."

She whirled, a half-dried dish in her hands. "No! Leave you—the baby? She's no Gentile. How could she get out? What Aryan family would risk sheltering a Jew baby?"

"There are some and you have a passport."

"Ha! Do you really think it would matter to the Germans? They've picked up hundreds of counterfeit passports. Or maybe, all passports are automatically considered counterfeit to them. No! I'll stay regardless of what you say or do."

He felt anger rising. He opened a hideous wound. "Maybe the SS (Schutzstaffel—Protection Detachment) will fumigate this building the way they did Number Seventeen, Gensia Street." He heard her gasp and she stopped as if frozen. The memory of 157 men, women, and children shot to death because the Germans claimed they were "filthy with typhus, fleas, and lice, and a menace to the community" sent a cold tremor through the room.

Her eyes flared with cold blue light and her voice was deep, "If it comes to that—ever comes to that—I'll meet it with you and our baby."

Josef sighed and sagged back hopelessly, holding Rose very close. She felt thin. Terribly thin. He placed the squirming baby on the floor, shrugged resignedly, and moved to a new subject. "We haven't had a single letter or package from your family for months."

"I know, Josef. The Germans steal everything and you know it. No one is getting mail anymore."

Before he could answer, there was a knock on the door. They looked at each other anxiously. But the knock was soft, not the fearful pounding of the SS or Polish Blues. Regina opened the door cautiously.

Jan Tyranowski entered. The newcomer strode across the room like a sergeant about to shout orders to his platoon. And, indeed, he had been a sergeant with Company A of the Bozny Mounted Brigade until his unit made a suicidal charge against a column of German tanks near Lodz. He was one of three survivors of his company. A big man, he still appeared muscular despite the work of two years of malnutrition. Clean-shaven with blond hair and blue-green eyes, he was very un-Jewish in appearance. A talented violinist, he occupied the first chair in the ghetto's fine symphony orchestra.

Jan's father, a concert pianist and professor of music at the university at Poznan, had been taken by the Russians in 1939 while lecturing at Brest-Litovsk. He disappeared with thousands of others in the Katyn forest. There were black rumors of a horrible massacre of tens of thousands of officers, teachers, and intellectuals. Jan's mother had died of exposure when the new governor general of Poland, an infamous Jew-hater named Hans Frank, had decided to enforce a policy of *Judenrein* (purging of the Jews). Hundreds of thousands of

Jews were routed from rural communities and concentrated in ghettos in the larger cities. Jan's mother was packed into an open railroad wagon in Poznan and transported to Warsaw in the terrible winter of 1939–40. Whole trainloads froze to death. Only four people of the sixty crammed into her wagon survived. The rest were thrown into an open pit just north of the *Umschlagplatz*—the great square at the northern edge of the Warsaw ghetto where a railhead had been built. Jan had been in the work detail that had unloaded the wagon and he carried his mother's stiff corpse to the pit.

Jan Tyranowski hated both the Germans and Russians with equal venom. He was Josef's best friend.

"There's a meeting tonight?" Regina asked, gesturing to a chair.

Jan nodded agreement and remained standing. "Yes. The prayer group."

"But you usually pray on Monday and Thursday nights," Regina insisted, naming the traditional market days and evenings for prayer.

Jan nodded his shaggy head like a big bear. "True. But we're trying out a new cantor. We need the whole group."

Josef knew something was up. He guessed it was not a prayer meeting at all. He suspected Jan wanted him to attend a meeting of the Kosciuskos, a new, secret resistance group Jan was forming. He had given it the name of Thaddeus Kosciusko. A famous Jewish fighter, Kosciusko had died with his entire unit defending Warsaw against a Prussian army in the eighteenth century.

"We need you to make our *minyan* (ten)," Jan said, turning to Josef.

The reference to the all-male group aged thirteen and above required by Jewish law to form a quorum for prayer brought an angry mask to Regina's face. "Can't you get someone else to make your *minyan*? Josef is working himself to death. He's on the *Judenrat* (Jewish Council) in charge of food, apartments . . ." She slapped her head. "And he's on the Education Committee, teaches the Torah, the Talmud . . ."

"Regina," Josef said, interrupting. "They can kill us, but our religion must live on or there will be no Jews. Our children must learn the legal part of the Bible and Talmudic law."

Regina spoke with an impatient wave of her hand, opening another old argument, "And celebrate Rosh Hashanah, Yom Kippur, Simchas Torah, Passover . . ."

"Yes! Yes!" Josef said, face flushed. "And thirteen-year-old boys must celebrate their Bar Mitzvah."

"Even if they—you are killed for it."

"That's how it's been since the destruction of the Second Temple and the Diaspora. We've been over this before."

Regina slapped the sink. "I know the damned history. Must you die for it? It's been going on for two thousand years." She waved at the baby. "All of us die for it?"

Josef looked at Jan who stared back silently. He turned back to his wife. "We are Jews and the children of Abraham. Like it or not we have inherited our past. Our lives would have no meaning without our law." He thumped the top of a packing crate for emphasis. "And you know it, Regina."

Regina was not finished. She stabbed a finger toward the front of the store. "You're working yourself to death in the hospital, you belong to a half-dozen committees and councils. You teach the Torah and the Germans would kill you for it. You need your rest and get none." She brushed an errant strand of hair from her eyes with the back of her hand. "The SS won't have to kill you. You'll do it for them." She turned away, shoulders shaking. Quickly Josef walked to her, took her in his arms. She turned away, but he held her and kissed her cheek.

Jan said, "Perhaps, you should skip the meeting, Josef. We can . . ."

Josef kissed an angry tear from Regina's cheek and then turned to Jan. "I'll drop out of the building committee and, perhaps, the *Judenrat*."

Regina stepped back, stared into her husband's eyes, anger fading. Her unsteady voice was conciliatory, "You promise to drop out of the building committee, the *Judenrat*?"

"Yes."

"Then go to your prayer meeting—if it's that important to you."

Jan said, "It will be a short meeting. He'll be home early."

Josef turned to the baby who sat quietly on the floor, smiling up at her father. He picked Rose up, kissed her tenderly, and placed her on the floor again. Then he pulled on an old wool jacket and placed a battered felt hat on his head.

Regina kissed him fiercely before he left.

The meeting was held in the basement of a century-old building on Pawia Street. A combination tenement and storehouse, the old structure had a large basement that had been partitioned into a dozen storerooms. A clandestine classroom that served as a prayer house had been established in one of the small rooms.

As Josef entered the room, which was dimly lighted by four candles, he could see a small pulpit at the far end. Covered with faded material, it had a Star of David embroidered at the top. Beneath the star, the words "God, Torah, Israel," which represent the three cardinal aspects of Judaism, had been stitched in gold. To one side stood a plain crooked cabinet, the *aron ha kodesh*—the sacred repository containing holy objects, relics, and icons. To the other side stood a Torah with its five Books of Moses inscribed on fine parchment and hanging from its walnut stand in rolls. Josef knew that here on this scroll resided the entire body of Jewish faith, social thought, jurisprudence, ethics, morality, culture. Here was the source of the richness of their life; here, too, was the source of their misery.

A long unfinished table with shelves filled with books stood against one wall. Some had beautiful, richly imprinted bindings; others were so worn their covers were beginning to crumble. There were three child-sized benches and a long table that had been obviously built with adults in mind. Josef and Jan sat at the end of this table.

There were eight other men seated on benches at the table. All were young and very thin. Without exception, their clothing was worn and shabby. Every head was covered. Seven wore dark felt hats while three bearded men wore linen *yarmulkes*, earlocks, and the black garments of the orthodox. All eyes were on Jan.

Jan opened the meeting. "This is a meeting of the Kosciuskos." His eyes roamed over the men like daggers. "If you feel you cannot resist the Germans, if you feel that you cannot keep what you hear a secret, even from your wives, leave now." No one moved except the orthodox who eyed one another curiously. Jan gestured to the end of the table where a stranger sat. "This is Natan Kagan," he announced. "The last Jew of Kutno."

Natan Kagan stood. He was a small young man with the face of a ferret and the eyes of a fox who had been driven to ground too many times. He was so thin, his wasted features seemed huge—his nose hooked and angular, eyes swollen, mouth enormous with wide colorless lips. He looked like a candidate for the next morning's death squad. Baggy and torn, his trousers were filthy, sweater ragged and as foul as his trousers, black hat rimless. He spoke softly, voice reminding Josef of the sound of wind rustling through dead, dry leaves. "The Jews of Kutno are no more. The village is gone."

"How do you know?" Henryk Laden, a young cantor, asked.

Natan Kagan eyed Henryk with rheumy eyes. "I was born there, lived there until the Germans came." The haunted eyes wandered over the intent faces. "Have you heard of *Einsatzgruppen*?"

The men looked at one another. "A task force," Zygmunt Warszawer, an apprentice carpenter, said, translating the word literally.

Kagan laughed, a hard, bitter sound that brought a chill to Josef. "Do you know what their task is?"

Silence. Kagan answered his own question, "Their task is to murder every Jew they can find. They are Heinrich Himmler's special SS exterminators. There were seven thousand Jews in Kutno when Himmler sent them. Some were taken to a camp they're building at Chelmno. They lined the rest of us up for inspection in groups of eighty and a hundred in front of old Polish tank traps. Then they shot us.''

A rumble of disbelief filled the room. ''Didn't you suspect? Run?'' Zygmunt asked.

''I suspected when they made us undress. Then it was too late.''

''But how could you escape?''

''My whole family held hands in a tight group. My mother, father, and two sisters fell on me. I wasn't scratched but almost drowned on my parents' blood. My father wasn't dead. They shot him in the head. Blew his brains into my face. I lay under my dead family until night . . .'' He stopped, reeled back and forth, and grabbed the table with bony, white hands. Two men leapt to their feet and steadied him.

''Sit. Sit, Natan,'' Jan said.

The Jew of Kutno shook his head. ''There is more.'' He threw back his shoulders and took a deep breath. Shook off the supporting hands and seemed to find new strength. ''There are rumors they're going to kill us all. Chelmno is to be an extermination camp and so is Treblinka and there are rumors of others.''

''Treblinka!'' ''Extermination!'' chorused through the room in horror. Thoughts of his family sent an icy hand to grip Josef's heart, cut off his breath.

''It can't be true!'' Zygmunt Warszawer cried. There were shouts of protest, wails of anguish. Warszawer continued, ''It's one thing to kill a few thousand Jews in a remote village, quite another to exterminate a population of nearly one-half million in a big city like Warsaw. It could never be kept secret. World opinion . . .''

Kagan interrupted with a dismissive wave, ''Hitler, Himmler, Heydrich, Frank, Eichmann, don't give one matzo ball for world opinion. They believe they're going to rule the world, anyway. Remember, 'Tomorrow the world,' they say. The Jews, Poles, and Slavs are *untermenschen* to them.''

"Subhumans fit for slavery or extermination,'' Josef offered. Natan Kagan nodded. Josef continued, "We'd heard of exterminations at Minsk and Vilna. But those were only Russians. Russians murdered my father. I wouldn't miss one of them.''

The Jew of Kutno laughed bitterly. "And Jews. Jews!'' Placing his hands on the table and leaning on them, Kagan stared around the room. "Oy! Are you blind? Can't you hear? Can't you read? Haven't you read *Mein Kampf*? He tells it all there. Look around you. You're all starving to death, thousands of you have already died. Do you think any of the Jews of Warsaw will be spared?''

A heavy silence crept through the room and hung in the air like the cold musk of a tomb. Finally, Jan Tyranowski broke the silence, "We should arm?''

"Yes,'' Kagan agreed.

Henryk Laden, the young cantor, came to his feet. "From the time of the end of the Second Temple, the *goyim* have tried to exterminate us. We've been accused of being witches, sacrificing Gentile children, bringing the Black Death. We've been slaughtered by Crusaders, Spanish Inquisitors, Cossacks, and dozens of others.'' He pounded the table for emphasis. "But the 'Chosen People' are still here and our faith is stronger than ever.''

"Ha!'' Kagan scoffed. "You're chosen, all right—chosen for death.''

"I don't believe that,'' the cantor said.

"You believe I do not tell the truth?'' Kagan asked, voice sharpened by hostility.

Laden the cantor looked the Jew of Kutno up and down, and said, "Except for the word of God, there is no truth, there are only varying degrees of lies.''

"You call me a liar?''

"I agree with Zygmunt Warszawer,'' the cantor said. "They wouldn't dare kill every Jew in Poland. Why that's three and a half million people—ten percent of the entire population.''

Kagan sighed. ''If God exists, my words are truth.'' There was a gasp at the near blasphemy.

Laden said to Kagan, ''We should wait. Obey the commandment, 'Thou shalt not kill,' which is a cornerstone of our faith. We have no right to take lives. We should resist with our faith, not guns, as we have down through the ages. We must wait for the Red Army to liberate us.''

''The Red Army is *kaput*. We will all die,'' Kagan said. He dropped into his chair.

Jan Tyranowski came to his feet. He spoke slowly and deliberately. ''There have been rumors of other exterminations and all of you have heard them. Natan Kagan has not told us anything we had not heard—suspected. We have just been deluding ourselves, refusing the truth when it has been here to see in Warsaw for over a year. Thousands of our own people have starved to death or been murdered in this ghetto, already. Last week the Germans shot one hundred fifty-seven people from that building on Gensia Street because they had lice.'' His eyes roamed the intent faces. ''We all have lice. I believe we're marked for death. I believe we should prepare to resist. I, for one, will not die like a dog at the feet of my executioner.'' He raised a fist and his strident voice filled the room, ''I will die facing him, fighting him, if only with a rock in my hand.''

Shouts of ''Hear, hear!'' and ''No, no!'' resounded from the walls.

Jan silenced the uproar with raised hands. ''Any of you who feels he cannot in good conscience resist to the death, please leave.'' Henryk Laden and the two other orthodox came to their feet and turned toward the door. Jan's harsh voice stopped them like the blade of a sword. ''Silence! This I demand. If any of you betrays us, I will have that man's life.'' He stared at the trio with death in his cold eyes. ''Do you understand?''

"We promise on our faith," the three men chorused and left.

The door had just closed, when Solomon Katz, a young painter, shouted anxiously, "The arms, where do we get them? Buy them?" He shrugged in a gesture of hopelessness. "We don't have ten zlotys among us."

"We must collect valuables—jewels. Trade them for weapons," Jan said.

"But where? Where? What *goy* would help us?" Zygmunt Warszawer cried.

Josef raised a hand. "I know a Pole named Bogdan Koz. Koz is an importer—deals in weapons. He lives on Bilowski Street and my father said he had a gun hidden under every brick."

"It would be dangerous to contact him," Katz said.

"It's dangerous to live," Josef said. "I'll go under the wall. If Bogdan Koz is alive, he'll deal with us. He'll do anything for money."

"No," Jan said. "You look too *Juden*, Josef. I'll go. After all, I have the look of the ideal Nordic, not an *untermenschen*." There was a brief chuckle. He continued in a serious mien, "We need recruits—fighters. Screen them carefully and see me before you bring anyone here. And start collecting valuables. Hound your families—your friends. Steal, if you must. We must barter." The blue-green eyes searched each face and there was a warning in them. "But be very careful. There are traitors in the ghetto and you know it." He gestured to a small young man slouching at the far end of the table, "Markus Lang, you're our electronics specialist. Before we leave, can you tell us of any news you've heard on your wireless?"

Lang, truly a genius, had built the ghetto's most powerful receiver in his basement. There were dozens of hidden wireless sets in the ghetto. Most were primitive crystal sets with limited range. But Lang had built a receiver with stolen tubes and transformers he had wound himself. When weather conditions were right, he could pull in stations from as far away as Switzerland, Turkey, Italy, Sweden, and England.

Markus Lang came slowly to his feet and spoke in a soft, almost effeminate voice filled with sarcasm, "As you know, international Jewish bankers started the war, Bolshevik Jews in Russia are helping to persecute Poles, Jews are traitors who have sucked the very life from honest Poles. Jews are 'Shylocks,' profiteers . . ."

"Yes. Yes, we all know Hans Frank's old slogans," Jan said.

"Polish radio is still filled with them," Lang said defensively.

Jan drummed the table. "What do you hear from England? From neutrals? How is the war going?"

Every man hunched forward eagerly. "The news from Russia is all bad," Markus Lang said. There was a sigh. He continued, "The Germans took Lwow and are nearing Kiev and Leningrad. The Red Army seems to be disintegrating."

"What can you expect?" Solomon Katz asked bitterly. "That maniac Stalin murdered all of his best officers in his stupid purges."

"The other fronts—the English?" Zygmunt Warszawer asked.

Lang said, "I have been picking up the BBC regularly. England seems to be safe from invasion. Hitler is too busy with the Russians. But things are not going well for them in North Africa. A new German general named Rommel has driven them all the way back into Egypt and a large force is besieged in a place called Tobruk. No, indeed, things are not going well in North Africa."

A dismal hush fell over the room and Jan gestured to the door. "We will meet here in one week," he said.

Slowly, the men came to their feet and shuffled out of the room. Josef and Jan were the last to leave.

VII

The Western Desert
August, 1941

BRIGADIER Lloyd Higgins hoisted himself through the hatch of the Matilda II tank, planted his feet on the thin cushion of his seat, adjusted his earphones, and unsnapped the top of his binocular case. Bringing his glasses to his eyes he swept the barren desert that stretched endlessly in every direction. Dug in on the reverse slope of Bir Fuad Ridge so that only the turret of his tank would be exposed to an advancing enemy, Lloyd's Matilda was the center tank of the nineteen survivors of the Fourth Armored Brigade. At two-hundred-foot intervals, he could see his command's cast-steel turrets stretching to the north and south like a line of armored pillboxes, two-pounders pointed to the west, commanders standing like statues, most with their binoculars to their eyes. Every man knew this brigade—now reduced to company strength—was the key to the Eighth Army's rear guard.

Lloyd regarded his Matilda like a man evaluating his long-time mistress—there were many things he liked about her, but, on the other hand, time had revealed many flaws he would change. Since, at the moment, she was the best the newly formed Eighth Army had to offer, he had to live with her. Lloyd liked her turret, which was cast, well-shaped, offering no shot traps to the enemy. Hydraulically driven, it had a 360-degree traverse. He liked her armored skirting protecting the five twin bogie assemblies on each side, the large return rollers, idlers, and sprockets. With seventy-eight-millimeter armor fitted to the front of the hull and turret and a high-velocity two-pounder gun, Matilda was as formidable as most of her contemporaries. In fact, her thick armor had made her all but impervious to any Italian or German guns until the devastating German eighty-eight appeared on the scene. But Matilda was slow; very slow, and as designed, she was incapable of bringing her weapons to bear on attacking aircraft.

Lloyd had personally modified all Matildas under his command. He had begged new high-compression pistons, raising the horsepower of the two Leyland diesels from 190 horsepower to 210. With modifications to the eight-speed gear box and injectors, speed was increased from sixteen miles an hour to twenty-two, which was three miles an hour slower than the Afrika Corps's Panzer (*Panzerkampfwagen*) III. The single coaxial machine gun fitted in the mantlet did not provide enough small bore firepower and its field of fire was limited to the plus or minus ten degrees of elevation of the two-pounder. He begged Besa Mark I, 7.92-millimeter machine guns from Supply in Cairo and had every tank in his command fitted with one on a post just outside the hatch where the tank commander could man it. Only 1,125 rounds of ammunition in four boxes could be carried, but the new weapon had an unlimited field of fire. In July the first Stuka was shot down by a squadron under air attack near Halfaya Pass.

The Italians had nothing that could stand up to the Matilda, but the Germans were a different show. The Panzer III was a formidable opponent, indeed. With excellent armor, a fifty-millimeter gun, and capable of twenty-five miles an hour, it could fight or run and there was nothing Matilda could do about it. It took clever tactics and direct hits on its flat shot traps to stop one of them with Matilda's two-pounder.

Something was afoot. When he had returned at the end of July, the siege of Tobruk was already three months old. Thirty-five thousand troops—Britons and Indians toughened by the Ninth Australian Division—were too hard a nut for Rommel to crack. With Tobruk denied him, Rommel had no forward base for his advance into Egypt. Axis ships were forced to unload at Tripoli and Benghazi and nearly two thousand tons of water and supplies had to be trucked daily hundreds of miles to the forward units. Nevertheless, in Rommel's last offensive, the Afrika Korps had smashed to the Sollum escarpment, destroyed the Second Armored Division, and sent the remainder of the Western Desert Force reeling back into Egypt.

Lloyd knew he had to hold Bir Fuad Ridge. New shipments of tanks, guns, trucks, and troops were arriving in Alexandria and the strength of the Eighth Army was growing under its new commander, Lieutenant-General Sir Alan Cunningham. Wavell had been sacked and sent to India. Lloyd knew Cunningham had made a name for himself in Abyssinia. But he had fought Italians there. Anyone could beat Italians.

Rommel was building up his forces, too. The coast road was kept in good repair by German *pioniers* (engineers) and it was crowded with trucks and tanks moving toward Egypt. Lloyd expected to see panzers before him soon. Rommel loved the Western Desert—a plateau 500 miles long and 150 miles wide that stretched all the way from Libya into western Egypt. Here in this barren, hot, featureless terrain, the master tactician could maneuver his tanks like ships at sea. Prodding, he looked for weak spots, always threatening one of his masterfully executed flanking sweeps despite his supply problems. Lloyd knew it was a question of who would be ready first—who would strike first.

Tactically, he was in a good position. To the north, a five-hundred-foot escarpment dropped to the sandy strip bordering the sea. Here, the Fourth Australian Division was dug in, backed by batteries of heavy artillery. Rommel would not strike there. A feint, perhaps, but not a full-blown offensive. No. He would seek the high plain of the Western Desert.

Lloyd's southern flank was formidable, too. The Northumberland Fusiliers were dug in with thirty-eight of the vicious new six-pounder antitank guns. First coming into action at Sollum, a single battery had destroyed four Panzer IIIs and two Panzer IVs in six minutes. Supporting the entire front on the plateau were two brigades of Matildas and divisional artillery of eight batteries of twenty-five-pounders and four of six-pounders. In the plain fronting the ridge, hundreds of antitank mines had been sown. The defenses were formidable, but all that was needed in the desert war was a crack in the line and the motorized enemy could pour through, making chaos of the best planned defenses. Nothing demoralized a soldier more than knowing the enemy was in his rear. This had happened to both sides numerous times. And there was nothing between Lloyd's line and Alexandria except partially completed defenses at El Alamein. Both Alexandria and Cairo would fall if the Bir Fuad line broke. But at the moment, the desert was deceptively peaceful.

Lloyd swept his glasses over the terrain. He found nothing but the usual dun-colored expanse strewn with boulders and sharp pebbles with occasional camel's thorn bushes pushing up through the wasteland. Although it could play havoc with tank treads and truck springs and axles, Lloyd had found crossing it was fairly simple. The biggest problem tankers and truck drivers faced was climbing the escarpment from the sea. Wheeled and tracked vehicles could only find a few passable routes up the cliffs. Lloyd's guns were "zeroed in" at the head of a wadi (dry streambed) where a trail snaked up the slope at a point where the cliffs made a sharp turn to the south and for a short distance actually ran in a north-south direction.

Lloyd chuckled to himself laconically. This was an excellent place to fight a war. You could hurt nothing except your enemy.

Lloyd had fought here since 1940 and quickly learned a man had to adapt to the desert or it would kill him before the enemy. A man developed a "desert sense" that told him to never try to tamper with this formidable environment but to use it or avoid its traps if he could. The desert set the pace, dictated direction, and planned the pattern. A wasteland devoid of almost all life except a few bedouin nomads, it was infested with poisonous scorpions, snakes, and clouds of flies that forced a man to eat under a net, a closely secured tent, or in a battened-down tank. Vegetation was scarce, only the scrubby, prickly camel's thorn could grow here. Without distinctive landmarks, traversing it was like sailing on an uncharted ocean. Tank commanders constantly steered by sun, compass, and stars. Days were unbearably hot, nights cold, and the weather unpredictable, wind storms striking without warning.

Sometimes with a velocity of a hundred miles an hour, the hot southerly *khamsin* shrieked out of the Sahara like a host of ravening furies. Driving impenetrable clouds of dust as fine as chalk, it clogged rifle bolts, artillery breeches, and carburetors. Men gagged on the chalky drift and it inflamed their eyes. It seeped into vehicles and tents, buried stores, and reduced visibility to zero. It could send temperatures soaring by forty degrees, overturn trucks, and whisk telephone poles from the ground. Cyclones of madly whirling dust generated electricity that sent compass needles spinning crazily. Once, an electrical discharge from a storm near the Gazala line ignited an ammunition dump.

The desert was a deceiver. On clear days mirages played magical tricks with a man's vision and imagination, deluding newcomers into believing they were approaching trees and pools of water. Every item a man needed to survive had to be trucked in. The temperature fluctuations were unbelievable. A man could suffer sunstroke at noon and then shiver with cold at night. Swings in temperature of sixty degrees in a single day were not uncommon. The desert forgave nothing. A mistake in rations, a mechanical breakdown, a misread compass, could lead to slow, horrible death.

Browns, yellows, and grays were its dominant colors. The Desert Force learned to take these colors for its camouflage. With practically no roads, the army shod its vehicles with giant balloon tires. The desert yielded water reluctantly, and then, when given, it was usually brackish. Generals and privates in forward positions learned to subsist on a gallon of water a day. The hot sands and desolate terrain could not be subdued or made livable. Instead, the troops became primitive and nomadic—truly creatures of the desert—and this is how they fought.

When Lloyd had first arrived, there were only Italians to oppose the British and victories were ridiculously cheap. The Italians had a proclivity for doing the wrong thing. Without adequate armor or transport, armed with cannons and rifles dating to the nineteenth century, the Italian army, at Mussolini's insistence, invaded Egypt and penetrated sixty miles before stopping. The halt was called at the coastal settlement of Sidi Barrani. Lloyd remembered his disappointment when his brigade was pulled back eighty miles to the miserable fishermen's village of Mersa Matruh. "When are we going to boff the Eyties?" he heard the troops grumble.

It had been a long wait. The Italians were unwilling to penetrate farther into Egypt. Instead, they fanned out from Sidi Barrani, building a semicircle of seven defensive camps. Here they rested, loafed, doused themselves with exotic colognes, built officers' clubs, drank Frascati wines from engraved glasses, and quickly tired of their lot. Settled in comfortable boredom and hoping for a static war, the Italians refused to accommodate to the desert. They were prepared for the siegelike warfare of the Great War. They were one war behind.

At the same time Lloyd's men were fed a spartan diet of

corned-beef stew—a brown concoction the men called "Mussolini's arse"—canned fruits, and strong sweet tea. The new Matilda II tanks, lorries, artillery, and Bren carriers began to arrive in large numbers. Training was rigorous, drills and maneuvers held continuously. The polyglot force of Englishmen, Ulstermen, Highlanders, Sikhs, Pathans, South Africans, and Hindus was welded into a superbly trained desert striking force. By December of 1940, the Western Desert Force was primed and ready.

Carelessly, the Italians had left a fifteen-mile unguarded gap between two of the seven outposts they had set up as a shield for Sidi Barrani. The two camps were Nibeiwa, which was south of Sidi Barrani, and Rabia, sited on the escarpment to the southwest. The fortified sides of all the camps faced Egypt. The British were quick to see that if a force could penetrate the Nibeiwa-Rabia gap, it could push to the rear of the Italian positions, wheel, and attack from the undefended rear. Lloyd's brigade was given the job of spearheading the penetration.

With his tanks spaced two hundred yards apart and on a two-thousand-yard front, Lloyd's brigade had finally moved out on December seventh. The Fourth Indian Division and the Seventh Armored followed. It took two days to travel the seventy-five miles before engaging the enemy. Not a single Italian aircraft was spotted, not one patrol crossed his track. Finally, on the morning of December 9, well behind the Italian works at Nibeiwa, Lloyd and his men breakfasted on canned bacon and hot tea topped off with a dram of rum— "battle rum," the men called it. Then, standing in the hatch, the brigadier waved his Matildas forward.

Lloyd would never forget that moment. Closing on the camp, he had actually smelled hot coffee and rolls; the Italians were fixing breakfast. They never ate it. Bren carriers shot their sentries out of their towers. Then Lloyd heard the skirling sound of bagpipes behind him as Cameron Highlander infantry charged behind his tanks. At this moment, he discovered all the Italians were not asleep. Thirty tanks clanked around the southern perimeter of the camp and in a ragged line advanced on the Fourth Armored Brigade.

This had been Lloyd's first tank-to-tank combat. The enemy armor was a regiment of Ansaldo CA/13 tanks. Slow, poorly armored, and mounting a forty-seven-millimeter gun, the CA/13 was no match for Lloyd's Matilda II with its superior speed, armor, and hitting power. Within minutes, the Italian tanks were shot into smoking scrap iron and the British smashed into the camp. The outpost fell in less than three hours and two thousand prisoners were taken. The rout was on.

Two days later, Lloyd led the Fourth Armored Brigade into Sidi Barrani. The advance had been so swift, the streets were still smoking from the preliminary naval bombardment. The advance continued relentlessly. Sollum and Halfaya Pass fell and the attack swept into Libya where Fort Capuzzo and Sidi Omar were taken. Thousands surrendered, sometimes entire divisions lay down their arms. And sometimes, stubborn men fought bravely.

Near Bardia, Lloyd crossed a battlefield fourteen miles wide, strewn with the debris of war. He would never erase the horror of that scene from his mind. The mix of dead vehicles and men made it seem worse than anything he had ever seen on the Somme. Every rise was littered with shattered, burned-out armor and wrecked field guns. Lying singly and in heaps, the dead were everywhere. Most of those who had died instantaneously had the "thrown rag doll" look to their posture—limp, casual, as if they were sleeping. Others had their arms and legs thrown out stiffly as if they had been staked to the desert floor by savages. Those who had died slowly suffered the usual muscle spasms, drawing up their legs and arms into the fetal position. Pain had clenched their fists and they remained balled even in death. Blankets of flies covered them, crawling into eyes, nostrils, and wounds where thousands of maggots boiled in a feeding frenzy. In the heat of the desert, the ghastly smell of death was overpowering, coating the back of Lloyd's throat and the roof of his mouth. Lloyd actually learned to prefer smoke and had his driver steer for it until clear of the killing ground. Burial parties wore gas masks.

It was here, outside Bardia in the carnage of that field, that the lesson of a battle's killing ground had been driven home. In France, Lloyd had found it at the receiving end of a bombardment or when advancing on enemy strong points with well-sighted machine-gun posts. Here, in the desert, it was the armor. Tanks were the most feared weapon, tanks attracted the fire, tanks took the killing ground with them. They killed and were killed in the greatest numbers. He could not fault infantry for shirking operations close to his brigade. "Bloody artillery magnets," the infantry grumbled.

Tobruk, Mechili, Benghazi fell. By February of 1941, the remnants of the Italian Army had pulled back to Tripoli and the British advance stopped 350 miles to the east at El Agheila. "Greece, Greece," began to be whispered. "They're going to ship us to Greece," raced through the army. The rumor had been accurate. Lloyd's brigade was pulled back and the Desert Army was stripped of some of its best units. Then came Rommel to fill the vacuum and the nightmare began.

Lloyd dropped his glasses impatiently and fingered the five-channel selector of his radio. He disliked running his radio and his hydraulic systems off of his two batteries. But his six-hundred-watt generator was noisy and gave off its own haze of blue smoke. Nineteen generators would give them away even to an Italian patrol.

The air was still, shimmering here and there with layers of rising heat. Nothing moved. Not a bush. Not a bird. He thumped the armor of the turret with a clenched fist. "Where are the Jerries?" he muttered to himself.

He had learned long ago that boredom was never in short supply in the desert. He had expected to hear the flylike drone of a German Fieseler Storch spotter plane by now. But the desert was silent except for the humming of insects. Then he heard another humming. He cocked his ear to the hatch. His young assistant gunner and radioman, Private Touhy Murphy, a cockney from London's East End, was humming "Lili Marlene." No doubt, in his boredom, he had tuned in Radio Belgrade and was listening to the favorite singer of all fighting men in North Africa—the silken, sexy-voiced Lale Anderson. The fact that Anderson was German made no difference to the British. She had a lovely, plaintive voice. She was a woman and they needed women. That was all that mattered.

As tradition dictated, Private Murphy was a true cockney born within the sound of the bells of London's Saint Mary-le-Bow. His crib and playpen had been a grime-coated tenement in a foul industrial pocket known as "The Isle of Dogs." Descending from Irish refugees of the potato famine, his father had been a "barrow boy," vending fruit on the streets. Growing up in the gutters where he fought with other boys for scraps of garbage, young Touhy had grown into a tough, burly young man. The vicious battle for survival had given Murphy a spark of independence Lloyd had never seen before. He was a nonconformist and a maverick who adapted to army discipline reluctantly and sometimes violently. However, with quick intelligence and an unshakable faith in his country, he was the best loader and radioman Lloyd had ever known. In an emergency, Private Touhy Murphy was equally adept as a gunner.

Lloyd's gunner was Lance Corporal Paul Dempster, a squat, husky, twenty-year-old lad from Teel on the Isle of Man. Paul's father had been a fisherman. The cold, windswept Irish Sea was an inhospitable place for fishermen and those who plied their trade were very hearty souls, indeed. Paul had begun his career in the boat when only eight years old. The hard work, danger, and constant battle with the elements had strengthened his body and toughened his spirit. Dempster's cold brown eyes were like natural range finders. He was a dead shot with an uncanny knack for calculating range and deflection. He never fired a ranging shot; every round was fired for effect. Glancing down into the turret,

Lloyd could see the brown-headed gunner leaning over the weapon, stroking the breech as if he were preparing a woman for a round of lovemaking.

Ahead of the gunner and below him in the center of the hull sat the driver, Sergeant Colby Powell. He was second-in-command to Lloyd. Tall, slender, and blond, Powell was a former draftsman with an architectural firm in Stoke Fleming, Devon. Taciturn and with a wry sense of humor, he contrasted with the boisterousness of the gunner and radio-man. Thirty-five years old, he was referred to as "Daddy" by Murphy and Dempster. Lloyd assumed they referred to him as "Granddaddy" whenever he was out of earshot. A close-knit group, Lloyd felt he had the best crew in the Eighth Army.

Sometimes, he felt they were too close. On infrequent liberties in Cairo, while Lloyd spent his time in "officer country" at the Continental Hotel or at Shepheard's, Dempster, Murphy, and Powell invariably frequented Cairo's lowest dives. Their favorite was the Melody Club where the band was protected from brawling patrons by barbed wire. Here the fabled belly dancer Hekmet performed. The acrobatic undulations of her hips frequently started riots among the sex-starved young men. The last time his crew visited the place, they had thrown three Argyles into the barbed wire, smashed the bar with the head of a Northumberland Fusiliers, and had to be subdued by a dozen club-wielding military policemen. Only by begging and threatening was Lloyd able to obtain their release from gaol.

The expected buzz came and the humming in the tank ceased. It rose over the escarpment like a big brown wasp. A Storch observation plane flying at the usual low altitude. Anxiously Lloyd fingered his binoculars but dared not bring them to his eyes. A glint of reflected sun was all that was needed to give away the whole show. He glanced down the line of tanks. Netting had been pulled over the rear of their hulls and camel's thorn woven in. Sprigs were even stuck into the pierced barrel casing of his Besa machine gun. Bloody lessons had taught them to sweep away all tracks behind tanks and vehicles. They were ready, as ready as they would ever be, and beautifully camouflaged.

He held his breath as the little plane flew not a thousand feet directly overhead and then to his rear. The German had guts. He would be target practice for a fighter. But, of course, the Desert Air Force was nowhere to be seen. Lazily, like a dragonfly over the Kentish downs on a hot summer's day, the Storch turned to the south and then made a wide sweep to the west. In a few minutes it vanished in the distant haze.

Lloyd heard Murphy's voice on the intercom, "Do you 'spect them bloody buggers saw us, Gen'ral 'iggins?"

Lloyd answered honestly, "I haven't the foggiest. But we'll know straightaway, if the Stukas pay us a visit."

Dempster's voice: "Don't send 'em an engraved invitation, sir."

Powell spoke: "I had enough of that lot at Fort Capuzzo."

Lloyd remembered the horror just outside the old Italian outpost. Eight Matildas and their crews had been blown to pieces by a squadron of JU 87 Stukas, with one-thousand-pound bombs. The attack had taken only three minutes and left nothing but huge craters and bits of smoking metal and flesh. The brigadier shuddered.

Something new on the horizon brought Lloyd's glasses to his eyes. Dust rising from below the escarpment. Vehicles were crawling up the wadi. He keyed the intercom, forced a jovial timbre in his voice that concealed the anxiety he felt. "Pull up your drawers, lads. The curtain's about to go up on the first act. You'll get more action than Hekmet's navel on Saturday night."

"I'll take Hekmet, sir," Dempster said. Murphy and Powell chuckled.

Lloyd dared not broadcast the sighting. He had imposed strict radio silence until the enemy was engaged. Instead, he looked to both sides, pointed, and pumped a fist two times over his head. The gesture was repeated by every tank commander. Higgins grunted with satisfaction. He said to Murphy, "Loader, load with APC (armor piercing capped)." Lloyd heard the clang of metal on metal as a two-pound projectile was pushed into the breech and locked into the firing chamber. "Driver, stand by to start engines and generator."

"Gunner ready, sir," Dempster said. "Tube loaded with APC."

"Driver ready, sir," Powell said. "Standing by to start generator and engines."

"Loader ready, sir," Murphy said.

Lloyd glanced down through the hatch into the turret. Murphy was seated behind the breech with a ready round of APC in his hands. Around him and beneath him, ninety-one more rounds were stored in lockers and ready boxes. Just to the right of the breech, Dempster sat with his eye to his range finder, hands gripping the elevating and traversing cranks of the cannon. His right foot was on the firing pedal. Seated in the front of the hull, Powell hunched over his controls and stared into his periscope. Only his back was visible. Lloyd felt a surge of pride. His crew was ready. "Bully, lads. Stand by. Our guests will be here shortly," he said, still masking his concerns and doubts with a show of confidence he did not really feel.

The cloud grew into a brown smudge on the horizon. Then the first enemy tank appeared, crawling like a clumsy beetle over the rim of the escarpment at least two miles away. It was a Panzer III. Quickly, it was followed by twenty-one more tanks. A reinforced company. Obviously afraid of mines, they formed a column of twos, advanced a short distance, and then stopped. Lloyd was sure his brigade was unseen, but why did the enemy halt?

Then he saw the half-tracks filled with infantry. They charged out of the wadi and streamed through the corridor formed by the tanks. Within minutes, a dozen half-tracks fanned out ahead of the panzers and advanced on Bir Fuad

Ridge. Obviously, the German commander was suspicious, and in the tradition of Rommel, he was conserving his tanks and risking his infantry first.

Lloyd wondered at the tactics. It was foolish to send fully loaded vehicles into a possible mine field. If the Germans suspected a trap—and they obviously did—they should dismount their infantry and send them ahead in a line of skirmishers. Rommel must be in a terrible hurry. He always was. Pursuing a retreating enemy closely. Perhaps, this time, too closely. Engines roaring and leaving clouds of dust, the half-tracks came on. What a dreadful waste of fine infantry.

Lloyd spoke into the intercom, "Stand by, Gunner. Fire on my command. Murphy and Dempster take out the half-tracks with APC, I will engage the infantry. I want the tanks. But we have no choice." Lloyd heard his commands repeated and acknowledged. Quickly, he unlimbered the Besa and grabbed the pistol grip. Swinging the perfectly balanced forty-seven-pound weapon around on its post mount, it felt as light as a feather. "Death is as light as a feather," he had heard an old soldier say once. He snorted. Now he knew what had been on the old man's mind. He snapped off the safety and trained the weapon on the advancing enemy.

Lloyd licked his lips as the big half-tracks entered the mine field. Nothing happened and the Germans bored in closer. They were so close Lloyd could see the goggled drivers through their open ports and the commander standing in the center leading vehicle. Their faces were brown with dust and their tunics were filthy. Only the helmets of the troops were visible swaying from side to side in the rear of the vehicles. The panzers remained stationary, engines idling. Then it happened.

The lead half-track was engulfed by a yellow flash that hurled it skyward end over end. Men were flung from the machine like rag dolls, wheels, hood, weapons, and chunks of wreckage arcing out from the yellow blast like the blooming of an evil flower of death. Then a second vehicle struck another powerful antitank mine and disintegrated like the first.

Instantly, the survivors stopped and the infantry poured over the sides. They were only four hundred yards from the ridge.

For the first time, Lloyd switched on the command circuit. Every man in his crew was on the circuit. Orders were only given once. "This is Rooney-oh-One. Rooney Command, commence firing! Commence! Commence!"

Obviously, Dempster's finger had been on the trigger and a target was in his sights. Preceded by only four rounds of tracers from his coaxial Besa, which bounced off a half-track almost directly ahead, the two-pounder fired with a vicious crack that struck Lloyd's eardrums like the end of a whip. The tank rocked backward from the recoil of the high-velocity shell and the half-track exploded, the armor-piercing shell boring halfway through its engine before detonating.

Every tank seemed to fire simultaneously. Flame rippled up and down the length of the ridge and a steady roar of gunfire boomed across the desert. Clouds of fine dust and brown smoke billowed and Lloyd coughed as the pungent smell of cordite filled his nostrils. It was time to report to division.

He switched channels and shouted into his microphone, "Scrooge, Scrooge, this is Rooney-oh-One." An incongruously calm voice acknowledged. Lloyd continued, "A force of twenty-two Panzer Threes with infantry and half-tracks on my front. Am engaging. Request artillery and aerial support."

"Roger. We have pressure on other fronts. Will send you what we can, Rooney-oh-One."

Watching the fire of his tanks rip through the German vehicles and staring at the waiting panzers in the distance, Lloyd said, "You'd better, old boy, if you want to spend your next leave in Cairo instead of a prison camp. Out!"

The quick-firing two-pounders engulfed the German line in explosions, half-tracks staggering, exploding, and burning. But the German infantry was well trained. Quickly the survivors spread out and went to ground, realizing they had stumbled into a major line of resistance. Through the din

Lloyd could hear the Germans shouting their battle cry, "*Heia safari!*"—Bantu for "Drive onward!"

Muttering "We'll see how bloody far you drive," Lloyd brought the Besa to bear on a squad of ten men rushing to a knoll. Four of them were carrying a light machine gun and two boxes of ammunition. He picked up the knoll with his bead first and then traversed back to the Germans.

Heart beating so fast he could feel the blood pounding in his temples, he pressed the trigger. The machine gun leapt and trembled in his hands like a live thing. Even through his earphones, the hammering clatter dinned on Lloyd's eardrums. Firing 750 rounds of ball a minute, the breech devoured the belt, bright brass shell casings spewing from the extractor, pinging and pattering off the turret and hull to the ground. His first slugs were short, kicking up small columns of dirt and clods. Following his tracers, he raised his sights and caught the first man with his stream. A burly sergeant, he stiffened as if frozen on the spot and dropped like a wind-blown board. Then Lloyd moved the weapon from right to left, bowling the soldiers over one after the other. Some leapt and flung out their arms, others whirled like dervishes, threw their weapons into the air, and tumbled to the hard desert floor to lie still in the embrace of death. Within seconds, the entire squad was down.

Releasing the trigger, Lloyd felt a familiar, disturbing tingling deep down inside, almost a sexual ache in his loins. Strange, how killing men could be so close to bedding a woman. Years ago he had felt this sensation in the Somme Valley many times during the Great War, and it was still with him. There was guilt, but it was over the reaction, not the dead men.

Murphy and Dempster were working the two-pounder like madmen, firing a round every two seconds. Within a minute every half-track had been hit by APC rounds and all were burning or disabled.

"Loader! Antipersonnel!" Lloyd shouted into his microphone. "Driver, start the generator and engines." He switched to the command channel, "This is Rooney-oh-One—Rooney Command, start generators and engines." The tank trembled as Powell started the generator and the two Leyland engines. The big diesels rumbled in slow idle. Glancing up and down the ridge, the brigadier could see blue exhaust smoke rising from every Matilda. He disliked idling his engines in the hot desert sun. Not only could they overheat, but the interior of the tank, which was an oven anyway, could become unbearable. Too often, crews collapsed from heat exhaustion. But he had no choice. The only relief the crew had was a small fan mounted at the rear of the turret. It did nothing but move hot air around the interior.

Murphy shouted, "Antipersonnel, sir," and the gun continued its rapid fire. But now, its shrapnel-loaded shells probed for troops huddled behind rocks and in small depressions. All of the tanks were searching out the infantrymen, explosions flinging dirt, rocks, men, and pieces of men into the air. Some Germans ran, but mercilessly, the hail of death followed them, cutting them down in their tracks. Guns were harvesting corpses the way reapers cut wheat.

"*Heia safari!*" Powell shouted sarcastically from his seat in the front of the tank. Murphy and Dempster laughed.

A black pall of death billowed into the sky and hung over the battlefield. Now the smell of cordite was mixed with that of burning oil, rubber, petrol, and the sickening sweet odor of burning flesh. There was a sharp fluting sound like the flight of a great insect past Lloyd's head. Then a ping as a bullet ricocheted off the Matilda and then another and another. Some brave German infantrymen were holding their positions and firing despite the murderous hail of shells and bullets. The commander in the Matilda to the brigadier's left flung up his arms and threw his head back as if in prayer, and dropped through the hatch, the top of his head blown away. Lloyd could taste the sour gorge of his bully beef lunch rise into his throat as a familiar cold hand clutched at his guts. But he could not "button up." Visibility from a secured tank was terrible and enemy infantry could sneak up and disable tanks with demolition charges. He would only close the hatch when engaging enemy tanks. He continued firing and the German response slackened and almost ceased.

Then, three Germans came to their feet and began to run back toward one of their vehicles with its right track blown off. There a machine gunner was firing and the trio obviously wanted to find shelter behind the truck. Lloyd cut down one with a short burst and then the firing pin clicked on an empty chamber.

Cursing, the brigadier released the ammunition box and threw it over the side. Frantically, he reached down into the hatch, grabbed a full box from its steel bracket welded to the side of the turret, fitted it onto its mount, and jerked the lid up. He released the lock on top of the Besa's breech and flipped the cover up, exposing the feed mechanism. Angrily watching the pair of Germans vanish behind the half-track, he grabbed the first brass-tag holder on the belt and passed it into the receiver. A quick motion of his left hand pulled the tag through until he heard a clicking sound. He slammed the cover down and pushed until he heard the spring-loaded locking device snap into place. Then, a quick pull of the cocking handle and the gib on the extractor grasped the rim of the first round. A second pull, and he heard the feed block clatter as the powerful return spring drove the first round into the firing chamber. The gun was ready, but there were no targets.

Now there were twenty-five panzers. They had deployed into five groups of five and had moved forward a hundred yards on a thousand-yard front. They had stopped and squatted patiently—waiting. And Lloyd knew why they waited.

Then he heard it. A low rumble high in the sky. Aircraft. The patent sound of Jumo engines. Even before he saw them, Lloyd knew they were Stukas. He brought up his glasses and he felt a sudden deadly tension that scraped along his spine like a serrated knife. They were unmistakable. Twenty-seven aircraft at perhaps six thousand feet approaching from the west. Gull-winged with spatted wheels, each had an awesome one-thousand-pound bomb slung beneath the fuselage on a crutch and a half-dozen smaller bombs racked under the wings. They all wore the unusual desert camouflage of the dreaded *Stukageschwader* One.

Nothing was as horrifying as a dive-bomber attack. Artillery shells and bullets could snuff you out in a blink, but a man never saw his death coming. The Stuka was different. It arrogantly paraded its killing power before blowing you to bits. It gave a man a chance to stare at the bombs tucked against its belly and wings and think about his own annihilation.

Lloyd's guts spasmed and he felt the tension race up his spine to his neck and scalp on the icy feet of hundreds of frozen insects. The hair seemed to rise from the back of his head. Fear, an old acquaintance, was back. He had known him intimately on the Somme and found him again in the desert. He wanted to hide—drop into the armored safety of the turret. But, instead, he caught his breath, threw his shoulders back, and clenched his jaw in a rictus of determination. Switching his channel selector, he called division, "Scrooge, this is Rooney-oh-One. At least twenty-seven Stukas preparing to attack my position and now I have twenty-five Panzer Threes on my front."

"Roger, Rooney-oh-One," the voice said.

"Where's the bloody Desert Air Force?" Lloyd shouted. "And I need artillery."

"There are other priorities."

"Other priorities, my bloody arse!" Lloyd shouted, watching the aircraft casually stack up in their usual oblique line that always preceded an attack. The brigadier switched to his command channel, "This is Rooney-oh-One. Stand by for air attack."

The command was unnecessary. Every commander of every Matilda already had his machine gun trained on the approaching bombers. Suddenly the pitch of the engines dropped as the pilots set their propellers at full coarse and Lloyd could see the hinged slatlike air brakes drop below the outer wings. They had less than a minute now. He felt like a drowning man with a cement block tied to his ankles. His wife, Bernice, gray, worn with years of worry, was there, eyes pooling with tears, lips trembling. His children, Bonnie and Trevor, smiled up at him. His dear brother, Randolph, flashed by, splendid in his blue RAF uniform. *Oh, for the RAF. If only Randolph and his Spitfires were here. They'd bloody well sweep the Stukas from the sky.*

The first bomber dropped off into its steep dive. Engine roaring, it hurtled downward like a thunderbolt from hell. Lloyd brought the Besa up and brought the bead of his sights on the first aircraft now followed by a half dozen more and the others were peeling off. The planes were headed directly for him. Lloyd had always had this feeling when under dive-bombing attack. All men did.

The shrieking began. Sirens—the British called them trombones—were attached to the landing gear. The howl was supposed to demoralize even seasoned troops. It was unnecessary. Every man was frightened out of his wits, but not demoralized. Anyway, there was no place to run—to hide.

The first plane released its bombs—a one-thousand-pounder and six smaller bombs. The black, pointed, finned missiles hurtled straight down on top of Lloyd's head. Immediately the pilot pulled the stick back. But Lloyd knew his momentum would carry him very low—within range. The Germans were careless. They still did not expect AA fire from British tanks.

The bombs shrieked and howled like a hurricane as they plummeted. The pilot had released too soon. The "stick" struck between the lines, about eighty feet in front of the Fourth Armored Brigade. The explosion of the one-thousand-pounder was cataclysmic. A burst of light that seared the retina of his eyes shot two hundred feet high from the desert floor, shrouded with boulders and dust. An earthquake struck the ridge, Lloyd's Matilda bouncing up and down on its treads like a frightened toad, dirt tumbling into the pit.

The Stuka was very low, pulling out of its dive with its belly exposed. Leading the aircraft like a hunter shooting partridge, Lloyd squeezed the trigger and at least six more machine guns unleashed a storm of tracers that stitched the German's belly. Trailing smoke, the Stuka banked off toward the Western Desert.

Lloyd heard another roar. A whine. The whistling sound of supercharged Allisons. Racing in from the east, high. Needle-nosed aircraft with huge air-scoops under their pylon-like propeller bosses. American-built Curtis P-40 Toma-hawks. Unmistakable. Not as good a fighter as the Spitfire, but still easily superior to the JU 87.

But hell was raining from the sky. Bomber after bomber released its bombs and pulled from its dive over the ridge. Two were hit and plunged straight on into the desert, dying in convulsive explosions and greasy black smoke. But their bombs made Bir Fuad Ridge a heaving inferno of hellfire. The tank next to Lloyd's shot upward at least fifty feet into the sky on the tip of a giant blast. More explosions shook and rocked the Matilda like a dory in a Channel storm. Lloyd cursed as his aim was spoiled and he sprayed the sky harm-lessly.

More Junkers screamed down. Would it ever end? To both sides Matildas were blown to fragments or whipped into the air like trash in a tornado. The ground quaked and the tank rocked and bounced, jerking the brigadier from side to side. Lloyd felt as if he were caught in the bowels of an erupting volcano. Screaming oaths into the bedlam, he fired in short bursts as Stuka after Stuka pulled out low and streaked to the south and west. Two more tumbled to the earth, disintegrating in long yellow smears of yellow flame and black smoke, flinging debris over hundreds of feet of desert. Lloyd jerked another box of ammunition from the turret.

Then a one-thousand-pounder struck just a few feet from the Matilda. The flash like a sun flare sent afterimages flashing across Lloyd's retinas and hundreds of tons of earth and rock heaved into the sky like a great curtain. The concussion struck like a sledgehammer, the earth itself writhing and convulsing like a mortally wounded creature. The Besa was ripped from Lloyd's hands and he was hurled to the side of the turret, impacting his ribs. Pain shot all the way from his neck to his toes and he dropped into the hatch. Grabbing the cover, he slammed it shut and fell into his seat.

Murphy grabbed his shoulders, steadied him while Lloyd held his side. Dempster and Powell both turned, Powell coming out of his seat. They all had the concerned look of children staring at a sick parent. "Bugger all, sir," Murphy said. "You ain't caught one, Gen'ral 'iggins?"

Lloyd caught his breath, shook his head while boulders rained down and bounced off the armor like shot. "No. No. Just a bruise, Private." He gestured. "Open the hatch and return to your post."

The cockney reached up, pushed hard against the cover, and flung it open. Dirt and clods rained in. Gritting his teeth against the pain, Lloyd climbed back up to the Besa. The tank was almost buried, but the engines still ran. They were still in fighting trim. He looked up just as the first Tomahawks roared over not more than five hundred feet high.

They were firing, streaking after the fleeing Junkers like lions after jackals. Lloyd waved a fist into the sky. "You're too late, damn your bloody souls." Four more JU 87s crashed into the desert far to the west. Then, just as quickly as they had appeared, the aircraft were gone, leaving the sky miraculously empty of both enemy and friend. An incredibly sweet silence descended on the desert.

Brigadier Higgins gripped his side. Even breathing was difficult. But he ignored the injury, looked up and down his line. He saw huge smoking craters, burning tanks, steel plate twisted into unrecognizable shapes, engines, turrets, treads twisted like warm spaghetti, bodies, pieces of bodies. He pounded the turret until his fist ached. "My lads—my lads. Oh, God, what have I done?"

Dempster's calm voice on the intercom jarred him. "Are you all right, General?"

Lloyd shook his head. Dempster had overheard him even over the rumble of the diesels. He took several quick, shallow breaths and cursed his momentary lapse. Felt composure return. He must present the iron spine, the steely resolve of command. And the men must not know about his severe pain. He spoke with his usual firm, evenly modulated timbre, "Quite well, Corporal Dempster."

"They're coming, General."

Lloyd stared through the dissipating clouds of dust and smoke and he could see the Panzer IIIs looming larger. His professionalism took over and suddenly the pain seemed to diminish. "APC."

"APC, sir," came from Murphy.

Lloyd keyed the radio. "This is Rooney-oh-One. Rooney Command, stand by to engage enemy armor. Acknowledge."

"Rooney-oh-Four standing by," "Rooney-oh-Two standing by," began to come through his earphones. In all, ten commanders acknowledged. Lloyd felt encouraged. He still had eleven Matildas, far more than he had expected. He remembered the Western Front and the stupendous bombardments of millions of shells that preceded attacks. Many times, he had emerged from his dugout into a moonscape of obliterated trenches, villages flattened to dust, forests stripped clean of every leaf, branch, and stump, even hills blown away and leveled. Invariably, he had been convinced that only he and those sheltered with him in his command dugout had survived in the entire sector. But when the attacks came, Tommies emerged from the desolation like ants from deep burrows and the Enfields, Vickers, and Lewis guns began to bark and stutter. Now, here at Bir Fuad Ridge, the tough Englishman was proving he was still very hard to kill. An old saying ran through the brigadier's mind, *The last are the hardest to kill*. He waved a fist at the approaching panzers. "Come on you bloody bastards. I've been killing you since 1914 and I won't stop until you're all dead."

"You bloody well tell 'em, Gen'ral, sir," he heard Murphy shout up from the turret. "We'll send 'em all to 'ell, sir."

Lloyd watched the approaching enemy. They were within a mile. Advancing in groups of five. The usual tactic. Three leading, two trailing to provide a fire base. When engaged, usually at five hundred yards or less, the fives would leapfrog, leaders becoming the fire base, trailing tanks taking the point. Now he could see more half-tracks and trucks pouring from the wadi and this time the infantry was deploying behind the tanks. This was no diversion. He grabbed his microphone.

"Scrooge! This is Rooney-oh-One. I have twenty-five Panzer Threes advancing on my front supported by infantry in battalion strength. I have sustained heavy casualties. Request permission to withdraw to Position Baker." Lloyd glanced over his shoulder. "Position Baker" was a low, long ridge of sand about six hundred yards to his rear. He could regroup, narrow his front, and concentrate his fire.

His earphones squawked with a harsh voice. "Negative, Rooney-oh-One. Hold your position."

Lloyd felt his guts contort with an amalgam of rage and frustration. He traced a finger over his sore side, trying to determine if any ribs were broken. He actually expected to find broken bones protruding, but there were none. His lips drew back into a grim line and he spat into the microphone, "I don't have the strength to hold. The enemy is making a major effort here. Get your bloody arse up here and see for yourself."

"Rooney-oh-One. Observe RT discipline. You are to hold."

"Then send me some support!"

"Rooney-oh-One. Out!"

Lloyd punched the turret angrily. He did not need his binoculars. The panzers were only eight hundred yards away, advancing slowly and deliberately. In fact, the leaders had already passed the first burning half-track and entered the killing ground. The battlefield was silent, only the rumbling sounds of idling engines could be heard.

The brigadier stared at his enemy. The Panzer III was familiar, now. He had destroyed a half dozen, inspected them inside and out: the wide four-hundred-millimeter tracks that gave excellent traction even in loose sand; six idler wheels and widely spaced return rollers supporting the heavy tracks; thirty-millimeter armor plate bolted to the twenty-millimeter mantlet front faces of both hull and turrets; to the left side the closed driver's visor in the hull; the powerful fifty-millimeter gun and two coaxially mounted 7.92mm machine guns; the turret with its high commander's cupola and its five vision ports now covered with sliding shutters. It was the equal of the Matilda II, perfectly adapted to the desert, and it outnumbered him more than two-to-one. They would be overrun, wiped out.

He was very exposed. Every instinct told him to drop into the turret and pull the hatch cover down. But he could see infantry crowding close behind the panzers. He had no choice. He must wait, remain at the Besa as long as possible. He wiped the perspiration from his forehead with the back of his hand as if fear was a mask he could rip from his face and discard. Breathing in sharp, short breaths and with trembling hands, he grasped the pistol grip and brought the bead to his enemy. He knew the feel of the weapon would calm him. Slowly, he pulled his lips back from his teeth and the leer was that of a death's head. He waited.

The Matildas of the Fourth Armored Brigade had two advantages—their diesel fuel was not as explosive as the Panzer III's petrol and they were dug in, offering only their turrets and the tops of their hulls to the enemy. Direct hits on the turrets, guns, or on the turret tracks—the small space between the turret and the hull—were necessary to disable. Lloyd keyed the intercom, "Gunner. Give me a range to the leading tank."

Glancing down into the turret, Lloyd could see Dempster with his eye glued to his split-image range finder. "Six hundred seventy yards, sir."

"Very well. Report every hundred."

More equipment was pouring up out of the wadi. Artillery. At least two batteries of howitzers were unlimbering on a small rise to the south of the mouth of the wadi. They were big pieces. Ten-point-five-centimeter field guns capable of attacking his line with plunging fire. This was something the fifty-millimeter guns of the panzers could not do.

"Scrooge, this is Rooney-oh-One," Lloyd said into his microphone. "I have two batteries of ten-point-five howitzers on my front. Enemy tanks and infantry advancing. In ten more minutes, there'll be a two-thousand-yard hole here."

The voice was flat and dehumanized, "Hold your position, Rooney-oh-One."

Uncontrolled rage burst through Lloyd's lips, "Up your bloody arse. I'll save my lads any way I can. Out!" The voice shrieked into his earphones, but he switched the circuit off.

"Six hundred yards, General," Dempster reported.

"Bernice. Bernice," Lloyd whispered to himself. "I've been a terrible husband. You deserved better."

There was a blast as a panzer struck a mine. Flung into the air, it rolled over onto its side and then toppled completely over. Treads still turning, it looked ridiculously like a turtle on its back. Two more struck mines and stopped, burning, crews tumbling out and running back to the protection of their own infantry. The odds were lowered but still heavily weighted against the Fourth Armored Brigade.

"Five hundred yards."

Lloyd switched on his command circuit, "Rooney Command, this is Rooney-oh-One. Commence firing! Commence! Commence!"

The Matildas fired almost as one. Because the Panzer III's front hull and turret armor was the thickest, each gunner selected a target to his right or left, aiming for treads, bogies, sprockets, or hull shot traps. With a tungsten carbide core, the two-pounder APC rounds were capable of penetrating forty-seven millimeters of armor at five hundred yards. However, if deflection increased over thirty degrees, penetrating power dropped off severely. Dempster fired on the first tank to his left.

His first round blew off a return roller and the panzer lurched to a stop. His second round punched through a flat spot in the hull just below the turret and flame and smoke shot out of ventilators and observation ports. The hatch popped open and a German with his clothes flaming rolled to the ground. Lloyd could hear his screams over the din of battle.

The Germans opened fire, flames racing up and down their line. A steady drum fire assailed Lloyd's ears and there were hissing sounds as if a bag full of snakes were suspended over his head. Then a deep-throated, fluttering roar began, booming through the sharp bark of the tanks' cannons like bass drums underscoring snare drums. The howitzers had opened fire. Hurled high into the sky, the thirty-two-pound projectiles plunged almost vertically into the ridge. The big shells parted the air with a shredding rustle and slammed into the hard-baked desert, ripping the surface with a shower of explosions. A haze of smoke and dust began to cloud the battlefield. Obscured by smoke and dust, the German infantry was not visible. Lloyd knew every one of his tank commanders would be killed in the next few seconds. He keyed the radio, "Rooney Command, button up, but keep a keen eye open for infantry."

He dropped down into the turret and slammed the cover down. He did not lock it. Men trapped in a burning tank did not relish fumbling with locked hatches.

Dempster had the two-pounder trained thirty degrees to the left and firing as quickly as Murphy could load. "I put the wind up the sod!" Dempster exulted. "Boffed him good. They're frying." There was a cheer.

"Ammunition count?"

"Under fifty rounds, Gen'ral," Murphy said.

"Very well. Make each one count."

Lloyd grabbed the handles of his periscope. A pain so vicious he groaned wracked his side. With sheer strength of will, he stared into his eyepiece and swept the field. At least nine panzers were disabled, most burning in pools of their own petrol. But a dozen or more were only two hundred yards from the ridge. There was a sharp metallic thud like a hammer striking a pot and bits of paint and dust rained from the turret top. They had been hit by a fifty-millimeter shell. Then another and another. But the tough seventy-eight-millimeter armor of the turret bounced them off. However, the heavy 10.5-centimeter shells of the howitzers did not bounce off.

Swinging his lens to the south and then to the north, he saw at least three more Matildas wrecked and burning. Survivors could be seen scrambling out of the wrecked vehicles and running down the reverse slope. He might have a half-dozen tanks left. He turned his channel selector. Ordered the brigade to back out. "But stay with me. Go when I go, stop when I stop."

Lloyd said to Powell, "Sergeant, back out at your best speed."

"Backing out, sir!" Powell pushed in the clutch, shifted into reverse, grabbed his tillers, and floored the accelerator. The tank lurched backward. With a best reverse speed of only eight miles an hour, the tank seemed to be crawling out of its pit and down the slope. Mercifully, they were free of the fifty-millimeter fire. But not the howitzers. The big shells continued to lob over the ridge and explode all around. The gunners were firing blind, missing the tanks but doing terrible execution among the British survivors fleeing their wrecked tanks. Boiling with anger and frustration, Lloyd swung the periscope around. He could only count five Matildas. He said to Dempster, "Let me know when we're eighty yards from the top of the ridge."

Dempster glued his eyes to the range finder. "Eighty yards, sir!"

The brigadier spoke into his microphone, "Rooney Command, halt. Targets of opportunity as they crest the ridge. Hit 'em in the guts."

Lloyd expected the Germans to be riding a wave of victory,

to crest the ridge at a high speed, exposing their soft under-bellies. He was right.

At full speed and shedding sand and dust from their treads in swirling clouds, three panzers fairly leapt over the crest of Bir Fuad Ridge. At only eighty yards, the British gunners could not miss the exposed undersides. All three panzers were hit simultaneously.

With the first hits, their fuel tanks exploded, great balls of flame like incandescent red balloons roiling into the sky, followed by greasy black smoke. The panzers skewed drunkenly and came to a halt, two or three crewmen tumbling out of their hatches and racing back to the crest. Then at least ten more roared over the crest, churning up a huge storm of dust like a small *khamsin*. Two more were disabled, but the survivors charged down the slope followed by infantry. Lloyd knew there was no escape now.

Suddenly a hail of large shells began to fall among the enemy armor. At first, Lloyd thought the howitzers were firing short. But these were high-velocity shells fired on a flat trajectory. "Must be twenty-five-pounders." There was a cheer as the men realized they were receiving support from the Eighth Army's most deadly field piece. Dozens of shells poured in, smashing the panzers and bringing their headlong charge to an abrupt halt.

The infantry fled back to the crest of the ridge, leaving heaps of dead and wounded behind to mingle with the British dead. They had taken the bait and been trapped. Frantically, the German drivers jammed into reverse and backed toward the ridge. Now the Germans sought the protection of the reverse slope where the big shells could not reach them. Only four of the Panzer IIIs made it to the ridge. The shelling stopped.

Lloyd stood and threw open the hatch. He felt a hot stab of pain, but reveling in the unexpected reprieve, he ignored it. Slowly, he pulled himself up and studied the slope. He could see nine destroyed Germans, three on the crest and six perhaps fifty yards in front of the Matildas. Most were burning and there were bodies scattered around them. An entire crew of five Germans stood behind a panzer with its treads blown off. They held their hands over their heads.

"Let's boff the bastards," he heard Dempster growl, turning the turret and bringing the coaxial machine gun to bear.

"They gets them Jenny Conven'suns," Murphy said.

"That's right. The Geneva Conventions," Lloyd said, correcting the cockney's pronunciation. "They're prisoners of war. Hold your fire, Corporal Dempster."

The brigadier looked around at his own command. The Germans' howitzers and fifty-millimeter guns had done their work, too. Two of his tanks were burning and a third was turned on its side. But the German howitzers were silent. They must be packing it up. He felt anguish well up and clot darkly in his throat. He wiped his cheek with his sleeve. It came away wet and smeared with dirt.

He heard engines behind him. Diesels. Matildas of a reserve brigade storming over Position Baker through at least four batteries of twenty-five-pounders. And behind the tanks he could see infantry: chamber-pot helmets, khaki shorts, Enfields at high port and tipped with bayonets. A new voice squawked in Lloyd's earphones, "Rooney-oh-One. This is Pygmalion-oh-One. You are relieved. Good show, old boy. You bloody well taught the Jerries a lesson."

Lloyd's voice was uneven as he spoke into the microphone, "Roger, Pygmalion-oh-One. I need medical personnel immediately. I have taken heavy casualties."

"They're right behind us, Rooney-oh-One. A great victory, truly a great victory."

Lloyd looked around the burning field, at his destroyed command. *A great victory*, ran through his mind again and again. As far as he could see, only one other Matilda of his brigade was undamaged. He began to laugh raucously despite red-hot flaming pains in his side. "A great victory. A great victory," he repeated, over and over. He became weak, knees bent and gave way. He sagged down into Murphy's arms.

"You've caught one, Gen'ral 'iggins. 'an you 'ave, sir." He lowered Lloyd into his seat.

Lloyd choked back his groans. "Dash it all. I told you, a sore rib or two—that's the lot, I'm sure." He was very weak and the tank seemed to be spinning.

Powell opened a side port and said to Lloyd, "Another bunch of Krauts, sir. Five more coming this way, sir. One has most of his clothes burned off. The others are carrying him."

Murphy grabbed the first-aid kit. "I'll see to 'em, sir."

"We owe the buggers nothin'," Dempster said.

"The Jenny Conven'suns," Murphy said. He looked at Lloyd. "Sir?"

Mind numbed by shock and pain, Lloyd lacked the energy to reason, exercise judgment. He just wanted to sit with his head in his hands and savor the thought he was still alive and every member of his crew was unhurt. This always happened to him when a battle was over and the killing lust faded. All survivors felt it. "All right. Carry on, Private Murphy," Lloyd said, sagging, head drooping.

The cockney scrambled up through the hatch.

"That's a jug full of rot, sir. He just wants souvenirs," Dempster said. "He'll sell them in Cairo, find a whore, and bonk his brains out. I'll lay my bit on that, General."

An insidious doubt nagged at Lloyd. Feeling slightly stronger, he forced himself to his feet and pulled himself up through the hatch. There was a roar of diesels and he saw the first Matilda of the relief force passing through his line. The commander waved at him. Lloyd waved back. He looked for Murphy and found him not more than twenty feet to one side of the tank. He was walking toward the Germans who had placed their wounded comrade on the ground and stood behind him. They were well clear of the coaxial machine gun that was still trained on the first group of Germans standing beside their tank.

Murphy dropped to one knee next to the German and opened his kit. Suddenly a corporal pulled a Walther P38 from his waistband and took careful aim. Lloyd shouted "No!" Murphy looked up just as the German fired. The nine-millimeter slug caught him between the eyes, the contents of his skull exploding from the back of his head in a yellow-gray gout. Arms outflung, he was hurled to his back by the killing force. His arms and legs jerked spasmodically in the strange way of the freshly killed. His sightless eyes were wide open.

One of the Germans knocked the pistol from the corporal's hand and punched him to the ground. Then the Germans seemed to be clawing for the sun, screaming "*Kamerad! Kamerad!*"

Shouts of "No! No!" "Murderers! Kill 'em!" came from the turret.

A blinding white light passed between Lloyd's eyes and brain. There was no conscious thought, no reality except Murphy's body, and he heard nothing. Felt no pain. He swiveled the Besa.

Screaming "*Nein! Nein!*" the Germans broke. Through his tears, Lloyd clamped down on the pistol grip and the Besa yammered to life, a bright bar of flickering light springing from its muzzle. The big slugs tore through the running men, breaking their backs, legs, and ripping life from them like a great scythe. They tumbled and rolled, blood and viscera cloying with the dirt.

But the corporal was unhurt, sitting next to Murphy's body and rubbing his jaw. He was staring at Lloyd with the wide, unblinking eyes of a madman. Lloyd felt a hand tugging at his trousers. Dempster cried through a broken voice. "Kill 'em! Kill 'em all."

"I'll give him the 'Higgins Convention,' " Lloyd said, bringing the bead to the German. He was blond and appeared younger than his son, Trevor. He stared back at Lloyd with wide blue eyes. The boy spit at him. Lloyd squeezed the trigger and the German was flung back by the steel torrent. Lloyd kept the trigger down, the body actually jerked along the ground on its back by the impact of dozens of slugs. He laughed gleefully as he moved the Besa back and forth, shooting off the top of the German's head and splattering his brains; broke his ribs and scattered chunks of bones, mangled flesh, slimy lungs, and detritus of entrails and viscera. Finally, the machine gun clicked on an empty chamber. The brigadier pounded the hot breech in frustration. ''I'm not finished! Not finished!'' he screamed. ''His balls! His legs!''

''I saw that, sir,'' a strange voice said behind the brigadier.

Startled, Lloyd turned and saw a captain of infantry leading the first squads of his company past the Matilda. The captain stopped. He was young and had the unwrinkled, polished look of a newly arrived replacement. ''Respectfully, General, Captain Courtney Hall of the East Sussex Rifles. I've got to report you, sir,'' he said. ''That was murder.''

Lloyd could not believe the words. And they came from a mere captain. Captain Courtney Hall must be mad. Or was he mad? No. They were all mad. Insanity was an essential ingredient of this business.

Silently, he stared at the battlefield; the shattered, burning tanks, scattered and piled bodies and pieces of bodies. The howitzers and twenty-five-pounders had killed with extraordinary violence. Perhaps fifteen escaping British crewmen had died on the field with the German infantry. In most cases it was impossible to tell them apart. Many bodies had been severed at the chest or waist, trailing viscera yards long, the dark brown effluvium of the newly killed spreading in dark patches on the desert floor. Torsos like dolls ripped by a child lay thirty to forty feet from the nearest legs and heads. Shattered bones, brains, and mangled flesh lay piled among the bodies. Here and there a wounded man propped himself up on his elbows and howled like an injured animal. Others, unable to move, cried out for their mothers. Above it all, hungry desert birds began to gather and circle on widespread wings.

The brigadier's eyes stopped on the rigid form of Private Touhy Murphy, lying in a pool of his own gore. His wide eyes were staring directly into the sun. Flies were already beginning to gather for the feast, several crawling across his eyes. Lloyd began to laugh. He laughed so hard tears ran down his cheeks. His side ached but he could not stop. The captain and a knot of his men stared up in alarm.

"Murder? Murder?" Lloyd gasped. "What's that?"

Then the terrible pain struck again and a black curtain was dragged across his eyes. His knees were suddenly limp as dead willow and he collapsed into the turret.

VIII

D URING September and October the papers reported unabated disasters on the Russian front. Despite an early winter, the Wehrmacht seemed unstoppable. Leningrad was encircled, Kiev surrounded, and four Russian armies were trapped. Over a half-million Russian troops surrendered. When Kiev was finally overrun, another 350,000 Russians laid down their arms. The German steamroller did not stop. It plunged on all the way to the Sea of Azov, cutting off the Crimea. Sevastopol was besieged. Other German units stormed toward the capital, crossing the Dnieper River and driving on Moscow.

Six hundred sixty-three thousand more Russian prisoners were taken with all of their equipment. The Moscow-Leningrad rail line was cut and the Germans captured a bridge over the Volga River intact. With German spearheads thirty miles from the city, the Russians began to evacuate Moscow and a state of siege was proclaimed. Hitler chortled in a speech at the *Sportspalast*, "This opponent is already broken and will never rise again."

America moved closer to war. Roosevelt ordered American destroyers to escort convoys as far east as Iceland and asked Congress to permit the arming of merchant ships. The American destroyer *Greer* was attacked by a German submarine off Iceland but managed to avoid the torpedoes. However, destroyer *Kearney* was not so fortunate. She was hit and eleven men killed. The U.S. Navy was ordered to shoot on sight. Late in October the American merchant ship *Lehigh* was sunk by a German submarine off the west coast of Africa. Then the nation was horrified when the destroyer *Reuben James* was torpedoed and sunk off Iceland while escorting a British convoy from Halifax. One hundred fifteen men were lost.

Roosevelt stated bitterly in a national broadcast, "It is the Nazi design to abolish the freedom of the seas and to acquire absolute control and domination of the seas for themselves." He said in a message to Congress, "Neutrality Act prohibitions have no realism in the light of unscrupulous ambitions of madmen." Averell Harriman and Lord Beaverbrook met with Soviet delegations in Moscow to determine Russian defense needs.

In the Far East, the Japanese pressed ahead in their war against China. As President Roosevelt had expected, the civilian government of Prince Konoye fell when the prince argued vehemently for the withdrawal of Japanese troops from the mainland. War Minister General Hideki Tojo formed a new government dominated by the army. Now the talks with the U.S. were hopelessly deadlocked and everyone knew it. Immediately there were ominous rumors of a Japanese buildup.

It was early November when Major Randolph Higgins returned to New York. He rang up Brenda immediately upon arriving at Grand Central Station. It was evening when Travers opened the door and Randolph entered the great house. Brenda held him, kissed him, and led him to the sitting room.

Betty, Marsha, and Ellen were spending a week in the Hamptons with old friends. However, Hamilton Babcock was seated in the room in a big easy chair, sipping a highball and smoking an Old Gold. The rancid odor reminded Randolph of Lloyd's old Egyptian Abdullahs.

Hamilton nodded briefly and muttered a terse, "You're back, Major?"

"Daresay, you never left, old boy," Randolph retorted.

"Now, boys, let's behave," Brenda chided. She waved Randolph to the sofa but before he could seat himself, Nicole entered.

"*Bonsoir*, Major Higgins. You look well, monsieur." The maid curtsied.

Randolph smiled. "You look lovely, Nicole." He took both of her hands and held them briefly. The maid curtsied again and left.

Randolph seated himself on the lush sofa and Brenda plopped down beside him. She clutched his big hand in hers. The Majestic was glowing in all its glory and Randolph could hear a show called "Your Hit Parade" coming through the big speaker. Mercifully, Brenda had the volume turned down.

"Lloyd's been injured," she said anxiously. "Bernice wrote me. He's home."

"I know," Randolph said. "Lloyd wrote me. He has three broken ribs." He snickered. "Said he got drunk and fell out of the tank. Claims he'll be back with his brigade soon. He's out of sorts because he's missing the show at Tobruk."

"That isn't what Bernice told me," Brenda said grimly. "Bernice got it from Whitehall. She has friends there."

"Daresay, I know," Randolph agreed. "She has a lot of pull there. In fact, Allanbrooke is her cousin."

"The chief of the Imperial General Staff?" Hamilton offered.

"Quite right." Randolph turned to Brenda impatiently. "And what did she say?"

Brenda continued, "There was an engagement at some ridge—Fuad, I think."

"Never heard of it," Randolph said. "Things have been quiet in North Africa." Hamilton nodded concurrence.

"I know. There wasn't anything in the papers. Just a minor thing," Brenda said. "But the truth of it is Randolph was wounded and his brigade almost wiped out."

"Lord, another bloody defeat. Rommel will be in Cairo soon."

"No, Randolph. Bernice said the British won."

Randolph's guffaw was devoid of humor. "What's funny?" Hamilton Babcock asked.

"The bloody arithmetic of war," Randolph said. "My brother's wounded, his unit's all but wiped out, and we have a bloody victory. Next they'll count Dunkirk as a bloody triumph of arms. It never fails to amaze me." He turned to Brenda. "I'll be back in England within a week. See Lloyd then and wring the truth out of him."

Brenda could not hide her shock. "Within the week?"

Randolph nodded. "I'm not returning by ship. I'm on temporary loan to Ferrying Command. I'm to fly a Hudson across the pond. Only Englishmen can fly the Atlantic, you know. Of course, the route is confidential."

Hamilton said, "From Newfoundland to Iceland for fuel and then on to England. The ferry route has been reported in the papers for months." He took a hard pull on his cigarette and expelled the smoke in a triumphant cloud.

"That will be such a long flight, Randolph," Brenda said.

Randolph ignored Hamilton and spoke to Brenda. "Nonsense, Brenda. The Hudson has good range and is a stout aircraft. Should be a piece of cake."

Brenda was not convinced. "A stout aircraft, Randolph?"

Randolph laughed. "Built by your Lockheed Aircraft Corporation in Burbank, California. It's a converted transport plane they called the Electra. Your Amelia Earhart disappeared in the Pacific flying one."

"That's encouraging," Brenda said.

"I build radios and RDFs for the Hudson," Hamilton offered. "You'll be talking through one of my sets."

"Was Earhart using your equipment?"

"Of course."

Randolph raised an eyebrow and twined his fingers into a steeple. He looked as if he were in prayer. "Fortunately, I'll be on radio silence."

Hamilton Babcock came erect, not quite sure if he had been insulted. Before he could answer, Travers swooped over the trio, handing Brenda a glass of Chateau Lafite-Rothschild and Randolph two ounces of straight Johnnie Walker Black Label. Hamilton accepted a sour mash whiskey and seltzer. He leaned forward and all three glasses touched.

"Cheers," Randolph said.

"Mud in your eye," Hamilton said.

"To Lloyd's recovery, a short war, and a stout Hudson," Brenda said. "No more Amelia Earharts." They all drank.

Randolph felt Brenda tighten her grip on his hand. "It's so good to have you back. I worry so. It seems I've spent most of my life worrying about Lloyd and you. If you aren't fighting Germans, you're testing airplanes or flying the Atlantic. There must be a safer way to make a living."

Chuckling, Randolph kissed her cheek. "I haven't been much fun as a brother-in-law. Have I, Brenda?"

"I wouldn't trade." She returned his kiss.

"Perhaps I should leave," Hamilton said with acid sarcasm. "Three's a crowd, you know."

"Nonsense," Brenda said.

"Suit yourself," Randolph added coolly.

"You know I've known Randolph for a quarter of a century, Hamilton. He's very special to me," Brenda said. "But you're special to me, too. Please stay."

Placated, the portly businessman grunted and drained his glass. His mottled gray-green eyes remained on the flyer as Travers handed him a fresh drink.

Brenda said to Randolph, "You know Rodney had a meeting with the president."

Randolph nodded. "I saw the lad in California. He was stationed in a BOQ in a place called Terminal Island—it's an island in Los Angeles Harbor. He couldn't say much about his conversation with President Roosevelt because it was off the record. But the president was anxious to find out about *Bismarck* and the engagement.''

Brenda nodded. "Yes. That's what he told me in his letters. He's very thrilled. He's a full lieutenant—promoted by his commander-in-chief personally.'' Her voice was filled with pride.

Randolph raised his glass. "To the little nipper. None of us could ever imagine this when we were changing his diapers and feeding him strained vegetables.''

They touched glasses and drank. Travers refilled all around.

"He's on his way to Pearl Harbor,'' Brenda said.

"I know. I saw him off just the day before I left. He was finally berthed aboard an army transport in Long Beach Harbor. Should be in Hawaii in a week or so.''

Brenda drank and placed her glass on the low oak table fronting the sofa. "Did you meet Kay Stockard? Rodney was very fond of her. For a while, I thought they would marry. She's a fine, talented girl.''

Randolph took a deep drink and squirmed uncomfortably. "He saw her.''

"And that's all?''

Randolph stared at his glass. "I really don't know. Rodney said very little and gentlemen don't ask other gentlemen about those things.''

Hamilton Babcock jumped in. "You mean women would?'' He sneered over his glass.

Randolph regarded him with glacial coldness. "If the answer to that is *yes*, then you would.''

Hamilton grunted as if struck, eyes bulging, face flushed like a man suffering from apoplexy. "See here . . .'' he sputtered.

"Please, you two,'' Brenda pleaded.

Hamilton rose. "Got to leave.''

"You don't, really,'' Brenda said.

Hamilton emptied his glass and tabled it. "Got to meet

two of my engineers. Electronics problems." He whirled on his heel and left without a word to Randolph.

"Sorry and all that, Brenda," Randolph said. "I fouled things up for you."

Brenda sighed. "Hamilton was thoughtless." She sipped her wine. "He's really a fine person, Randolph."

"But jealous."

Brenda smiled. "I'm afraid so."

"Do you love him?"

"I don't know."

"Will you marry him?"

"No."

"Will you ever marry?"

Brenda's smile revealed her perfect white teeth like polished ivory. "You're a fine one to be asking that."

"Touché!" Randolph said.

Travers refilled the glasses and Brenda dismissed him. Before the butler left, he placed a silver tray with the liquor on the oak table in front of the pair.

After the butler closed the door, Brenda moved closer and Randolph could feel her hip against his. The old yearning began to build.

"Have you found anyone, Randolph?"

"You mean love?"

"Yes."

"I'm not sure."

"Oh!" she said with surprise, arching an eyebrow. "Do you mean you're not sure of knowing what love is or you don't care to marry?"

"Perhaps both. But I know a young girl. She's—ah, very unusual. Elisa Blue. I told you I was shot down. Well, a German fighter dumped me into her garden. She took me in—made me happy for a few moments."

Brenda smiled knowingly. "Happy? I understand."

"No, Brenda. You don't understand. It's not what you think. She's different. She doesn't belong in that world— that world of killing, of slaughter." He stared into her eyes and his eyes were cold. "England is not what you remember, Brenda. Will never be the same again."

"You want to marry her?"

Randolph shook his head and his face hardened. "I learned long ago, when there's a war, there is no future, Brenda. I couldn't do that to any woman."

Brenda sighed. There seemed to be relief in the sound as if she had been freed of a great worry. Her words contradicted her attitude. " 'There's only one happiness in life, to love and be loved.' "

"That's a quote."

"George Sand, Randolph. She knew what she was talking about." She drank, held her glass up, and studied the rich liquid. "Take what's offered, Randolph, and make no demands on the future."

"Who are you quoting now?"

"Brenda Hargreaves."

"My favorite poet," he said, grinning broadly. He touched her glass with his and they both drank.

She stared at him over the rim of her glass. "War or not, you need a wife, dear brother-in-law."

"And you a husband, dear sister-in-law."

"*Touché*, yourself, fighter pilot," she chided. They both laughed.

"Your son, Nathan, joined the Marine Corps?"

"Yes. He's in Camp Pendelton, California, completing his training."

"Does he like it?"

"He doesn't complain except they cut his hair right down to the scalp." Randolph grinned and nodded.

A troubled look clouded her eyes, straightened her lips. She turned her glass, examining it like a collector mulling a purchase. He caught her sudden mood change, remained silent. She finally spoke and took him by surprise, "You love your brother?"

"Of course. Lloyd and I are very close. You know that."

She snickered bitterly, drank. "And my sons would kill each other."

"Kill?"

"Rodney and Nathan." She told him of the terrible fight.

He tugged at his ear, sipped his Scotch. "Those things can happen between brothers."

"They hate each other."

For a long moment he knuckled his forehead and stared down at the plush Oriental rug under his feet. He spoke slowly and deliberately, "Brenda, love and hate are two sides of the same coin."

"I know."

"I don't think you do. They live in our heart side by side, one always ready to overwhelm the other. Just think, Brenda, husbands and wives have been killing each other as long as there's been an institution of marriage."

"Then you really believe there's still love between them?"

"Quite right. As intense as the hatred that shocked you so. And it'll break through. Mark me. Especially now that they face a common enemy—a common peril."

"War is a hell of a way to solve a family problem."

"I'm sorry, Brenda, but I know Lloyd and I have never been so close." He wanted to tell her how he was driven by the prospect of death ending it for one or both, but dared not. He could only say, "They'll find their love again, Brenda."

Sighing, she poured more wine and added to Randolph's drink. He knew it was time to move on. He hesitated, drummed the table, and spoke reluctantly, "And Regina?"

She turned her lips under and took a deep drink. "Oh, Randolph. We still haven't heard a word. No mail seems to be going in or out of Warsaw. There have been terrible rumors—I'm so worried."

He slipped an arm around her. "Rumors. That's all they are. I've fought the Hun in two wars and I hate him. But he always observed the Geneva Conventions." Coop Hansen's butchered body came back, but he let the lie stand.

"But the rumors of atrocities?"

"Just that. Unverified stories. Why Hitler wouldn't dare. He'd be daft to—ah . . ."

She finished the sentence. "Kill Jews—exterminate."

There was shock in Randolph's voice. "Good Lord, no, I say! Not even Hitler can ignore world opinion. Why, he'd lose his allies—the lot."

She kissed his cheek. "You make sense, Randolph. I do so hope you're right."

"You jolly well know I'm right." He remembered the horror on the faces of his Polish pilots when they told him of the letters that had been smuggled from their homeland. But not a hint of the misgivings he felt showed on his face.

Tactfully, he changed the subject. "Your sister Betty has a son?"

Brenda welcomed the change, brightening. "Anthony Borelli. He's just been commissioned an ensign. He grew up in Los Angeles, you know. Went to college there. I have never seen much of him."

"Dash it all. I could have looked him up."

Brenda laughed. "Not really. He's at Treasure Island in San Francisco awaiting a ship."

She finished her wine and reached for the cut-glass decanter. She filled her glass and poured more Scotch into Randolph's. "I expected you back much sooner, Randolph."

Randolph sipped the strong liquor and began to enjoy the spreading warmth. "We had problems."

"With that North American fighter?"

He nodded. "The P-Fifty-one, Mark One. For some reason, the prototype I tested was a little heavy in the controls."

"You flew out of Burbank?"

He shook his head. "Do you know Southern California very well?"

"I've spent vacations there."

"I flew mostly out of Clover Field in Santa Monica."

"Oh, yes, a small beach town near Los Angeles."

He nodded. "Also hopped over to March Field, Mines Field, Edwards."

"Took the grand tour."

He laughed. "Could say so. But we finally found the problem. Now she handles like my old S.E. Five. A real fighter. Your air force will build the Rolls on contract here. Your Packard Corporation is already producing the engine." He licked his lips. "Love to have a squadron of them."

She drummed the table. "I thought you were going to test-fly a fighter out here—ah, that plane built out on Long Island."

"The Republic XP-Forty-seven. I'll fly one out of Mitchell tomorrow. One flight only, and . . ." He glanced around uneasily. "And I'll be gone the day after tomorrow."

She clutched his arm. "No. Not so soon." There was anguish in her voice.

He stared at his glass and his voice was heavy, "I'm sorry, Brenda."

She placed her drink on the table and put her chin on his shoulder. "Something is always taking you out of my life, dear Randolph."

He felt her breast against his arm. He dared not look at her. He spoke to his glass. "It isn't cricket, is it, Brenda?"

"I want you to stay tonight."

He turned to her, startled. He remembered long ago after he had been badly burned in a crash in no-man's-land. He had considered his scarred body as hideous as that of a lizard. Brenda had offered herself to him. But it had been done in pity, a woman's way of convincing him he was still an attractive man. He had turned her down ruthlessly. The scars had faded, but not the memory. From that day on, he had had his regrets, too. He still desired her—always would.

"There are two other chaps in my delegation, Brenda," he said, controlling his voice with difficulty. "We have rooms at the Waldorf. I'm their superior officer. It wouldn't do for me to stay away all night while they observe a ten-o'clock curfew I've ordered."

She spoke, her lips only inches from his. Her great blue eyes were misty. "Do you remember when I first met you? You asked me to meet you in Trafalgar Square."

His expression was grim. A memory as vivid as yesterday flashing like a cinema in his mind. "On the stairwell. We met on the landing. I—I told you about my digs in Kensington." He turned away. "It was beastly of me. I was a randy cad trying to take my brother's wife to bed."

Her smile had the dust of years of longing on it. "You almost succeeded, Randolph. You should have been just a little more persistent. Oh, you were a glorious young man."

Randolph drained his glass. "I must have been off my wick. My brother Geoffry with only a few months to live and I . . ."

"Please, Randolph. We can't condemn ourselves for being human. After all, we never betrayed anyone—ever." She ran her fingers over the back of his neck. They left tingling trails as if they were charged with electricity. "And after you were burned, I did go to your flat in Kensington and . . ."

"And you offered me charity."

Her eyes flared and she moved away. "It wasn't charity."

"Then what was it?"

"My expression of my love for you."

"You didn't love me that way—not romantically, not like a lover."

"I did then. And you told me you loved me." The blue of her eyes was heightened by moisture. "You needed me, I know. But there was one thing you overlooked, Randolph."

"What was that?"

"My need for you."

He stared and she riveted her eyes to his. Unconsciously, his arm circled her narrow shoulders. She kissed his neck, his cheek, and, finally, his lips. The tip of her tongue circled his lips and darted into his mouth like a wet, hot serpent. It found his, slithering, dueling with a tip of fire. The kiss struck him like a powerful aphrodisiac, fanning a hunger in his guts and causing a burning ache in his loins. Gasping, she broke the kiss. "Please stay with me, Randolph. While this world goes insane, let's have our one night together. We owe it to ourselves."

Gripping both of her shoulders, he leaned back. He saw Elisa Blue and then Brenda's eyes and the consuming heat eroded his doubts, all conscious thoughts from his mind except Elisa. Then she, too, began to fade. Brenda stood and took his hands. He let her pull him to his feet and lead him to the stairway. Following her, he marveled at the tiny waist, the full hips, and the sinuous walk. She was still like a young girl and he knew she would be in every way. The heat rose and seemed to engulf his being. He had loved her for so long. Had wanted that maddening body next to his. For years he had dreamed of her, fantasized about her in his bunk, on lonely patrols. Had discarded scores of women because none could be Brenda—none came close to Brenda.

Silently, they began to mount the stairs, yet Elisa Blue would not be banished. The face was brilliant, smile sad, so innocent and filled with love it deserved a halo. The strength of the memory struck with physical force. He stopped in midstride. He slipped his hand from Brenda's.

"What's wrong?" she asked in confusion.

"Don't rightly know." He sighed. "But I do know this isn't right. It has always been wrong for us and still is."

She took his hand again and moved very close. He could smell her perfume and the blue eyes engulfed him like the sea and the lips like rose petals were very close and parted. Her intuition and incisive intelligence startled him again as it had for all the years he had known her. "It's the girl, Elisa Blue, isn't it?"

He looked away. "Yes. She follows me."

"She's here?"

"Yes. Everywhere. I'm sorry."

She was so close, the hard nipples of her breasts pressed against his chest. "It would be a betrayal?"

"I don't know."

"Then you must love her. Follow your conscience, dear Randolph."

Randolph stared into the blue depths. He felt lost. A rudderless plane in a strong wind. The will was slipping and he cursed his weakness. She took both of his hands. For a long time he remained motionless. Finally, he said, "Brenda. My conscience tells me to have another drink."

He took her hand and they walked back into the sitting room.

IX

WHEN Randolph leapt from the cab carrying his single canvas duffel bag, Lloyd met him at Fenwyck's great doors. He embraced him with one arm. The other was strapped to his side, which was heavily taped. "Million-dollar wound," Lloyd quipped, quoting a phrase popularized in the trenches during the Great War.

Lloyd's appearance was shocking. He looked even more desert worn than before. The arid wind and fierce desert sun seemed to have burned off the last of his flesh, leaving only desiccated skin stretched over his bones. The skin of his face had been darkened as if stained by walnut. It was scored and riven with new lines of pain and worry. The entire visage was that of complete exhaustion. It was emphasized by the bloodshot eyes sunken deep into dark eye sockets like craggy hollows, underscored with bruised purple smudges. Randolph had heard that the dehydration of the desert could preserve corpses like tanned leather. With a start, he realized his brother's appearance reminded him of Egyptian mummies he had seen as a boy at the London Museum. But the toughness was still there like finely tempered steel—a resiliency that could give but never break.

Close behind was Bernice. She held Randolph close and kissed him. "My brother-in-law. My beautiful brother-in-law. You're back safe."

Randolph chuckled into her ear. "Why quite so, Bernice. It was only a short hop over the pond."

"Uncle! Uncle Randolph!" came from the huge entry hall. In a moment, Trevor and Bonnie surrounded him. Bonnie in his arms kissing him, Trevor pounding his back with unabashed joy.

Randolph had forgotten how beautiful Bonnie was. Her features were as delicate as fine porcelain, white skin glowing with good health. She had all of Bernice's beauty when she had been a young girl courted by Lloyd, but exuded boundless energy Bernice had never known. Her black hair shimmered and reflected the sun like newly mined coal, hazel eyes kindled by excitement. She was with her uncle. She worshipped him. It was obvious.

Trevor had put on weight. As tall as his father, he appeared beefy in comparison. His thick reddish brown hair was brushed back from a wide, unlined forehead. His features were well formed and proud. He was every inch the navy officer from his black leather shoes to the double-breasted reefer with its stand-and-fall collar, two rows of eight gilt-metal buttons. The two gold lace rings and narrow half stripe of lieutenant commander decorated his cuffs and shoulder straps. He was over thirty years old and an experienced naval officer, yet, to Randolph, he still had an air of boyish vulnerability about him.

"You've done well, nephew," Randolph said, shaking Trevor's hand vigorously while Bonnie and Bernice fought to hold his other hand. "Did you get your destroyer?"

"Yes, Uncle. Finally off the beach. Got the *Terrier*. She lost her bow to a mine off Norway, but Swan Hunter has completed repairs. She's berthed at Portsmouth and ready for sea."

Randolph glanced at the stripes. "You've added a half stripe."

"Quite right, Uncle. I'm her new number one (executive officer). I'm due aboard by seventeen hundred hours."

Randolph slapped Trevor on the back. "Bully for you, nephew."

"Thank you, sir."

Dorset met him with his usual grave demeanor. But, as usual, the moisture in his eyes gave him away. "Welcome home, sir," the old man said.

"Always good to see you, Dorset," Randolph said. He gripped the old butler's shoulders briefly.

Lloyd said, "Let's have a tot, brother." He gestured. "The library."

"Right-oh, brother," Randolph said. "Stand you a Scotch." Everyone laughed.

Stepping into the entry, he shook Chef Andre Demozay's hand and nodded as Bernice's personal maid, Emily Burns, curtsied. The woman's face was as blank as the face of Buddha. Within minutes, the family was seated in the library and Lloyd was pouring drinks from the crystal decanters on the Regency sideboard. He handed Randolph and Trevor Scotch, the women wine, and sank behind the massive serpentine writing desk stiffly and slowly like an old man. He clutched his own double Scotch. Carefully, he freed his bound arm, lit a Lucky Strike, and exhaled a huge cloud of smoke. Randolph sat on the couch flanked by Bonnie and Bernice. Trevor took a large leather chair to one side of the desk.

"To HMS *Terrier* and her new number one," Randolph said, holding his glass high.

"Hear! Hear!" everyone shouted. They drank.

Randolph asked Bonnie about Blake Boggs. "He's in the army, you know. He's a lieutenant with the Forty-first North Midland Rifles."

"Do they have any equipment?"

She shook her head. "Lost most of it at Dunkirk. But they're being reequipped and they are at full strength."

"Will you marry him?"

She blushed. "I don't know, Uncle—I really don't know."

Trevor downed his drink and rose. "Got to be leaving, Uncle Randolph," he said, gesturing at the regal Carlin long-cased clock. "The number one can't afford to be over leave. Terrible example and all that."

Bonnie came to her feet, explaining she had the evening duty at the Chatham Naval Hospital. She kissed Randolph while Trevor pumped his hand. The young people mumbled a few words softly to their parents and took their leave.

The door had hardly closed when Randolph said, "Dash it all, Boggs isn't worthy of her." Smiling, Lloyd and Bernice exchanged a glance. "I'll wager four bob he'll botch the whole thing the first time the Midlands go into action."

"Don't be too harsh on the lad, Randolph," Bernice said, standing. "After all, you only met him once."

"Once was enough."

She spoke to her husband. "I've told Crag Watson I'd meet him in the hothouse. He needs help with the orchids."

Lloyd said to Randolph, "Watson's the best grounds man in Kent and you know he's an absolute magician with orchids. We should win the East Ashford Flower Show this year. We have a Cattleya and a Miltonia in full bloom, by Jove."

"I say, you've lost me, brother."

Bernice interrupted, "You know orchids are tropical. And these species grow only in Central America and Brazil. It's like a miracle." She left.

"War be damned, we'll always have our flower shows, brother," Lloyd said, holding his glass high, knuckles like knobby raised roots.

"You're bloody well right, brother," Randolph agreed. "Someday we'll stick a bouquet of bluebells up Hitler's arse." The brothers emptied their glasses and Lloyd refilled them. He sank back and smoked thoughtfully for a moment.

He asked about Randolph's trip, the new American fighters, America and American attitudes, and Brenda and her family.

Randolph talked of Brenda and her family, but did not even hint at the passion of their last few moments together. However, he felt his face warm as he talked with just the thought of her. He noticed Lloyd studying his glass with unnatural intensity as if he had found a chip on the lip and was pondering the jagged edges. Randolph felt that damnable sixth sense that seemed to tune into his thoughts, especially his guilts, like a WT to his brother's consciousness. *Lloyd suspected. No, Lloyd knew.* The flyer's thoughts became confused, words garbled. He took a deep drink.

Quickly Randolph assembled his thoughts and switched to America's amazing industrial potential and the strong antiwar sentiment evident in her papers and on the wireless. Lloyd nodded gravely. There was bitterness in his voice, "Lend-Lease, the 'Arsenal of Democracy,' the whole lot. But Englishmen must still do their dying for them, Randolph. Just like we did in the first one."

Randolph took a mouthful of liquor, swirled it around his gums and through his teeth before swallowing it, enjoying the strong burnt taste and relaxing slightly with the impact of the strong liquor. "They've lost some men. After all, they're escorting convoys."

"They should have been at Bir Fuad Ridge."

"What about Bir Fuad Ridge?"

Lloyd described the battle, the horror of losing most of his brigade that he was convinced was used as bait. He condemned General Sir Alan Cunningham's tactics bitterly. He said nothing of the German prisoners he had killed and the investigation he suspected was under way. "You don't throw away good men like that," he added. "An army's spirit can be broken by those bloody, expensive victories. Pyrrhus learned that lesson over two thousand years ago against the Romans. We British haven't learned it in two world wars." He drank, puffed on his Lucky Strike, and fell silent. He poured Scotch into his glass for the third time.

"But Cunningham's been sacked, and the Eighth Army's on the move."

Lloyd's demeanor brightened. "Right, Randolph, Auchinleck replaced that dolt Cunningham with a good officer, Neil Ritchie. We've taken Sidi Rezegh and soon Tobruk will be relieved. The bloody bastards are on the run." His face clouded again. "But Rommel'll be back again. It's been like a bloody tennis match—back and forth, back and forth." He moved his head as if he were watching an imaginary game at Wimbledon. Tiring quickly, he sagged back into his chair and gulped half the contents of his glass.

"You need a rest, brother," Randolph said.

"You sound like my wife."

"You have three broken ribs. You can't go into action with broken ribs. And most men retire from business at your age, let alone from war."

"Quite so. But my ribs are almost mended and look." He waved both arms over his head. "A man with shattered ribs can't do that."

"You're aching to go back."

"Aren't you?"

"I'm not injured."

"You report to your squadron tomorrow, don't you, Randolph?"

"Quite right."

Lloyd went on the attack. "You still have something to settle, brother?"

"Kochling. Yes. He's a murderer."

Lloyd sighed. Drew on the Lucky Strike and began his fourth double. "Some people would say the same about me."

Randolph came erect, eyes wide with shock. "What do you mean?"

Lloyd told him of Private Touhy Murphy's tragic death and the killing of the prisoners at Bir Fuad Ridge.

"But you were justified, Lloyd," Randolph protested.

"They surrendered and murdered your man." He was interrupted by Dorset who knocked politely and then entered. "An officer to see you, sir," he said to Lloyd. "Brigadier General Gilbert Fraser, sir."

"Fraser? Fraser?" Lloyd said to himself meditatively, staring at the smoke hugging the ceiling. He turned to Randolph. "A 'Pommy' bastard and equal to my rank. Something's up. I'll lay my bit you'll find out about Bir Fuad, straightaway." He gestured to Dorset. "Show him in."

Brigadier Gilbert Fraser entered. In his late fifties, he was a stocky little man with narrow, baleful eyes tilted up at the corners like those of a hawk. Sparse brown hair shot through with gray crowned a high domed forehead and a beaked nose that added to his birdlike aspect. The flesh of his face was as pallid as a gravestone. He wore all the accoutrements of the staff officer: meticulously tailored uniform, glistening Sam Browne belt, black leather of his shoes burnished like mirrors, even a polished blackthorn swagger stick with a silver band was tucked under his arm. Randolph could smell the Kiwi polish even through the tobacco smoke. Both Lloyd and Randolph stared at the newcomer with the suspicion and distrust all front-line soldiers carry for "staff."

Fraser walked to a point directly in front of Lloyd's desk and stood rigidly, swagger stick tucked smartly under his right arm. "Brigadier Gilbert Fraser, here," he said in a high, brittle voice. "I'm a member of General Archer's staff—Intelligence."

"I know. We met at Whitehall at a briefing in 'thirty-nine," Lloyd said. He gestured to Randolph. "My brother, Major Randolph Higgins, commanding officer of Number Fifty-four Squadron."

Randolph rose. The general nodded stiffly, but did not extend his hand. "I've heard of you," Fraser said matter-of-factly. He gestured to the door to a young captain who had entered so quietly, Randolph had not even noticed him. "Captain Nigel Davenport, my aide," Fraser said. All spit and polish like the general, the young officer stared at the brothers. He was obviously ill at ease and Randolph knew something distasteful was afoot. Everyone ignored the captain and Randolph sat.

Lloyd did not offer a drink or a chair to Fraser. In fact, he glared up at him with unabashed hostility. Randolph knew his brother hated "staff" almost as much as he hated the Germans. "Bloody dugout queens," he had called them back in '17. He had never changed. If anything, the hatred had intensified.

"My mission is distressing, even more so because of your wounds, Brigadier Higgins," Fraser said with forced concern.

Lloyd sneered. "Don't let my wounds upset you, old boy. Front-line troops are often wounded. Daresay, sometimes killed. You should catch the show, sometime. Jolly good fun."

Randolph sniggered and sipped his drink, never taking his eyes from Fraser.

Fraser glared down at Lloyd, face a map of rage. The gleam in his eyes was that of a hawk about to pounce. "We can dispense with your sarcasm. I'm here to inform you we have eyewitnesses to your execution of five prisoners of war, Brigadier Higgins."

Lloyd snapped back, "Do you have eyewitnesses to the execution of my brigade? Of my loader Private Touhy Murphy? Is Cunningham on the dock for his stupid tactics?"

"I know nothing of General Cunningham's tactics and would not pass judgment on them if I did. As for Private Touhy Murphy, I have nothing in my report concerning him."

"Ask his parents. They got the letter from the Crown."

"I regret your losses. But we can't tolerate the killing of helpless prisoners. We are gentlemen who observe the Geneva Conventions."

Lloyd hunched forward and stabbed his cigarette at Fraser as he spoke, "Understand this, General, I have always observed the Conventions. But when one of your men is murdered while giving aid to a wounded enemy, it is time to act.''

''Not like a savage, General.''

The blush came through Lloyd's sun-darkened skin. The deep-set eyes seemed to bulge from the hollows like polished gemstones. He half rose. His voice seemed to rumble up out of his throat, ''See here, you uppish gamecock. Mind your tongue or I'll cut it out and stuff it up your arse.'' And then sarcastically, ''Just think, you could get the DSO for being wounded in 'inaction.' ''

Fraser rocked as if he had been hit by a board. ''I bloody well won't take that,'' he snarled. ''There'll be a hearing in a fortnight. You'll receive official notice by courier.'' He whirled on his heel and left, Davenport trailing like a trained dog.

''Bloody dugout queens!'' Lloyd shouted after them.

A silence so sweet it reminded Randolph of the stillness following a battle filled the room. He rose and refilled his glass. Sinking back into the soft folds of the sofa, he stared at his brother who smoked and drank with fury in his eyes. ''You think I botched it,'' Lloyd said.

''On the contrary, you were superb, brother.''

''Put the stupid sod in his place?''

''Quite right. Never saw it done so delicately and discreetly.''

Lloyd's uproarious laughter exhaled a cloud of smoke. And then seriously, ''They'll have me on the dock, Randolph.''

The flyer shook his head. ''Can't afford to lose experienced officers. Especially in desert warfare. They'll sneak some meaningless reprimand into your record to satisfy staff and the Swiss Red Cross and ship you off to Egypt. Mark me.''

Lloyd arched an eyebrow and the harsh lines of concern softened. ''You really believe that?''

''Quite so, brother. And don't forget, Allanbrooke is Bernice's cousin. They wouldn't dare tamper with either of us.''

Lloyd sighed and sank back. ''Got to get back. The lads need me. Now we'll have a lot of replacements . . .''

"I know, I know," Randolph interrupted. "I've been trying to keep new chums alive for two wars, too."

Randolph glanced at the clock and fidgeted restlessly. A terrible emptiness had been gnawing at his guts from the moment he had arrived in England. Again, Lloyd startled him. "You miss the girl?"

"You mean Elisa Blue?"

"Quite. Do you intend to see her again?"

Randolph nodded and shifted his eyes away from his brother's face. "Yes. I intend to leave in a few minutes."

"Don't remain on my account, brother," Lloyd said. "Have you rung her up?"

"She doesn't have a telephone."

"Then you'll surprise her?"

Randolph smiled enigmatically. "I don't believe anything could ever surprise Elisa Blue." He rose and walked from the room while Lloyd smiled behind him.

She was standing by the door when Randolph turned the Jaguar from the dirt road and parked. She was dressed in a filmy green frock pulled in at her tiny waist by a black patent-leather belt. Her marvelous hair was pulled back and held in place by a yellow silk ribbon. She was smiling, her entire being appearing to light up with some inner illumination as her eyes clung to him. Again, Randolph was struck by the way sunbeams seemed to be attracted to her. They played in her hair, turning it into a glossy cap that changed color from the burnished iridescence of platinum to the rich glow of polished gold. She was stunning. Breathtaking.

He took both of her hands and stared down into her eyes that were as blue as the deepest part of the Atlantic on a summer's day. "I was expecting you, my major," she said.

He took her into his arms and she reached up eagerly for his lips, her soft body becoming malleable, shaping itself to his so that he could feel her against him from thighs, to hips, to small hard breasts. Her lips were parted and hungry but the urgent demand of Brenda's kiss—and for that matter, the other women he had known—was not there. Instead, he found the sweet longing for a beloved realized at last. He kissed her cheeks, her forehead, her temple, her hair. Finally, he whispered, "You knew I was back?"

"Yes." She stepped back but kept his hands captured in hers, eyes searching his face as if they had experienced a starvation of their own.

"How?"

"I knew." She gestured to the door. "Some peach wine, Major?" He followed her into the cottage.

It was a rioting with color. There were the bluebells, lilacs, daisies, heliotrope, and ferns he remembered. But a new exquisitely delicate bloom stood majestically in a corner. He waved at it as he seated himself on the couch.

"It's an orchid," she said. "You brought me a half dozen when you were on your last leave. I wanted my own. They remind me of you."

He ran a hand over her cheek and through her hair. "But they only grow in the tropics or in hothouses under constant care."

"I keep it in the shade and move it to my little greenhouse when it's warm. I've been very lucky." She disappeared into the kitchen and returned with a bottle and two glasses. Seating herself close to him, she filled the glasses with the deep yellow wine. She touched his glass with hers and caught his eyes. "To peace, when love tunes the shepherd's reed," she said. He was sure the verse was part of a couplet but he could not place it. They drank.

"That's Byron," he hazarded.

She kissed him and he tasted her laugh as refreshing as raindrops. "Scott," she said. "And I corrupted the poor fellow."

"There's more."

She averted her eyes. "I can't remember the rest." Quickly she asked him about his trip. He told her of America, the planes he flew, and the long journey home. He said nothing of Brenda and her family.

"You return to your squadron soon?"

"Tomorrow."

She bit her lip. "Duty. It's your white whale. It takes all of you. And you'll be gone again."

He sipped his wine and studied the golden liquid and the reflected light from the rounded glass. He spoke thoughtfully, "You're right, Elisa. A man can travel to the ends of the earth, to every byway, to the end of his days, but nowhere can he lay down his duty, shed his past, and walk away from it. That's how I am—will always be."

"I don't understand—can't understand. It's not right, it's against life. All I know is that I've missed you so—so very much, my major."

"My field is near Detling. It's actually only minutes away by Spitfire." He kissed her and she kissed him back fiercely. He spoke into her ear, "I'll buzz by, if I get a chance. Give you a personal wave from the RAF. Would you like that?"

She reared back. "You'd risk your life to wave at me?"

He threw his head back and laughed. "Not at all, Elisa. Safer than driving my Jag on some of these beastly Kentish roadways."

"Fenwyck is only an hour from here."

"Quite right."

"Will I see you when you're home on leave?"

"Every time."

She kissed him again. This time her mouth was open, warm, and wet. "I love you, my major," she said breathlessly. "Stay with me. We'll walk in the forest, I'll pick flowers for you, we'll soak our feet in the brook, plant, reap what we have sown. We'll dedicate ourselves to life instead of . . ." She caught herself, stopped in midsentence, her hand to her mouth.

"Instead of death, Elisa?"

"Yes. Instead of death."

He turned away. "I'm sorry, my darling. You know . . . ."

She interrupted him, "I know it's impossible." There was utter defeat in her voice. She clutched his arms with hands like claws. "I love you. I can't bear the thought of losing you." She stabbed a finger upward. "I told you before, the sky will take you from me. I know it! I know it!" She began to sob bitterly on his shoulder.

He stroked her hair, kissed her forehead, the salty tears streaking her cheeks. "Please don't, my darling," he soothed.

The sobs abated and she looked up into his eyes. "I'm your darling?"

"Yes."

She dabbed at her cheeks with a dainty lace handkerchief. "Do you love me?"

He cupped her face with his big hands and searched her eyes with his. "I don't know. I'm twice your age, and I have known, ah . . ."

"You've known a lot of women."

"Yes. Many."

"And loved none?"

He turned to the table and refilled his glass. Drank. "Perhaps one."

"Where is she?"

"Far from here." He stared at a fern on the far windowsill.

"Why didn't you marry her?"

He sipped his wine. "Because it wasn't right. In fact, it would have been dishonorable." He expected her to probe further, to ask about lovemaking, bedrooms. Most women would. She took him by surprise.

"Then you've known love," she said with relief in her voice. "They haven't destroyed you." Her hands found the back of his head and she stared into his eyes. "If you've loved once, you can love again." She kissed him and pulled him down on the sofa. He ran his hands through her hair, tasting the sweetness of her mouth. Sighing and moaning she pulled him down on her until his body covered hers. "Remember the last time," she gasped through his kisses. "I had you to myself—all of you. Completely."

"How could I forget. It's haunted me."

She laughed happily and gently pushed against his chest. Then she rose slowly and the strength and promise of the look in her eyes brought him to his feet like a magnet. She took his hand and led him to the curtained doorway.

When he left, it was dark. As he shifted into second gear, he glanced back and saw her standing in the doorway. A penumbra of light from a lamp behind her filtered through her hair and surrounded her head with a diffused golden glow. It was a terrible, wrenching feeling of parting he had never known before. He could still feel the hot warmth of her flesh, and the perfume of her hair still lingered. Then a thought struck him. It was the poem by Sir Walter Scott she had quoted. The entire couplet came back: "*In peace love tunes the shepherd's reed, but in war, he mounts the warrior's steed.*"

X

December 7, 1941

LIEUTENANT Rodney Higgins stretched his big bulk uncomfortably in the meager confines of his bunk on the battleship *Arizona*. In the eerie gloaming between sleep and wakefulness, he squinted through one partially open eye at the brass clock mounted on the bulkhead. It showed 0545 hours. His subconscious told his conscious mind to sleep; he still had two hours before he was due to relieve the quarterdeck watch. However, twisted by the lingering effects of too much alcohol and prodded by troubling thoughts, images flashed from the subconscious to interrupt his craving for more sleep.

It had been a wild party. At the Royal Hawaiian Hotel. His roommate, Lieutenant Donald "Stud Horse" Colburn, had rented a suite after meeting a young secretary named Katherine Newby at the submarine base. She had brought three of her young friends along for the party. Two ensigns from Rodney's fire-control section, Dick Jordan and Paul Stolz, leapt at the chance to attend. "We can take care of those broads, Mr. Higgins," Stolz had said. "Just you wait and see. I'll make a pussycat out of ol' Stud Horse."

With one table ladened with liquor, mixers, pretzels, and crackers, and with a record player blaring Tommy Dorsey, Kay Kyser, Duke Ellington, Benny Goodman, and Glenn Miller, the party had become instant bedlam. Rodney had paired off with a slender blond named Joyce Brockman while Dick Jordan and Paul Stolz became immediately enamored with Christine and Sylvia—Rodney never did learn their last names. There was jitterbugging on the floor, on the tables, in the kitchen, and eventually in the two bedrooms.

Joyce Brockman vaguely reminded Rodney of Kay Stockard. Her hair was blond, but her eyes were hazel and set too far apart and her features were sharp instead of soft. But her tight satin dress emphasized her slender hips, small waist, and large breasts. She was very sexy and was quite aware of it. She drank her whiskey with Coke and after two drinks her dancing became so close Rodney's arousal became an embarrassment. However, all four couples were dancing close, arms wrapped around each other, a mating ritual more than a dance. After his fourth drink, Rodney felt everything slip away except the feel of the slim body pressed to his. "Nothing but foreplay," Stud Horse had smirked into Rodney's ear.

As midnight approached, Colburn slipped into one bedroom with Katherine while Paul Stolz and Sylvia rushed into the other. Watching the doors close, Joyce whispered into Rodney's ear, "Let's get out of here. They'll be in there all night."

"We can wait," Rodney said.

"I can't." She took him by the hand and pulled him to the door.

They hurried through the lush gardens down to the beach where the surf crashed under a bright moon shining in a clear sky. The star-studded skies held that spectacular kind of beauty one can only find in Hawaii. Rodney spread his tunic on the sand in a spot sheltered by an outcropping of rock. They made love. It had been so violent, so devoid of emotions except for the hunger for release, the young lieutenant had felt like a rutting animal. Joyce clawed, whimpered, and finally shrieked so loud a SP came running.

"Nothing at all. Nothing at all," Rodney managed, coming to his feet and pulling up his trousers. "Sat on a rock. That's all." Joyce crammed her panties into her purse, stood, and straightened her dress.

The SP looked them both up and down and said, "I understand, sir." He saluted and left. Rodney could hear him chuckling.

Rodney had called a cab, escorted the girl back to her apartment in Waikiki, promised to phone, and left. He knew he would never dial that number.

His mind wandered through the shadows of half sleep and Kay Stockard was there again. He would never forget the last time he saw her. It was the night before he met his uncle Major Randolph Higgins at Clover Field in Santa Monica. He had decided to surprise her—could not wait for the delighted look on her face when she first saw him. He found her house on Franklin Avenue in Hollywood—the house actually owned by the designer Gertrude Foot.

He remembered entering the big airy frame house with the dark wood interior so loved by Californians. Gertrude Foot was big and burly with features fashioned by a hatchet and piercing eyes that glowed with latent malevolence. She looked to be about forty. She was dressed in slacks and a blouse that was more like a man's shirt than a woman's blouse. Kay, as lovely as ever with the folds of her long blond hair flowing almost to her waist, had taken both his hands in hers and kissed him on the cheek. She avoided the full mouth kiss and he did not seek it. She was obviously disquieted, perhaps embarrassed. Her cheeks were the color of sunset when she asked him to have a drink.

He took a chair facing a couch where Kay and Gertrude sat. He and Kay had talked of New York, family, friends while Gertrude glowered. There was a challenge in Gertrude's eyes, and possessiveness dwelled there, too. Kay asked about his duty, station, length of stay. Galled by growing discomfort, Rodney had answered quickly and excused himself early, promising to phone. Then he left, and although he was to remain at the BOQ on Terminal Island for three more weeks, he never phoned Kay. He could never forget the picture of the two women in the doorway as he left; Kay standing in the porch light with a tortured, defeated look on her face, Gertrude close behind with her hands on the girl's shoulders, grinning triumphantly. He had heard the price of success in Hollywood could come high, but the amount Kay was paying was exorbitant.

He wondered about himself and women. Certainly, his cousin Marsha had left him with a self-loathing that had endured. Then, Kay, a stunning woman who he had truly loved. He had heard of women who loved women, but it had seemed like a disease that struck others in a distant country. He knew there were men who preferred other men to women. In fact, he had punched one in a Manhattan bar after the creature had patted him obscenely. But to lose Kay to another woman was not only the loss of a beloved, but a blow to his manhood, an insult beyond measure. Clearly, she had enjoyed him in bed. Then where had he failed?

He had wanted Joyce Brockman and had made love to her fiercely. No. With Joyce it had been a coupling. A frantic hunger for release that had left him weak, drained, but strangely unsatisfied. There had been no attachment to the girl. He was convinced he was incapable of love. Craved release, true. Why not just find a whore and be done with it? No complications. A lot of his shipmates found it that way. Maybe they knew something he didn't know.

He turned in his bunk and an ache just behind his eyes began to exact its toll for the excesses of the previous night. The eyelid fluttered open and he found the clock. It was only 0630 hours and the big lieutenant rolled away from the light streaming in from the room's single porthole. The pain diminished. His mother was back and then his Uncle Randolph.

They loved each other. He was sure of it. Yet, they seemed to hold each other at arm's length.

He had watched his uncle put the new North American Mustang fighter through its paces. Flying out over the sea, Randolph had climbed until he became a speck in the vast vault of the sky—even in Rodney's seven-ten binoculars. Then the screaming power dive and pull-out low over Santa Monica Bay, the rolls, stalls, brutally sharp turns. When Randolph had landed, Rodney accused him of trying to tear off the fighter's wings.

"You're bloody well right, nephew," Randolph had said, laughing. "If you have a Messerschmitt on your arse, that's exactly what you've got to do."

With the dull throb banishing sleep, he laced his fingers behind his head and stared at the sagging springs of Colburn's bunk overhead. His mind wandered to his mother's letters. She wrote him at least three times a week and her last letter had been four pages long. His mind riffled through the pages. Uncle Lloyd's wounds were healed but he was still at home in Fenwyck on recuperation leave. He was involved in some sort of investigation into an incident in North Africa. Rodney knew his uncle was itching to return to action in North Africa where the Eighth Army's Operation Crusader had driven the enemy back into Libya. Uncle Randolph, too, was home and back in the air with Number 54 Squadron. But with the Germans bogged down in Russia in the grip of the coldest winter in 140 years, things had been relatively quiet over the Channel. But in some ways, Rodney knew his uncle better than his mother. Rodney was sure Randolph would take his Spitfires in over Occupied France and hunt the Germans down, if they refused to come to him. His grandmother was well, Aunt Betty in good health, and Marsha still attended Columbia. Marsha. The overheated bitch. He actually felt hatred for his cousin.

Nathan was still training at Camp Pendleton in California. Rodney had been surprised to read Nathan had actually been promoted to corporal. His cousin Anthony Borelli was an ensign and had been sent to Florida for small craft training. He would probably get one of those new submarine chasers. They were very small, wooden, and Brenda considered them very dangerous. "Not safe like that big battleship you're on," Brenda had written.

The saddest parts of all the letters were in his mother's anxious scribbles about Regina. Still no word from Warsaw. There had been horrifying rumors of mass killings and Brenda believed them all. Rodney would assure her in his letters that the rumors must be false. Atrocities could not be hidden from the International Red Cross. But he could never convince his mother.

Colburn's voice from the upper bunk interrupted his reveries. "Hey, mate, time to rise and shine. It's almost oh-seven-hundred." Rodney looked at the clock. He was amazed. Almost thirty minutes had slipped by unnoticed.

Colburn's long skinny legs dangled down from the upper bunk. With a shout of "Look out below!" the young officer dropped to the deck. He was dressed in white skivvies that were exact duplicates of those worn by Rodney. "Got to meet the gunnery officer in number two turret," Colburn said. "Number one rammer isn't working right. And I'm the turret captain. So when the shit hits the fan, you know who's in the middle of the breeze. That goddamned rammer has never worked right."

"You didn't have any trouble with your rammer last night, Stud Horse," Rodney said, coming erect in his bunk and rubbing the sleep from his eyes.

Chuckling, Colburn walked a few steps to the tiny head, switched on the light over the mirror, and reached for his shaving mug. "If the breech were a pussy and my dick was the rammer, that goddamned gun would be automatic. Yes, sir." Laughing, he rotated and shook his hips in a series of bumps and grinds. "Just like ol' dad, man. Just like ol' dad." And then, gesturing at Rodney, "You did all right yourself, Ol' Biz," Colburn said, stopping the dance and fixing his eyes on his reflection. Colburn had attached the sobriquet "The *Bismarck* Kid"—usually contracted to "Ol' Biz"—to Rodney the day they met. Every man in the crew knew of Rodney's presence on *King George V* during the engagement with *Bismarck*. Rodney did not find the notoriety unpleasant. In fact, he rather enjoyed basking in the limelight of being the only man on board who had been in a major engagement between capital ships.

Rodney was troubled with a sudden unsettling thought. "I thought you were going to move that black powder? There's a ton of it on the second deck. It belongs in the magazine, not on top of it," he said.

"Tell it to the gunnery officer, I just work here. Just another powder monkey, Ol' Biz. He says 'stack it,' we stack it. He had the whole turret crew piling the shit for two days." Colburn reached into a small cabinet above the sink and removed a shaving mug.

"It's against regs. Isn't it?"

"You're fuckin' A," Colburn said, whipping up a lather. "But it would take a fourteen-inch shell to set it off. So don't abandon ship yet, Ol' Biz. This old battlewagon'll still be here tomorrow."

Whipping lather on his face over a reddish stubble, Colburn leaned close to the mirror, staring at his reflection. Everything about him was red. His hair flamed like a forest fire, his brown eyes had a reddish tint as if they reflected the fire, and freckles were scattered across his nose and cheeks as if splattered by a careless painter's brush dipped in red paint. The tiny nose, slightly tilted eyes, pointed chin, and mischievous grin gave his face a subtle air of good humor like a pixie about to play a practical joke. And, indeed, he was a joker. He had played only one joke on Rodney.

Late one night, Rodney had returned on board after playing poker and drinking with a group of junior officers in the officers' club at the destroyer base. He found a condom filled with at least a quart of water under his sheets. Donald Colburn was snoring in his bunk. The snores were too loud. Rodney broke the condom over the turret captain's head. There were screams of protest, laughs, but no more jokes.

In the ten weeks the pair had shared the cabin, Rodney and Donald Colburn had become very close. Don's ready smile, quick wit, and boundless generosity made him easy to like. Under the jocularity, he had a deep respect for Rodney and never carried his kidding to the point of antagonizing his roommate. In front of senior officers and enlisted men, Lieutenant Donald Colburn was the model of decorum. It was always "Mr. Higgins," or "Lieutenant Higgins." Rodney considered him his best friend and felt he had known the young man for a lifetime.

The grating sound of a boatswain's pipe screeched from the bulkhead-mounted speaker. "Get your ass in gear," Rodney grumbled. "They just piped the forenoon watch to chow and I've got the oh-eight-hundred quarterdeck watch."

"Christ, I can hear. Don't get your balls in an uproar, ol' shipmate. Almost finished." And then with uncharacteristic seriousness, "Roosevelt's really cruising for a showdown with Adolph."

"What do you mean?"

"He scrapped the Neutrality Act, didn't he?"

Rodney felt anger begin to stir. He had managed to keep his interview with the president secret. He had even sworn his family to secrecy. He was determined the specter of presidential favoritism would not haunt his career. However, he could not help but feel an attachment to the president; empathy for a man faced with the greatest problems in the history of the world. And the brilliant Roosevelt seemed to be handling it despite sometimes violent opposition. "Congress did it, and they had no choice," Rodney said.

"We're going to be in the middle of this thing yet."

"So? What do you get paid for?"

Donald turned from the mirror. "Hey, man, cool it. It's no big deal." He turned back to the mirror. "Anyway, the Heinies are stopped outside Moscow. Hear they're freezing their asses off." And then thoughtfully, "But you know, those goddamned Nips have a wild hair up their ass."

Rodney nodded. Washington had issued three war warnings in five weeks. Every officer on *Arizona* had been briefed. Now there were ominous reports of Japanese convoys moving south. Everyone concluded the most practical objectives of a Japanese attack, if, indeed, one were imminent, would be Malaya or the Netherlands East Indies: Malaya for its rubber and strategic location, the East Indies for the oil that flowed from the ground in some places so pure it could be burned without refining. "They're up to something. That's for sure. Probably the N.E.I," Rodney said.

"They won't screw with us."

"No way. They wouldn't take on this battle line," Rodney agreed.

"They'd have to be nuts," Colburn offered, wiping his face with a small towel and stepping back.

"Okay, Bismarck Kid. You're up." Patting his face with bay rum, Colburn walked to the tiny closet and pulled his white service uniform from a hanger.

Yawning, Rodney walked to the basin.

Rodney had time for a cup of coffee and two doughnuts before relieving the watch at 0745. Leaving the wardroom, he entered the typical glorious sunlight of a Hawaiian morning. He blinked his eyes and rubbed his forehead where a dull ache still persisted. Walking aft on the starboard side of the ship, he cursed the antiquated repair ship *Vestal* that was moored alongside. Tied up forward, she cut off the breeze and filled the air with fumes from her auxiliary engines and odors from her bilges. Across the harbor the young lieutenant could see naval housing on McGrew Point and the Naval Supply Center. Despite *Vestal*, all of Southeast Loch was visible and the submarine base with a half-dozen fleet boats nestled in groups of three. Behind the submarines were fueling and supply docks. Across the loch, he could see the Naval

Shipyard where *Arizona*'s sister ship *Pennsylvania* and two destroyers sat on their blocks in the great graving dock. Cranes, backs bent like arthritic old men, hunched over the ships while in the background row after row of huge warehouses, barracks, and shops stretched in an ugly sprawl like an unplanned city built for giants. Forward of *Arizona*, battleship *Nevada* squatted low and gray. However, the *Arizona*'s upper works obscured the five battleships moored astern.

Reaching the ship's quarter, he grasped a ladder and climbed up to the boat deck. From here the view of Oahu was spectacular. Rodney never tired of the beauty of the island. The sky was patchy so that the water and shoreline was dappled with sunshine and shadows. However, to the east the sun was brilliant in an arching blue amphitheater of its own. To the north, low-lying Ford Island showed thick growths of green undergrowth along the shore. The hangars of her airfield were busy already. He could see mechanics working on three PBYs (Consolidated Catalina flying boats), four or five transports, and a pair of observation planes. Four Brewster Buffalo Marine fighters and a half-dozen Grumman F4F Wildcat Navy fighters were lined up neatly on the tarmac.

Crossing the deck he stared at the mountainous interior of Oahu looming behind Ford Island. Sunlight streaming through the broken clouds heightened the green of the foliage mounting the escarpments like a great verdant staircase behind Honolulu and Aiea, blending into the majestic grandeur of the Koolau Mountains. The infinite shades of green and splashy colors of blooms were breathtaking. Cane fields stood out like trays of emeralds. Stands of acacias, banana, mango, guava, and the slender elegance of bamboo added their subtle greens and yellows. Rodney knew hibiscus, orchids, plumeria, ginger, epiphytes, and hundreds of other varieties of flowers crowded in the shade of the trees, but at this distance the rioting colors of their blooms were not visible. Raising his eyes, he stared at the enormous buttresses and citadels of sheer rock of the Koolaus rising in the center of the island. Here, dominating like great silent sentinels, Mount Tanalus and Mount Olympus were wrapped with their usual moisture-laden clouds. Driven by the northeasterly trade winds, they swirled around the mountaintops like lacy nightcaps, the morning sun painting them with delicate strokes of apricot and gold. Here and there rainbows flashed as pregnant clouds pushed high by the slopes of the mountains dropped their moisture in glinting, slanting sheets like ground rhinestones. He sighed, thinking of home. The mean concrete, steel, and brownstone warrens of New York City were suddenly carnal and vulgar.

He passed the crane amidships, two whaleboats, and the captain's skiff. Forward, the tripod mast and great foretop with its huge main director and array of antennas blocked the view to the east. Astern, the aft mast with its director, where he manned the range finder at general quarters, soared high into the sky on its three steel posts. Below the director and level with his head was a Vought OS2U Kingfisher observation plane tied down on its catapult on top of number three turret. Rodney could see the three fourteen-inch guns of the turret inclined slightly upward in battery position. The other nine fourteen-inch guns of *Arizona* were not visible.

As he reached the port ladder, he glanced astern at "Battleship Row." In pairs he saw battleships *West Virginia* and *Tennessee, Oklahoma* and *Maryland*. Then cruiser *Honolulu*, and close to Ford Island battleship *California*. He felt a thrill of pride as he viewed the massed power; sixteen-inch and fourteen-inch main batteries pointed fore and aft, dozens of snouts of five-inch guns pointed at the sky like stubby gray logs. Senior and junior partners in a corporation of death and the first line of defense of his nation.

He descended the ladder and walked to his station at the quarterdeck, which was actually a small platform at the head of the accommodation ladder. Here, a lieutenant j.g. named Martin Lebow waited impatiently with two enlisted men. Dressed in service whites matching the uniform worn by Rodney, Lebow was a short pudgy young man with a keen sense of humor and a rainbow of a laugh. Rodney had taken an immediate liking to him. The two officers exchanged salutes while the pair of enlisted men stood at attention next to a small table with a log, a telephone, and a stack of pamphlets. The enlisted men looked at the hatch to the mess deck anxiously for their own reliefs.

At that moment, there was the thud of shoes on steel and two enlisted men in undress whites and wearing duty belts emerged from a ladder leading up from the mess hall. Rodney recognized petty officer of the watch Quartermaster First Class Jay Mendel who had been aboard *Arizona* for a decade. Close on his heels and almost running was a young seaman second class named Marvin Bollenbach. Mendel had the typical look of the "old salt"; squared and "winged" white hat, tailored uniform, face darkened to the color of tobacco by years of salt spray and sun. Even the oiled brown hair slicked back from his temples had reddish silver streaks as if it, too, had been burned by the sun. Rodney had heard Mendel had an enormous bouquet of roses tattooed on his chest with "Mother" inscribed beneath it. In fact, the men joked that the whores on Hotel Street referred to him as "Rosie."

Fresh out of boot camp, Bollenbach had only been aboard for four weeks. With a severe acne problem, he had the timorous look of a high school junior looking for his first date. Both enlisted men saluted the officers and chorused, "We relieve the watch, sir."

"Very well," Martin Lebow said. He turned to his men, "You're relieved, boys. Chow down." The two men saluted and hurried to the hatch to the mess hall. Immediately Mendel and Bollenbach replaced them.

"Orders?" Rodney asked.

Lebow smiled and handed Rodney a small pamphlet. "Here are your standing orders, Mr. Higgins."

"I'm familiar with them."

Lebow spoke in a businesslike monotone, "Here are your orders of the day. The commander of Batdiv One (Battleship Division One), Rear Admiral Isaac C. Kidd, is aboard. Captain Van Valkenburg (*Arizona*'s captain) is on board and is in his cabin. The executive officer is the duty officer. Bridge manned by communications personnel only, all weapons secured, boilers and main engines secured, we're on auxiliary engine number two. Boilers three and ten are down for descaling. The ship is at condition five. Mooring lines and draft reading just checked and okay. Damage Control Center reports all secure except for a leak in a saltwater line in number one engine room. Should have it shipshape in an hour or two." He pointed to a large board mounted on the bulkhead just forward of number three turret. It contained three rows of switches and a telephone and a microphone, which hung on hooks beneath it. "Your Com-One. You can communicate with the exec, radio shack, any department, or all stations. The switches are marked."

Rodney nodded understanding. He was bored but knew the ritual had to be repeated regardless of the number of times he had heard it. "Very well," Rodney said. "I relieve you."

"I am relieved," Lebow said, unsnapping his duty belt and handing it to Rodney. A holstered Colt .45 hung from the belt.

"Armed to the teeth," Rodney said, grinning. He gestured at Mendel. "The petty officer of the watch usually wears this," he said.

Martin Lebow shrugged. "Captain's orders." He smiled wryly. "Keep in mind, Lieutenant, you have the only loaded weapon on board this great floating fortress."

Strapping the belt to his waist and patting the automatic, Rodney quipped back, "Rest assured, Mr. Lebow, if the Nips try to board us, I'll fight to the death."

They both laughed and Rodney could hear the enlisted men chuckle. Then, quickly, salutes were exchanged, Lebow signed the log and vanished forward.

Rodney walked to the rail and stared down at the platform at the foot of the accommodation ladder. It seemed to be down by the head. It definitely was out of trim. He turned to Quartermaster Mendel but before he could say anything, young Marvin Bollenbach said, "They've two-blocked Blue Peter, sir."

Glancing at the foremast, Rodney saw the large blue signal flag with the white square center fluttering high at the ship's yardarm. Immediately a boatswain's pipe skirled "To the Colors." It was 0755 hours and men on every vessel in the harbor were readying ensigns to be hoisted at the bows and sterns. "Stand by for colors," the lieutenant said. The pipe fell silent and across the harbor he could hear church bells in Honolulu calling worshippers to eight o'clock services.

"I hear engines, sir," Bollenbach said suddenly.

"Yeah," Mendel affirmed. "Lots of engines."

Rodney heard the rumble. It seemed to be coming from all points of the compass. Shading his eyes he stared up at the sky. Then he found scores of aircraft streaming toward Pearl Harbor over the Koolau Range. "Must be the air groups from the *Enterprise* and *Lexington*."

"Air groups?" Bollenbach said.

"Our carriers usually send in their air groups before they stand in," Mendel explained.

Rodney squinted. Something was wrong. He pointed at two streams of at least twenty planes that were wheeling slowly toward the harbor. "Some of those planes have fixed landing gear."

"Doesn't make sense unless some of 'em are army, sir," Mendel offered.

"Look! They're making practice dives on Ford Island," Bollenbach shouted excitedly, stabbing a finger into the sky.

"Those assholes are showing off," Mendel said.

A mottled green aircraft with fixed landing gear hurtled down on the island. It was followed by a stream of other planes.

Suddenly a PBY vanished in a great ball of flame and black smoke.

"My God," Mendel groaned. "That goddamned 'flat hatter' dropped his bomb by mistake."

"Bull shit!" Rodney screamed. "That's a Jap! See the meatballs on him?"

Mendel and Bollenbach stood paralyzed with disbelief as bomber after bomber released its bomb and pulled out of its dive, some roaring mast high over *Arizona*.

Rodney snatched the microphone from its cradle and shouted, "All stations! All stations! Air raid! Air raid! Sound the general alarm." And then the phrase that was to become the most quoted of the day, "This is no drill!"

Only a few minutes were required for the destruction of the Ford Island strip. Within seconds, the line of four Brewster and six Grumman fighters had been blown to pieces, and two hangars had been blasted with the flames of burning gasoline leaping high into the sky. Even the tarmac seemed to be burning, fueled by burning gasoline. Then graceful white fighters with black cowlings swept over the field, machine-gunning anything that moved. One pulled out so low it almost scraped the runway with its belly. Engine barking at full throttle, it banked just a few feet over Rodney's head. The canopy was open and the lieutenant could see the pilot quite clearly. Wrapped around his head, he wore a white band with a red dot on the front. He actually waved and smiled.

Rodney punched the bulkhead. "What the fuck's going on," he screamed. "Wake up! The whole fuckin' world's gone crazy."

Finally, after an eternity, *Arizona*'s PA system came to life. "Now hear this! All hands man your battle stations. This is no drill. Set Condition Zed." The short staccato blasts of Klaxons filled the air and reverberated throughout the ship's 608-foot length. Through the bedlam, Rodney could hear the clang of watertight doors slamming shut the length of the warship. Then, somewhere, deep in the vessel's bowels, an electrician's mate threw a switch, stopping every blower.

"Get to your battle stations!" Rodney shouted at Mendel

and Bollenbach. Both men raced forward as the lieutenant ran for the ladder to the boat deck and his battle station in the aft director. Taking the wrungs two at a time, he bounded to the boat deck. Here he was stopped in his tracks by the spectacle of Pearl Harbor under attack.

There were hundreds of aircraft circling overhead like buzzards about to pounce on carrion. To the south great clouds of black smoke billowed skyward from the fighter strip at Hickam Army Air Base where dozens of P-40s and P-36s had been parked in neat rows. He could see the same mottled green bombers with fixed landing gear and the white fighters swooping over the stricken field, blasting the crowded fighters to burning junk and strafing. To the south at least forty large monoplanes wearing green-brown camouflage were turning toward Battleship Row and lining up their runs on Merry's Point and Southeast Loch. Fearsome torpedoes hung from their crutches. "Why? Why?" Rodney screamed, waving a fist. "You have no right."

He started for the ladder leading to his station in the director when a shriek overhead stopped him and he craned his head back and stared skyward. Dive-bombers. A half-dozen dive-bombers were plunging directly down on him, Lieutenant Rodney Higgins. Each had a huge bomb slung under its fuselage. Fear, a deep-rooted dread, wrenched the bottom from his stomach and he began to tremble, his whole body turning cold as if he had been caught naked in a snowstorm. Frantically he leapt over the last rung and huddled under a ventilator in a fetal position. *A nightmare. A nightmare*, he told himself. *I'll wake up in a minute. This can't be happening.*

The sounds of the engines reached a crescendo, then a shriek, a blast that shook the ship, raining water. Another blast. Tons of water poured down on the entire aft part of the ship. Near misses. A series of explosions followed by a shattering detonation that shook every frame and plate in the ship, clanging, ripping sounds of metal blasted and tortured by high explosives. This was no near miss. This time metal rained, clattering on the deck, bouncing from the ventilator. Bits of plating, chunks of armor, tubing, and sheeting, and soft pulpy debris bounced and splattered.

Gagging on the nitro-acid stench of high explosives, Rodney crawled to his feet. The after director was askew with a huge hole blown in its side. The *Kingfisher* had been blasted from its catapult and hung by a single line over the port side, nose down into the water. Littering the deck around him were shards of metal, pieces of range finders, glass, electronics gear, and pieces of men. Half a skull, brains, arms, legs, teeth. The largest piece was the lower half of a torso with its entrails stretched for at least two yards across the boat deck. Rodney felt his gorge rise and scald the back of his throat. His battle station had been destroyed along with the crew. This was how it must have been on *Bismarck*. The wheel had turned full circle. "No! No!" he screamed. He ran to the starboard rail.

Clutching the rail, he stared hypnotized at Southeast Loch. Swarming low, the torpedo planes stretched in a column miles long all the way to Diamond Head. They were starting their runs, their big radial engines pointed at him. The leaders were close on the water and less than a mile away.

Shouts turned his head. Beneath him in the gun galleries he could see *Arizona*'s frantic gun crews cranking their five-inch guns down. They were screaming for ammunition. It was locked below in the magazines. The ship's eight fifty-caliber guns were still silent, too. Rodney pounded the rail in an agony of frustration.

The first half-dozen torpedo bombers released their glistening steel cylinders and roared over Battleship Row, one banking sharply and barely clearing *Arizona*'s stack. They were big planes and he could see their three-man crews staring down curiously. The steel cylinders dropped into the water with small splashes. Immediately six more planes bore in for the kill. The narrow waters of the loch were like a bowling alley and the Japs were rolling their torpedoes into the stationary pins of Battleship Row. Horror-stricken, he watched the pencil lines of tracks race for their helpless, immobile targets. Not an American gun had fired. Not an American fighter was in the air.

There were detonations all up and down the row and water shot into the sky. *Oklahoma* staggered and rocked as the first torpedo struck her amidships. Immediately she listed. In quick succession, *California, West Virginia*, and *Nevada* were hit. Oil hemorrhaged from the stricken warships, flames spread across the water—black, oily smoke billowing into the pristine blue sky. The sulphurous stench was suffocating.

Then it was the turn of *Arizona*. Two of the white tracks headed straight as doom for her starboard side. They passed by *Vestal*, which had drifted away after her panicked crew had chopped her free, and struck *Arizona*. It was a one-two punch that rocked the 31,400-ton ship like a surprised fighter slugged against the ropes. Two great columns of dirty water soared into the air and the ship twisted and convulsed like a mortally wounded whale. Rodney was ripped from the rail and hurled to his back. Stunned, he came to his hands and knees. He heard stuttering, sharp barks. AA guns were firing at last. The sky was pockmarked with drifting bursts. Tracers streamed and arched. Coming to his feet, he saw a torpedo plane lose its wing and cartwheel across the harbor, disintegrating in a huge spray of water. But more came on, boring in relentlessly.

Oklahoma's list had increased, starboard rail almost underwater. *California* and *West Virginia* were settling in a sea of flames. *Nevada*, down by the head, was moving out into the stream, guns blazing, hounded by swarms of bombers. Flames were everywhere, spread by the flaming oil. He was in an inferno, the bowels of hell itself. The sounds of engines, blasts of gunfire, and booms of exploding bombs and torpedoes were like the crash of a storm surf on a rocky shore, the wild beat of a demented drummer, the fevered pulse of a sick, mad world. A stifling cloud of acrid smoke swept over the boat deck and he retched and vomited up doughnuts and sour coffee. A breeze swept it away and engines overhead turned his eyes skyward. He wiped his mouth with the back of his sleeve.

At least forty high-flying bombers. Stretched in a long single line. Making a run on the anchorage. Glistening in the sunlight like icicles breaking from spring eaves, the bombs began to fall. They dropped slowly in perfect parabolas, shrieking through the din like banshees gone berserk. Mouth agape, frozen by this new horror, Rodney stared upward still disbelieving. The first three missed. Two struck off *Nevada*'s starboard side simultaneously, shooting towers of water a hundred feet into the air. The third hit fifty feet from *Arizona*'s bow. The fourth did not miss. It plunged into *Arizona*'s forecastle, into *Arizona*'s heart.

Arizona did not die in a millisecond flash. Her death began with a convulsive vibration and deep rumble like a volcano preparing to erupt. Then the sound like a force-twelve wind and the entire forward part of the ship detonated with a retina-searing flash of a newborn sun and a roar that shattered eardrums. The great battleship surged from the water, pulling her moorings loose and hurling debris in a half-mile radius. Incandescent fireballs boiled from her forecastle followed by flame-lashed clouds of brown and black smoke. The concussion was so mighty, many crewmen drowned in the blood of their ruptured lungs. Others were crushed when catapulted against bulkheads, while others hurled from the decks died screaming in the burning sea. Even automobile engines on Ford Island were snuffed out.

The shock hurled Rodney upward and then he crashed down on the deck, rolling under a whaleboat that had been partially knocked from its davits. His brain burst into bright colors and stabbing lights. He tasted his own blood, thick and metallic. *The black powder. The magazine*, broke through his dazed mind.

He tried to dig his fingernails into the steel deck as the great warship crashed downward, pitched, wallowed from side to side, settled quickly with most of her bottom forward of amidships blown out. Peering out from his shelter, Rodney could see giant fireballs roiling skyward hundreds of feet like a desert sunrise. The foremast tilted forward and everything forward of the mast was obscured by boiling flames and black smoke that churned furiously into the sky. A huge strake of armor plate smashed down, bouncing and scraping across the deck, ripped out the lifeline and a half-dozen stanchions and flew over the port side, splashing into the harbor. Fearfully, Rodney scurried farther under the boat. More ringing, clattering sounds as wreckage rained down onto the deck and bounced off the boat. Then there was an enormous crashing, ripping sound and something crushed the boat and black curtains were drawn on the world of Lieutenant Rodney Higgins.

Rodney Higgins hated summer nights in New York City. He could never sleep well in the oppressive heat. Why was Travers shaking him and calling his name? The butler never shook him. It didn't make sense. And it was so hot. The nightmare began and the butler kept on calling and shaking him. He was dead and hell was a burning ship. No! The nightmare was reality and New York the dream. The voice belonged to Seaman Second Class Marvin Bollenbach.

"Mr. Higgins. Mr. Higgins. Please, sir. Don't die, too."

Rodney opened his eyes. He saw the distraught, bloodsplattered face of the young seaman above him.

"Thank God. You're alive," Bollenbach said. He helped Rodney to his feet. "They're all dead—everyone's dead," the young seaman said, voice quivering on the edge of hysteria.

Rodney gripped his head, which was a ganglia of screeching, spastic nerves. Then he shook it, spit blood, and looked around, not believing what he saw. The whaleboat had been crushed by the entire side of a cabin, complete with porthole, which was still dogged shut and unbroken. It was a miracle he had not been crushed with the boat. He had been saved by the crane that had taken the brunt of the impact and had been crushed down over the whaleboat like a giant spring. Looking forward, he saw the entire foremast had sagged even farther forward in the intense heat of the still-raging fire. An inferno of yellow-orange flames stormed upward from the forecastle, sending smoke rolling in black thunder clouds thousands of feet into the sky, blotting out the sun and bringing darkness in the morning. Even the sea seemed to be burning, blazing oil slicks drifting out into the harbor in huge pools. The air was heavy with the sulphurous stench of burning oil and the smell of cordite. And the blast-furnace roar of the flames, rumble of engines, and bark of gunfire were ear-numbing. But it was real. He was here. In Pearl Harbor and the ship had been sunk. And the deck was hot. Very hot.

He thought of Donald Colburn. He must be dead. Number two turret was gone. And the young ensigns Jordan and Stolz could never have survived in the director. No one could.

Something was wrong with his right eye and his head throbbed. Gingerly, he touched his forehead. His hand came away covered with blood. "A fuckin' Purple Heart," he said to himself.

"It's your blood, sir," Bollenbach said. "You have a gash over your eye." He ripped off his black kerchief and handed it to Rodney. Gingerly, the lieutenant wiped the blood from his eye and wrapped the kerchief around his head. Then he spit blood again and carefully ran his tongue around his mouth. He found torn tissue where he had bitten himself.

He looked at the seaman. His whites were discolored with soot and coagulated blood, face tight with shock, eyes blank and uncomprehending like balls of glass. He was staring at Rodney as if the lieutenant were a god who could snatch him from this hell. He appeared unhurt despite the blood. The blood must have belonged to others. Rodney shook his head, took some deep breaths, and treaded from one foot to the other as the heat grew under his feet. Strangely, he felt his nerves calm and resoluteness course through his veins as if fear had gone beyond fear in a full circle back to courage. Maybe it was the responsibility he felt for the safety of someone besides himself that did it.

"You okay?"

"Yes, sir."

Rodney's voice was as calm as a man ordering lunch, "Let's haul ass, Bollenbach."

"Aye, aye, sir."

Rodney started for the ladder, but staggered in the grip of dizziness like a drunk. Bollenbach grabbed him and steadied him. "Okay, sir?"

"Yeah. Yeah," Rodney said, gritting his teeth and setting his jaw. His head seemed to clear and he felt strength begin to seep back into his muscles. Stepping over wreckage and pieces of bodies, he led the seaman to the port ladder. Looking down, he could see the ship had sunk below its main deck forward and was rapidly settling by the stern. He noticed a new odor; the sickening sweet smell of burning meat. Looking toward the bow, he could see two five-inch gun tubs with flames curling up around them. Bodies were piled around the guns. The tubs had become cooking pots, slowly cremating the corpses of their crews.

But a tub almost beneath the ladder showed movement. Bollenbach shouted, "Look, Mr. Higgins. Some of the guys are alive!"

Descending the ladder ahead of the seaman, Rodney was unable to hear the roar of engines. "They're gone," he said hopefully as he stepped onto the main deck.

Marvin Bollenbach waved skyward. "No, sir. They're still there." Rodney shaded his eyes and saw them. A cloud of specks high in the sky, circling. He cursed.

The five members of the gun crew walked toward Rodney with the dazed looks of zombies. They were as helpless as conscious men could be. All were blackened by smoke and soot, appeared in shock, but unwounded. Higgins recognized three of the men. The oldest was Chief Gunner's Mate Bill Farris, a middle-aged, twenty-year man. The other four were very young. Only one was rated, Storekeeper Third Class Fred Bagsby. The remaining three were seamen. The lieutenant knew one, Seaman First Class Kenneth Nemhart. The last two, lagging behind the others and side by side, were fresh out of boot camp. Both were short, appearing fair despite the soot covering them. *Children*, Rodney said to himself. *Nothing but children*.

Marvin Bollenbach turned with the gun crew and stared at Rodney like supplicants at a deity. They were alive and they were looking to him for leadership. He felt strong again. Someone had to survive *Arizona*. Colburn, Stolz, Jordan, and hundreds of others were gone, but he would save these men. It would be his only victory over the cowardly Japs.

"Lay aft!" he shouted, gesturing to the liberty launch ladder that was afloat, flush with the main deck.

"But there ain't no launch," the chief said.

"Then we'll swim."

"I think my arm's broken, sir," Bagsby said matter-of-factly, holding his right elbow with his left hand.

"Then, goddamn it! I'll tow you," Rodney said. "Now haul ass, on the double, before we're all fried." Pushing his way through the group, the lieutenant led the way to the gunwale.

He heard a bell. And then again a bell coming out of the smoke. "A whaleboat," Chief Farris shouted. Everyone cheered as a gray motor launch charged out of the smoke obscuring Ford Island and headed for *Arizona*. In a moment a member of its three-man crew threw a painter to Nemhart who secured it to a bent stanchion while the coxswain clanged his commands to the engineer by ringing a small bell attached to his conning platform. Another line was put over and the two young seamen began pulling the stern of the boat to the battleship.

Then they heard the clanging. It sounded like sledgehammers striking the very deck under their feet. At first, Rodney thought he was hearing the sounds of the ship breaking up. But the sounds were rhythmic, controlled by intelligence. Three short and three long over and over. "SOS," Farris said in a heavy voice. "Some of our guys are down there! They're dying by inches."

Bollenbach dropped to his knees and began to scream and

pound on the deck with his fists. Grabbing the seaman's arms, Chief Farris pulled him to his feet. "I'm okay. I'm okay," Bollenbach pleaded.

"If you do that again, I'll punch your fuckin' teeth out!" the chief spat.

"Let him go," Rodney said. Sobbing, Bollenbach turned away. "We can't get them out," Rodney continued. "We'll need acetylene."

Chief Farris showed new enthusiasm. "That's it, sir. Maybe we can get torches on Ford Island."

But there was no chance and Rodney knew it and he was sure the chief knew it, too. It was all an act. The battleship's great strength in deck and side armor made rescue impossible. The men in their steel-sealed tombs would never be saved. They would die the most horrible deaths; suffocation or slow drowning in boiling oily water as the ship flooded. But Rodney tried to put on a mask of enthusiasm as he ordered the men to board the whaleboat that was now secured alongside. He fooled no one.

"Our ship's a graveyard!" Nemhart screamed, tears washing white tracks down his cheeks. The two teenagers began to sob.

"Shut up! You're supposed to be men, not babies. Now get your asses in that boat before I kick 'em in," Rodney shouted.

Followed by the clanging dirge played by their doomed shipmates, the seven survivors tumbled into the whaleboat. With a ringing of bells, the boat charged toward Ford Island. A sudden gust of wind turned the greasy columns of black smoke to the south. Every man in the boat had a view of Battleship Row. They saw a cataclysm. *Nevada*, low in the water, had abandoned her attempt to put to sea and was beached on Waipio Point. *West Virginia* had sunk and was burning, her flames spreading to *Tennessee*. A hose-equipped garbage lighter was spraying seawater into *West Virginia*'s flames. *California* was sinking and her ruptured fuel tanks were adding to the flames spreading across the harbor. *Mary-*

land, too, was aflame and *Oklahoma* had vanished. All around the ships, men were in the water, clinging to wreckage, desperately trying to swim away from the burning oil. Everywhere, whaleboats and small boats darted into the inferno, pulling men from the water and taking crewmen off of the dying ships.

One of the seamen shouted, "The *Okie*'s rolled over!" He pointed at the long red bottom of *Oklahoma* sticking out of the water like a great dead creature. Men could be seen on her overturned hull. Then the scream, "They're killing 'em." Transfixed beyond horror, the men stared as first one graceful white fighter and then another made leisurely strafing runs the length of the hull. Brown smoke trailed as their guns flamed cherry-red and men were shot from the hull like tenpins. The men screamed, waved fists.

"We'll remember this!" Rodney shouted. The men quieted and stared at the lieutenant. "It'll be settled someday!"

Abruptly the sky seemed almost empty of aircraft, only a pair of bombers circling high and to the north. Rodney glanced at his watch. It was 0840 hours. He shook his head. All this damage had been done in only three quarters of an hour.

He felt a bump as the boat came alongside the wharf at Ford Island. At a run, he led the men through the shrubs and onto the airfield. The place was a flaming madhouse. Every hangar was shattered. Wrecked aircraft were scattered in flaming heaps. Dead marines and sailors were lying in heaps and in rigid solitude. Wounded were screaming, frantic corpsmen bending over some and rushing to others with their big kits slung over their shoulders. Groups of smoke-blackened marines were stacking sandbags, wreckage, and crates furiously, building antiaircraft platforms for machine guns. Others crouched with their Springfields at the ready.

"My God," Nemhart said. "They've had it."

"But this island can't sink," Chief Farris said.

A roar and then a whine high in the sky turned seven pairs of fearful eyes upward. Hundreds of aircraft were hurtling down on the harbor from the north. Another wave plunging into new, intense antiaircraft fire. Scores of guns were firing, stitching the sky with tracers and the brown pox of exploding shells. A half-dozen fighters banked toward Ford Island. "Here they come!" Rodney shouted. He waved at an undamaged maintenance building where an old SOC-3 (Curtis Seagull) amphibious biplane was parked. "Take cover!"

With the chief leading, six figures raced for the shelter. But Rodney was frozen to the concrete, staring upward at the glistening white fighters. The leader did a graceful half roll and plunged into a dive. The other five followed. As the planes screamed downward and steepened their dives, they separated, pointing for different targets like a handful of lightning bolts hurled by a vengeful god. The leader headed directly for Lieutenant Rodney Higgins.

Staring upward, a wild animal took possession of Rodney. Fear, logic, and reason were gone, only a primal hunger for revenge remaining. He had been a frightened, hunted animal, groveling, crying, praying. He would hide no more. Run no more. Lips drawn back in a rictus of determination, he unholstered his Colt, pulled the action back, and chambered a round. Raising the pistol with both hands, he planted his feet and growled, "Come on you yellow son of a bitch."

"For Christ's sake, take cover, Lieutenant!" a marine sergeant with a BAR (Browning Automatic Rifle) braced on a pile of sandbags shouted. "You can't do anything with that peashooter!"

Rodney ignored him. Brought the plane into the V of his sights. It seemed that time slowed and his senses concentrated his vision to brilliant clarity. The fighter grew in his sights, black cowling, radial engine, knifelike edge of the wings, canopy, and the pilot, hunched behind his range finder. Marine BARs, rifles, and machine guns began firing all around from behind wreckage, vehicles, pits on the edge of the runway. Flame spurted from the wings and cowling of the fighter, shells exploding to Rodney's left and marching through a weapons carrier, exploding its gas tank and killing a pair of marines firing from its bed.

Rodney got off two rounds and the thunder of the fighter's engine changed to a staccato blast as it whipped past, banking into an astonishingly fast turn, almost scraping the runway with a wingtip. The noise of the engine drowned out all other sounds, the plane passing so close, Rodney could feel its backwash. Whipping around with it, Rodney got off two more quick shots. The canopy was open, the helmeted and goggled pilot staring at him. The same white band with the red dot he had seen on the other pilot was wrapped around the man's head. Pulling back on the stick, he rocketed out of range.

Low on the runway, another fighter flashed past at the same time to Rodney's right. Lining up on the old SOC-3 parked in front of the maintenance building, it blew the observation plane to pieces with one long burst that shot out the front of the building, too. Banking, the fighter climbed with the same incredible speed of his leader.

Rodney noticed heaps of bloody white cloth scattered in front of the building. Screaming "No! No!" he ran to the building and the burning SOC-3. At a full run, he tripped over a chest, bloody and with ribs protruding, falling head-on to the tarmac, slick with thick black blood and entrails like cooked spaghetti. They were all around him; Bollenbach, Farris, Bagsby, Nemhart, the two young seamen. Torn and ripped by twenty-millimeter shells and bullets. They had been dismembered, butchered like cattle. All dead. Rodney pounded the cement, screaming "No! I've lost them. I've lost everything."

The marine sergeant and a private grabbed his arms and pulled him to his feet. They dragged the protesting officer from the bodies. Rodney could only moan, "Why this? Why? Why?"

"Easy, sir," the sergeant said. "Your men are dead. That's all there is. A lot of good men have died this day—a lot of mine."

A shout of "We got one of the fuckers!" turned every head.

Staring skyward, Rodney felt a surge of joy as one of the fighters plunged downward, trailing smoke. Frantically, the pilot tried to pull up, but the plane streaked down onto the strip from west to east, hitting perhaps two hundred yards from Rodney. It disintegrated into thrashing, tumbling pieces of burning, smoking wreckage that flew high into the air, whirled, and rolled toward the lieutenant like a flaming cyclone. Its engine tore loose and spinning like a great sparkling pinwheel rolled across the strip and crashed into a burning PBY. There were choruses of hoarse cheers. Something smoking, flopping loosely, and leaving a red trail tumbled toward the lieutenant. It stopped rolling only a few feet from Rodney. It was the pilot in brown, fur-lined flight clothes. The clothes were ripped and smoking. Rodney, the sergeant, and a private ran to the body.

Both legs had been ripped off at the trunk and most of one arm was missing. But the face was remarkably untouched, goggles up, helmet, and the same white band with the red dot wrapped around the head. Ideograms were brushed on the cloth with black ink. Two narrow brown eyes stared up at Rodney with the crystal-hard, unblinking stare of the dead that had become so familiar this day. The thin lips were pulled back from fire-blackened teeth in a ghastly, mocking grin.

Rodney stepped over the body, straddling its chest. He pointed the automatic at the cadaver's head.

"Sir! No!" the private shouted.

"At ease, Private," the sergeant said grimly. "He has something he must do. Leave him be."

Rodney pulled the trigger. The weapon fired three big 230-grain bullets, shattering teeth, blowing out an eye, and the third punched out the red dot, splattering pieces of bone and the yellow-gray contents of the skull on the concrete. Then the .45 fell silent, clip empty. "Now grin, you fuckin' butcher," Rodney hissed.

The sounds of engines began to fade and wordlessly the men looked skyward. "It's over," the sergeant said.

Rodney stared at his immolated ship and then at his dead men. The anguished voice came from a tortured soul, "It'll never be over. Never!"

The next week was an extension of the nightmare. Rodney was taken to an emergency hospital set up in a warehouse just back of the graving dock and shipyard. Part of his head was shaved, scalp wound closed with twenty-two stitches, and he was assigned to a bunk in an improvised BOQ in a Quonset hut next door to the warehouse. The hut was filled with survivors from the battleships. Donald Colburn, Dick Jordan, Paul Stolz, Jay Mendel, and Martin Lebow were missing. In fact, over a thousand members of *Arizona*'s crew were dead or missing. Rodney knew they were all dead. He saw only one other officer from *Arizona*—an ensign from communications named Norman Marcky. Because telephone communications with the mainland were prohibited, he sent a heavily censored telegram to his mother assuring her he was well. He followed the telegram with a letter that was also censored.

The entire area stank of disaster. To the north, the burned-out hulks of destroyers *Cassins* and *Downs* sat in the graving dock with the almost untouched battleship *Pennsylvania*. Just to the south at Hickam Field, the wreckage of scores of fighters and hangars reeked with the smell of burned gasoline, oil, solvents, and explosives. And a new odor began to seep in from the harbor. Rotting meat. Despite the efforts of a fleet of small boats, bodies and parts of bodies still drifted in the harbor. And more bodies popped up from the depths each day as the dead always do, filling with gases and finally breaking free from the mud of the bottom.

Everyone felt a Japanese invasion was imminent. Concertinas of barbed wire were unrolled at the beaches, mines laid, artillery sited, and marines and army troops dug in to repel the enemy. Boeing B-17 bombers and PBYs were flown in from the mainland and constant patrols were maintained, covering every sector. It was rumored hundreds of fighters and thousands of troops were outbound from the mainland. Carriers *Enterprise* and *Lexington* were out hunting the Japs and *Saratoga* was on her way. But the spirit was that of despair. The battle line was shattered—shattered so easily its destruction had almost been casual. Every man was crushed by the knowledge his enemy possessed lethal power that could kill with speed and near impunity. Across the harbor the specters of Battleship Row were there to haunt them.

It was a week filled with disasters. Following Roosevelt's "Day of Infamy" speech, Congress declared war on Japan. Germany and Italy declared war on the United States and the U.S. declared war on them. Japanese aircraft caught MacArthur's air force on the ground at Clark Field in the Philippines and destroyed most of it. Japanese forces landed in Malaya and Thailand. Manila, Singapore, and Hong Kong were bombed. Guam fell and Wake Island was under attack. However, the greatest disaster occurred off the Malaya Peninsula on December 10 when the British battleship *Prince of Wales* and battle cruiser *Repulse* were sunk by Japanese aircraft. The German withdrawal from Moscow and the relief of Tobruk did nothing to relieve the gloom.

On December 14 the surviving officers were addressed by Captain Thomas Flanigan from the staff of Admiral Kimmel. The meeting was held in a conference room shaped like a small amphitheater. Completely bald, Flanigan was a fiftyish man with a florid face and the large red pockmarked nose of a man with a weakness for alcohol. Harsh lines of fatigue coursed downward severely from the corners of his eyes and mouth. Flanked by his aide, a young lieutenant, and a yeoman who sat at a small table with a pad and pencil, he mounted a platform at the front of the room. Speaking in a whiskey-addled voice, the captain told the men they would be returning to the mainland for survivor's leave. He cautioned them about secrecy. "The enemy must not know about the extent of the damage to the fleet."

"He's got to know, Captain," a commander said. "My God, he has eyes and he must have had cameras."

"True, but he won't know the details—how extensive the damage was."

"Then not a word to our families?" another officer said.

"Of course. Complete secrecy. We must keep this information from the Japs and we must consider civilian morale, too."

"The press, sir," Marcky said.

"They're restricted."

Marcky waved in an encompassing gesture. "But the hills, sir. Anybody can see . . ."

Flanigan cut the ensign off with a dismissive gesture. "We have the cooperation of the media. The only descriptions of damage they will report will be those provided by us." He punched a palm with a big beefy fist. "Minor damage will be reported and that's it."

There were a few cynical snickers, but the captain ignored them. Then there was a discussion of damage. Only *Arizona* and *Oklahoma* were completely lost. Salvage and repair crews were already working on *Tennessee, Maryland, Nevada, California*, and *West Virginia*. *Pennsylvania* had sustained little damage. Six of the eight battleships would be returned to service soon. No one in the audience believed this.

The meeting was dismissed, but to Rodney's surprise, Captain Flanigan asked him and Ensign Marcky to remain. He dismissed his aide and the yeoman who had been taking notes. Obeying the captain's gesture, the two officers sat at the small table. Flanigan took a chair opposite them.

Drumming the table with short pudgy fingers and averting his eyes, the captain began, "This comes straight from Compacfleet. *Arizona* was lost because a bomb went down her stack, exploded her boilers, and set off her magazines."

Rodney felt a wave of anger storm from his guts and burst

from his lips in a shout. "That's a lie! It was that goddamn black powder. Illegally stored on the second deck. That's what killed the crew!" He came half-out of his chair. A wide-eyed Marcky pulled him back.

Surprisingly, the captain retained his composure and answered in an evenly modulated timbre, "That may be true, Lieutenant Higgins. But the damage is so cataclysmic, so complete, we may never know the true reason."

"I know the true reason," Rodney said bitterly, clutching his bandaged head, which had suddenly started to throb viciously.

"Perhaps. Someday the reports must be made and next of kin must be informed and we owe it to them to at least give meaning to the deaths of their loved ones."

"You mean we don't want them to know they died because of our own carelessness. Died for nothing, Captain. Cover it up."

The big nose flamed scarlet and tiny veins made their first appearance like a latticework across the nose and cheeks. The captain showed his first loss of patience. "This is an order, Lieutenant. A bomb went down the stack of the *Arizona*. Is that clear?" He did not wait for an answer. "If it isn't clear, you will remain here for the rest of the war assigned to the boondocks!"

Rodney fumed like a volcano on the verge of eruption. He could feel Marcky's hand on his arm. He calmed himself. "I obey my orders. But this one under protest."

"Protest all you like, Lieutenant. But both of you remember what has been said here when you board that transport for the States."

"When, sir?" Marcky asked eagerly.

"Tomorrow. You both leave tomorrow."

XI

December 27, 1941

RODNEY arrived in Grand Central Station on a Saturday afternoon. The complexion of the place had changed, uniforms everywhere in the crowd, servicemen and their women saying tearful farewells. Armed Military Police patrolled in pairs and there were two Red Cross stands dispensing coffee and doughnuts to men in uniform. He phoned his mother and refused when she said she would send a car. Instead, he told her he would hail a cab. After he hung up, he pulled a slip of paper from his wallet, called the long-distance operator, and asked for a number. Within seconds, his call was completed and a woman's voice said, "This is the White House. Marguerite LeHand here."

Rodney spoke for a few moments, finally smiling and saying, "Monday afternoon at fifteen hundred hours. Got it." He replaced the telephone on its hook. Then he walked out to the curb and climbed into a cab.

Wearily, he settled into the back seat with his single barracks bag. He was wearing a new set of blues he had bought in Long Beach after he had disembarked from the transport. However, he was still unable to wear his hat because of the tenderness of his wound that still showed swollen, red, and discolored through the short growth of hair. Although the sutures had been removed, stitch marks were still clearly visible. He carried his hat under his arm. He had earned the Purple Heart, but, somehow, as he thought of his dead ship-mates, wearing it seemed like a vainglorious attempt to appear a hero—to be the wounded, indomitable warrior personified by the film star John Wayne. The thought was nauseating.

Brenda, Travers the butler, his aunt Betty, grandmother Ellen, cousin Marsha, and Nicole met him at the door. Brenda wrapped her arms around her son and sobbed on his shoulder. "It must've been horrible," she cried.

"Oh, no, Mother. They did very little damage, really," he said, mouthing the well-rehearsed lie. "It's all been in the papers—just minor damage."

"Your head!"

"Just a scratch. Tripped over a ladder."

"Your ship?"

"Ah, some damage. Nothing that can't be fixed."

Then he was engulfed by his grandmother Ellen and aunt Betty while Travers, Nicole, and Marsha hung back, looking for an opening. Finally, Travers grabbed his hand, his aunt darted in for a quick kiss followed by Marsha. Rodney turned his head quickly and took his cousin's lips on his cheek.

His mother gestured to the sitting room and walking past Nicole, he stopped and embraced her. She kissed his cheek and cried, "Welcome home, monsieur."

Within a few minutes he was seated on the sofa with his mother on one side and his grandmother on the other. Word-lessly, Travers handed Rodney a double Scotch and seltzer. Nicole hung over his shoulder and the other women pulled up chairs. Everyone, including his grandmother, held a glass.

Ellen raised her drink. "To a quick victory over the cow-ardly Japs."

"Hear! Hear!" was chorused. But Rodney saw his mother bite her lip before she drank.

"Your head looks like a jigsaw puzzle," Brenda said, staring at the wound.

Rodney laughed. "Just a scratch, Mother," he said. "I told you."

"Won't it ever end?" Brenda anguished. "I've lost two husbands—Randolph and Lloyd both have been fighting since 1914 and carry the scars on their bodies and their souls. And, my God, now my sons. The world is mad! Mad! Mad!" She brought her fist to her mouth but could not stifle her sobs. Ellen began to cry and Betty dabbed at her eyes with a handkerchief. Even Nicole and Marsha were misty-eyed.

Rodney held Brenda close. "Mother, I have a month's leave." He avoided the word "survivor." "I'll be around here until you get sick of me."

Brenda dabbed at her eyes and forced a smile. "You'll spend every minute here, with me."

Chuckling, Rodney held up his glass and Travers and Nicole raced to fill it. Nicole won. He looked at his mother. "Every minute, Mother." He drank. "Except for Monday and Tuesday, I've got to report to the Pentagon—a report and stuffy things like that." He tried to make the lie sound flip but failed.

"A report?"

"Of course, Mother. I'll be back by Tuesday—Wednesday at the latest."

She held him very close and her tears left little wet spots on his new uniform.

The president looked as if he had aged ten years. The moment Rodney stepped into the Oval Office, he was gripped by the funereal atmosphere. Roosevelt looked like a man who had taken giant strides toward his own grave. The face was haggard, creased by new lines, eyes bloodshot and swollen from the lack of sleep. Even the pince-nez seemed to droop low on his nose and the cigarette holder hung out of the corner of his mouth. A half-empty cocktail glass was on the cluttered desk. The job would kill Franklin Delano Roosevelt. Rodney was absolutely sure of it.

There were two other people in the room; the secretary, Marguerite LeHand, seated at the small revolving desk next to the president and an elderly man in a blue business suit who was seated to the president's left. With sandy gray hair, the man was of medium build and his face looked as tired and drawn as the president's. He held a drink in his hand and rose when Rodney entered.

"Lieutenant Rodney Higgins," the president said, beaming and waving his cigarette. "It's good to see you, son." He gestured to the stranger, "This is my secretary of the navy, Colonel Frank Knox."

Colonel Frank Knox was well known to Rodney. An ex-Rough Rider and publisher of the internationalist-minded *Chicago Daily News*, he had been the Republican vice-presidential candidate in 1936. Rodney grasped the colonel's hand. The grip was firm and the look in the man's eyes was warm and concerned. "You've been wounded," Knox said, staring at Rodney's head.

"When the *Arizona* . . ." Rodney caught himself and stared at the secretary.

Roosevelt spoke up, "It's okay, Lieutenant. Missy hears nothing, repeats nothing. We can discuss anything here."

Rodney completed his sentence, "When the *Arizona* blew up I got clobbered—knocked out. A seaman brought me around, probably saved my life."

"Brave fellow," Roosevelt said. "He deserves a decoration."

"He's dead, sir."

There was a long silence. Roosevelt broke it. "Then, by God, we'll award it posthumously. Give the details to Missy."

Rodney quickly described Seaman Second Class Marvin

Bollenbach's part in reviving him and Bollenbach's death on Ford Island.

"Terrible. Terrible," the president said, voice deep and filled with grief as if he had lost a member of his own family. Then his voice became apologetic, "I'm sorry. I'm remiss as a host. A drink, Lieutenant?" he said, pouring a generous shot of Johnnie Walker Black Label into a glass. Roosevelt smiled. "See, I remembered. You're a Scotch drinker." Missy rose and brought the drink to Rodney. Roosevelt refilled his cocktail glass with a martini from the same pitcher Rodney remembered from his first visit and dropped in an olive. He stubbed out his cigarette, selected another from a pack of Camels, screwed it into the holder, and lighted it with his gold lighter. He took a long drag that he sucked deep into his lungs and drank half his martini in one gulp. The president stared at the young officer through the haze of smoke. "You wanted to see me, Lieutenant?"

"Yes, sir."

Roosevelt nodded at Knox. "Well, we wanted to see you, too." He took another drink. "You know a board of inquiry is studying the attack and its consequences. I assume you will be called eventually. We even have divers down, studying the damage, and salvage operations have begun. And I, personally, have interviewed a dozen senior officers who were witnesses. But we would be interested in precisely what you saw." The voice dropped and the eyes were averted, "You know there were very few survivors of *Arizona*—especially officers."

Rodney emptied his glass and Missy refilled it. Slowly and deliberately Rodney Higgins described the events of December seventh. As he spoke, the horror, fear, and rage all came back. He had trouble controlling his voice. The president and the secretary of the navy listened, both staring at the young man with remorse and anger on their faces. Marguerite LeHand took notes furiously, glancing up occasionally. "And it was the powder, a ton of black powder stored on the second deck that set off the main magazines—killed most of my shipmates," Rodney said in a harsh, husky voice. His hand was trembling. He paused to drink and compose himself while everyone stared uneasily. He continued, the timbre of his voice acid with bitterness, "Carelessness killed them. That's what it was."

Silence seeped through the room like the oily waters of Pearl Harbor, coating everyone and everything. Frank Knox and the president exchanged a long enigmatic look. Finally, Knox spoke, "You can't accept the theory that a bomb went down the funnel?"

Rodney felt the frustration and anger of three weeks of hell begin to boil over. His eyes were wide and he waved the drink, spilling some of the Scotch. "Could you? That's the story I got at Pearl. It's ludicrous, Mr. Secretary, and you know it as well as I do." Trying to calm himself, Rodney took a large swallow of Scotch. "And those bombs weren't that good. The torpedoes did most of the damage to the other ships on Battleship Row."

The president and the secretary of the navy eyed each other with surprise. "You're right about the bombs, Lieutenant. They were finned forty-centimeter shells. One penetrated the second deck of *West Virginia* and failed to explode. We've been studying it," Knox said.

"The armor stopped it," Rodney suggested.

"Correct."

"And a forty-centimeter AP shell would carry a small explosive charge—probably about seventy pounds."

"Sixty-six and a half pounds," Knox said.

"You're very knowledgeable, Lieutenant Higgins," the president said.

"It's my business, Mr. President." Rodney turned back to Frank Knox. "Then, at the most, the bombs might have penetrated two decks? Correct?"

Lips drawn in a thin hard line like a gambler who had just seen his bluff called and his stake scooped from the table,

Frank Knox nodded. He took a large drink. He almost whispered his answer, "Yes."

"So the stack—down the stack with the miracle bomb. The unlucky hit. The one-in-a-million shot." Rodney's wound began to throb and he rubbed his temple gingerly. "That should throw next of kin off of the truth, protect the navy from criticism."

LeHand shot a surprised look at Frank Knox and then at the president. But the colonel was drumming his armrest mutely and the president remained silent, smoking and drinking and staring at the young officer.

Frank Knox's face hardened and he said to Rodney Higgins, "You mentioned next of kin."

"That is your primary concern, isn't it?" Rodney shot back. "Political expediency." LeHand gasped and dropped her pencil.

"Now see here, Lieutenant," Roosevelt said. "That was below the belt."

"And my shipmates are below the surface."

The secretary stared at Rodney with shock in her eyes. Obviously, she had never heard anyone talk to the President of the United States like this young officer. Knox was aghast and stared silently as if his vocal cords had been frozen. He reached into a briefcase and pulled out a document. He finally managed to speak in a thick voice, "Perhaps you're right about the powder. But there is a black powder magazine forward, right, Lieutenant?"

Rodney nodded agreement. "Yes. On all battleships. Ours was in compartment A-four-one-five-M on the first platform deck, thirty feet below the upper deck and shielded by the second armored deck and the third splinter deck."

Knox pressed on. "But it is possible a bomb could have penetrated that far. A hit on that magazine could have set off the powder bags of the six main battery magazines."

"Negative."

Surprised by the blunt response, Roosevelt interrupted, "Why do you disagree, Lieutenant?"

"Because the black powder magazine is behind and partially below the barbette of the forward turret. And don't forget I was watching those bombs drop. They were dropped from high altitude and the angle of impact was seventy-five to eighty degrees. No less. To hit the black powder magazine, the bomb would have had to somehow avoid number one turret and the barbette—come in at fifty to sixty degrees. Impossible. Absolutely impossible."

"And you contend . . ." Knox said, continuing the young officer's thought.

"I don't contend, I *know*, sir. As I told you, I *know* a ton of black powder was stored illegally on the second deck—precisely in passageway A-four-one-six—and the armored hatches must have been left open or unsecured. The men were still working there on Sunday morning. That was the only way a bomb could have penetrated, set off the magazines." He took a large drink and stared at his glass.

Roosevelt and Knox looked at each other, obviously disconcerted by the intelligent young officer's knowledge and ironclad arguments. Finally, Roosevelt said, "Look at it this way, Lieutenant. *Arizona* is lost. Nothing can ever change that. Why the entire bottom from, ah . . ." He looked at the secretary of the navy for help.

Knox came to the aid of his chief. Slipping on a pair of glasses, he glanced at a document. "Our divers report from frame sixty-two forward to frame ten the ship's sides were blown out almost to a horizontal position and from the base of the funnel to the first barbette the decks collapsed all the way down to the armor belts. The structural material that was not blown away was smashed and buried in the mud."

Roosevelt halted Knox with a raised hand and picked up the argument, "The destruction is so complete, we'll never raise her, never be able to accurately assess what happened." He stabbed his cigarette at Rodney. "I can understand how you feel. You're convinced the lives of your shipmates were thrown away and you want the truth to be known. Well I want the truth to be known, too. But not now—not if it further demoralizes a shocked nation. Why torture fathers, mothers, wives, sweethearts with conflicting stories? We must stand united in our nation's greatest peril. We need heroes, gallantry, victories, not charges of inefficiency, recriminations that will split us, damage our war effort—our very chances for survival."

Rodney tapped his glass and stared over the rim at the president. The arcane aura of authority, the supreme confidence of his president, had been torn away. It gave Rodney a queer twinge of conscience to see Roosevelt reduced to a pleading old man, unable to move from behind his own desk, unable to cope with the terrible truths and responsibilities that had struck him with one hammer blow after another. The illusion of the brilliant statesman with the quick decisive mind that could pierce the clouds of the most complex problems and come up with quick solutions was gone. He actually felt sorry for the man. But he knew his president needed help. "You want me to hold my tongue?"

"Don't you think that would be wise?"

The young lieutenant sipped his drink while three pairs of eyes stared. "All right. No one will believe me, anyway."

"Good. Good," Roosevelt said. "It's the patriotic, the military thing to do, Lieutenant." Roosevelt smiled; the broad, satisfied, complacent smile he reserved for victories.

Rodney was not finished. He could not, would not be that easy. He spoke boldly, "Two conditions."

The smile vanished and Roosevelt raised an eyebrow. Frank Knox hunched forward. Rodney continued, "First, I will not be called to testify before any board of inquiry, and second, when this is over, I'm free to tell my story as I feel it should be told. The truth as I know it."

Roosevelt and Knox both nodded in agreement and relief was on their faces. "Of course, agreed, Lieutenant," the president said.

Frank Knox said, "You're a good man, Lieutenant." He glanced at his watch. "With your permission, Mr. President, I'll excuse myself. I have a meeting with the chief of staff."

Roosevelt nodded and the secretary of the navy left. He turned to his secretary, "Missy, you may leave. Please type up your notes and place them on my nightstand."

"Yes, sir." She left, eyeing the lieutenant with curiosity and wonder. Rodney began to rise.

"Please remain, Lieutenant," Roosevelt said. "I would like to chat for a few minutes. You're a very interesting young man." He held up a bottle and Rodney walked to the desk. Roosevelt recharged the glass and the lieutenant returned to his chair.

Roosevelt lit another cigarette and slumped back, sipping his martini. He held the cigarette up, adjusted his pince-nez, and stared at the glowing end of the Camel thoughtfully as if he were gazing at a beacon in the fog. He seemed to be having trouble holding the cigarette steadily. He was feeling his drinks and Rodney, too, could feel the warming, comforting effects of the Scotch spreading and relaxing his body at last. The enfolding leather of the chair suddenly felt as comfortable as satin and the young officer sagged back.

Roosevelt tapped some ashes into an ashtray and spoke words that jarred Rodney erect, "I'm to blame. I'm responsible for all of it." He waved the cigarette in a wide arc. "I killed them all—your shipmates, all of them."

"That's not true, Mr. President."

The big head shook negatively. "I'm the commander-in-chief. I bear the responsibility. It goes with the job."

Rodney hunched forward, "We had war warning after war warning, Mr. President. You couldn't be expected to . . ."

Roosevelt interrupted, "I should have pressed for more alertness everywhere."

"On the local command level—bases, ships? Sir, as CIC, that's just not your job and everyone knows it. Your subordinates were expected to do that job and the commanders were warned that the Nips were on the move, were expected to attack. I was briefed, too."

The big head nodded, and a slow smile broke the lines of wrinkles. "Thank you, Lieutenant. You are very knowledgeable about naval matters, have an uncanny knowledge of ordnance, but you don't understand the jungle of politics.'' He drew on his cigarette and sipped his drink. ''Someday—mark this—my enemies will contend that I deliberately provoked the attack to plunge us into the war.''

Rodney stared wide-eyed. Obviously, the president had had too much to drink. He was not even rational. ''That doesn't make sense, sir.''

''It doesn't have to. Not with my enemies.'' He stabbed the cigarette at Rodney like a dagger. ''They'll come around to even saying I knew the Jap carriers were coming, perhaps, even had some kind of communications with the Jap High Command. It's already being whispered on Capitol Hill.''

''But, sir, where is the logic? Provoking a war with Japan was the last way to lead this country into the war. Why, Japan wasn't involved in the European war. Officially, she wasn't at war with anyone—not even China. The Tripartite Pact is not a true mutual aid agreement or she would have declared war on Russia last year. If Hitler and Mussolini hadn't declared war on us, we wouldn't be involved in the European war.'' Rodney drank while Roosevelt stared at him with a slight smile curling the corners of his mouth. Rodney continued, ''And another thing, sir, American public opinion screams for revenge—to kill the cowardly Jap. There is no way you could change that, guide us into a war with Germany, if, as your enemies say, that's what you wanted.''

The tiny smile broadened to a grin. ''I take back what I said about your lack of political acumen. You're a very astute observer, Lieutenant.'' He stubbed out the cigarette and did not immediately reach for another one. ''But you must understand, Lieutenant, logic, intelligence, and reason are not to be found in a large part of my opposition, in American politics, for that matter.'' He chuckled unexpectedly. ''But you know, Lieutenant Higgins, I believe a man's stature, his achievements, can be measured by the venom, the thunder of his enemies.'' He laughed. ''It can almost be measured in decibels.''

Rodney chuckled, emptied his glass, and the president refilled it. Walking back to his chair, his step was slightly unsteady. He was happy to be off his feet again and took only a tiny sip of his drink. Roosevelt reached for his cigarettes and lighted a fresh Camel. He stared at Rodney for a long moment. "Lieutenant," he said. "After you recover" —he pointed the cigarette at Rodney's wound—"I'll see to it you get a new battleship. A brand-new ship of the North Carolina class or the Indiana class, if that's what you'd like."

Rodney shook his head. "Thank you, sir. The day of the battleship is over."

The president arched an eyebrow in surprise. "Because a few of our older ships were caught by surprise, sunk in peacetime?"

Rodney set his jaw. "Isn't that proof enough, sir?"

Roosevelt sighed. "We still need a balanced force of capital ships—big-gunned ships and carriers. That's what we're building." His face fell into a crisscrossing pattern of tired lines. "But it'll take time—so much time. Two years at least before our building program is felt." He drew on his cigarette. "You'd like a carrier?"

"I'm applying for submarine duty, sir."

"Submarines?"

"Yes. I had duty on an old S-boat when I first got out of the Academy. I think our subs will sweep the Nips from the sea. And they can start doing it now, not two years from now."

Roosevelt laughed, and a new spark showed in his eyes. "I like your attitude, Lieutenant. If we had a million of you, this war would be over in a month."

It was Rodney's turn to laugh. "Thank you, sir. You are very kind."

"You'll get your boat," the president said. He gestured at the wound again. "But not until navy doctors clear you. Not until March or April of next year, I would guess."

"Maybe February."

Roosevelt laughed again. "We'll see." He became suddenly serious and stared at the bric-a-brac that cluttered his desk, picked up a ceramic pig, and examined it. "The last time I saw you, you asked about Warsaw, rumors of atrocities. You told me you have a sister in Warsaw?"

Rodney felt his stomach drop. "Yes, sir. Regina. She married a Jew."

Roosevelt placed the pig carefully back on the desk and kept his eyes on it. "I have bad news for you. We have reports of atrocities."

"Killings?"

"Yes. And this is top secret." Rodney nodded. "We got it from British Intelligence that has been gathering information from the Polish underground. Jews, Poles, and Russians have been shot."

"No!"

"Several thousand. In Latvia, Estonia, Lithuania, Poland, and Russia."

"Organized exterminations?"

"We don't know. It seems to be random, depending on the German units involved. In fact, seems to be the SS in most of the cases."

"And Warsaw?"

The president looked away. "There have been thousands of deaths from hunger and disease and some have been shot."

Rodney downed the contents of his glass despite an empty, sick feeling. "Oh, Lord. Lord, no."

"I'm sorry, Lieutenant. But I knew you were concerned and I owe you this."

"I appreciate the information, sir."

Roosevelt slapped the desk in his first display of anger. "And damn it, Lieutenant. There's nothing we can do."

"But there is, sir."

"Oh?"

"Yes, Mr. President. Win this goddamned war just as fast as we can."

Roosevelt drank and smiled. "Be sure to phone me at the end of your first patrol. You're a fountainhead of information, Lieutenant, and I like talking with you."

"Thank you, sir." Rodney sipped his drink, stared into the shadows behind the president's desk. The liquor had relaxed him but at the same time had played tricks with his brain. Weird things were happening. He was seeing things in the shadows. Then they came into focus. Just a glimpse like images flashed in a millisecond from a projector in a recognition class, yet very clear. They were standing behind the president. Stud Horse Colburn, Dick Jordan, Paul Stolz, Martin Lebow, Jay Mendel, Marvin Bollenbach, Bill Farris, Fred Bagsby, Kenneth Nemhart. All of them in bloody whites, eyes fixed on him like coals in a hot fire, and then they were gone. Rodney stared at the president with eyes that glowed balefully like the eyes of a wolf lying in dark ambush. Anger and grief had carved his handsome face into an ugly mask—all hard, deep, down-slashing lines. "Kill those fuckin' Nips. Kill them all," he spat.

The smile vanished from Roosevelt's face. He stared back silently in confusion and wonder.

XII

**The Warsaw Ghetto
February 1, 1942**

IT had been a harsh winter in the ghetto. Deaths averaged
nearly five thousand a month. The survivors became hardened to the skeletal figures with yellow swollen faces and
bloated abdomens that sat propped up against the walls of
buildings. Eyes puffed and slitted, they reached out with
hands like bent roots to indifferent passersby for food. Others,
already dead, lay rigidly on the curbs awaiting the death
squads to haul them off to the mass graves. Children too weak
to walk crawled on all fours like tattered crabs, snatching
food from pedestrians, swallowing as much as possible before
they were caught and struck. When a ''snatcher,'' or *khapper*
as he was called in Yiddish, dropped a jar of broth, soup,
milk—any liquid food—there was a mad scramble of tiny
skeletons and a horde of *khappers* lapped up the food, mud,
particles of glass, and all while the screaming owner kicked
them. There were even rumors of cannibalism.

Yet, to the Nazis' rage and frustration, the bulk of the
Jewish population found ways to survive. The smuggling

grew and proliferated, became highly organized and efficient. Refuse collectors left with garbage and trash in their wagons and returned with food. Cows and goats were herded over the walls on especially constructed mobile ramps. Chickens were passed over the wall or through cracks. A pipe running from the roof of a building on the Aryan side to a building in the ghetto was used as a funnel for milk. Workers, especially women who passed to the Aryan side to their jobs, reentered the ghetto with food hidden on their bodies. Children darted through small openings in the wall to buy or beg food. Many were shot, but the practice grew.

Clandestine industries expanded, providing goods for sale on the Aryan side. Raw materials were smuggled in to supplement the tons of wastes collected on the inside. Trousers, shirts, dresses, and sweaters were fashioned from rags and smuggled bolts of cloth. Slippers were manufactured from woven cardboard, paper, and wood fibers. Brooms and brushes were made from hair, feathers, and recycled bristles. Shoes, wallets, and handbags were created from the leather covers of old ledgers and books.

Consequently, most people continued to survive causing consternation among their Nazi masters. The Yiddish theater continued to give performances and the symphony orchestra gave regular concerts. Schools, though forbidden, thrived, serving children and adults in attics, cellars, and in any place hidden from the eyes of the police.

Despite the horrifying rumors of mass killings in Poland and Russia, most of the people felt a glimmer of hope, even of optimism that they would somehow survive. They even found reassurance in the news from the Russian front. Markus Lang's wireless and a hundred others monitored reports from the fronts and supplied the news to a half-dozen underground newspapers. The Germans had been stopped outside Moscow and hurled back two hundred kilometers. Russian forces had recaptured Mozhaisk and Rostov, and Sevastopol and Leningrad were still holding out. "We'll just hold out until the Red Army frees us," they told each other.

But Josef Lipiski, Jan Tyranowski, and many other young militant Jews believed none of it. Natan Kagan, the last Jew of Kutno, had died. But his story of annihilation had not. In fact, other refugees had brought reports of mass murders in other parts of Poland. The Kosciuskos had grown in strength and numbered almost a hundred men and a dozen women. The Pole, Bogdan Koz, had been contacted and a steady stream of small arms had been smuggled from his home on Bilowski Street—but not without loss. Early in February Solomon Katz was caught on the outside with a Luger under his coat. The SS hung him from a lamppost by his feet and emasculated him. "Circumcised right down to the crotch, balls, and all *Jude*," a burly sergeant laughed. Then they cut his throat and let him bleed to death like a butchered animal.

In January the Kosciuskos traded an emerald ring for their first machine gun. It was an old Italian Fiat-Revelli, Model 1935. It took three weeks to smuggle the forty-pound weapon and a thousand rounds of ammunition into the ghetto. It was hidden in the Kosciuskos' meeting place in the cellar of the storehouse on Pawia Street with an arsenal that had grown to sixty-three rifles, twenty-seven pistols, and four boxes of German grenades. When Josef patted the cold steel of the breech of the Fiat-Revelli, he felt a strange feeling of power, of assurance. Regina thought he and the rest of the Kosciuskos were mad.

Unknown to Josef and Jan, a new organization called the Jewish Fighting Organization (*Zydowska Organizacja Bojowa*) or ZOB was formed. Word filtered quickly through the packed ghetto and a meeting was arranged. It was held in the apartment of Mordechai Anielewicz, the twenty-four-year-old leader of ZOB. Because *Anielewicz* was derived from the Polish word for angel (*aniol*), Mordechai was commonly called "Angel" by his followers. He radiated charisma and commanded great respect and loyalty from his followers. As head of the even more militant Kosciuskos, Jan Tyranowski and his chief lieutenant, Josef Lipiski, joined Anielewicz and two other men unknown to Josef in the tiny apartment at Zamenhof 32 in the central ghetto.

Seating himself at a battered table next to Jan and across from Mordechai Anielewicz and the two strangers, Josef noticed Mordechai wore the new battle dress of ZOB: threadworn gray jacket, knickers, and golf socks. The ZOB leader's thin, dark face was cast in grim, down-turning lines like a bronze too long in the heat. His brown eyes moved first from Jan and then to Josef.

"It is good that you are here. We must unite our efforts against the Germans," Mordechai said. Josef could feel the force of the man's personality. He and Jan nodded.

"How many members do you have? Weapons? Are your people ready to fight to the death?" Josef asked.

Mordechai held up a hand defensively. "Nearly two hundred members, all young, and, yes, all ready to fight to the death. We have twenty-two rifles and ten pistols."

"Machine guns?"

"None. And you?"

Jan explained their membership and described their arms. Mordechai nodded approval. "We must unite," he said.

Jan looked at Josef who nodded almost imperceptibly. "Agreed," Jan said. "We must coordinate our efforts, but I insist on keeping command of my own."

Josef almost snickered. The two leaders sounded just like jealous generals arguing over authority. Mordechai Anielewicz yielded quickly. "Of course," he said. "But we must conduct joint meetings, share information, and . . ."

"But we don't share weapons," Jan said.

"All right," the ZOB leader agreed grudgingly. But there was a hard glint in his eyes—a glint that told Josef the argument was not finished.

Mordechai drummed the table uneasily and said, "We have word Karl Brandt (chief of the Gestapo's Jewish department in Warsaw) has been ordered to plan special *aktions*. That's why ZOB was formed."

Jan and Josef exchanged a confused look. "Round up Jews

for resettlement," the ZOB leader explained. He gestured to the strangers. "This is Yitzhak Schneidmil," he said, gesturing to the first and then to the second, "and Abraham Zuckerman." Both men nodded at Jan and Josef. Josef looked at the lined faces. Both men could have been very young. It was hard to tell, anymore. Starvation and disease made old people of everyone. There seemed to be a mask of terrible pain that had been fitted to every inhabitant of the ghetto— every Jew in Poland, for that matter. And the torn and threadbare clothes looked the same. Yitzhak Schneidmil was very fair with blue eyes. As un-Jewish in appearance as Jan Tyranowski.

Before Mordechai could continue, there was a knock and an old rabbi entered. Josef recognized Rabbi Yochanan Rosenfeld, a prominent member of the Judenrat. He was a bent old man so devastated by time and suffering he seemed crushed into a shape so singular Josef was reminded of a lame monkey he saw once in the Bronx Zoo heaving with difficulty across the sand of his cage. But the black eyes sunken in dark hollows were hard as steel and showed strength despite the frail body. Limping across the room, he sagged into a chair next to Mordechai. He wore the drab black of the orthodox. Josef did not trust the rabbi and wondered why he would be attending a meeting of a group of men pledged to fight the Germans.

Mordechai introduced the rabbi and explained, "Rabbi Rosenfeld is my uncle and has been aware of our activities since the beginning. He requested to be here. You can give him your trust. He has mine."

The rabbi's rock-hard eyes ran over every man in the room. "You're still determined to fight?"

"Yes, Uncle," Mordechai said. He gestured to the strangers. "You must hear from Abraham and Yitzhak."

Abraham Zuckerman stood. He spoke with Yiddish distinctly flavored with the rolling Russian spoken in the Ukraine. "I am from Kiev—that's where I was born." Irony twisted the young-old face into a frightening leer. "I want to tell you of the Germans' beautification efforts." The men shifted uneasily. "There's a ravine outside Kiev, it's called Babi Yar. The Germans decided to fill it—fill it with the corpses of every Jew in Kiev."

"But how do you know?"

The man snickered and drooled and there was a touch of madness in his eyes and in the squealing timbre of his voice like a stuck pig. "As you can plainly see, I am a coward. I hid in the forest just to the west of Babi Yar. In just two days all the Jews of Kiev, over thirty thousand, were marched there, forced to disrobe, lined up at the edge of the ravine, and shot." The dark eyes moistened and looked down at his clenched fists resting on the table. "Including my mother, father, two brothers, and my sister." He slumped down into his chair, drooling and sobbing into his fists. He began to gasp over and over, "I'm afraid—so afraid . . ." No one reacted, no one tried to console the broken man. Everyone had seen too much horror, too many tears, too much agony. They would let Abraham sob himself out.

Mordechai turned to his uncle. "Now do you believe? We've had reports that *Einsatzgruppen* A alone has killed over two hundred thousand Jews in Latvia, Lithuania, and Estonia. And it's been reported Jews have been rounded up and shot at Smolensk, Kharkov, Minsk."

"Reports! Reports!" Rabbi Rosenfeld said. "You young bulls want to believe all the worst. Find some reason to fight."

To Josef the old Rabbi Yochanan Rosenfeld represented all of the obstinate, blind members of the ghetto who refused to believe they were marked for destruction even when it was before their eyes. Angered by Rosenfeld's intransigence, Josef asked with irony and feigned naiveté, "Do you believe the corpses you see on the sidewalks every morning, Rabbi? Do you believe the starving children? Do you believe the mass graves?"

"Enough!" Rosenfeld shouted, flaring like a struck match to the insult. He pointed a bent finger at Josef. "Of course

I believe. Thousands have died. But to suggest organized exterminations is another matter. It is absurd—irrational.''

Mordechai gestured at Yitzhak Schneidmil. Yitzhak stood. His diction was just as distinct as Abraham Zuckerman's, but was spoken with guttural German inflection instead of Russian. "I am from Berlin. For most of my adult life I passed for Aryan under the name of Heinrich Wacht. I worked as a clerk in the War Ministry. One of my superiors became suspicious. I had to flee." He stared at the rabbi. "We are all doomed. It has been decided. There was a meeting at a place called Wannsee in January. The butchers were all there—Adolph Eichmann, Reinhard Heydrich, Heinrich Muller. They decided on a 'Final Solution.' They're going to murder every one of us. That's their Final Solution for us, their Jewish problem. I saw the notes."

"And just how will this be done? Just how will they murder three and a half million people," Rosenfeld asked, voice edged with sarcasm.

"It's already being done. With gas—they've decided on prussic acid that they call Zyklon B and the bodies are incinerated."

"There's a rumor people are being killed at Chelmno," Jan said.

Yitzhak nodded agreement. "It's an extermination center. And the biggest is being completed at Auschwitz-Birkenau and there are others at Belzac, Sobibor, and Treblinka."

"Treblinka!" Josef shouted. "My family is there."

Yitzhak set his jaw in a hard line. "I'm sorry, comrade. They are probably dead. The gas chambers are finished and test groups have been run through. Most of the Jews of Warsaw are destined for Treblinka. That's why it was built."

Josef felt Jan's hand on his shoulder and he dropped his head so that the other men could not see the tears pooling in his eyes. He wiped his nose with his sleeve. Jan said to Yitzhak, "When will the exterminations begin?"

"They're behind schedule. Much of the work was sabotaged by Jews, Poles, Russians, and other *untermenschen*.'' He drummed his temple. ''I would say by June—July at the latest.''

Rabbi Yochanan Rosenfeld came to his feet as fast as his infirm legs would permit. ''I won't listen to this madness,'' he said. ''The next thing you'll discuss is your revolution! Have you forgotten the Law of Moses? The Pentateuch. Does the commandment 'Thou shalt not kill' mean nothing to you? May God in his infinite mercy forgive your folly.'' He hobbled across the room and left, slamming the door behind him.

''He's blind! Blind!'' Josef cried, looking up with wet eyes.

''And so are most of them,'' Jan agreed.

Mordechai sighed deeply and sank back. ''We must fight, but we have practically nothing—perhaps two hundred fighters and a few weapons. We can't take on the Wehrmacht, the Luftwaffe.'' For the first time he showed despair. The cloak of confidence sloughed away. Dropping his head on his clenched fists, he spoke to the table with a voice as soft as a wailed psalm, ''And there will be no help from the Russians, British, Americans. The Americans, British, and Dutch can't even handle the Japanese in the Pacific and the British can't drive Rommel out of North Africa. No. There will be no help. We are on our own and we have nothing.'' He looked up, the brown of his eyes heightened by a film of moisture.

Jan came erect, eyes as hard as the rock of Zion. ''Don't say that. We'll buy, steal more arms. Dig bunkers. Plan a line of defense. We won't be ready to fight this summer, but we'll recruit, build our forces, and strike out at them even if it's with our fingernails. We have two advantages. We can choose how and where we die and we'll be fighting on our own ground.'' He circled a finger overhead in an encompassing gesture. ''We live in a labyrinth—our own catacombs. We'll knock down walls in the attics, between cellars. We'll be able to shift positions, retreat, attack at our choosing, bring up supplies through our maze without the Germans seeing anything." He slammed his fist down hard on the table. "They won't exterminate us all with impunity—without cost."

Josef stared at Jan with awe. He saw in him the tortured yet ultimately triumphant Jewish spirit—the spirit that had kept the "Chosen" alive through two thousand years of oppression and dispersion.

Mordechai's eyes were on Jan, too, face alight with new resolve. Josef could see the young man's confidence flowing back, hear it in his voice. "Yes. You're right, Jan. We'll build for that day. Fight them in the streets, gutters, buildings. Kill some of them."

"We're not sheep," Jan said. "We'll build interconnecting bunkers with air vents and stock them with food and water. We'll plant mines, make Molotov cocktails, steal more grenades, and rain them on the Germans. The British stopped them at the Channel. We'll build a channel of our own."

Josef spoke, "And if we only had our own RAF."

For the first time tiny smiles were seen on the faces of the men. Abraham Zuckerman had stopped crying. Looking up, he stared at the other men over his clenched fists. His eyes shone with the hate and fear of an animal trapped by predators that finally turns and lashes back at its killers. "Kill them!" he shrieked, spraying spittle and coming erect. "That's the only way. Kill them all!" Then, shouting unintelligible oaths, he bolted through the door. The men could hear his maniacal laughter echoing through the building.

XIII

**England
February, 1942**

JANUARY and early February had been frustrating for Number 54 Squadron and the entire RAF. Randolph led patrols daily, scanning the sky hungrily for the orange-and-green-striped ME 109 of Major Erich Kochling. However, *Jagdstaffel Vierter* had not been seen since the first week of December and as the early days of February slipped past, Randolph began to suspect Kochling had been transferred to the Russian front where most of the Luftwaffe had been concentrated. Fighter Command, too, had been weakened with a dozen squadrons transferred to the Middle and Far East. There were a few nuisance raids, but, in general, the air war had become a deadly bore. Massed dogfights seemed to have become a thing of the past.

On January 17, Flight Lieutenant Cedric Hart bagged a mine-laying Junkers JU 88 over the Thames estuary, but Randolph, flying cover, did not have a hand in the kill. It was the squadron's first victory in five weeks.

The next afternoon while making an instrument check,

Randolph flew at treetop height over the farmland in eastern Kent. Throttling back just above stall speed, he roared over a small cottage like a gem in an elysian setting; a brook and forest on one side, verdant fields on the other. She was there. Elisa Blue, standing in front of her house, waving a wide-brimmed hat and scarf. Looking down, his entire being ached for her and he realized he had not had her in his arms for almost a month. He circled twice, waving, then turned for home. Flying back to Detling, he maintained a low altitude. The weakening rays of the sun intensified the colors beneath him. England had never looked so beautiful, so peaceful.

Then came the foolish raid of January 19. The German battle cruisers *Scharnhorst* and *Gneisenau* and cruiser *Prinz Eugen* had been based in the French port of Brest for repairs and refitting. *Prinz Eugen* had helped dispatch the mighty battle cruiser *Hood*; the *Scharnhorst* and the *Gneisenau* had sunk the carrier *Glorious* and sent 115,000 tons of merchant shipping to the bottom. Here on the Bay of Biscay they posed a constant threat to break out into the Atlantic. Surrounded by the continent's heaviest concentration of flak batteries and nests of fighter squadrons, the flotilla posed a difficult target. Bomber Command mounted a series of night attacks—nineteen hundred sorties that dropped nearly two thousand tons of bombs. Dropping their bombs out of the darkness that was ripped by hundreds of flak guns and staring into the glare of a belt of searchlights, the bomb aimers had little success. In fact, most bombs did not land within five miles of the target. Forty-three bombers had been lost in the raids. But fear and the hunger for revenge drove the War Office to brash, ill-advised decisions.

Bomber Command's AOC-in-C (Air Officer Commanding in Chief), Air Marshal Sir Richard Peirse, decided to mount a giant daylight raid with 102 Whitley, Hampden, and Wellington bombers from Number Two Group and Number Three Group. This was one fourth of the RAF's entire bomber force. Every available fighter in southeast England was to escort the bombers. When Randolph opened the envelope with the bright red seal marked, "Top Secret, Immediate Action," he was astonished. The plan was stupid. With only a range of 395 miles, his Spitfires would be pushed to the limit to reach the target. In fact, a strong headwind would eliminate his squadron. At best, he would only have a few minutes over the target if he ever did reach Brest. Adequate fighter protection would be impossible.

The raid was a disaster. Desperately, Number 54 Squadron and ten other squadrons of Fighter Command Group Eleven tried to fight off the swarms of German fighters that suddenly materialized. Randolph shot down one ME and Fifty-four Squadron accounted for three more. Randolph lost one of his new chaps before low fuel tanks forced Number 54 Squadron to turn for home. Ack-ack and the Luftwaffe had a field day, shooting down thirty-two of the slow bombers. There were reports of bomb hits on the enemy ships, but the major doubted the veracity of the claims. "A bloody muck-up," he told his adjutant, Captain Edwin Smith.

Randolph felt frustration compounded upon frustration. Apparently, the German ships had escaped serious damage and he had caught a glimpse of Kochling's green-and-orange Messerschmitt while fighting for his life in the midst of a dogfight. He had had no chance to engage the killer. Coop Hansen was still unavenged and on German radio Axis Sally and Lord Haw Haw gloated over the heavy British losses. "Thanks for the target practice," Axis Sally had said, closing her broadcast.

For almost four weeks, Randolph flew three patrols a day, but the Channel was peaceful and calm. The storm had passed. Again he heard rumors that *Jagdstaffel Vierter* had been transferred. But now he did not believe them. Kochling was still there. He felt it in his guts. Sensed the man like a hungry animal sniffing the breeze for his enemy—his prey, his killer. He was there. He knew it. Somehow he would flush him out. Hunt him down.

By the end of the month, the constant patrols had exhausted Randolph and the squadron doctor threatened to ground him if he did not take a leave. "Get some rest, old boy," the surgeon had said. The adjutant, Captain Edwin Smith, had joined in, "We can jolly well run the war without you, sir. Take a few days. I'll instruct the lads not to chop Kochling. We'll save him for you."

Randolph knew they were right. His alertness had slipped and his reactions were slowing. He had fatigued himself to the point of being a menace to himself and his men. He had done it before. He knew the signs. He was worn to the bone and he yearned for Elisa Blue and Fenwyck. Lloyd was still home recovering, but Randolph knew his brother would soon be gone. And things were very slow. He took a three-day leave at the end of the month.

When Randolph arrived at Fenwyck, he found Lloyd's three broken ribs had healed faster than his reputation. The flyer was well aware of the vicious report the enraged Brigadier Gilbert Fraser had submitted to General Archer—a scathing account of his interview with Brigadier Higgins concerning the killing of the five POWs at Bir Fuad Ridge. Fraser described Brigadier Lloyd Higgins as ". . . callous, belligerent, and unrepentant with no viable explanation for his actions at Bir Fuad Ridge."

General Archer had convened a board of inquiry and three witnesses were brought from Libya to testify: Captain Courtney Hall of the East Sussex Rifles who reported the incident, a corporal from his company, and Sergeant Colby Powell, Lloyd's driver. It was not until January that Chief of Staff Viscount Alanbrooke intervened—just as Randolph predicted—declaring Brigadier Higgins "not culpable in any respect." Randolph suspected there had even been some gentle prodding from 10 Downing Street. However, the taint on Lloyd's reputation remained like an ugly stain on one's finest shirt. As Randolph had expected, a letter written by General Archer was inserted in Lloyd's record describing the incident, absolving him as "acting under extreme duress," but falling short of justifying his actions. There was no mention of his bravery, clever tactics, and dogged, tenacious conduct on the field against overwhelming odds. In effect, it was a reprimand. Randolph had not seen Lloyd's copy of the letter.

Lloyd read the letter to Randolph in the study while seated in his usual place behind the serpentine desk. The brothers laughed and toasted each other while Bernice sat quietly on the sofa sipping her Bordeaux. "You were right, brother," Lloyd said, holding his glass high.

"Quite right. Let them write their bloody letters," Randolph said. "It's a lot of rot. I remember in 'sixteen when I chopped that septic butcher August von Landenberg. He had seventeen kills, over twenty good English lads dead. There was a blizzard of letters and endless twaddle from the 'dugout queens' just because I scragged him at altitude zero. It wasn't sporting to dispatch the Hun on the ground. Swiss Red Cross and all that. The letters are still in my file. 'Not cricket,' they said."

Lloyd nodded with the memory. "I'll never forget. You bagged the sod over the Somme. Two stretcher bearers were carrying him. You sent the whole lot 'west.' " He held up his glass. "Good show!"

"Just one long burst," Randolph said proudly, warming with the memory. He answered his brother's salute and they both drank.

Bernice drained her glass and stared at her brother-in-law, her delicate jaw in an unusually hard line. She had heard the story many times and disliked it more every time she heard it. Reaching for a cut-glass decanter on a Regency table next to the sofa, she refilled her glass and took a large drink.

The mood sobered as the conversation inevitably swung to the conduct of the war. In hushed tones the brothers discussed the events of the past three months. Although the Russians had stopped the Wehrmacht outside Moscow and actually pushed the enemy back, the Japanese were running wild in the Pacific. Reports from Washington were guarded and obviously heavily censored, but the Americans had apparently suffered an appalling defeat at Pearl Harbor. It was rumored the entire battle line had been sunk or damaged and terrible casualties sustained. But Rodney was safe. Letters from Brenda had assured them he was home and well with ". . . just a bump on his head."

Lloyd refilled the three glasses, lit a Lucky Strike, and spoke in funereal tones. "Those little yellow men have had it all their own way. *Repulse* and *Prince of Wales* sunk, Hong Kong gone and Singapore is next."

Randolph winced. Elisa Blue's father was in Singapore with the East Surreys. She must be upset. He had to see her. Would see her before the evening was out.

Lloyd continued the litany of disaster, "Why they've invaded Burma and even Ceylon and India are threatened."

Randolph nodded. "And the Netherlands East Indies are gone—write them off. They'll have all the oil they need."

A patina of anguish shone from Bernice's face. "It'll go on forever, won't it, Lloyd," she said. "This war feeds on itself—grows like a cancer."

"Please, love," he soothed. "The Yanks are in it early this time and the Russians are doing better than anyone expected."

Randolph joined in. "You know I've seen American aircraft plants, Bernice. Their capacity is unbelievable. They crank them out like Fords. Soon we'll outfly, outman, and outgun them on every front." He did not mention the fact that most American plants he had seen were still "tooling up" and his belief that a two-year lag was inevitable before American production would be felt.

Bernice slumped back and sullenly sipped her Bordeaux. Lloyd continued in his somber mood. He was disturbed by the news from the Western Desert. The fighting in North Africa had been confused and indecisive and losses had been heavy. With close friends in high posts in Whitehall, the brigadier was privy to information not available to the public. Waving his cigarette for emphasis he compared the wily Rommel to an elusive fox in a briar patch. But General Ritchie was after him, clearing Cyrenaica and relieving Tobruk. Then a surprise counterattack drove the Eighth Army back to the Gazala-Bir-Hachim line. Ritchie rebounded to take Bardia and Halfaya Pass and then the armies rested like two exhausted stags, horns still locked but lacking the energy to destroy each other. "Ritchie's a good man," Lloyd concluded. "But the Eighth Army needs more aggressive field commanders. It's like fighting sea battles. Often there are no lines at all. Commanders must make decisions on the spot without really knowing where the enemy may be. Often he's in your rear, and by the same token, you can be in his rear." He shook his head. "Not a place for inexperienced officers." He took a drink and then punched the desk and spoke before he considered the impact of his words. "Blast it all! This waiting about can get on a man's wick!"

Bernice came erect, eyes wide, passion modulating the timbre of her voice to low, harsh tones. "You want to go back—you've got to go back to the desert, don't you, Lloyd? This is how it's always been since 1914. Then it was the Coldstreams who couldn't survive without you, now it's the Fourth Armored Brigade and the whole blasted Eighth Army!"

Lloyd lit another Lucky Strike and sipped his drink. "I'm recovered from my wounds and quite fit. I expect orders to return. It's my duty, love."

"You're a broken record, Lloyd. War! That's all we've known. Now my son is in the North Atlantic hunting for U-boats—or are they hunting for him? My husband carries the scars of two wars, is at an age when men retire . . ."

"Men don't retire from honor, Bernice."

"Don't give me that bloody drivel, Lloyd." Then her words shocked Randolph to the marrow of his bones. "Plain and simple, you—both of you—love war. Live for death." She stabbed an accusatory finger at her husband. "You've been untrue to me. Kept your mistress. That whore war is your mistress! I've never had a chance against her. You've slept in her bed all these years." She slammed her glass down on the small Regency table so hard the stem broke and the contents spilled across the walnut top with shards of broken glass. Sobbing, she left the room.

Lloyd sighed and emptied his drink. He spoke softly, "I have my orders, brother. I leave for North Africa at the end of the week. They're going to fly me in." He nodded at the door. "I couldn't tell Bernice. She's obviously out of sorts —got her wind up. I'll wait till the end. She'll never understand." He poured more Scotch into his glass.

Randolph held up his glass and stared at the amber liquid thoughtfully. He spoke slowly, "No woman can. They weren't made that way—to understand."

Lloyd smiled at his brother's insight and turned a lip under and dampened his lips with the tip of his tongue. "You're still hunting Kochling?"

"Quite. You know what he did. I told you about Coop Hansen."

"Kochling may be gone."

Randolph shook his head. "No. He's here." He took a drink. "I can smell him."

Lloyd's nod indicated understanding. "You're awfully keen to kill him—murder him?" he said wryly.

Randolph nodded affirmatively. "In his cockpit, in his parachute, in the water." He raised his big hands, fingers extended clawlike. "With these, if I could. I'd prefer it that way."

Lloyd chuckled. His voice was filled with irony. "I say, brother, they'd call it murder."

"Is stepping on a cockroach murder?"

The brothers stared into each other's eyes and laughed. Then they raised their glasses in a single unified motion and emptied them.

Seated on the sofa with Elisa close to his side, Randolph stared at the red wine glistening in his glass. "It's strawberry, my major," Elisa said.

Randolph sipped it. "It's nectar," he said, savoring the liquor. "Fit for Zeus."

Elisa smiled but her usual Madonnalike serenity was not there. "Singapore will fall," she said simply.

He tapped his glass with a single finger. "It's quite possible, Elisa."

"Now I'll lose my father. They've already killed my brother." She turned away. "Maybe my father's dead, too."

He wrapped a big arm around her narrow shoulders. He would not lie. "Actually the fortress is cut off. It's a siege. Casualties have not been heavy but they may be forced to surrender. The lot of the POW is not all that bad, Elisa. There are the Geneva Conventions, you know."

She turned back to him. "It's better than fighting, isn't it?"

She needed reassurance and he leapt in. "Why of course. The war would be over for your father. He'd live in a camp until this lot is over. And it's only a question of time before the Yanks clear out that whole blasted nest of Japs." He did not mention the amount of time; the years and years of blood and carnage he knew lay ahead.

She snuggled closer and seemed to relax. "I need you, my major. It's so thrilling when you fly over. It's like looking up at a beautiful pigeon come home to roost with his mate. And I know you're safe—you're still . . ."

She turned away, unable to finish the sentence. He kissed her forehead, her eyes, and found tears on her cheeks. He kissed them away and then she raised her lips. Soft as velvet, they were parted and warm. The kiss was long and hard and then they clung to each other and he could feel her quick breathing on her ear. "Stay with me. Live with me," she pleaded.

"Please, my darling. You know I can't . . ."

"So did my brother, my father know. It's your damned duty, your white whale." She leaned back and there was a fierce look in her eyes he had never seen before. "There are so many good reasons to die, so few to live." She kissed him savagely with a hungry, physical urgency. They locked together, tongues twisting, kneading, pressing like attacking reptiles in their fervor. Pulling up her thin cotton blouse and sliding his hand over her hot silky flesh, he became acutely aware of every plane of her back. He traced the smooth curve of muscles on each side of her back and ran his hand up and down the ridge of her spine. It felt like a string of polished pearls.

"Stay with me. Stay with me," she repeated breathlessly. "The sky will claim you. I know it will." She pulled away and her eyes were misty.

He felt the hollow emptiness of hopelessness well deep in his guts. He felt like a man with his arms tied to two Clydesdales pulling in opposite directions. There was no solution, no resolution, only agony. And Bernice came back. Her anguished face. The terrible words. *You love war!* But that was insane. He agonized over each lost boy. Died with them. Flew to save his lads and punish the enemy. And he wrote the painful letters to next of kin. First Bernice and now Elisa. He loved them both but they would drive him mad. He drained half his glass and stared at the table in front of the couch. "Please, my darling. Please," he pleaded. He rubbed his forehead with a closed fist.

She sighed and sank back. "I'm sorry, my major. I torture you every time I see you."

"Oh, no, my darling. Don't say that."

"It's because I love you so much." She pointed skyward. "You were sent to me."

He looked up, finally freeing his mind from the vise of Bernice's words. "Perhaps you were sent to me."

"Do you love me?"

"I'm not sure."

"You need me?"

"You know I do."

"That's enough." She found his eyes and held them with the power of her gaze. "Love is as strong as death," she said.

The phrase was familiar, but his memory failed him. "Which poet?" he asked.

She smiled. "The Bible."

He drank his wine. She recharged his glass from the bottle on the table in front of the couch. He spoke thoughtfully, "Perhaps when this is over we can talk of being together, can speak of . . ."

"Can talk of love then, Major?" she interrupted, lips tight, eyes flashing, cheeks rouged by passion. "Is there so much hate in this world love has become a transient thing, Major? Is hate immune to the onslaught of time—raging, destroying, immutable? Must the call of the last trumpet sound in our ears till the end of time?"

Momentarily, he was taken aback by her words, but collected his thoughts quickly. "You know that isn't true. It's just that these times are too uncertain. I haven't been fair to you."

"You mean I've lost enough."

He tabled his glass and stared into her eyes. "Quite right. That's the harsh reality of it."

Her mood softened and she stared into his eyes. The little girl was back. "But I've already been everything a woman can be to you. We've taken everything there is from each other. If I lose you, I lose everything."

Her circular logic baffled him. There were no openings. He grasped her arms and he could feel her hands on his shoulders. The dark blue of her eyes glowed like sapphires held to candlelight, penetrating all the way to the essence of his being. There was love there; full, brimming, enveloping like a warm summer breeze. He kissed her again, hard and demanding. Wordlessly, they stood together and walked to the curtained doorway.

Within minutes she had disrobed and stretched herself on the bed while Randolph threw his uniform on the floor like a pile of discarded rags. He dropped down beside her and enfolded her in his arms. He ran his hands over her neck, swollen ruby-tipped breasts, tiny waist, sculpted hips, thighs. He kissed her neck, ears, breasts, her fine skin like hot satin under his lips and fingertips. She breathed in short choking gasps; cooed and chortled with joy as he kissed her again and again while his hands explored and caressed. She twisted, writhed, and trembled, finally rolling to her back and pulling him with her. Spreading her knees, she raised them high and he lowered himself between them. He heard her gasp and groan as he finally found her depths.

In contrast to the other nights, tonight's lovemaking was wildly urgent. His body deep in hers, he plunged, rocked, thrust while her hips met his assault with power that belied her frail body. His former reservations were swept away like a stick in a flood and he was carried beyond his sense of self. Locked in the rood of her arms and legs, he was completely hers, seemed to blend with her so that their very blood seemed to mingle and pulse with the same beat—the beat of a single heart. And it was her breath that filled his lungs, her thoughts that glimmered in his mind. They moaned, thrashed, and although his mouth was glued to hers, somehow he heard her say, "I love you, my major. I love you."

He gasped into her ear, not sure it was his voice or hers, "I love you, my darling. I love you."

XIV

**Number 54 Squadron
February 11, 1942**

THE meeting was held in the officers' mess. A small room, it appeared even smaller crowded with eleven pilots; the squadron adjutant, Captain Edwin Smith; squadron clerk, Lance Corporal Timothy Evans; and two batmen serving coffee, cocoa, and liquor. There was a relaxed atmosphere, the pilots lounging, smoking, and talking. Every flyer was dressed in RAF blue.

Three, the ready pilots, were in flying kit, wearing their helmets; parachutes and Mae Wests stacked on the floor behind them. Actually, they were the "Wolf Blue" section, led by Flying Officer Michael Sturgis—a former flight sergeant with nine victories. Sturgis's wingmen were both flight sergeants who had been with the squadron for over six months; Gilbert McCarthy with one kill, Dwight Tambler with two. With their fighters parked in the nearest dispersal area a hundred yards from the mess hall and a lorry waiting just outside, they sat near the door where they could board the vehicle in seconds and be airborne in minutes. But Sector

Control had not reported a single "bandit" in nearly a week. No one expected a scramble.

When Randolph entered, the babble of voices stopped and every man came to his feet. The squadron commander walked to the front of the room where there was a small platform in front of a blackboard mounted on rollers. Corporal Evans with a pad and pencil sat to one side of the platform while Captain Smith took his usual post at the other side. Everyone looked at the squadron commander expectantly.

"Carry on, gentlemen," Randolph said, mounting the platform, and the men returned to their seats with the sound of chairs scuffing over the rough unfinished wood planking of the floor. Randolph's batman, Sergeant-Major Forrest Woodhouse, raised a bottle of Haig and Haig inquisitively. Randolph shook his head and indicated a pitcher of steaming cocoa instead. Quickly, Woodhouse poured a mug and handed it to the major. Randolph eyed his pilots over the mug as he took his first sip and then placed it on a small table in front of him. There were two new faces in the room. Two pilots who had reported the day before while he had been on leave. They looked so young. They seemed younger every time. A strange phenomenon because they were always eighteen or nineteen years old. Rarely, did he ever get a pilot over nineteen unless a veteran transferred from another squadron.

He had met the new pilots that morning in his office in the farmhouse. They both held the lowest commissioned rank of pilot officer. They had stood rigidly at attention in front of his desk as new pilots always did when first introduced to their squadron commander. It tore Randolph's heart. He had welcomed so many young men to their graves—generations of young men in two wars.

The first was a slender, fair reed of a lad named Robert Burroughs, a barrister's son from Bideford, Devon. A law student destined to follow in his father's footsteps, Burroughs had left college to join the RAF. His gray eyes held an apprehensive, almost-frightened look and his left eye twitched nervously whenever he felt stress. At that moment, it had been ticking steadily. He would bear watching. Randolph was sure the lad stood a good chance of killing himself long before the Germans got the opportunity. He was eighteen years old.

The second was Milby Davenport, the scion of a well-to-do family in Birmingham. The son of a steel broker and exporter, Davenport was short and stocky with a compact athletic build that attested to his prowess on the soccer and rugby fields. In fact, he had played semiprofessional soccer for the Birmingham Lancers at the age of sixteen. However, his father had talked him into his office where the boy had languished unhappily until his eighteenth birthday. The day after his birthday, he joined the RAF.

Eyeing the two youngsters from behind his desk, Randolph had asked his first question. Except for the aircraft, it never varied from pilot to pilot, war to war. "Number of hours in Spits?"

"Seventy-two, sir," Burroughs answered in a high, wispy, almost-effeminate voice, eyes fixed on some obscure point a foot over Randolph's head, left eyelid still fluttering. Randolph shifted his gaze to the other new chap.

"Seventy-seven, sir," Davenport said in a deep voice that was almost theatrical in its resonance. His brown eyes were on his squadron commander, steady and confident.

Randolph smiled. Things had improved. At the height of the blitz, he had taken aboard men with as little as eleven hours in Spitfires. With greater experience and a lull over the Channel, these chaps had a far better chance to survive, unless they escorted another foolish raid to Brest. He dismissed them after reminding them of the afternoon's meeting.

Now he was staring down at them; the two bright new faces and the nine other veteran pilots. Veterans. A veteran was a man who survived because of skill and luck. Some said good luck played the most important part in survival. Certainly, during a man's first month of combat fortune's smile had been indispensable for survival—especially during the Blitz. But now they all had a chance, a good chance for staying alive—if that idiot Air Marshal Sir Richard Peirse had learned his bloody lesson at Brest.

Peirse reminded Randolph of Sir Douglas Haig and his stupid offensives of the Great War that sacrificed hundreds of thousands of England's bravest and finest uselessly on impenetrable German defenses of barbed wire, machine guns, and preregistered artillery. In so many ways Englishmen insisted on repeating history. Few seemed capable of learning from it. But Major Randolph Higgins had learned. He would not throw away these priceless young men.

He looked first at the new pilots, Pilot Officer Robert Burroughs and Pilot Officer Milby Davenport. Then his eyes encompassed the entire room. These were his men; the best. He spoke slowly and softly, making the same basic speech he had directed at young men flying the flimsy crates of two world wars. Subconsciously, he used a mixture of idioms and slang that had crept into his vocabulary from both conflicts. "Some of you have heard this many times, but I have rules—rules that we must all follow if we are to stay alive." Timothy Evans moved to the blackboard and wrote as Randolph spoke. "No lone wolf heroics or you'll just be another RAF roundel on some Kraut's tail fin—a round of schnapps at some Krauthead mess." He stared at one of his older pilots, Flying Officer Anthony Bowman, who stared back with narrow, unblinking eyes. Randolph continued, "Remain in your sections of three unless ordered to individual combat. Keep the sun behind you; always carry out an attack once you have started it; fire only at close range—under two hundred yards if possible. Always remember you only have sixteen seconds of firepower. Fire in short bursts, long bursts will overheat your weapons and there's a good chance they'll jam. No full deflection shots unless within eighty yards. Don't waste the Crown's ammunition trying for the miracle shot. Attack from behind at minimum deflection and look for your enemy's blind spot; every aircraft has them. *Never* fly straight and level in a dogfight or you'll get buggered with twenty-millimeter and seven-point-nine ball in a brace of shakes. Jink, weave, don't make an easy target of yourself. Remember, you're a target the minute you belt yourself into your Spit, so don't bugger all and make it easy for the Krauts to prang you."

He sipped his cocoa. "Think before you attack. Hit the JU eighty-seven from below. It's cold meat. The HE one-eleven and the Dorniers from above or head-on. They can only fire back with seven-point-nine mgs. But don't get too bloody eager. Some of our lads got the chop because Heinkels looked like cold meat but were decoys for the ME one-oh-nines hanging about in the sun. Look out for the Hun in the sun," he warned again, just as he had over twenty years earlier.

His eyes wandered over the intent faces. Every eye was riveted on him. He continued, "Another thing, if a Jerry dives on you, don't dive. Turn to meet him. You bloody well can't bring your armament to bear if you show him your arse." There was a chuckle. "Always remember the Messerschmitt has fuel injection while we use carburetors. In a steep dive, your Rolls can conk out while the Daimler-Benz can purr along like a randy pussycat after a night of bonking in an alley." Another chuckle rumbled through the room. He could hear Burroughs's high titter over the rest. He stabbed a finger at the new pilots. "Don't give Jerry any advantages, use your strengths, hide your weaknesses. Your enemy's weakness is in his wing root. The ME doesn't have the wingtip to wingtip wing spar the Spit has. So aim low at the cockpit. If you miss the pilot, you may hit the wing root. A burst in the wing root can break the whole bloody lot loose." He moved his eyes from Burroughs to Davenport. "Remember, we can't dive with the ME and he can outclimb you, but we are faster and more maneuverable. If you use your wits, you can get behind an ME and if you get your arse in the twist, you can always outrun him and make it home." He nodded to himself. "You can always come back to fight another day. That's better than having your family awarded your DFM

(Distinguished Flying Medal) posthumously.'' There was no laughter.

Randolph sipped his cocoa and placed the mug back on the table. ''If you want to live, remember the prevailing winds are westerly, especially when we make sweeps over the continent. This will work against you on the way home. And for all that's holy, remember altitude is your most priceless possession. It can always be traded for speed and speed spells 'life.' '' He took another large swallow of cocoa.

He nodded at Davenport. ''Pilot Officer Davenport, you are assigned to Wolf Yellow Section under the command of Flight Lieutenant Archie Rhoads. Your other wingman is Pilot Officer Meredith Hammes.'' Hammes, a burly ship-fitter's apprentice from Liverpool, looked pained. Then Randolph shifted his eyes to Rhoads, his most valuable man and second in command.

Flight Lieutenant Archie Rhoads was Freddie ''Coop'' Hansen's replacement. At twenty-seven years of age, Rhoads was a distant second to Randolph in age. Of average build and balding prematurely, he looked to be ten years older. In fact, he looked more the part of a college professor than a fighter pilot. Holding a degree from Oxford in civil engineering, he had left his profession and joined the RAF in 1939 on the day war was declared. He had fallen in love with flying as a youth and had joined the Oxford University Flying Club as a fledgling ''aeronaut'' when only seventeen. Rhoads became an expert with the Hart Trainer airplane and by the time he was eighteen he was putting the sturdy little biplane through wing-bending acrobatics. Throughout the Blitz he was assigned to Fighter Command Group Thirteen in the north and flew Hurricanes out of Sunderland in Durham with Number 27 Squadron. Opposed by *Luftflotte* 5 operating out of Norway and Denmark, action was sporadic as few German raids originated across the North Sea. Still, Rhoads had shot down four bombers and a single ME 110. Hungry for more action and a chance to fly a Spitfire, he had harangued Fighter Command until he was transferred to Number 54 Squadron.

Immediately, Randolph had been impressed by the man's aeronautical skills, dazzling panache, and insouciant verve when in combat. Since joining the squadron in July of '41, he had added two Heinkel 111s and three ME 109s to his skein of kills. Randolph was delighted with him. He was a killer. If anyone could keep Davenport alive, Rhoads would do it.

Major Higgins moved his eyes over the faces, stopping on Flight Lieutenant Cedric Hart, his starboard wingman. "Lieutenant Hart," Randolph said. "You will fly wing with Flight Lieutenant Mason Wykoff in Flight Lieutenant Rhoads's section and"—he gestured to Burroughs—"Pilot Officer Robert Burroughs will take your place in my section." The news brought a grimace of distaste to Hart's face, a smile of delight to Burroughs's.

Randolph turned to the ready pilots. "Unless you have questions, return to the dispersal hut." Sturgis and his two sergeants rose, gathered up their parachutes and life preservers, and left. The commanding officer turned back to the remaining pilots. "Any questions?" His eye was caught by some movement to his left.

Randolph smiled as he acknowledged Flying Officer Anthony Bowman. A short, round man with an unruly plume of brown hair falling forward over his forehead like a wild growth of brambles, Bowman had an intensity about him that doubled his size. A zealous trencherman and drinker with the palate of a gourmet, he was revolted by the squadron's food and stuffed himself in London's finest restaurants whenever on leave. A small paunch told all of his weakness. By some miracle, he had an inexhaustible supply of Havana cigars padlocked in his foot locker. In fact, it was an exhaled jet of blue smoke and a waved cigar that caught Randolph's eye.

A capable, workmanlike fighter pilot, Bowman was famous and somewhat notorious for an unauthorized lone-wolf attack on the German fighter base at Wissant on the Pas de Calais. The attack had been carried out after his wingman, Clyde Millford-Davis, had been shot down by Major Erich Kochling and machine-gunned by the German while he drifted in his dinghy. In a blind fury, Bowman had actually attacked the wrong air base. Kochling's was known to be near Hardelot Plag while the enraged Englishman pounced on the first airfield he saw. The unfortunate airdrome happened to be the fighter strip at Wissant. Bowman destroyed two fighters on the ground and shot down another ME 109 as it tried to take off. In the usual British schizoid approach to unauthorized bravery, he was both mentioned in dispatches and reprimanded at the same time. Randolph had exacted a solemn promise from Bowman that the act would *never* be repeated without authorization and support. "Any news about our friend Kochling," Bowman asked in a soft voice as he came to his feet.

Randolph gritted his teeth and turned his lips under. "Intelligence would have us believe *Jagdstaffel Vierter* is on the Russian front."

"What do you believe, sir?"

Randolph dropped his jaw and rubbed his cheek with an open palm. "I can smell the bloody bastard."

"I say, bully for you, sir," Bowman agreed. "I can smell him, too." He looked down at his wingmen, Flight Sergeant Melvin Greentree and Pilot Officer Ernest Krasney, who were seated beside him. The three men exchanged smiles and nodded at each other. Bowman jammed the cigar into the corner of his mouth, dropped into his chair, and began talking to his wingmen in excited whispers.

"Any other questions?" Randolph asked. The pilots looked back silently.

Randolph nodded, satisfied. "Then inspect your aircraft —every nut and bolt. We have the best 'plumbers' (armorers) and mechanics in the RAF. But your life hangs on that prop, not theirs. I'll join you shortly. Only after your inspection will you return to your quarters and get some rest." He finished off his cocoa. "Things are quiet. It's a good time to get some relaxation."

Never had the squadron commander been so wrong.

* * *

He was awakened before 0500 hours by Sergeant-Major Forrest Woodhouse's frantic voice. "Sir! Sir! You're wanted in the operations room. Something big is astir."

Quickly, Randolph, dressed only in trousers, undershirt, and slippers, bolted down the stairs to his office. A sleepy Edwin Smith was already there, pulling on his tunic and sipping a cup of coffee. Anxiously, Sergeant-Major Timothy Evans, who had the duty, rose from his chair behind his desk and handed the major a handwritten sheet. "Signal from Group, sir. Just got it by telephone."

Randolph froze in the middle of the room as he read the document. *Scharnhorst*, *Gneisenau*, and *Prinz Eugen* had broken out of Brest with at least seven destroyers. Unbelievably, the flotilla was headed up the Channel. Every fighter squadron in Fighter Command Group Eleven was ordered into the air as soon as the weather permitted. Surprisingly, takeoff was at the discretion of the commanders.

"Weather?" Randolph shouted.

"Scattered clouds, rain, and fog, sir. A four-knot wind from the northwest gusting to eight, Major," Evans answered.

"Blast it! Full squadron scramble!" Randolph ordered. "Crew chiefs start warming up engines. Pilots to the mess hall."

Evans pushed three buttons setting off alarms in pilots' and enlisted men's quarters. Then he grabbed the telephone.

Randolph bounded up the stairs to his room where Woodhouse already had his flight kit laid out on the narrow bed. A mug of steaming hot coffee was on the nightstand. First Randolph pulled on a white roll-necked knitted pullover that he pulled down over his belt. Then, seating himself, Woodhouse helped him pull on his white knitted socks and tucked the trouser legs into the tops. Brown suede flying boots with rubber soles were pulled on next and zipped securely in place. Quickly the major stood and Woodhouse helped him shrug his way into his sheepskin-lined flying jacket followed by his yellow Mae West. Then he pulled a type C flying helmet made of brown chrome leather and lined with chamois down over his head. Antiglare goggles followed, pulled down only to his forehead where the elastic band held them securely in place above his eyes. Then he stuffed two maps into his boots, grabbed his parachute, and rushed through the doorway. He had not touched the coffee.

When he ran out of the door, he was appalled by the weather. Now he knew why takeoff was at his discretion. If his squadron was lost because of foul weather, he would be blamed, not Fighter Command. The politicians and generals would be secure. He looked around anxiously. Low banks of fog were sweeping across the airfield, blotting out the feeble efforts of dawn and casting everything in the deep darkness of midnight. The tarmac was wet and the air smelled of fresh rain. At first, he thought that all of his haste had been wasted. But there were breaks that appeared like dim lights held behind blankets. Once they took off, they could climb above the weather and be in the clear. Maybe find Kochling. He knew what his decision would be—had to be. He felt his pulse quicken, and strangely, he saw Bernice's haunting eyes, ravaged face ruined by hard down-turning lines. The terrible words came back. "You're wrong. Stop haunting me," he cried to himself. *Am I going mad?* he asked himself. He shook his head and she vanished.

Entering the mess hall, he found eight pilots talking and drinking coffee or tea. They were all standing. "Seat yourselves," Randolph said. As he mounted the platform three more pilots entered. Davenport and Burroughs were the last to enter.

Woodhouse handed the major a fresh cup of coffee and this time Randolph was able to sip the hot liquid. Quickly Randolph told his men of the breakout of the German warships that, by now, were well into the Channel. "Only a few heavy units of the Royal Navy are available and they're based at Scapa Flow," he said. He looked around at the tight, expectant faces. "I doubt if they can intercept," he added.

"Only the RAF, destroyers, and motor torpedo boats stand between the Germans and escape and you can bloody well bet your bit every German fighter on the continent will be up there."

He knew he was redundant, the "squadron telegraph" had already informed every man but he gave them the details anyway. He had to be sure every pilot knew the object of the mission. He gestured skyward, "The Krauts have got to be up there already. We'll climb through this muck on full throttle on a heading of one-six-zero and at thirty-second intervals. This way we won't come up under a staffel. Assemble when we break into the clear and then we'll turn toward the Channel. Kraut fighters should be swarming over their ships and our bombers will be trying to make their runs. We've got to protect the bombers. If our field's closed in by weather when you return, land on any available field." He waved a hand overhead. "As you can see, we have a heavy overcast and the wind is from the northwest at four knots—but it's gusting to eight."

He took a moment to take a last look around at the young, intense faces. How many would he lose? How many would die? He choked back a rising lump and shouted a phrase that had been an epitaph for so many, "Man your aircraft and good hunting!" Suddenly his stomach was empty and sick.

The cheering pilots ran to the door. Randolph was the last to leave. He was not cheering. As he ran to the waiting lorry, Elisa flashed in his mind's eye and he felt a sudden inexplicable yearning for her. But just as inexplicably, Bernice crowded her out. This time she came out of the darkness like a demon, a witch, a harpy, howling on the cold wind from the north. He wondered if he were going mad, felt like a flood victim clinging to the straw of his sanity. "Leave me alone, damn you," he spat as he grasped the hand grip next to the vehicle's tailgate. Ian McBride had a startled look on his face as he extended a hand and then hesitated. Randolph muttered, "I didn't mean you, Ian." The Scotsman grasped his arm and pulled him up into the vehicle. As Randolph seated himself, Ian stared curiously but remained silent.

Four lorries charged off into the dim light as the feeble sun battled its way through the clouds and fog. The front was weakening and the ceiling lifting sluggishly. Now he could see shreds of it hanging from the control tower, hangar roofs, and the tops of the poplars lining the field. Within minutes, Randolph's lorry stopped in front of a hardstand two hundred yards north of the last hangar. The major dropped to the ground, the weight of his parachute almost toppling him onto the wet grass. In spite of his heavy clothing, a gust of cold wind cut through him like a sword. Within seconds, McBride and Burroughs had dropped beside him and the lorry roared off into the gloaming.

The three Spitfires of Randolph's section, Wolf Red, were parked in a sandbag-protected hardstand just off the perimeter track. Each aircraft was in its own protected area, shielded from the others by a six-foot-high wall of sandbags. With the engines already warmed, they had been turned off to save fuel and prevent overheating. In this enclosure, they were safe from low strafing attacks. Only direct hits by bombs could destroy them. At the back, or closed end of the dispersal, the ground crewmen had built shelters for themselves out of scrap lumber, corrugated iron, tarpaulins, and old packing crates. Struggling with his chute, Randolph jogged to his aircraft where his crew chief, Sergeant Everette Harrington, awaited him, crouched on the wing.

An old professional with over twenty years in the RAF, Harrington was probably the best crew chief in England. He was a short, white-haired, jolly man, who if he had had a white beard could have passed for Santa Claus in greasy overalls. This morning he wore a heavy fleece-lined jacket but still shivered as he held a gloved hand down to his pilot. "Big show today," he said, pulling Randolph up onto the wing.

Puffing, Randolph said, "Jerry's got his wind up."

"Take some of it out of his sails, sir," Harrington said, checking the canopy lock.

Grunting, Randolph fastened the leg straps of his chute. Carefully, he placed his booted foot into the slot at the side of the cockpit and Harrington gave him a heave up. He lowered himself into the cramped cockpit. Cursing, he pushed and pounded the parachute pack into its seat box and then adjusted the inflatable dinghy that was actually his seat. While Randolph plugged in his oxygen mask, microphone, and headset, he felt the crew chief tug at his shoulder straps that felt too tight and then fasten them without loosening the straps. Randolph knew this was wise, the distraction of loose straps could prove fatal in a dogfight. He worked the stick, rudder pedals, and checked his rudder, flaps, elevator, and ailerons. Everything was proper.

"Engine warm, mixture closed off, pitch control all the way, half inch of throttle. Are you taking off in pairs today, sir?"

Randolph looked around at the clouds that had lifted to perhaps eight hundred feet. The heavens had brightened and there was no rain or fog. He was encouraged but shook his head, thinking of his new pilots. "Singly. At thirty-second intervals."

Harrington dropped to the ground and waved a half-dozen other crewmen away from the Spitfire. He remained close to the fighter's wing. Randolph looked to his right at Burroughs. Belted into his cockpit, the young pilot grinned back, a ghastly, frightened grimace. The tic in his left eye was so rapid, he looked as if he were trying to impress a strange girl. Randolph felt his stomach drop but gave him a confident thumbs-up sign and the young man answered with his own. A quick look to the left at his other wingman of over a year, Pilot Officer Ian McBride, and the same exchange of signals. They were ready. Randolph circled a finger over his head and then stabbed it upward four times to represent all four sections. Harrington picked up the signal and a man in one of the shacks spoke into a telephone. Immediately a green flare arced up into the clouds from the control tower.

Randolph released his brake and then reset it. Then he threw two switches, turning on the battery and magneto. Immediately his instruments sprang to life. His hands moved quickly, hitting first the starter and then the fuel booster. There was the usual high electrical whine and then the first cylinders banged and popped, the three-bladed propeller jerking and turning spasmodically while Randolph primed the engine with his booster pump. More pops and bangs and the propeller picked up speed, the engine's barks gradually blending into the rich rumble of the idling Rolls Royce Merlin. The blades became a gray-blurred disk. Randolph increased manifold pressure slightly and nodded with approval as the big Rolls changed its pitch just as it should have. The engine was perfectly tuned, he could feel it in his feet, his hands, the seat of his pants. He glanced to his right and to his left. Both his wingmen were gunning their engines.

A final check. Gradually, he increased throttle until his rev-counter read seventeen hundred. He checked his instruments; twenty inches of manifold boost, oil temperature eighty, pressure seventy-five pounds, coolant temperature 101. Nodding approval, he throttled back and waved Harrington away. The crew chief shook his head in understanding, jerked both thumbs outward, and two men pulled the chocks free and ran to the back of the enclosure. Randolph looked to his right and then to his left, again. Both McBride and Burroughs nodded and held a thumb up. Randolph answered the gesture, stabbed a finger straight ahead, released his brakes, and increased throttle. The fighter slowly bumped along the ground and taxied out of the blast pen onto the taxiway.

Followed by McBride and then Burroughs, Randolph taxied toward the southeast end of runway one. Passing the other dispersal pens, the squadron commander picked up the other nine members of his squadron like a mother hen leading her chicks. He could see the flagman standing at the end of the runway. He was waving both flags in a sweeping gesture toward himself. Slowly Randolph passed the flagman and turned off of the perimeter track onto the runway. He brought the aircraft into take-off position at the end of the runway, set his brakes, and stared at the flagman. "Blast it. Let's get on with it," he shouted into the roar of the engine.

A single flag dropped and Randolph jammed the black knob of the propeller lever forward into fine pitch and released the brake. Then hard open on the throttle and the lithe fighter leapt forward. Roaring at take-off power with the rev-counter crowding twenty-six hundred rpms, the Spitfire gained speed, tires drumming along the runway, vibrations of the airframe quickening, the oil-stained concrete of the runway flashing beneath him. With the huge engine and wings obscuring his forward vision, Randolph always felt queasy at this moment—like a blind man running down a strange alley. Gently, he pushed the stick forward so that his tail wheel left the ground and his nose lowered. Now he could see over his wings and engine and the aircraft was ready to return to its natural habitat. Gently, he pulled back on the stick and the Spitfire roared off of the runway and climbed into the clouds.

Climbing with the throttle pushed to its next to last stop, Randolph broke through the clouds at nine thousand feet; much lower than he had expected. Looking back, he could see the other Spitfires of his squadron bursting through the clouds, wispy trails of vapor clinging to their airfoils like ghosts reluctant to release them. A quick look around found a clear sky and he keyed his radio and spoke into his microphone, "This is Wolf Red Leader. Wolf Flight, form up on me."

Throttling back slightly, he reduced his climb while the other fighters formed up in their familiar echelons of three; his leading with McBride and Burroughs close on his elevators. To his left and slightly above, the three Spitfires of Flight Lieutenant Michael Sturgis bounced on the rough air but still managed to hold a tight formation. Covering the right side was Flight Lieutenant Anthony Bowman's section while pulling up for top cover was Archie Rhoads with Hammes and Davenport keeping their wingtips close to their leader's elevators.

Quickly Randolph scanned the sky with his usual short jerky movements. To the south and east there were only scattered clouds and the arching blue vault was limitless, the blinding orb of the sun low on the eastern horizon, painting the few stringy clouds with deep reds like the blood of a mortally wounded man. However, all of England except a small part of the south coast and what appeared to be the Isle of Wight were still obscured by a solid blanket of clouds. The Pas de Calais and northern France were covered with the overcast. Here the sun played tricks, too, reflecting from fluffy pinnacles with the glare of Alpine snow while plunging the valleys into deep grays with occasional crevices as dark as lampblack.

To the southeast, he could see the Cotentin Peninsula and the great seaport of Cherbourg and the Channel Islands. As he turned his head, thousands of square miles of the channel were visible opening on the Atlantic to the west. Here the slanting rays of the sun were reflected by the chop, a spectacular display glinting like chips of mica sparkling on a blue mat. It was too riotously colorful to be natural. But beauty was not on Randolph's mind. Today was a day for killing men. Anxiously, he searched inland over central France that was free of clouds. As usual, it appeared peaceful in its pastoral splendor. At the moment, it looked as if Number 54 Squadron owned the sky, but not according to the radio.

He switched to Sector Control but heard nothing but the hiss of the carrier wave. It was weirdly quiet. Number 54 Squadron must be on their radar. But the bomber circuits were alive with frantic voices. "Where are those Kraut ships?" "I can't see my nose in this bloody muck." "Kraut fighters! Fighters! Three o'clock low." "Where are our bloody glamor boys. Freddie's bought it. We need fighters!"

One bomber squadron commander shouted sarcastically, "Never have so many owed so much to so few who aren't here."

Randolph pulled back on the stick and banked to the east toward the Channel, his squadron following as if they were attached. Abruptly, his fighter circuit came alive with the familiar disembodied voice of the control officer.

"Wolf Red Leader, this is Cricket Control. Fifty plus bandits in sector one-five-seven at angel six. Your vector zero-eight-zero. Intercept."

"This is Wolf Red Leader. Roger. But fifty!" Randolph said. "I could use a bit of help, old boy." He pushed the safety cover from his firing button and threw a switch, bringing his electric reflector sight to life.

"Roger. On the way, Wolf Red Leader. Out." Then he heard more commands as at least a dozen more fighter squadrons were vectored in on the fight below.

Turning Number 54 Squadron toward the new heading, Randolph's mind analyzed the information. RAF bombers were apparently attacking the German ships just east of Dover. The German ships had made incredible speed. Enemy fighters were pouring in and RAF fighters were racing to intercept. But everything was confusion in the low clouds and banks of fog hugging the sea. There was a brawl going on down there and he could not see a thing.

Pushing up his goggles, he dropped his port wing and stared down. He saw flashes light up the clouds like the blinks of weak light bulbs. Flak or bombs? Probably both. Suddenly the clouds parted narrowly over the Channel like a partially opened theater curtain and the scene it revealed was melodramatic, stagy, and horrifying like a Shakespearean tragedy. Low-flying Hampdens, Beaufighters, Wellingtons, and Blenheims were streaming toward the long gray shapes of at least ten German ships that were barely discernible through the mists. But the huge hulks of *Scharnhorst, Gneisenau*, and *Prinz Eugen* were unmistakable; long, broad, gray shapes leaving white, streaking wakes behind. The big ships were boiling with the flashes of ack-ack while destroyers steamed close alongside, lending their own gunfire support. German fighters like black sharks were racing in. As Randolph watched, a Wellington lost a wing and cartwheeled across the sea and disintegrated. Another bomber pulled up, engine streaking bright yellow flames like a blowtorch. Then the clouds moved in and the curtains closed.

Randolph shouted into the microphone, "Wolf Flight, this is Wolf Red Leader. Bandits at ten o'clock, low. Follow my lead but look out for our own bombers. It's a bloody muck down there." His section leaders acknowledged but before he could punch his throttle into war emergency power and roll into his dive, the control officer's voice stopped him.

"Wolf Red Leader, this is Cricket Control. Change of orders. Twelve plus bandits east of you twenty miles at angel ten. Closing fast. Intercept!"

Randolph squinted through his goggles at the sun and found the enemy just to the north and below the glaring sphere. Black dots headed for the fight below. Tiny fly specks that were growing rapidly. A staffel of fighters below them. Apparently they were so intent on the battle, they had not picked up Number 54 Squadron. If he had led his men in a diving attack into the melee below, this lot would have fallen on their tails and massacred the squadron. Obviously, Sector Control recognized this danger. "Roger, Cricket Control. I have them. Am engaging. Wolf Red Leader out." And then to himself, "We'll give those bloody bastards a jig-a-jig they won't forget."

He keyed his radio and spoke into his microphone, "Wolf Flight, this is Wolf Red Leader. New target at two o'clock. At least a full staffel. We'll engage." Again, the quick acknowledgments from his section leaders. Craning his neck, he looked up at Rhoads's section two thousand feet above and behind. He could see no Germans in top cover or up-sun. He needed every gun. "Wolf Yellow. Join the party."

Rhoads's voice scratched in his earphones with the usual wry humor no situation could defeat, "Thanks awfully for the invitation, Wolf Red Leader. Wolf Yellow on its way in black ties and tails.''

One last look around. The sky was clear. "Tally-ho!" Randolph shouted into his microphone, punching the Rolls to war emergency power and banking sharply toward the enemy aircraft. They were ME 109s. And his heart jumped into his throat when he saw the black and white chevrons on their vertical tail planes. They were flying in threes with the orange-and-green-striped Messerschmitt of Major Erich Kochling leading. *Jagdstaffel Vierter* at last. He felt his hate for Kochling boil up. It was a tangible thing that sat heavily on his heart and lungs and cut his breath to shallow, labored gasps, tingled his fingertips, and poured nervous strength into his arms and legs. He hunched over his controls and there was suddenly no saliva in his mouth. He dampened his lips with the tip of his tongue.

Streaking toward the enemy, Randolph scanned his instruments with a minute glance. The needle of the rev-counter had passed the red line at 2850 and was crowding 3000. The engine temperature was climbing slowly toward its red line at 121 but was still within a safe range. The airspeed indicator showed 360. He could hold this speed for five minutes and no more. The glycol would overheat and burst out through the safety valves. The Merlin would burn up. But he cared nothing about his engine, his aircraft, not even his life. Only one thing possessed him—to kill Kochling.

Good, experienced leader that he was, Kochling was leading his staffel in a shallow climb directly toward the hurtling Number 54 Squadron. The Spitfires' advantage in altitude had been erased. The first pass would be head-on at a combined closing speed of seven hundred miles an hour. Randolph knew his wingmen would have no chance to stay with him in the free-for-all to come. He disliked seeing his new chaps on their own, but had no choice. It would be every man for himself. He spoke into his microphone, "This is Wolf Red Leader. Individual combat."

The two squadrons streaked toward each other like two

lances hurled by hateful giants, Kochling's ME expanding with explosive speed in Randolph's gun sight. The Englishman brought the yellow spinner into the center of the sight and squeezed off a quick burst just as flame blinked like yellow blossoms from the ME's cowling and wings. Glowing strings of luminous beads whipped past as the two fighters raced together spinner to spinner. Burroughs and McBride were firing and the other sections had opened up, Rhoads diving down to join the battle. Laced with tracers, the shrinking space between the two squadrons appeared filled with white threads that were pulling the enemies together. Kochling's ME filled Randolph's windscreen.

At the last instant, the German pulled back hard on his stick, kicked rudder, and the Messerschmitt's wings flicked almost vertical, continuing over into a punishing right turn. His wingmen shot past to the left and right while the remaining three sections of the staffel bored on through the British formation.

A Messerschmitt collided with Flight Sergeant Melvin Greentree's Spitfire in a cataclysmic explosion of flying debris—chunks of wings, torn aluminum skin still attached to formers, wheels, an engine, a complete tail assembly, the lower half of a pilot still strapped into his seat. An incandescent ball of yellow flame swirled in the air for an instant like a boiling apocalypse, sending a black cloud storming upward. And then there was only falling, smoking wreckage and wind-whipped smoke to mark the extinction of two young men.

Immediately, all order, organization, was lost; the sky filled with snarling, brawling aircraft, tumbling, firing.

The fighter circuit was filled with shrill, frenzied voices. "Kraut at three o'clock. Break right, Tambler!"

"See the bastard!"

"Krasney! Two at eight o' clock high. I'm coming in from your left."

"See them, Sturgis! Take the one on the left! I've got the other."

Randolph was worried about Burroughs and Davenport, but there was nothing he could do for them now. He brought the stick back sharply with his left hand, balancing with his left foot for rudder control. He was matching Kochling's maneuver, upward and into a tight turn. Randolph screamed to release pressure as the g-forces slammed him down in his seat and for a moment his vision blurred. But not his mind. He knew Kochling would be wracking his ME around so that he could bring his guns to bear as quickly as possible. A tight turn costs a plane a lot of speed, but he knew the Messerschmitt would lose more than the Spitfire—could risk a high-speed stall. Kochling would be dropping his nose to regain speed before pulling up for his shot. Try to catch the Spit in the belly.

A Messerschmitt burst into flame, rolled onto its back, and curved slowly into its final plunge into the sea, leaving a black banner of smoke behind. Randolph heard Rhoads's shout of triumph, "Chopped the bastard. Welcome to Oz, Krauthead."

Then McBride's voice, "Look 'oot, Hammes. One-oohnine, five o'clock low! Break left, laddie! Left! Left!"

"See him! See him!"

But Hammes did not turn soon enough. Randolph saw Hammes's fighter break from the dogfight and turn toward home, streaming smoke while McBride stormed after the ME that had damaged Hammes and was streaking after the smoking Spitfire for the kill. McBride fired a two-second burst that hit the German's left wing root and tore the entire structure free. With its left wing fluttering behind it, the ME tumbled grotesquely across the sky like a grouse that had taken a full load of buckshot. The pilot tried to bail out, but he was slammed by the remaining wing and swatted across the sky like an insect struck by a board. His parachute never opened.

McBride's voice came through the circuit, "Pranged the Heinie bugger. Hammes, hightail it. Sure an' I've got your arse covered."

Hammes answered, voice controlled and calm, "Roger. Thanks much, old boy. The old Rolls is heating up a bit."

Randolph felt a jolt of panic, heart pumping against his ribs like a caged animal trying to burst out. He had guessed wrong. Kochling had not dived, but, instead, he was coming around in a tight turn onto his killing angle, risking a stall. Frantically, the Englishman made a quarter turn to his right, rolled out, and pulled the stick back brutally, whipping the Spitfire into a wrenching loop—a loop the Messerschmitt could never follow. A hammer pounded low on his fuselage and then the controls leapt in his hands as slugs drummed into his tail. The German was a great marksman, firing in a turn and at one-half deflection with an aircraft that must be mushy in the controls. However, he had lost too much speed and Randolph broke free, coming down flat out of the loop and barreling into a wing-bending half roll and onto Kochling's tail. But the German had anticipated Randolph, split-essing into a dive.

With the Spitfire hard on his tail, Kochling dove. Randolph knew the ME would pull away and he had to kill the German now or he would escape. He brought his sight to the German. Jammed the button with his thumb. The guns jittered and the airframe vibrated, flames leaping from his wings and the brass casings tumbled into the slipstream.

The German seemed to be reading his mind. At the moment Randolph opened fire, Kochling steepened his dive and jinked to the left. Randolph cursed as he saw most of his tracers fly off into empty space. But then he felt a surge of joy. Kochling was trailing a fine mist. Coolant. He was hit.

Burroughs's high girlish voice in his earphones jolted him. "Major! A ME diving on you, four o'clock high!"

Randolph turned his head so fast and hard he felt a pain streak down from his neck to the base of his spine. A black Messerschmitt with a yellow arrow painted the length of its fuselage was diving on him. And he was close with a good killing angle. Tracers whipped past and Kochling was pulling away. Then another presence, above and to the left. It was Burroughs. Diving and closing on the black ME. Both fighters converged on Randolph's Spitfire while a desperate Kochling flattened his dive over the Channel and turned his wounded fighter toward France. He was on his own. The cloud cover was far to the north.

Doggedly, Randolph bore in to a hundred yards. His hunger to kill Kochling was so voracious, so overwhelming, he ignored the mortal peril charging in from his right rear. At zero deflection he opened fire, his tracers smashing into his enemy's engine. A twenty-millimeter shell blew the hood off, there was a puff of smoke, the yellow flame of burning petrol, and the ME rolled on its back. A black figured dropped out of the cockpit and a white parachute blossomed.

A blow struck the Spitfire like a pneumatic tool. Abruptly the Plexiglas panels were punched and rent open, wind pouring in and raging about the cockpit like a ravening beast. Randolph's instrument panel dissolved and exploded in his face and he was suddenly sprayed with blood. He screamed, fear and icy despair clutching and squeezing his guts. Instinctively, he rolled away from the burst. Frantically, he ripped off his goggles and wiped his cheeks with the back of his glove. Hydraulic fluid. A line had been severed by thirteen-millimeter bullets. Immediately Randolph felt the drag of trapped air. He must have been damaged in the fuselage, back of the cockpit, too.

Correcting his trim with stick and rudder, Randolph continued his roll into a dive without reducing throttle and glanced into his rearview mirror. The black ME was boring in closer for the kill and Burroughs was racing in from the German's port side. The young man was firing and the German suddenly ignored Randolph and turned to meet the new threat. Burroughs never wavered, never changed course, his attack as true as the arrow painted on the side of the Messerschmitt. He charged into the ME.

"No!" Randolph screamed. The Spitfire's spinner slashed into the ME's cockpit and the two aircraft enveloped each other like two lovers maddened by passion. The impact hurled the locked aircraft across the sky in a single spinning mass that shed huge chunks of aluminum and broken, bent debris. There was a flash. Flames. And the two locked fighters whirled and tumbled into the Channel like a great flaming pinwheel.

Pulling out of his dive, Randolph pounded his combing in anger and frustration, his soul riven by a silent scream of anguish. Another young man dead. Poor Burroughs with his nervous tick and frightened voice. Had he frozen at the controls, misjudged his distance, or actually rammed deliberately to save his commanding officer? He would never know. What he did know was that the lad's sacrifice had saved his life. Had attacked bravely with dash and verve. You could never tell what stuff made up a man until his life was on the line and you fought by his side. This would go into the letter— the blasted, bloody letter.

Forcing the horror from his mind, he choked back the sour gorge in his throat, reduced throttle, and looked around. The sky was absolutely empty and the fighter circuit quiet. This miracle happened so often in the most ferocious dogfights. One moment the sky would be filled with snarling, twisting, burning fighters, the next it was empty. The fight had taken him far to the southwest. He could see the Cotentin Peninsula just a few miles to the southeast. To the far north the clouds were still thick as if God was cooperating with the Germans and covering the escape of the enemy warships. Where was Kochling?

Banking and losing altitude, he leaned over the combing. There was something down there in the Channel. Something large and gray that bobbed in the water like a buoy. Dropping beneath a thousand feet, Randolph nodded to himself. A German rescue float equipped with blankets, rations, and medical supplies. The enemy anchored them in the Channel close to the French coast in hopes that downed flyers could paddle to them in their dinghies and await rescue by small craft. There was a parachute floating nearby and a man was sitting with his back to the float's small tower. He was blond and very white. Kochling. It had to be Kochling.

Randolph's lips pulled back from his teeth in a hard line and his mouth was suddenly filled with saliva as if he were savoring a gourmet meal. Slowly he swept around the float in a complete circle and then turned in to bring his armament to bear. Kochling stood, pulled a pistol from his holster, and pointed it at him. The man was no coward. Randolph throttled back just above stalling speed. With his reflector sight shot out, he would use the top cowling panel for his open sight. It would be easy. Kochling would die the same way Freddie "Coop" Hansen died.

He pushed the red button. The first bullets and shells hit short. A slight pull on the stick marched them into the float, blasting open the tower and hurling Kochling against it. Torso ripped open, entrails pouring onto the deck, he slid across the small platform. As Randolph passed over, the eviscerated corpse slipped from the float and plunged into the water, held on the surface by its life preserver. The German floated head down in the water, arms and legs extended in a ragged cross the way all dead men float. A stain began to spread in the blue water like a red dye marker. Kochling looked just like Hansen. Nothing separated them in death. Here, all men are equal.

Randolph was startled by a voice in his earphones. It was scratchy with static. He looked around but could not find even a sea bird. Despite the interference and the wavering carrier wave, he recognized Rhoads's incongruously gay voice carried from beyond the horizon. He was singing a song popular with the RAF. "We're off to see the wizard . . ."

With Rhoads's voice in his ears, Randolph looked down at the corpse one last time. Staring at the German, he felt a warm glow inside, a fullness, the same feeling as after making love with Elisa. But instead of Elisa, he saw Bernice. He laughed until he felt tears on his cheeks. "You're right, Bernice!" he screamed. "You're right."